DAMANÉ

ISBN: 978-0-9559807-0-1

© 2008 Harriet Talbot

Contents

Stolen	5
Just A Dream	13
Watchers	18
Lost	24
Trolls	26
News	30
Forthum	34
Zobor	39
Protection for a Dark Hope	46
Zale	53
Heat and Temptation	58
Magic	68
People of the North	77
The Prophecy of Man	82
The Pass	90
Marshes	100
The Pit	105
Galzan	109
The Passage	114
Domai	118
Passage through the Mountains	126
Stories	131
The Rostauru	139
The Forbidden Valley	148
Lose One, Gain Two	157
Dragons	169
More Than a King	179
Reinforcements	186
Broken Borders	190
The Last Battle	195
Survivor	198
Mercy	202
The Maze	212

Snolye Forest 216
Death and Shadows 223
Life 230

Stolen

It was the darkest night Damané had seen for many years. A thick layer of cloud, the colour of the night's ocean, covered both of its smooth, silver moons. Not a single sliver of starlight had the strength to pierce the unnatural blanket. A wind was blowing through the narrow streets, rocking the trees like a baby's cradle. An eerie silence had fallen over the land, as though the city had been disconnected from its surrounding villages. Not even the leaves, rustled up in a whirlwind, made a sound. The cool white stone houses looked ashen in the shadows, as though they had battled some great unseen fire. The surrounding hills lay bare and peaceful, completely deserted except for the cool wind softly caressing them.

No one noticed the clip clop of horse hooves upon the cobbled ground, belonging to the stallion that carried Xannon through the sleeping villages. He appeared as a small speck of black against the grassy hills that were now cast into shadow. It was, of course, the sorcerer who had used his powers to create this foreboding darkness, for in the Land of Light it is a rare thing to see clouds and find all things to be still. He meandered along the path with apprehension as he passed the first houses of the city. Xannon's face was not full of life and optimism like those who lay asleep all around him in their beds. His was one of fear and caution. He was on a mission, sent by Lord Jabari to steal one of Damané's ten sacred crystals that keep the land in equilibrium. If one ever went missing, the Land of Light would perish and the unity of time would be forever broken. None dared even speak of such an atrocity, let alone conceive someone walking through their midst to carry out the task. The crystals had been in place longer than any could remember, forged by the Rayden's themselves long ago when they once lived as a people on the White Islands. They had long since left the lands to men and travelled back to their home land to the West.

Xannon rode up the pebble path towards the Tower of Light. His hazel eyes peered through the windows of every house he passed, through the gaps in the curtains, trying to make out the bodies in the rooms. He wanted to turn back, but his master's voice echoed in his head, cursing all sorts of punishments if he returned empty handed. All around him, Xannon thought he could see eyes watching him, judging him. The houses about him became larger and more spaced out the further into the city he delved. The path before the sorcerer opened onto a large square lined with delicately placed shops and bars, their windows boarded up with shutters for the night. The square had a feeling of majesty about it as in its centre rose a grand statue. It was of a beautiful woman, her arms raised to the sky. In the palms of her hands hovered a yellow crystal glowing with a light that now seemed to be unnaturally forced inwards. From the woman's hands shot jets of water that sent a cool mist into the air as they collided with the crystal. Her hair was a silver waterfall that plunged into the depths of a pool below. The pool was surrounded by shallow steps, the ground radiating from them as slabs of slate instead of the uneven cobbles. Xannon rode cautiously round the statue as if he feared she would awaken to find him there. He looked at her with sadness in his eyes, for he knew his spell was suppressing her true beauty.

Leaving the fountain behind him, the sorcerer continued on between even larger homes than before, these with front gardens full of blossoming flowers. Small white fences marked the boundaries of the owners' land. Above the front doors of these larger homes was engraved a different symbol, depicting the resident's status within the city. Xannon tried to translate them, but was left to wonder what they all meant. Perhaps a sentry lived in one of the homes? Or a lead guard? Maybe some were the homes of accountants or actuaries. Xannon longed to know more and be a part of the magical world he was trespassing in, though he knew he must continue and remain an outsider. The sorcerer would never come to learn the meanings of the symbols of the enchanted city.

The path around these larger houses was wider than that which led up to the city, allowing Xannon to feel more relaxed as the fear of an impending trap was lifted from him. The cobbles transformed instantly to cool, white marble as he neared the tower. Once again, the path opened before him, though this time there was a set of steps stretching out in either direction leading up to a great square building. There were hollows in its walls, which Xannon presumed were windows for the rooms inside. A magnificent archway cut through the building, leading directly to the gardens at the base of the tower. Its design was unclear due to the pressing darkness, though the sorcerer could see its intricacy. Xannon pressed on warily and rode beneath its arches, whispering *desgardire* under his breath so as to place anyone left inside the building under a spell. It was designed to make them forget what or where they intended to go if they tried to leave or peer inquisitively out of the windows. As he passed along the passageway, Xannon could sense the knowledge that was embedded within its walls. He knew instinctively that this was a place of learning and record keeping. He so longed to creep inside and find the hidden books of the White Islands, learn its history, its origins, its wars, and where he came from. The thought of Lord Jabari pressed in on him again and he shook off the temptation.

As he approached the palace, he trembled at the site of its great white, stone exterior. The highest room seemed as though it were piercing the sky, able to feel the stars upon its roof. He had never seen the tower before, only memorized its interior layout. As he saw how its shape went from being as wide as a valley at its base, to a narrow column, no wider than three great men, he found it hard to catch his breath. *Focus* he told himself. *You must focus. Get it over with, but do not be careless.* Yet, try as he may, he still found himself staring at the mighty tower. It was built in stages. Its base was wide and square, littered with patrolling archers on its roof, ready for any attack. Ten metres into the roof was built the next section, and ten metres into that was the next. It towered above the land like circular steps. Upon each step were other archers, tired from hours of watching the keep. Each step was at least twenty metres tall. The walls were covered in evenly spaced hollows that made windows. Hovering in each window was a ball of blue light, illuminating the night sky. When the tower became about fifteen metres wide, the stepping stopped and the tower grew upwards, tall and slim, until its peak, where a spear-like roof tickled the heavens. Surrounding its base lay an opalescent sea of botany, delicately arranged to show of the magnificence of each species of plant. A thin slate path slithered within the array of flowers, dividing them into sections that could be more closely admired.

 Xannon eventually pulled his eyes off the tower and continued to approach his destination. The darkness concealed his black-cloaked figure. As he neared the guards, he dismounted and lowered his body to the ground so as to not be seen. The thick plants and trees surrounding the tower hid him, just as he had planned. The smell of cherry blossom and wild roses hung in the air like a dense fog around the sorcerer, as though the flowers themselves were trying to force out the rancid darkness. He was startled to feel his horse nudging him in the side. Panicked, Xannon spun round and shooed him away, then eagerly looked to the guards to see if they had heard the sound of his stallion's hooves. Luckily, the sound was muffled by the wind whispering through the leaves. Xannon's mind was once again buzzing with what his Lord had said as he had set off.

 'If you return without the crystal, you will be severely punished. And Xannon, do not try to run. If you do, I will have you tracked down and killed.'

 The punishment for returning empty handed was that Jabari would have Xannon's powers removed. Xannon shivered at the thought of it. This is a painful process whereby the sting of a giant doybon fly is used to drain his powers. It is a long, slow procedure. The more power the fly takes, the brighter its skin glows. The tiny creature goes from its repulsive look of five eyes the size of acorns, mud brown body, and long, black, spindly legs covered in mucus, to a beautiful golden glowing butterfly the size of a man's fist. After this has happened, the fly is locked away, waiting for the day when it can give back the powers. This is only when Lord Jabari has decided that Xannon no longer needs him to be his slave. He has threatened Xannon with this being over one hundred years.

The guards of Damané's tallest tower were patrolling the front gates, ever watchful for danger. The unusual atmosphere was unnerving and they were sure something was about to happen. They could feel it in their bones. One of the guards thought he saw something dash behind a bush. He went over to it but could see nothing. As he walked away, sure he had imagined the incident, Xannon directed his long, thin fingers towards the man and muttered *tirandae,* placing him under a spell that put him to sleep. The guards heard their comrade's body fall to the ground and rushed to his aid, but Xannon was too fast for them. Before they knew what had happened, they found themselves under the same spell as their friend. He then hid the bodies and stepped towards the tower's entrance.

Xannon opened the great oak doors with a wave of his hand and stood for a moment to take in the site of the tower's great hall. It was as high as an old oak and had images carved into its stone walls. The room now stood empty, absent of the scholars and soldiers whom in daylight hours roamed across its pale stone floor. Xannon could only guess as to the whereabouts of his sleeping foe. His greatest fear was one restless being waking prematurely to discover him as he endured his secret quest.

The room around him appeared to glow, as candles as long as his arm reflected light off the white walls. Xannon's scar that ran from his left eye to his chin shone silver in the light and his sharp features were cast into wild shadows. He walked forwards, his long black hair flowing out behind him, and inspected one of the carvings. It was the image of a group of men that at first glance looked like nothing more than a pack of strong warriors remembered through extravagant artwork. As Xannon's eyes became more accustomed to the flickering light however, he noticed other more unusual attributes visible on the men's grave faces. Shimmering scales stretched across the hollows of their cheeks until they faded into pale skin. Bright white spikes tipped their ears like deadly mountain peaks. It was as though, Xannon thought, that these men somehow had the blood of the Domai running through their veins. His fear of the Domai pulsed through him as he thought of their clawed warriors and their powerful magic-wielding guards.

A gust of wind swept through Xannon's hair, waking him from his trance. He felt it best not to look around so crept up the winding marble stairs. They began as shallow steps that could stretch from one side of a villager's house to the other. Then they became narrower and steeper. If Xannon reached out with his arms to either side he could touch both walls. He hurried past the various shaped doors that held so much mystery for the aging spell weaver.

The light here came from orbs of blue fire hovering in small hollows in the cool wall, but these were few and far between. There were times when Xannon crept on in pure darkness. It was in one of these moments that that his fears were brought to life. He heard footsteps, soon accompanied by heavy breathing, making their way down the stairs towards him. He slithered into an alcove in the wall, hoping to be passed by unnoticed. What he did not count on though was the suit of arms he backed into which clanged loudly, alerting the midnight walker to his presence.

'Who goes there?' came an aged, demanding voice. Xannon froze, breath barely escaping his lips. 'Show yourself!' A short rustling of fabric followed this command, and then the sound of a liquid being shaken in a bottle. Just feet from Xannon, a greying man came into view as a glass vial in his hand began to glow with a powerful golden light. His eyes shone an unnaturally soft green and a well kept beard hugged his cheeks. It was apparent from his silver trimmed black robes and the sparkle of magical arrogance in his eyes that he was an alchemist of the tower. Xannon lifted his hand in preparation for the working of his magic, but his foe was too fast for him. The man threw the vial to the floor and it exploded with a blinding flash. He began to run back up the passage away from the fumbling sorcerer. Xannon had shielded his eyes with one hand and with the other instinctively cast a silencing spell. *Stelasae*. Upon hearing this, the alchemist, knowing no more words could pass his lips, stopped running. He was alone, the only man now able to defend the city.

Xannon had been blinded by the sudden light and so reached out in front of him, his eyes shut tightly. The sound of the man slowly approaching filled his ears. Xannon stood stock still, aware that every ounce of noise was vital to his defence. The alchemist's breathing deepened, as though he was preparing for some great task. Xannon drew himself to his full height and let his hands fall gently to his sides. An almost silent brush of metal informed the sorcerer that a blade had been unsheathed. A dark cloud covered Xannon's mind and with it a slight smile spread across his cheeks. In an instant, his eyes were open and his arm was raised. *Unaeri*. The alchemist's eyes opened with shock at Xannon's power. The sorcerer's first spell had been quite a simple one, but the next was lethal. All the air was sucked out of the man's lungs, leaving him gasping soundlessly as he collapsed onto the cold stairs. Xannon stood over his dying enemy until he moved no more. Coming back to his senses, Xannon was filled with a desperate hate for what he had just done. *I am not like him. I will never be like him!* He knew now that he must hurry so hastened up the stairs, leaving the innocent man's body far behind. Harsh voices began to whisper in the sorcerer's mind, speaking of evil magic and past enemies. It was all Xannon could do to force them back and push his magic that he could now feel on his fingertips deeper within himself.

Once he reached the middle level, Xannon stopped climbing and slipped into a chamber to his right. He desperately tried to catch his breath and wiped the beads of sweat from his forehead as he examined the chamber. It seemed even more spectacular than the entrance. He could see all ten crystals floating on air twenty metres above him. Each was giving out a different colour light that was reflected off the white marble walls. It was as though they rested upon invisible perches at various heights. Xannon thought that perhaps the height of the crystal symbolised its importance, though he could not fathom who or what held them there. It would take too much energy for any creature he knew of to maintain them for so many years. The walls, unlike in the entrance, had no carvings on them at all. Neither did they have any windows. He could hear a faint noise filling the room. It was a type of chant, sung in the Ancestral Tongue of the Land of Light. The words were calming. They spoke of times of peace and a great power that watched over Damané. The sorcerer presumed this was just a tale of old, kept alive by the magic that seemed to vibrate all around him. It was a magnificent sight. He knew that each crystal had a purpose and its own special powers but he did not know what they were. The song and light was so beautiful it engulfed him. Xannon stood entranced for a moment, until the voice of Jabari re-entered his mind. With his master's echoing words, the beauty seemed to darken and grow cold. Xannon rose up, using magic to lift him off the ground, to the one crystal that could be concealed by night. It resided above all the rest, so close to the ceiling that Xannon thought he would not reach it. As he drew near, he could see that the crystal was as large as his head, the scent of fresh lilies exuding from its smooth exterior. It was a deep blue with what looked like tiny stars scattered across its surface. The light given out by it looked like a mist of black. A shiver went down the sorcerer's spine. For some reason, he feared this crystal, but Jabari had been adamant that he had that one crystal brought to him. Xannon looked around at the other crystals. None of them held the same foreboding as the crystal before him. Almost two metres below him, the sorcerer spotted another dark crystal, this one an even deeper black than the one Jabari had requested. He flew down to it and noticed there were no blemishes to its rich colour. Nor was the light a black mist, but rather a truly dark light shining from it. '*The light makes it more difficult to hide,*' thought the sorcerer feebly, '*though I would be more willing to take this one. Has Jabari ever seen the crystals? Would he know that this was not the one he had asked for?*' He was about to take the beautiful black crystal he was now next to when he glanced one last time at his true goal. As he looked at it, he thought that for a moment he could see the image of his brother who was long since dead. Confused, he got closer to the crystal to get a better look. Xannon reached out and took it from its invisible perch. Instantly, the other crystals dimmed and the room became the colour of the dawn sky. The chanting was replaced by what sounded like a whisper. He could not understand what it was saying, but he knew that he had to leave at once. He stared down at the crystal he held and saw that the image had gone. A crimson mist began to filter down from the top of the room, just above Xannon's head. It reached his hair, singeing some of his wisps of black. The sorcerer drew away from the burning cloud. The whispering grew louder so he turned and flew down to the door. His exit had turned into a scorching white gold, the handle melting in his hand. He stifled a cry of pain as he withdrew his burnt palm and muttered *ouvaria* to open the door. He passed through it just in time. The door swung shut behind him, as if trying to catch the hem of his cloak and trap him. Xannon's heart pounded as he ran down the stairs, past the alchemist's now cold body, and left the tower as fast as he could, never stopping to gawk at the images he so wanted to understand. He found his horse waiting by the oak doors looking darker than ever. Xannon noticed its coat had become even more of a rich black and thought for a moment that Lord Jabari himself was staring at him through those jade green eyes. He shook off the feeling and fumbled for a brown sack he had tied on the saddle. Xannon hastily opened it and put the crystal inside. He threw it over his shoulder and rode through Damané to its eastern border, no longer caring if he was seen. He paused for a moment on the brow of a hill, took one look back, and continued on his way.

  His horse slowed to a walk once the Land of Light was out of sight. The tired sorcerer stopped only briefly on his journey by a pool of water in which to dampen a piece of cloth and sooth his wounded hand. It took him four whole suns to reach the dark Forbidden Valley which he travelled through cautiously. The ground was not green and moist like in Damané, but dry and scorched. Once again he had the feeling of eyes upon him. He hurried through, muttering under his breath *disaaparoh* to cloak his path and become one with the background. He knew that if he did not do this, there would be no stopping the creature that lies in the bottom of the valley from killing him. At the end of it, Xannon came to a ridge and saw his Lord's domain, still disguised to those of sin. Xannon had thought that he need not hide it from everyone as it is only children who can see through the shield, and it would only be those who have sinned who would go looking for him. *There's no need to use more of my power than need be* he had thought to himself, already feeling the drain from the amount he had used. He paused and took out the crystal. He examined it for a moment, searching for his brother's face. Disappointed at seeing nothing, he passed through the shield and felt safe knowing that he had accomplished his task.

On the steepest side of the Valley, a boy with brilliant blue eyes stood by a beautiful grey horse. His name was Bazyli, and he had followed Xannon from Damané to Jabari's domain.

Just a Dream

The Land of Light awoke from an unusual night of darkness with an air of unrest. The people of the city of Damané are ones full of happiness and optimism, yet something did not rest well in the air. Even so, women woke their children from undisturbed dreams, smiling happily as they looked to the sky and saw the weather was promising. The white sun slowly rose above the distant Minar Mountains, which were capped with snow during this winter season. They wear the icing all year round, though during winter the snow creeps down the mountain side until it strokes the borders of the outer villages of Damané. The colossal pine forests could not be seen through the white now and the frozen streams glistened like beacons to warn away travellers. Streams of white smoke from the farmers' wooden houses gently puffed into the air from brick red chimneys as the women lit the morning fires to warm their husband's breakfast. The men began preparing their animals for a day of labour, seeing as there were few days left before the weather changed for the worse. The sun was always bright in Damané, though once the snow tickled the village borders, a strong icy wind would batter against the walls and the morning would wake to a frost. It would soon be time to lock up the barns and hide the oxen and horses away in the warmth. Firewood could be seen stacked up against the hay in the barns, left to dry out before the cold.

A line of children and young adults began to make their way along the winding dirt tracks leading towards the centre of the city pulling carts laden with fruits, meats and trinkets to sell at the market. The unusual atmosphere did not stop them from laughing and joking as they always did on their way to work. It was always a wonderful sight to see. The girls wore dresses of all colours that flowed out behind them as they skipped along, their long hair dancing with ribbons in the wind, whilst the boys looked scruffy next to them in their muddy trousers and torn shirts. They would try selling each other some of their load as early sales for discounted prices, but everyone there had all they needed to survive on. Besides, they new what the trinkets were really worth, and it was not all that much! The real money came from the 'city folk' as the farmers liked to call them. The villagers were not keen on the hustle and bustle of the city as everyone made their way to 'easy work' as they called it. On rare occasions, a curious teen would leave their peaceful home next to the mountains and try to find work in the city, though more often than not they would return after but a few weeks to live out their life as either a wife or a farmer.

Further towards the centre of Damané, the weather never faltered. It was warm all year round, with the sun high in the sky from the early hours of the day. The previous night's clouds did not linger for long as the people opened their curtains to let in the new day. The market stalls had already started to arrive and began to open as men kissed their wives lightly on the cheek before setting off to the Masdour for the day. The Masdour lay at the base of the Tower of Light. It was the large, square building, made of the same white stone as the houses close to the centre of Damané, which Xannon had seen the night before. It was full of dark rooms used as offices to keep records of merchandise sold within the Land of Light and for keeping records of its inhabitants. Any who worked in the market had to register with the Masdour and inform those who worked there of any transactions that took place each day. It was then up to the men of the Masdour to make sense of the data and calculate how much the farmers needed to grow in the way of crops in the coming seasons. It also allowed them to work out what minerals needed to be mined and in what quantity. The workers of the Masdour also took a percentage of the silver earned in the market by those who had registered with them. It was not much, but each member of the Masdour had many clients, so it added up to a lot. Those in the Masdour who had the clients then paid those who worked with the data. There were only about five or so of these higher-ranking officials for the entire city. For this reason, they were paid a lot of silver and lived in the larger houses closer to the Tower of Light.

Even though the city appeared to be split into these three different groups of people, everyone was treated equally. No one was left to fend for him or herself. If anyone needed some help of any kind, whether it was financially or socially, everyone was willing to help. However, that day was different to most. No one, in or out of the city, would be able to give aid to their neighbours during the time that was about to come to pass, since known as the 'Dark Hours'.

The sun could be seen over the peak of Benza, the tallest of the Minar Mountains, when the Tower's guards changed shifts that still morning. Luca, the Bringer of Light and ruler of Damané, sat awake in her chamber. A stream of light filtered through the gap in her curtains onto her great, four-poster bed. The posts were made of the finest ivory and seemed to twist in on themselves like old trees. The canopy of her bed was nothing more than one delicate piece of white silk. There were only two other things in her room. On the wall opposite her bed, there was what looked like a picture, yet there was no frame. It was merely a sheet of glass, inside of which there was a waterfall of white sand. These were the Sands of Time. It was Luca's duty to ensure that the sands never stopped falling; else the land would turn to ruin.

The second item in her room was an area of white feather cushions on the stone floor in a far corner. Surrounding the cushions were hovering glass cases that glowed when the room was dark. If anyone looked closely enough, they would see small villages of Fairies inside the cases. Luca was their carer as the Fairies were a dying species. Since the time of Luca in her chamber that morning, however, a miracle has occurred, giving back the Fairies their homelands.

The Fairies were glowing at that moment because the light of the morning had not yet reached their homes. By now, however, the six hundred year old queen was bathing in a pool of light. It looked as though her whole body was glowing. This is how it always was when the light hit her. Her long blonde hair licked her white gown as it stirred in the breeze. The rings, representing her royal status, on her middle fingers glistened against the crystal lining of her robe. Luca's soft features looked more beautiful than ever, yet she did not seem her happy self as she had been disturbed by a nightmare. She had dreamt that one of her sacred crystals had been stolen. Whilst thinking back to her restless night, Milon, her personal guard, came rushing into the room. His expression was grave.

'Are you alright Your Highness?'

'I'm fine Milon,' she said in her soothing voice. It was as soft as water bubbling in a pool. 'I just had a bad dream. It has not helped waking up to this dry air. Can you feel it Milon? It's as though something's missing from it.' Milon looked back into his Lady's deep, blue eyes. Luca smiled at him to reassure him that everything was all right, and then continued. 'It felt so real. My dream I mean. I dreamt that one of the crystals had been stolen.' She gave a short laugh. 'Isn't that strange?' She looked up at him. 'What's the matter? You look as if it's true!' Milon had a confused expression.

'But Your Highness, that is why I came in as I did. One of the crystals *was* stolen this night! The guards were put under a spell and could do nothing!'

'What! Impossible! Is this some sort of joke?' Luca stood up abruptly. Though her body was slender, she was just as tall as Milon. Her eyes seemed to be on fire as rage seeped into every corner of her soul. The sun roaring behind her gave her whole body a red hue. Milon cowered away from her slightly, afraid of what she may do to him for bringing this bad news. He was one of the few who knew how powerful she was. When he spoke, his voice was almost inaudible and trembled with his body.

'I'm afraid it's true. Check the sands.'

Luca's face turned to absolute fear. She could see that the Sands of Time had stopped falling.

'But no one could possibly take a crystal! There's no way of doing it! The crystals are guarded day and night! No one would even want to steel one! There's nothing to gain! No one could possibly do it other than...' Realisation flickered across her face as she thought of it, draining the anger from her body. She now looked deathly pale, as though a ghost had passed right through her. *He wouldn't dare. Or would he?* Milon stared at her curiously, and then, choosing to be brave, he whispered words that floated to Luca's ears that no one else could dare ask.

'Other than who Your Highness?' Milon could see that Luca was more disturbed by what had happened, now that she knew who was responsible. He stood there, staring at his Lady, hoping he had not angered her further by probing into her thoughts. Luca's mind was frantically searching for another explanation, but nothing came to her. After a few moments, she looked back into her guard's grey eyes.

'Lord Jabari.'

'But he was banished.'

'That's precisely why he would have done it.' She began pacing the room, her robe billowing out behind her. 'He wants revenge. And besides, he has his sorcerer to do his dirty work. Milon, I'm going to need to call upon all of our allies. Send word to the distant lands. I will especially need Zale and Harden. Warn the Elements. Find them quickly. Jabari will know I wish to call upon their aid. I fear what he will do to them to block their passage to these lands.'

'Yes Your Highness.' As he turned to leave, Luca addressed him again, forcing a smile so as to calm him.

'Thank you, Milon, for bringing this news. You are my most trusted guard. I know you will not fail me.' Milon bowed respectively and made to move back towards the door. 'Wait Milon,' Luca continued. 'Was anyone hurt?'

'There were a few grazes and injured heads from falls,' said Milon in a quiet voice, 'and one death Your Highness.' Luca blinked back tears.

'Who?' she asked, her voice almost inaudible.

'Shethar, our head alchemist. It seems as though he tried to stop the intruder.'

'I will go to his family shortly and give them the news myself. He was a very brave man.'

With a final bow, Milon left Luca to her troubled thoughts and fled down the stairs. Men and women were bustling in and out of the entrance now in dark robes, preparing for another working day. They hurried on in silence, sensing the troubled air and not wanting to be in the way. Rumours were already spreading of a death within the Tower. Milon cut a path through the alchemists and historians, and assembled his men outside the great oak doors. He sent them off in all directions, instructing them to contact all the kings of the land that showed allegiance or debt to Luca, though he knew she would not want any forced into service. There was to be Zobor, a gathering of all allies to help retrieve the sacred crystal and restore the unity of time. The ancient meeting had not taken place since before the Histrims, hunched men-like creatures, had left the shores of the White Islands where Damané resides. Luca ruled over the islands but allowed men their own domains and kingdoms. Though this evil would affect all, she knew a smaller, more select group would have a better chance of retrieving the crystal, but she still wanted to offer the choice to aid in the plight to all the kingdoms of the islands.

Luca drew back her curtains and looked out of her window. She could see the effects of what had happened already. Storm clouds were gathering on the horizon. Not even she, a half-blood Rayden, would be able to keep the light filtering through. She sat muttering to herself.

'Jabari, what have you done?'

Watchers

    Word spread quickly. On the slopes of Mount Nigh, the smallest of the Sincre Mountains, Harden and Zale were sitting on two large boulders, celebrating their recent victory. Their swords rested on the bloodstained ground, spent arrows piercing the soil around them. Five Nicars lay slain by the men's feet. The murky grey creatures of the air had been plaguing a nearby village for years, camouflaged by their surrounding swamps and preying young children who wandered too far from their mothers. At times, when the Nicars has gone days without a feed, they would use their long snouts and sharp teeth to pry open windows at night and steal children from their beds. Their blood red eyes would bear into their victims, paralysing them where they stood. The two men had stumbled upon the restless village more than a week before and had been offered a great rewards if they could kill the terrible foe. Some of the village farmers had spotted the two men as specks upon the mountainside and named them the Watchers of the Wild. They had preyed the men would come to their aid and found their deities gracious.

    It had taken suns to lure the Nicars out from the swamps. The warriors used meat from fresh kills to tempt the beast with an easy meal. With the villagers locked away day and night in their main hall with enough provisions to last them a month, the Nicars soon gave way to their hunger and crept out in the shadows. Once in the open, Zale managed to pierce the lead Nicars heart with a swift arrow, followed by Harden removing its lolling head. The others were thrown into panic and took to the air, shielding themselves from Zale's deadly arrows with their tough hides. As they swooped down in an attempt to retrieve Zale's bow, Harden would spring on them with his sword, slicing at the joints of their wings. Once grounded, the two men battled with their foe, never allowing their gaze to wander to their freezing eyes, until each moved no more.

    The pair now sat drinking and laughing in the sun counting their gold pieces. Money was of little value to them, though it would pay for more arrows and fresh boots when needed. They were both tall men, Harden in his mid-thirties and Zale ten years younger. Zale's long, black hair curled softly round his ears, an inherited trait from his mother. Though strong, he was a fairly thin man, and as such he could run at great speed and had expert agility. He was son of Tre'ath, the late king of Morsenden. Zale's older brother, Lokar, now ruled as Zale chose to leave in search of adventure and become a part of the tales he had read of as a child. He had met Harden just two years earlier, soon after he had left the kingdom, and had travelled with him ever since. Harden had roamed the great lands since his early teen years, rarely staying in one place for more than a few days. He was more muscular than Zale and equally strong. His dark eyes often seemed to hide behind his straight brown, chin-length hair. He was skilled with a blade, though did not share Zale's accuracy with a bow. The pair of them wore black, long-sleeved shirts and long, brown jackets made from animal skins with a belt. Knee-high boots, strapped to the top by crossing laces, half covered their black trousers and they wore full-length, hooded black cloaks to hide them at night. They were solitary men who enjoyed their peace and freedom. They laughed and joked as they recounted the battle they had recently fought.

Nicars, Nicars
Slain now you be!
Foolish were you
To think you better than me!

Zale began to sing merrily, stamping his foot and clapping his hands to create a beat.

The stink of your rotting flesh
Fills the air!
No more shall you plague us!
No more of your evil stare!

Harden continued, standing up and marching round the dead bodies before him.

You plague the villages
Far and wide!
Yet never shall you
Escape our stride!

Stealing children
From young and old,
You wreak havoc,
So we are told!

But now with delight

We raise our swords to the sky!
Never again shall you haunt us!
Never again shall you fly!

They continued like this for some time until they collapsed on the floor, breathing heavily after all their laughter. They poured some of their ale on the rotting bodies and set them alight to rid themselves of the stench that now clung to the air. The flames roared up in front of them, plumes of black smoking rising into the sky, signalling to the village that the task had been done. The small clusters of thatched-roofed huts was situated a league away to the west past a great forest that tickled the foothills of the Sincre Mountains. The colossal giants stretched out across the south-western edge of the White Islands, becoming parallel with the Minar Mountains by the most western cliffs of the land. To the east of the two men rolled grassy hills dotted with shrubs and wild flowers, beyond which rested another forest said to be home to some great power.

Zale stared at the snow-capped mountains that rose up behind him, his pale blue eyes glistening in the sun. He and Harden had traversed them for three moon cycles before happening upon the village. He thought back to the long nights spent sheltering in damp caves to get out of the sharp, cold air. Harden, taking a swig of water from a pouch carried on his belt, felt no need to dwell on the past. His contained too many evils to want to remember, so he had taught himself to look to nothing but the future. Upon the boulder, he sat enjoying the warmth of the sun on his face. Beads of sweat rolled down his cheeks. The two men were leagues away from any land claimed by any of the kings that ruled on the White Islands. It was how they liked it. They felt no obligation to any of the arrogant rulers of the land other than to Luca as she was queen of all that they called home. She kept the peace in the land and allowed any man his freedom when others would have him bound to a lifetime of service. Harden was very fond of the immortal queen, having known her during his upbringing. Zale, however, also felt some duty to Morsenden as it had been his home for many years and royal blood flowed through his veins. Tre'ath had always dreamed of Zale ruling Morsenden, but Zale had not wanted that responsibility at his age when his father died. He had died when Zale just turned twenty. It was tradition for the youngest son to become ruler so long as he had reached the age of adulthood, eighteen years. It was thought that if the youngest were to rule, they would stay upon the thrown for longer and so would learn the desires of the people better. Lokar was only two years older than him, so the people accepted him as the new king without complaint. They understood how Zale felt and knew that if he were not ready, it was not their place to force the title upon him. Zale looked back down on the Nicars and felt his chest swell with pride. He felt that he had accomplished so much more out in the wilderness with Harden than if he had stayed in Morsenden. Lokar had always been interested in politics, spending his days shadowing his father. Zale thought back to the many days he had spent reading about hidden treasures and creatures of magic, and other days where he had set out on his horse at dawn and not returned home until the onset of night. He smiled to himself, cherishing the adventurous memories he now had. Harden noticed Zale's pleasure and began mocking him, saying how young he looked when he grinned in such a manner. Laughter echoed around the mountains as they continued to drink lazily in the sun.

A chill breeze soon swept down from the mountain forcing the men to pull their cloaks around them tighter. The sun was well past its peak and beginning to slip away into dusk when they decided it was time to find shelter and make camp. They collected their packs which were hidden in the undergrowth on the border of the forest and marched a little way up the mountain. They found a cave they had spotted that morning and checked it for animals. Sure there were no beasts lurking in the darkness, the two men rolled out their bed mats and made a fire. Harden pulled out a few strips of dried meat from his pack and handed some to Zale. They greedily chewed on the salty deer hide, washing it down with some water. A distant memory of hunting with his father flashed into Harden's mind, but he soon pushed it away again. His father was long since dead and nothing would change that, so Harden chose not to think of him at all. Zale was imagining what challenge the two of them may face next, eager to continue to develop his swordsmanship. Harden had taught him the basics along the way, though Zale had learnt many skills within the palace walls growing up. Harden looked at him now and thought back to himself in his twenties. He had been travelling most of his life, not through choice, and here was a man with the opportunity to be great and have power, but who had chosen to make his own adventure. Harden admired him for that. Without another word to each other, they lay themselves down by the warmth of the fire and closed their eyes.

The night was still young when Harden woke. The fire still crackled lazily next to him. Zale was crouched by the entrance of the cave, his blue eyes peering out into the shadows.

'What is it?' asked Harden in a gruff voice, snatching up his sword as he went to Zale's side.

'Someone's coming,' said Zale quietly. 'I can hear horses. Over there, in the trees.' Harden strained his eyes and noticed a slight movement in the trees across the plain. Moments afterwards, the two men could see torchlight and a few men riding out of the forest.

'The fire!' said Zale urgently, but the men had already been seen. The riders headed straight towards them with hast. Zale and Harden immediately reached for the hilt of their swords. They could now make out the three men riding towards them. Two were leading an extra stallion each at their side. They bore delicately crafted swords, the lead rider with a bow slung across his chest. Instantly, Zale and Harden rose to their feet, swords unsheathed.

'Who goes there?' Harden called threateningly to the approaching riders.

'Please, lower your swords. We come in peace. We have been sent by Luca, Bringer of Light, to ask for your help.' The man who spoke was leading the other two. They all wore the red and black uniform of Damané's guards and red cloaks. They looked weary, as though they had been travelling for days. 'If you are Harden and Zale that is.' The lead guard looked the two men up and down and seemed content with what he saw.

'What's the matter?' asked Zale urgently, replacing his sword.

'One of our sacred crystals has been stolen.'

'What! Who would do such a thing?' demanded Zale, knowing full-well what the threat meant. He had read tales of the crystals and their powers as a boy but had never thought anything would happen to them.

'No one saw the intruder, though my lady believes it to have been planned by Lord Jabari.' When he heard this, Harden's expression turned to that of fear and hate. His body tensed and his heart began to pound rapidly.

'What is it? Do you know of him?' Zale could not understand why Harden seemed afraid. He did not know much of Harden's past but thought he knew all that Harden feared.

'Yes, I know of him. He killed my father, many years ago. He is the reason why I live out here.' The air was filled with silence. None of the men looked at each other, especially not to Harden. Zale was shocked. He thought that Harden would have told him something like that, though he knew how Harden seemed to hide from the past. Then Harden seemed to shake himself from his thoughts and returned to the matter at hand.

'Is Luca safe?' he asked, his voice filled with apprehension, eager for the response.

'She is fine. It appears the thief went no further than the Tower of Light's middle level. All of your questions will be answered in due time. Are you willing to help retrieve the crystal?'

'Yes!'

Harden was suddenly filled with an anger that he had not felt for many years. Zale had no say in the matter, though he too was eager to help. He and Harden were given the reins of the two stallions. They gathered their packs and mounted the horses. The guards turned as one and began to lead the two men back towards Damané.

The journey took three days of non-stop riding through The Silent Valley and past the Great Sea. All the men sensed a feeling of unrest, as there was no sign of life. No birds. No animals. Not even the wind dared move. They all knew that, slowly, the life was being sucked out of The Land of Light. Clouds were already creeping across the sun. The men did not talk as they galloped towards the city. Each of their minds' was possessed with the thoughts of what would happen to the land if they did not retrieve the stolen crystal. Harden had seemed to slip into a daze, shutting out the entire world, consumed by his thoughts of Jabari. Only he knew how dangerous the magic-weaver truly was.

Lost

An unusual silence had fallen upon the city of Damané. The air was still and the sound of birdsong had died away. It was as though the animals could sense a change for the worse approaching and waited with apprehension. The Tower of Light, however, was full of movement and energy. It appeared more grand than normal with the hive of activity. There were more archers patrolling the rooftops and whispers were circulating of some strange beings wandering through the tower. No one knew where they had come from. It was as though they had sprung out from the walls themselves. The rumours of what had happened and the secret creatures had spread beyond the Masdour and throughout the city. It would not be long before the neighbouring villages would hear of the danger that they all now faced. Security had been increased, though Luca knew there was no real need for it. Jabari had got what he was after and had no need to attack any further. The people of the city, however, felt reassured by the sight of the Damané guard patrolling the streets in pairs, passing on words of comfort to its inhabitants. The people tried to go about their days as normally as possible, though they spoke in hushed whispers and glanced nervously at the approaching clouds. The soot-coloured blanket loomed darkly over Damané's borders, as though waiting for the right moment to strike. Distant claps of thunder echoed across the hills and through the villages. With the hovering shadow came an icy wind that enhanced the ominous atmosphere. Shops were open for fewer hours than normal, everyone feeling safer staying in their own homes. No-one entered or left the city. Those outside feared an attack on the capital, whilst those within feared the dangers that could be lurking just beyond the border.

Luca had been acting strange since she had been given word that a crystal had been stolen. She was seen hurriedly gliding through the tower, darting between alchemists and guards, historians and archers. She needed to know all forms of defence available to her to prevent any further attack to the city and was searching hopelessly for some means of retrieving the crystal without putting her people in danger. The healers of the tower were called to her and instructed in ways to prepare for any wounded men that may return from the attempt to retrieve the crystal. She rummaged through maps and dusty records in an effort to locate Lord Jabari. She once knew him so well, until he asked of her an unthinkable request. She shuddered now at the thought of it and of the crimes the magic-weaver had committed since the day she refused his offer and banished him from her lands. She had sent her best men to capture him, but none had ever returned. Soon after, he had gone into hiding, no one knowing of his whereabouts. Foolishly, Luca had assumed he had fled the White Islands as she had demanded. Luca stared down at the map before her and cried out in frustration. She collapsed to the floor and buried her face in her hands.

'My Lady?' called Milon as he rushed into the room. He feared the worse had happened, but was relieved to find Luca alright. 'MyLady, what's the matter?'

'It's hopeless,' muttered Luca bitterly as she looked into Milon's eyes. Her personal guard could see the hate and anger in the queen's gaze. 'I cannot find him. I can barely even sense the crystal anymore. It's like a fading speck of light in my mind. Why didn't I stop him when I had the chance? I had the power to do so. My people have capabilities beyond any human's understanding, and yet I let him slip away! Now he is taking my power from me as he knows it is bound to the light due to my impure blood.' Luca's anger was growing. Milon shook his head sadly and knelt before his queen. He took her hands and spoke to her softly.

'You are the greatest queen any have known. Your mother was proud of what you had achieved before she passed the thrown to you. You know she would not have done so if she did not feel in her heart you were ready. Your actions are nothing to mock. It was your pure heart that let him go, just as you still know it was the right path to choose. Your people respect you for it.' Luca looked back at him and the anger seeped away from her. A sudden peace washed over her with her guard's reassurance and the mention of her mother. How she longed to be with her again and have her guidance. She had felt so young when she discovered the crystal was gone, as though all her power had been drained from her body. Now, her mind was clear and her strength returned. She stood up tall and thanked Milon. He bowed respectively and stepped aside, ready to follow any course of action Luca chose to take. She swept past him and headed straight for her chamber. Once there, she knelt by the fairies' home and a dozen fist-sized creatures flew up to her. Their disproportionally large wings beat furiously behind their human forms as Luca made her request. Instantly they darted out of the nearby window and shot off in different directions.

'Where are they going?' asked Milon. Luca rose and turned to her personal guard.

'They are going in search of Lord Jabari and to find out what else he has been up to.'

Trolls

As Zale and Harden rode on with haste, another three guards were approaching the Elements' domain. The large wood had a thin, moat-like plain around its borders, encircled by a great forest. The Sea of Life crashed against the precarious cliffs of the Tuli Moors a little way to the south. During the winter seasons when the wind howled between the trees and echoed between the rocks, the sharp scent of salt could be caught on the air within the forest. The animals would hide themselves away from the cold in dens in the undergrowth and nests in the trees. Deep burrows would home families of rabbits whilst natural crevices in the bark would house squirrels and birds. The air would hum with the sound of life and the forest would remain restless all year.

As the guards made their way through the sparse trees of the forest however, they could not hear a sound. Signs of animals were everywhere, though now they stayed in hiding, shying away from the sunlight. The guards felt exposed. It was unnatural for the forest to be so quiet. It was as if life itself had been silenced by an unseen danger. The guards travelled cautiously along an old dirt path. They were on alert, investigating every sound of a twig snapping under their horses' hooves. The stallions whinnied nervously, steam issuing from their nostrils. The guards picked up the pace to move across the eerie plain. There were no birds in the sky, not even the smallest fly skimming across the grass. As the men entered the wood, the trees loomed darkly over them, each taking on the form of a great giant ready to ensnare any trespassers. Thicker and thicker the shrubs seemed to become, barring the way with sharp thorns that caught on the horses' flanks. They drew their swords and battled through the undergrowth. Vines caught around their stirrups and had to be sliced away to allow them to progress. The sound of running water came to the guards' ears as the trees finally began to thin. Light could be seen a little way ahead, suggesting there was a clearing. A strong stench hung in the air like rotten flesh. The guards encouraged their horses on faster as they heard what sounded like a battle taking place. As they made their way through the trees, drawing their swords, great bursts of coloured light could be seen coming from the clearing. Creatures, three metres tall, were fighting the four Elements. They used clubs as weapons and wore straps of animal skin. Their muscular feet stumbled recklessly on the ground laden with rocks, their grey skin oozing green fountains of sweat. They were trolls. Though they were strong, the Elements' powers were not enough to fight off the nine trolls' great arms, which swayed here and there. Their human bodies were fragile and they had been taken by surprise. None of them had the time to draw on their own element to use it in their defence. Instead, they had resorted to using Ancestral spells, which the guards saw manifested in the form of light directed from the Elements' hands. They silently manipulated the energy before casting it out towards their foe. The trolls seemed to be shrouded in some form of protective enchantment, preventing any damage from the battle magic. The Elements soon learnt, however, that the trolls were still susceptible to physical attack. Rings of fire blocked the path of another wave of trolls, seemingly kept alight by Nare, Lady of Fire. Her companions had distracted the trolls long enough for her to draw upon the heat from the sun and convert it into flames. The dry foliage caught easily as she expected, though it was taking a lot of concentration to keep it under control. Her golden hair and red silk gown fluttered in the gusts of wind that emerged from rays of pale blue energy near her. The light came from the left palm of Baaron, Prince of air, as he heaved his great sword above his head, his movements slowed slightly by the armour suited for a king adorned upon his muscular body. His fair face, crowned with rich brown hair, was now fierce and full of concentration as he battled with his enemy. The wind he created was strong enough to slow the trolls, but still he had to evade heavy clubs as they crept closer. Arrows, precisely aimed at the trolls' heads, flew from the Princess of Earth's slender bow intermittently as Acacia, for this was her true name, switched between magic and weapon with incredible speed. She delicately twisted her agile body so as to avoid a collision with a wooden club. Sachiel, Angel of Water, fired sapphire jets of magical energy at the great beasts, all the while keeping his eye on the others, ready to rush to their aid if need-be. Such a time came quickly as Nare, distracted by something through the trees behind her, was knocked to the ground by an accurately swung club. Sachiel ran towards her broken body only to find himself and Acacia suffering from the same fate. Four trolls had pushed forwards through the bombardments of mystical light, gaining enough ground to be close enough to hit the two Elements. Warm blood now trickled down their fair cheeks. Baaron, enraged by the fall of his friends and filled with determination, slashed his sword through the air with deadly precision. As it met the putrid skin of the first troll, its blade shone with a crimson hue. Its edge slid effortlessly through the necks of the four trolls, leaving their bodies to collapse to the floor headless. He turned to face another three trolls and sheathed his sword. As if clinging to some great invisible stones in front of him, Baaron's face turned to that of furious concentration. The air around him was drawn to his hands, accumulating between his fingers. A tornado sprang forth from the palm of each hand, heading straight for the foe before him. The mighty wind touched nothing other than the three beasts which were thrown into the air. After only moments of being held there, their great bodies crashed to the ground and were still. Now drained of energy however,

Baaron was not prepared for the blow from another club to the back of his head. His tired form fell onto that of Nare, the Elements now helpless against the remaining two trolls.

The men from Damané charged at the mighty creatures. The trolls were thrown into confusion by the unexpected threat and started to scatter. Acacia and Sachiel were left unconscious on the ground as Baaron and Nare were dragged away by two trolls that remembered their goal. The guards galloped towards them but it was too late. The trolls were already too far away and Acacia and Sachiel needed help. They watched bitterly as the trolls slung the two Elements' bodies over their shoulders and stumbled off through the trees. The guards turned to Acacia and Sachiel and checked them for their necklaces. The teardrop pendants on silver chains are always worn by the Elements. Each pendant looks as if it contains an entire galaxy of stars. If ever one of these was to be broken, all four Elements would die and the control of fire, water, earth and air would be lost.

'Can you hear me?' One of the guards was trying to rouse Acacia. Her long dark hair hid the soft features of her face as it clung carelessly to the blood that still trickled from her wound.

'There's no use, they're completely out of it.' The captain looked solemnly after the trolls as they clambered up the nearby mountain, slipping on the damp rocks. Though they appeared to be quite slow, the captain knew that trolls are excellent climbers and can travel at great speeds if they wish. 'Put them on their horses and we will guide them back. You,' the captain pointed to the younger of the two soldiers, 'ride back to Damané as fast as you can and tell Luca what has happened.'

The boy did as his captain ordered and set off. Throughout his whole journey, he could think of nothing else but what he had seen and his orders. He had to inform Luca. He had never even come within one hundred metres of her, let alone spoken to her.

As he rode, his captain and fellow guard cleaned up the wounds that had been engraved on the Elements' faces.

'Come on,' said the captain in his rugged voice, 'help me lift them onto the horses.'

'But sir,' said the young guard slightly confused, 'there are no horses here.'

'Is that so?' said the captain with a slight grin. He tilted his head towards the trees and watched the guard's reaction. Galloping into the clearing came two magnificent mares. Their black coats glistened in the light, one with a blue shine and the other with a hint of green. They were the most magnificent creatures the young guard had ever seen.

'How did they know to come?' asked the guard with wonder.

'Now, that I do not know. They always seem to know when they are needed. You see the one with the blue in her coat?' The guard nodded. 'She belongs to Sachiel. Let's get him on her first, and then attend to Acacia.' With that, the two men carried the wounded Elements to their horses and carefully strapped them on the creatures' backs. The senior guard knew the mares would follow them all the way back to Damané and so set off back through the woods. The journey at first was slow as the two guards had to slice a wider gap through the trees. They felt guilty knowing they were damaging nature with the Princess of Earth unconscious behind them. Once they made the open plain, the picked up the pace, constantly checking to ensure the Elements were still secure. The trees of the forest were widely spaced out making it easier for the group to travel. When the finally emerged from watching giants, it was a clear open path all the way back to Damané. For most of the way, the young guard kept looking back at Acacia, unable to believe how beautiful she was.

'You've never seen an Element before, have you?' asked his captain as they gently cantered up a slope. The guard shook his head.

'They are the most beautiful of all creatures. They look just like men and women, yet their skin shines like silver in the light and their eyes look like pearls. You can tell which element they control by their eyes. Do you know how?' Once again the guard shook his head.

'Each is a different colour you see. The Element of fire: red with a swirl of orange. The Element of air: white with a swirl of blue. The Element of water: the deepest blue you have ever seen. And finally, my favourite, the Element of earth: emerald green with a mix of jade. Beautiful.' The captain reminisced for a moment, thinking back to when he first met the Elements during a royal visit to Damané. 'Why anyone would want to harm them I'll never know. They are the kindest of creatures.' The captain then looked back at the two bodies slumped over the horses behind him.

'Which is the Element of earth?' asked the guard.

'She's the one you've been keeping a close eye on,' his captain said with a smile. The guard smiled back and then fell silent. He hoped that they would be all right. They still had a two-day journey ahead of them and their injuries needed attention.

After another half day of travelling however, the guard noticed that the wounds on the Element's faces had almost healed with no sign of a scar. 'Magic,' said the captain simply, 'nothing more than magic.'

News

Luca waited alone in her room for the return of the fairies. Milon approached her once to offer her some food, but she simply remained quiet as she gazed out of her window. Her body was glowing unnaturally. The sun still shone above Damané so Luca used it to her advantage. She was drawing upon its energy, slowing the approach of the clouds. As the warmth filled her being, she felt stronger both physically and mentally. She began to stretch out her thoughts amongst the creatures beyond her borders, searching for any sign of Lord Jabari. There was a shroud of fear to the most eastern reaches of the island that came to her as a foul taste like poisoned water. Her mind could sense gathering movement to the North and she saw an image flash before her eyes of waves crashing about a mighty ship. She ran her hand along the air before her and felt the cool touch of scales beneath her fingertips. The sensation began to burn, forcing her to draw back from the premonition she was calling to her. Her mind wandered further, through the mountain valleys and over great lakes. It took her beyond the cliffs and over the open sea. It reached smaller lands that were still her own, tied to her by ivory threads. She then drew her thoughts back across familiar hills and past rich forests. Her deep blue eyes searched endlessly for anything that was out of place.

Luca had been stood at her window for many hours when a sharp wind woke her from her trance. It stirred her long blonde hair into a frenzy before leaving it to rest upon her shoulders once more. The city was quiet. Stars now littered the saphirine sky and the two moons shone brilliantly upon the tower. Luca looked to the east and saw twelve glowing specks come together and head straight for the highest room of her palace. The fairies dashed into Luca's room and all started speaking at once. Their voices were deep and mellow, yet they spoke with such speed Luca could not keep up.

'One moment my friends,' she implored, 'one at a time.' She moved over to her bed where the fairies gratefully sat down and folded their wings neatly behind them.

'We have grave news,' said the fairy sitting closest to Luca. She had high cheekbones and dazzling green eyes that Luca found hard to look at for too long a time. She had been informed of what each of her companions had discovered and prepared to tell Luca all that they knew. She straightened her crimson dress and tried to tidy her dark silky hair. When she was ready, she took a deep breath and began.

'We could not find Jabari anywhere. We searched the whole island and he could not be found. Not in the forests, not in the mountains, not in any natural cave we could find. The other islands have never heard of him either. They had not yet received word of the threat, so we told them all we could and they are readying to defend themselves if Jabari chooses to attack. We think he is far in the east, however, as the animals have gone into hiding. Jabari is gathering an army. Ships have been seen on the horizon and dark creatures are stirring that haven't been seen for centuries. A hooded man has been going from village to village to purchase strong horses and tack tough enough to carry great men. He has been seen speaking with the blacksmiths of the cities, swapping handfuls of gold for swords and armour. We tried to follow him, but he is a man of dark magic. He can conceal himself entirely. Though there was something else strange about him. We fairies can sense the beings around us as their forms move the air. This man was something we could not sense, not even when we flew next to him.' Luca's mind started to process all the information she had been given. Where was Jabari gathering an army from? As far as she was aware he had no allies other than the sorcerer Xannon. This man the fairies spoke of must surely be Xannon or his manifestation of some form. How he could create an entirely new form of himself that could be communicated with, she did not know. The magic of a sorcerer was far beyond anything she could contemplate, though she knew it was weaker when the sorcerer was young and Xannon had not taken breath too long before. If Jabari was calling the island's dark creatures to him as well then whomever she sent in to retrieve the crystal would have a more dangerous journey ahead of them than before.

'That is not all,' continued the fairy quietly. She could see Luca's mind working and did not like to interrupt the queen's thoughts.

'There's more?' asked Luca. 'What else could Jabari be up to?'

'Shaynar has gone missing. His people have searched for him, but their lands are cast into darkness with his disappearance. They called upon the mountain dwellers for assistance but they are under attack from Wyrms.'

'It appears no one is safe from Jabari,' stated Luca sadly. She rose from her bed and began to pace the room. The fairies, knowing their task was done, fluttered over to the corner of the room and settled themselves back in their homes, the glow leaving their bodies. Luca despised Jabari for what he was doing to the land. She, like her mother before her, had sworn to protect the White Islands and keep the peace between all the creatures that lived there. Now a man who had once been her friend and ally was turning his power against her to destroy all that she loved and cared for.

'Milon,' called Luca. Her personal guard instantly appeared at her door. 'The Wyrms are attacking in the mountains. Send as many men as you can spare to aid in the fight against them. I will need our friends' help in the battle to come. Your men must travel by stealth. I cannot have Jabari focusing his attention on the mountains and threaten our aid. Tell them to keep watch for a stag. They are to keep away from any they see but must go to the valley to the north and inform the people there of the sighting.'

'The valley to the north?' questioned Milon. 'But that's...'

'I know. They will have to be cautious. Tell them not to approach from any direction but north.' Milon bowed and left the room to pass on the orders. The queen glanced back out over the city and marvelled at how peaceful it was. If she did not know better, she would have said there was nothing to fear at all. At least her people were still able to sleep soundly in their homes. She moved away from the window and left her room. Luca felt another vision drawing near her and slipped into a trance. She slowly walked down the tower's steps, seeing images flash before her eyes. There was a purple glow and a cry of pain. The voice was uncomfortably familiar to the queen. She saw an arrow, and then everything went red. The colour seeped away and Luca found herself stood on a bare plateau. A strong wind irritated her silk dress and danced her golden hair around her face. It whipped at her soft features, marking her cheek with a line of crimson. The queen looked about her. The sky was clear but the land was barren. She could not tell if it was the past or the future. Four ribbons of light danced around her; green, blue, yellow, and red. She turned and saw a dark crystal hovering before her. She recognised it immediately and then knew which crystal had been stolen. The land started to spin and all the colours melted into one. There was a soft voice on the air. *Waken.*

Luca's vision cleared and she was back in the tower. There was a thin scratch across her cheek that disappeared almost instantly. She had wandered down a corridor on the third level and found herself staring at a pine door with a star-like symbol engraved upon it. It was a place she did not recognise. She could hear a child's voice coming from inside the room whispering words she recalled from a distant dream. Luca gently pushed the door open and immediately the child went quiet, staring at her.

'Where did you learn that?' asked Luca in a hushed voice. The girl's dark eyes seemed full of knowledge and understanding beyond Luca's imagining.

'It is a gift,' said the girl simply, her dark hair falling carelessly around her shoulders.

'A gift?' questioned Luca. She stepped into the room and noticed that the girl's gaze did not follow her. 'Can you see me?'

'I can see, if that's what you mean,' stated the girl, 'though the time at which I see is not your own. A keeper of time should know what I am.' Luca remembered something her mother once told her centuries before and realisation flickered across her face.

'What makes me worthy to have one such as you in my presence?' Luca asked in awe.

'I am a gift. Onofre sent me.' Luca looked at the girl with wonder. She paused, not sure of what to do. Then the queen turned, closed the door, and prepared to listen.

Forthum

Five valleys to the north, a further three guards of Damané were approaching the Great Hall of Kings in order to inform Caden, General of Forthum, of the situation. They rode with haste along the main road towards centre of the port city. They had had to pass through the gates of the outer wall; a wall that enclosed all the farmland of Forthum. Now there were freshly ploughed fields all about them dotted with barns and stables to shelter the working animals. The boundaries of the General's domain could not be seen on either side in the distance. The haze, caused by the scorching heat of the sun, rose up from the ground like transparent snakes, distorting the appearance of a cluster of trees set in the middle of one of the fields. A layer of pollen clung to the air, hovering like a protective mist before the inner wall. As opposed to the five sentries watching over the outer gate, this wall was patrolled by no less than fifty men clad in heavy body armour. They each carried a bow at their side, ready to make aim whenever the sign of a threat emerged. At that moment, six arrows were trained on the Damané guards. As the guards drew closer, the archers could make out their uniforms and signalled to someone on the ground below. The mighty oak, reinforced gates slowly creaked open to reveal four cavalrymen waiting to escort the guards through the city.

'Welcome, men of Damané,' called the lead rider as the guards drew near. 'We are honoured to be visited by the ruling city.'

'Thank you,' responded one of Damané's guards. 'We are here on official business representing Queen Luca.' There was no further delay as the cavalrymen encircled the guards and began to guide them to the centre of the city.

Within the inner wall resided the homes of all the people of Forthum. The population had grown to fill the entire grounds dominated by General Caden. The houses were wooden, like small ships cast upon the shore in a treacherous storm. They lined narrow dusty tracks and the air smelt of fresh salt. Water could be heard to the riders' left, washing up against a shore. Children in dusty woollen clothing were seen darting between the houses, laughing and joking, playing with small toys crafted from timber gathered from a nearby forest. Every-so-often, an aging woman would open the shutters of her house and demand silence, sending the children giggling off in another direction. The guards' horses trotted through a patch of muddy ground where a new spring has forced its way to the surface. They could see a group of heavily built men attempting to cut off the flow and quickly build a temporary well around it.

Closer to the Great Hall that marked the centre of the immense city, the buildings turned to red brick; taverns, butchers, blacksmiths. Plumes of black smoke billowed out of soot-covered chimneys as the men laboured away. Grey-white smoke melded with it as the women bakers, covered in a thin layer of flour, baked the last loafs of bread for the morning and finished off decorating buns with sweet syrups that the children liked to snack on. A group of beautiful women dressed in finely cut silk dresses glided past the riders having just purchased some fresh venison from the oldest and most respected butcher in Forthum. As they rode on, one of the guards commented on the women.

'It is strange to see women such as they in an area like this,' he said to the cavalryman riding next to him.

'Indeed,' he replied in a smooth, deep voice. It matched his chiselled features and clean-cut hair. 'I would have questioned their motives if Caden's sister had not been among them.' The guard looked surprised.

'Caden's sister chooses to buy from here herself and not send someone in her stead?'

'Oh yes,' laughed the cavalryman, 'she is a very independent woman. No man has yet laid claim to her, and some say they never will. She's a free spirit that one.' The guard glanced back at the women one last time, his gaze catching the eyes of whom he assumed to be the General's sister. The brown orbs sparkled mischievously as she flicked her golden hair behind her.

The dirt road steeped upwards, leaving the shops behind, for the final lead up to the General's residents. The road was trimmed with grand mansions spread far apart, ivory creeping up their cream walls. This gave the guards a clear view of the docks that opened up onto the Great Sea of the North. They bustled with life as men and women alike organised the docking, repair, loading, and launching of dozens of ships a day. Four mighty crafts where moored there now, dark wooden cranes towering above them as they shifted cargo that was to be traded with distant lands. The sails of one of the ships were being tied in tightly whilst a plank was set down to allow its crew back onto steady ground. The sailors looked tired and battered after weeks of crossing the distant oceans. A couple of woman adorned in beige cotton dresses hurried over to them laden with fresh fruit and water. Another ship had just finished being loaded as the guards neared the top of the slope. The ropes keeping it moored were set loose and twenty broad men pushed against its tough undercarriage to force it away from the cranes and into open sea. It took a few moments for the ship to be clear before it dropped its sails and brought out the ores. Thirty men hidden below began to row with all their might in order to turn the mighty vessel and catch the wind.

Between the docks and the Great Hall stood the barracks, busy with soldiers training with swords, both on horseback and on the ground. Fresh cadets, as young as thirteen, were queuing up excitedly, eager to start their first day of training. A man stood before them and started taking their names, looking them over, and then deciding if they were to join the infantry or the cavalry. It was the way the new recruits had always been selected. Some were not fortunate to be chosen at all and so had to remain a farmer, blacksmith, or dock-boy. Those who ended up working on the docks often went on to become sailors for some years whilst they were still young so they could explore the world. The boys who were selected to be infantry were sent straight to a captain to start training immediately, whilst the cavalrymen were first given a young horse and instructed on how to care for it as it was going to become their greatest and most trusted friend. Higher ranking military officers hid themselves away in large tents as they pondered over maps and assessed threats from the surrounding cities and neighbouring lands they were trading with.

The escorting cavalrymen left Damané's guards as they were greeted by five foot soldiers standing watch by the mahogany door of the Great Hall. Damané's guards dismounted and saluted the men respectively. The soldiers let them pass without question, two escorting them to the general. The small group travelled along a wide corridor, passing numerous rooms with people disappearing in and out of them almost constantly. The corridor was filled with light coming from hundreds of flickering candles held in great wooden chandeliers dangling from the ceiling. It reflected off the smooth cream walls and cold slate floor. They soon came upon the centremost room, that which gave the building its name. Its size and the statues of past rulers impressed most that saw it, but the guards of Damané did not give it a second thought. It was nothing compared to The Tower of Light. It was empty but for the statues against the walls that rose to the ceiling, made of a grey stone. From the ceiling, flags baring the shield of Forthum fell to the height of two grown men. Dotted around the room were hollows in the walls containing candles that burned with a brilliant white light. Scholars could be seen huddling around them so as to read scrolls of parchment. The men would pause, read a scroll, and then leave the hall with hurried feet, past the many guards lining it. In the centre of the room was a raised stone platform with at least fifty steps leading up to it on all sides. The steps were shallow but as wide as a house. Caden was sat on a great gold thrown perched in the centre of the platform surrounded by guards. A grand mahogany desk rested in front of him, covered in maps, scrolls, quills, and pots of black ink. Caden was concentrating on a map of a neighbouring island and listening to an advisor who stood to his left. Damané's men approached him, bowing respectively as they neared. The advisor stepped out of ear-shot and gestured to his guards to do the same. Damané's captain spoke in a hushed voice to explain why they had come with no warning. He did not go into details as he knew that all could be explained once they reached Damané. When he heard the news, Caden rose suddenly, putting all of his guards on alert. Believing Damané's guards were threatening him, they surrounded him at once. With a wave of his hand they backed down.

'Captain Selvon! Prepare the armies at once! We go to Damané's aid!' With the general's orders, Captain Selvon bowed and turned on his heel, leaving the hall with haste.

'I am sorry I cannot offer you a meal and a night's rest, but the situation is dire,' apologised Caden to Damané's guards.

'Do not worry. We did not expect anything of the sort. The sooner we reach Damané, the better. Things I'm afraid are not looking good.' The captain stepped aside and Caden walked down the steps before him. He was tall and proud. From a distance, seeing Caden clad in blue and gold, no one would have been able to tell he was not king himself. Forthum, however, had not had a king for many years. It had been decided long ago that the bravest and most skilled of their warriors would be their leader.

'Catrana,' called Caden in a booming voice. When there was no answer, he waved over his advisor. The tall slim man glided over to the General, his navy and grey robes billowing out behind him.

'Dalorn, where is my sister,' asked Caden quietly. 'I need to inform her of the situation before I leave.' His advisor glanced at some of the guards in search for an answer.

'I believe we saw her in the city,' said Damané's captain stepping forwards. 'She was with a group of women having just made a purchase.' Caden did not look surprised, though he was frustrated.

'One day she will be here when I need her,' said Caden. 'Dalorn, find her and inform her of what is happening. Tell the men that she is now in charge. All orders she gives must be followed, understand?' Dalorn nodded and disappeared from the room.

Damané's guards followed Caden out of the great hall and back along the grand corridor. Once outside, they were greeted by Caden's army. The guards were impressed by the speed at which they had been prepared. The cavalry had been the only ones to assemble as they would travel faster and the city still needed protecting. They had pulled on their armour, mounted their steeds, and ridden up the hill from the barracks to the Great Hall. Captain Selvon had brought Caden's stallion from the stables which the General mounted quickly. Damané's guards retrieved their own horses and the mass of men left for Damané at once. Forthum and Damané had been allies for generations. It was Luca who had saved the city from the Bangai dragons seven years before. There had been no way to repay her until now and Caden was determined to do all he could for the suffering queen.

The sight of his army travelling across the great land was spectacular. To watchers from afar, it looked as though a new sea had formed in the valleys as the soldiers' blue cloaks billowed out behind them. Their swords and arrow tips glinted silver in the sunlight. As they travelled, Caden asked the guards from Damané countless questions about the events that had taken place. What he was interested in most was what Luca had planned for the retrieval of the stolen crystal. The guards, however, knew nothing of her intentions. They were not even aware that she had called upon the service of Zale, Harden and the Elements. After half a sun Caden gave up his interrogations and rode on in silence.

Zobor

By the time all the parties had arrived, Damané was looking grim. Dark clouds lined the sky and, in the distance, forks of lightning stretched like fingers across their azure bellies. Thunder echoed around the peaceful villages, which were now cast entirely into shadow. High up on the Minar mountains, blankets of white hid the great rocky peaks, the thick snow glistening ominously as it encroached upon the city. The wind cut through the farmers' clothes like shards of ice, leaving a glassy coating upon all it touched. As the horses carried their loads towards the tower, their hooves skidded precariously on the frost bitten cobbles. The mystical fountain now looked pale, a distant expression on the once beautiful woman's face.

The Elements had been briefed about the crisis when they had woken just one sun earlier. They had soothed the remainder of their injuries with enchanted water, created by Sachiel from nothing more than leaves lying in a river they had passed. They arrived in Damané half a sun after Zale and Harden. Each party had been offered a room in the Masdour to rest in, though none of them could sleep. They were all eager to speak with Luca and plan a course of action against their common enemy. Caden and his army approached the city a few short hours after the Elements. He commanded his cavalry make camp on the bordering hills whilst he set off with Captain Selvon towards the tower. Damané's guards showed them to another room in the Masdour where they would wait to be summoned by the queen. The people of Damané were grateful for the site of Caden's men watching over them from their camp.

The day wore on slowly and still the allies heard nothing from the tower. One by one, Damané guards were arriving back at the city, riding up to the Tower of Light and rushing inside to Luca. Once all had returned, the queen finally informed Milon she was ready to speak with those waiting. Milon hurried to the Masdour to gather each party and escort them to his Lady. Caden asked Captain Selvon to await his return, knowing Luca would want to speak with him and any other leaders in private. He made his way through the beautiful gardens to stand with the others. Before entering the tower, the allies greeted each other respectfully and realised that Luca must truly fear Jabari if she thought she needed help from ones such as the Elements to retrieve the crystal. Harden was the only one who had some knowledge of Jabari and Zale had realised that Luca shared his dread. Since arriving, Zale had asked his friend why Lord Jabari was to be feared as much as he was, but Harden did not want to discuss the matter until after they had spoken with Luca.

They stepped through the great oak doors, leaving the magnificent gardens that sill clung to summer's breath behind, and began their journey up the winding stairs, just as Xannon had done. When they reached the top chamber, they found Luca sat in a large, white marble thrown. In turn, they each bowed and then found themselves marvelling at the room. It was very light as everything was made of white marble, even the walls. Arches towered twenty metres above them, spaced evenly apart. Lining the walls were sixteen metres tall statues of the previous rulers of Damané. Acacia looked a bit closer at the walls and noticed that, carved in the Ancestral Tongue, there were the stories of how each ruler had lived and died. The immortal Elements had often visited the great tower when Luca's mother ruled, though none had ever entered that chamber. Zale could not believe the size of the room, as from the outside it only looked fifteen metres wide, yet when inside, it felt three times as large.

'Thank you for coming.' As she spoke, everyone's attention turned to Luca. They could see that she did not have her usual glow. Her skin was very pale and her eyes had lost their sparkle. Even her voice sounded empty.

'As you may have noticed, Damané is dying, as am I. The Land of Light needs your help. I had hoped more of our allies would come, but I know of the troubles that litter the land and that each ruler must look to their own people. However, this danger that presses against us now shall affect every creature beneath our sun. Lord Jabari has used his sorcerer Xannon to steal one of our sacred crystals. Harden, you of all people knows what he is capable of.'

'Yes, I know what he is capable of.'

'Where is he?' asked Caden importantly.

'All I know is he has the crystal somewhere beyond the eastern border of this land.'

'How is it that you know this?' Zale was the one who spoke this time. He was new to the powers of the land and had already been surprised to find that there were ones who controlled the elements. He had only dreamed of magic and mythical creatures when he was a boy, never suspecting that all the stories were true.

'I can sense each crystal and thus I know where it is in relation to the others, though the feeling is weak. Lord Jabari has used dark magic to suppress my abilities in an effort to hide it from me.'

'I will take my army and leave at once!' As Caden turned and began to head for the door, Luca spoke again.

'No brave General. Where you are going you cannot take your army.'

'Where is it that you would have me go, My Lady? My army can traverse any ground at great speed. I would have your crystal back in a matter of days.'

'No Caden. Your army will not go where you must. To find the crystal, you must go through The Forbidden Valley.' A murmur spread throughout the chamber.

'But that is home to the Domai.' Caden had fear in his voice. His strong demeanour now turned to one of a fearful child, his sandy blond hair seeming to add youth to his face. He had been General for more than two decades and feared nothing other than what lay within the Forbidden Valley. His armour was all that now kept his appearance of authority.

'Yes. For this task you will need their help.' Caden tried to protest but Luca raised her hand and silenced him. Unaffected by the mention of the Domai, Acacia stepped forward and bowed.

'Which crystal was stolen, Your Highness?'

'The Crystal of Death.'

A murmur spread throughout the chamber for a second time. The Crystal of Death is the one crystal with dark powers. Each crystal controls some part of the lives of Damané's people. There is a pale blue crystal called the Crystal of Lensen that controls the rain. There is also a brilliant yellow crystal that gives out a golden light. This crystal, the Crystal of Sunar, controls the sun. The Crystal of Death decides who will die, when and how. Any who touch the crystal have sentenced themselves to death. Xannon had not known this when he stole it. It had not been his brother that he had seen in the crystal, but himself. Some day soon he would die. The Land of Light is in a perfect balance as long as all ten crystals are in place. With the Crystal of Death missing, the land would be turned into chaos. Eventually, the land would be destroyed by the very things that sustained it.

'Elements, I called upon you as I had hoped that you could keep the land in balance until the others returned. However, I have been informed that Baaron, Prince of Air, and Nare, Lady of Fire, have been taken. Lord Jabari must have known that I would ask for your help, just as I had feared. Now I ask you to travel with these men and help them when the elements battle against them.'

'Of course Your Highness. Sachiel and I would like to help in any way possible. We would like a chance to save our fellow Elements,' said Acacia, bowing.

'There is an ancient prophecy that all used to know and fear. Most, however, did not even know what it meant. I myself had forgotten its words and its existence, until after the crystal had already gone missing. It was recited to me by one who knows more of these things than any of us can imagine. They are here today for you all to hear so you have some understanding of what may happen. From listening to it, you shall see as I have that some of it has already come to pass. Please, step forward.' Luca gestured to a child standing by the wall to the group's left. It was a young girl with long, brown hair. Her eyes were dark and mysterious and her robe was the colour of the night's sky. None of the allies had noticed her there. Sachiel and Acacia looked upon her with wonder, realising what form of creature she was; a being with powers that far outweighed their own. The girl bowed to Luca and began. As she spoke, her eyes turned a glassy white, as if in a trance, and her voice echoed throughout the room.

When the moons are full and the keepers don't waken,
Then shall the shining secret most sacred be taken
By the enemy once dear to all,
Then the royals begin their call.

All that was light will be cloaked with dark,
And the land itself shall be broken at heart.
Come will the allies from distant lands,
The fate of the people in their hands.

Those of sin shall be blinded from their task,
Until the young are looked to at last.
On their journey they will be touched
By the Elements in evil's clutch.

The sun be high on that fatal day
When the young are heroes and their life gives way.
Rivers are formed from strangers alike,
When the ancient enemy use their might.

All the world be healed by love
When the dear one is taken by Disuff.
But remember those that were sacrificed
And a miracle shall come forth and bring life.

When it was over, the girl went back to where she had been standing before. She stared oddly at the opposite wall, her face full of knowing and wisdom.

'It speaks of Disuff!'

'Yes Sachiel. That is why I wanted you to hear it. When the name of the creature of death itself is mentioned, I do not ask any to go on this quest lightly. It took me a long time to decide what to do. The thought of this winged black wolf haunting your path does not sit well with me.' As she thought of it, Luca could almost see his blood-red eyes and yellowing teeth in front of her.

'We knew when you called upon us that we may have to face him in the end,' said Harden. He looked sadly into the queen's eyes but did not hold her gaze.

'If any of us were not willing to face these dangers, we would never have come.' Acacia's words comforted Luca slightly. The others all nodded in agreement with the Princess' words.

'What did it mean by the young are looked to?' asked Caden, showing he had no reservations about the journey ahead.

'No one knows, Caden,' said Luca, turning her thoughts away from what may come. 'I only give the prophecy to you as a warning. The first two stanzas have come to pass. As soon as you are rested, you must leave at once. Already the unity of time has been disrupted. Now there is almost no light touching the land. I must warn you though; it is likely that Xannon has placed a spell on Jabari's keep to hide it from your eyes. My scouts could find no sign of it, though they heard rumours of Jabari gathering an army. They will see you before you see them.'

Moments after she had finished speaking, a boy with brilliant blue eyes ran into the chamber followed by ten guards.

'I am sorry Your Highness. We tried to stop him.' The guard speaking was the one who had summoned the Elements and was heavily out of breath.

'It is alright Captain Bynach.' Luca raised her hand and Captain Bynach bowed and left the room in silence. A kind smile spread across Luca's face as her eyes fell upon the boy. 'Why are you here child?'

'I am sorry Your Highness,' Bazyli did the biggest bow he could and continued breathlessly, 'but I saw a hooded man riding fast out of Damané late at night eight suns ago. I had been riding, as my horse was restless. It did not seem right for someone to be leaving the city alone after dark so I decided to follow him. He travelled for four suns in total.' Bazyli took another deep breath.

'It is alright child, take your time.' Bazyli looked up at Luca and her smile broadened. He slowed his pace and continued.

'The late on the third sun he spent creeping through the Forbidden Valley. I recognised it from maps I have seen in the Masdour. I stayed high on the slopes so he would not see me. I feared to travel through the valley itself for there were strange noises that came from its mouth. I lost track of him along the way, but eventually caught up with him on its eastern edge where he stopped. Ahead of him was a great lone mountain guarded by dragons. At its base there looked like a maze of stone. The man paused for a moment and took out what looked like a large crystal from a bag over his shoulder. It was black and he studied it closely as if he were looking for something. Then he took another two steps forwards and looked relieved. That was when I turned and rode as fast as I could back here. It was all I could do to make it back so soon.'

'Xannon,' muttered Harden with anger.

'Yes. It seems as though I was right about the spell.' Luca paused for a moment, lost in her thoughts. 'But for some reason, this young boy can see through it. What is your name?'

'Bazyli, Your Highness.'

'Where do you live? Your parents must be worried.'

'My true parents have gone, Your Highness. They died two summers past. I am now in your charge. I care for your gardens whilst I live with Shethar. He is one of your alchemists, Your Highness. He was a friend of my parents and has taken me in.' A deep sadness touched Luca's heart as she heard this. Bazyli did his best to smooth out his matt of black hair and wipe the splatters of mud off his face. His clothes were made of beige cotton and seemed to be three sizes too big. His entire body seemed to be covered in dirt, as if he had travelled through a marsh of some sort at great speed. After a moment of thought, Luca spoke again.

'I am sorry about your parents. Can you do something for me?' Bazyli nodded. 'Can you tell these men, and woman, exactly where you left the man?'

'It was dark. I won't know the way. It was my horse who tracked him.' There was a long pause and everyone in the room looked as though all hope was lost. The eastern border of the Forbidden Valley stretches for leagues down the island. It would take days, even weeks, to find the location of the keep, especially as the men would not be able to see it.

'I understand,' said Luca to Bazyli. She then turned to address the others. 'I will need time to think on this. At worst, you will have to travel to the valley and hope the Domai have seen signs of the keep. Now, it has been suns since you all had some rest. You must stay in the tower for half a day and refresh before your journey. I would say that you should stay the night, but I do not know when the sun shall settle back behind our neighbouring mountains. Our days are growing longer. Please, wait outside until the guards call you. Enjoy the fresh air while it lasts.' With that, the group of warriors knew it was time to leave Luca to her thoughts and ask her no more questions. They all left the great room to wait outside the tower. Fear gripped each of them for the uncertainty of their mission would surely be the downfall of them all and the end of the White Islands.

Protection for a Dark Hope

The warriors had left the chamber in which Luca sat, the young girl following in their wake unnoticed, leaving Bazyli gazing around at the carvings on the walls as he drifted towards the exit. Bazyli had just reached the door to go in search of Shethar when Luca stopped him.

'Have you been living in Shethar's quarters?' the queen asked him.

'Yes, Your Highness,' he replied. 'I am on my way there now to let him know I am alright. He must have been worried as I haven't returned in so long.' Bazyli thought he saw a tear in Luca's eye, but it was gone almost as soon as it came so passed it off as his imagination.

'May I join you?' Luca paused, still sat watching Bazyli. 'I am afraid I have some difficult news for you.' Bazyli froze. He recognised the tone of voice Luca had used. He had heard it just two years before. His heart began to race, the sound of it thumping in his head like an uncontrollable drum. Hoping she would not continue, he simply nodded and left the room. Luca was not far behind him. He travelled down the seemingly endless stairs with hurried feet. With his speed, the orbs of blue fire seemed to pulse as though they chose to mimic his own racing heart. When he was a few floors down he shot off to the left down a narrow corridor. He glanced into the rooms that opened onto it, peering through the glass vials and strange measuring equipment that were set upon high tables. He saw familiar faces of alchemists working away. A couple saw him and gave him a sympathetic look that hurt him deeply. He felt uncomfortably hot, desperation seeping into his bones. At the end of the corridor was another set of winding stairs, this one even narrower than the first. He darted up them two at a time, his breathing fast and sharp. Down another corridor he went, the world around him becoming a blur as he broke into a run. Door after door he fled by, until at last he came across a room to his left with a deeply engraved mahogany entrance. The young boy darted inside.

'Shethar?' he called as he looked around the small room. It had a double bed in the far left-hand corner, a pile of cushions heaped on the floor at the end of it. A glass table stood to Bazyli's right covered in various vials each with its own brightly coloured liquid. Other than that the room was bare. Bazyli turned to Luca.

'He must be working. He's always been a hard worker. I didn't check the workstations properly. He must have been in one of the store cupboards or advising a colleague.' There was panic in the young boy's voice. His eyes darted nervously around the room like an animal falling into a trap.

'Shall we go and sit on the bed?' asked Luca softly.

'We can wait for him there I suppose,' replied Bazyli. Once he had sat down, he started to rock slightly back and forth, staring at the floor. Luca placed an arm around him and looked into his young face.

'He was very brave,' she began quietly. 'He was trying to stop that man you followed. He was trying to protect Damané, and you.' Tears silently rolled down Bazyli's face. 'He couldn't have known how powerful Xannon was.' Luca paused so that the young boy could take it all in.

'He left me.' Bazyli's words, so quiet, so soft, echoed in Luca's mind.

'What..?'

'They've all left me.'

'No Bazyli, no one has left you,' said Luca kindly. 'They are still with you, and always will be. He did not mean for it to…'

'Then why do they all go? Why am I alone?' Bazyli's glance at Luca caught her off-guard. There was so much hate in that boy's eyes that it felt as though she had been burnt. Bazyli then buried his face in his hands.

'Why didn't they get out of the house?' Bazyli's voice was muffled, almost inaudible. 'Why didn't she leave? She never gets hurt, never! Why didn't she stay and be with me?' Luca could barely sit there and listen. There was so much pain in that boy's voice. It was as though he was there as it was all happening again. She was not sure who he spoke of, but she could feel his loneliness as if her whole life had just been stripped from her. 'Why did he have to fight? Why didn't he think of me? He could have just come back to me. Why didn't he want to have me? Why does no-one want to have me?' Bazyli's words then faded into sobs of tears. Luca held him in her arms as he cried, releasing all the pain that had swelled inside him for all those years. As his tears subsided, Luca spoke again.

'He knew that by stopping that man he could be with you.' Luca forced Bazyli to look into her kind eyes. There was no hate in his gaze anymore. She was simply looking down at an innocent child who felt alone and defenceless. 'Xannon could have hurt you, and Shethar knew that. He was protecting his son.' Luca was not sure if she should have named Bazyli Shethar's son without fully knowing how close they were, but Bazyli seemed to understand. He dried his face with the cuff of his sleeve and hugged the queen tightly.

'Then I want to help,' he said at last.

'You already have,' said Luca, 'by letting us know what lies at the end of our allies' journey.'

'But I can help in another way,' continued Bazyli, fiddling with his sleeves and looking away. 'If Shethar wanted to stop Xannon, then I do too. I can lead them to him.' Luca pulled back with shock. She had never dreamed that one so young would be willing to make such a sacrifice.

'You know how dangerous that would be, don't you?' she asked, hopeful that he would change his mind.

'Yes,' said Bazyli firmly, 'but there's no other way, is there?' There was truth in his words and Luca knew it. She shook her head sadly.

'I don't know if I can allow it.' Luca was thinking back to the prophecy that was already unfolding and fear was creeping into her heart. As she recalled its words she felt she almost had no choice in the matter. Their best hope rested with this boy and she could not deny it. She silently nodded her head and Bazyli jumped up.

'Well then, I will go and get my horse ready.'

'Not so fast,' interjected Luca. 'If you are to do this, then I will send someone to protect you. You will be the most important person on the quest, for it is only you who can guide them.' With that, she got up and left the room. Whilst she was gone, Bazyli went over to the glass table and selected a small wooden case. He then spent a few moments choosing twelve specific vials and placed them carefully in delicate holders within the case. They were secret concoctions the alchemists had created for use in healing, making light, and defence. Shethar had shown him what each vial did when either shaken or broken, but Bazyli always thought that they could do more somehow. He had only taken ones that Shethar had ever permitted him to use. The case was necessary to stop the liquids being shaken around and activated. Shethar had once told Bazyli that a secret charm had been placed on the case many centuries ago that would preserve all that was placed within it's protective walls. Bazyli slid the willow case into his pocket, sat back down on the bed, and waited for Luca to return. The red and gold silks around him that had once brought him so much warmth now felt cold and dangerous. The distinct smell of Shethar's clothes hung in air as it always did; a mixture of chemicals and smoke. It was as though he had only moments before left the room and would return shortly. Bazyli desperately wanted to leave. He could feel a lump in his throat as he pushed away further tears that threatened to come with memories that now flooded back to him. When Luca finally returned, Bazyli was on the edge of fleeing the room but relaxed with curiosity as he saw that she was followed by an unusual man.

'This,' said Luca, 'is Lysias, one of the Kai'rae, protectors of my people.' The man wore a sleeveless, cerulean tunic with a cream belt. From the belt hung two curved swords, one on each side, and a quiver of arrows was strapped to the man's back. His tanned, muscular arms befitted that of a great soldier, as did his powerful legs, though they were covered by cream trousers that matched his belt. High, leather boots protected his feet and shins. They looked old and worn, as though they had already seen many battles. It was when Bazyli studied the man's face that he realised that he was not a man at all. His features were as fair as Luca's, his white blond hair resting naturally in tall spikes like mountain peaks. This, however, was not what was unusual. His eyes were completely black, except for the very corners where the darkness faded into a brilliant white. His ears were tipped with deadly sharp, pale spikes. Shimmering sea-green scales stretched across the hollows of his cheeks until they blended into skin and disappeared completely.

'What kind of creature is he?' asked Bazyli after staring at his features for a while.

'As I say, he is a Kai'rae. They are creatures that have similar traits with both my own people and the Domai. Only five remain on the White Islands. He is the most capable being I know of to protect you on your journey.'

'I will do all that I can to prevent any harm coming to you.' Lysias spoke with a calm, deep voice. It sounded almost enchanted, as though he were weaving some ancient magic melody.

'Thank you,' said Bazyli in awe of Lysias.

'Now you have been acquainted,' said Luca, 'we must inform the others of the new plan. I am sure there will be some protest, but that cannot be avoided.' With that, Luca led Bazyli and Lysias back down the small winding stairs that lead to another part of the entrance hall and out to the gardens of the tower. Bazyli had never appreciated crisp fresh air as much as that moment. It was as though he were breathing out all of his pain and simultaneously taking in the first breaths of a new live. Everything around him seemed more vibrant. Now he knew his life had a definite purpose and it enthralled him. He could hear the allies' voice more clearly than he ever remembered hearing another sound. The group of warriors were huddled beneath a willow tree, icy mists escaping their lips as they talked together.

'It has been decided,' declared Luca as she approached, snapping them all to attention, 'that Bazyli, a very bold and courageous boy, shall lead you to Jabari's keep.' They all looked at each other as if they had miss-heard what was said. Luca knew that this announcement was about to start a debate and simply winked at Bazyli reassuringly.

'Absurd! We cannot be responsible for a child!' Caden was outraged by the suggestion.

'There's no question of responsibility,' said Sachiel. 'It is just so dangerous. Is there really such a need to risk the life of one so young?'

'Precisely,' said Caden. 'If it can be avoided, which it can, then so it should. I do not want to carry the guilt that follows a child's death.'

'But Caden,' said Zale as the General began to pace up and down, 'what are we going to do when we get there. Even if he tells us exactly where Jabari's keep is we still won't be able to see it. We won't know what's waiting for us just on the other side. It is his choice. He has as much right to defend Damané as we do, maybe more.'

'I agree with Zale. If he is willing, I think the boy should travel with us. If you like, as I am the only female, I will look after him.' Luca looked at Acacia with pride. She had known that the men would be uncomfortable with a woman around, especially one as beautiful as Acacia. She had long dark hair and skin the colour of the earth itself. Her green eyes captured the gaze of all who looked at them. She wore a strap of black leather that only covered her chest and tight black trousers. Her bow and arrows were worn across one shoulder and a long sword hung by her left side. All the men knew that she was a powerful woman and none dared challenge her.

'I appreciate that,' said Luca, 'and I would ask that you all look out for Bazyli. I am also, however, sending another with you specifically to watch over him.' For the first time the warriors noticed Lysias standing behind the queen. He stepped forwards and bowed respectively to them all.

'A Kai'rae,' said Sachiel admiringly. 'You have been greatly honoured Bazyli. You could not be in better hands.' Lysias bowed again, Sachiel reflecting the gesture.

'I do not mean to sound ignorant,' began Zale, his cheeks turning slightly ruby, 'but what is a Kai'rae?'

'We are the protectors of the Rayden,' explained Lysias. 'We took an oath many centuries ago, before either we or the Rayden came to these shores, to watch over their people and save them from harm. My people, like the Rayden, have now left the White Islands, their location unknown. Only twelve of us remained. Since those days, seven of my companions have fallen, leaving myself as the leader of our group.'

'Surely you cannot spare one of your true protectors,' said Caden suddenly, 'especially not the lead warrior.'

'I can spare whomever I wish good General,' said Luca.

'I will be honoured to fight by your side,' said Harden from the back of the group. Luca smiled and the others nodded in agreement, but Lysias seemed almost confused by the remark.

'Then it is settled,' announced Luca, not noticing the words' affect on Lysias. 'Bazyli will be your guide. Before I take my leave, there is one last thing. I have asked the help of the Dûr'baëns. They themselves do not know where the crystal lies, but I believe you will need them before the end. They have their own battles to face now, but I hope they will be resolved by the time they are required. Once you have located the keep you must find some way of informing them of where to meet you. Their home lies in the wild forest situated in the fork of the Réligh Mountains.'

'I will ensure the task is done,' said Acacia importantly.

'Thank you, I know you will,' replied Luca gratefully. 'Harden, I have something else to say to you.' The warrior stepped forwards and looked hopefully into the queen's eyes. Luca dropped his gaze and spoke in a hushed voice. 'Sino baria unu das mer chantin lay mursanda tor onley.' Zale, Caden and Bazyli looked puzzled, but Harden simply nodded and bore a face of gratitude. Sachiel, Acacia, and Lysias looked completely shocked, and Acacia gave Luca a concerned look. Ignoring this, Luca continued, 'Your rooms should be ready for you soon. When they are, a guard shall call you.' Luca then turned on her heel and left the group standing there. None other than Lysias and the Elements knew who the Dûr'baëns were, but they were sure Luca would not have asked for their help unless they were powerful creatures. Zale kept wondering whether he should ask Harden what Luca had said, but decided that if she had wanted the others to know, she would not have spoken a strange tongue.

Now with the knowledge of what was to be done, Caden found Captain Selvon and instructed him to send half his army back to Forthum and order the remaining men to stay and guard Damané. Captain Selvon was keen to know what had been discussed in the tower, but he kept his emotions hidden and did not question his General. Caden returned to the gardens to find the group stood in silence. The wind swept past them and up to the peak of the tower, carrying fallen blossom in its invisible hands. Acacia and Sachiel looked at the dark clouds gathering on the horizon and knew that Damané would soon be cast into shadow. They began talking with words the others did not know. Zale noticed that it was slightly different to that which Luca had spoken with, though to him it was just as strange.

'Se treo cus don mino so krin sythin. Bi forg pillias dewar don hyl, vars dre nai. Se xenna bi wachi dre jool,' said Acacia in a soft voice. She looked upon the villages below her as she said it.

'Gre dre se Acacia, ins laysa doon se treo cus Nare ers Baaron. Se harge fe Acacia. Se harge don sielle noi pre fe skillia. Se noto fe drenna,' replied Sachiel with a note of pain in his voice.

'Ers se noto Baaron drenna, ins bi wach dre naizin cus varen ni don monienta. Vars opda ly don yarsa vu Grentianna Sondellio.'

A single tear rolled down Acacia's cheek.

'Do not fear so for these people,' said Lysias, catching Acacia off-guard. 'They are strong and have their own allies on these shores that I believe will come to their aid before the end. Nare and Baaron are also very strong. You know this. You will see them again.' Lysias then stepped away from the group and looked out at the Minar Mountains. Acacia took comfort in his words. She and Sachiel were wise, but she knew Lysias had so much more knowledge and experience of the world, and for that she trusted him.

The group stood in silence once more, each member overwhelmed with thoughts of Jabari and the road that lay before them all. With Bazyli to guide them, hope touched them once more, but it was a dark hope.

Zale

The sun was still high above their heads, even though over an hour had passed and it should have been closer to the Sincre Mountains from where Zale and Harden had come, when the silence was first broken.

'I need to talk to Luca for a while,' said Harden turning to Zale. 'Stay here with the others. I will not be long.' Zale nodded and watched Harden re-enter the tower.

Harden uttered a few words to the guards inside and proceeded up the great stairs. Once he reached Luca's chamber, he knocked quietly on the blue topaz door. When there was no response, Harden pushed the door gently and stepped into the room. Luca was sat on her bed, just as she had been eight suns earlier when the crystal was stolen. She was looking out of her window, untouched by the light filtering into her room.

'I was wondering when you would come back to talk with me Harden, son of Pysira.' Luca did not turn her head to address him but merely lifted her hand and beckoned him in.

'Your Highness,' began Harden, bowing in respect. 'I fear that many lives will be lost in the days to come. I beg of you, leave these shores. I cannot protect you from so far away, and now with you sending Lysias with us I fear even more for your safety. If a Kai'rae must come with us, send another in his stead. You know Nerina is just as capable.' Harden's voice was pleading and desperate.

'Harden, I have many guards. Milon is especially an excellent man to have in times of need. By sending Lysias I can be sure Bazyli will be safe. I must do all I can to protect him from the prophecy. Besides, where would I go? The lands where my people reside have been kept secret from me my whole life. The truth of their location died with my mother.' Luca paused, thinking of how she longed for her mother's wisdom now. She knew she would have consoled her and known the best action to take. Still not looking at Harden, Luca continued. 'I need you to do this for me, as I know that only you can see it is done. After all, you have another to protect. You must train him to fight and defend himself. He must also learn the ways of magic. Can you do that for me?'

'Yes Your Highness.' Harden dropped his head. 'He is a great warrior. He will be ready when it is time.'

'Good. But Harden, he must never know of his fate. You must only guide him to it. Only he can decide with an honest heart. If he does not do it out of love for his people but merely out of what is expected of him, he shall fail.' Luca turned to face Harden as she spoke her words of warning. Their eyes locked for a moment and a ghost of the sparkle that had faded from Luca's eyes appeared for an instant. She looked away and it was gone.

'Send him up to me Harden. I wish to speak with him. There is something I must give him for his own protection.' Harden bowed and turned to leave.

'Wait Harden,' Luca rose from her bed and walked to the door where he stood. She looked into his eyes and then kissed him. 'Stay safe my love.' Harden placed a hand on her cheek and then with it followed the shape of her body down to her stomach. There it rested and he looked at her white robes beneath his fingers. Luca looked down with him and placed her hand on top of his. Harden then turned and left her alone in her chamber.

Luca sat back down on her bed, silent tears rolling down her cheeks. She muttered a prayer under her breath and wiped her face dry. Sitting up straight, she smoothed out her robes and pat down her hair. There was the sound of footsteps approaching her door. When they stopped outside she called for the person to come in.

'You asked to speak with me Your Highness?' Zale stepped into Luca's chamber, his black hair falling untidily to his shoulders.

'Yes. Come, walk with me.' Luca's voice was calm and steady. She walked past him and out of her chamber. Bewildered, Zale followed. As they walked in silence down the steps, he noticed how graceful Luca was. She appeared to float over the ground and every time the light hit her, she seemed to glow. When they reached the centre level, Zale thought he could hear a whispering. He had heard it when going to Luca, but thought he had imagined it. Now he was sure. It appeared to be coming from the only door on that level, but guards surrounded it so he could not investigate. Luca noticed he had stopped and smiled.

'Come Zale. Do not worry yourself with that room. It is merely the home of the crystals. Once one is taken, none may enter unless they carry the one crystal that is no longer present. It is sure death otherwise.' Zale took one last look at the door, and then followed Luca down the remaining stairs.

Once in the great entrance hall of the tower, Luca turned left and walked up to the wall. It was the only part of the wall with no inscription. All that was there was a jade leaf, no larger than Zale's palm, trimmed with gold. It seemed to grow out of the wall itself. There, Luca stood and began to mutter some words under her breath in the same language that she used when speaking with Harden. *Ravlea ton sescrata.* To Zale's surprise, the leaf split in two and the wall parted to reveal a secret tunnel. Without a word, Luca entered it and Zale followed obediently. It began as a set of marble steps leading underground, but soon turned into a rocky passage with a thin film of water on the walls. Zale could hear a low rumbling ahead of them and began to feel nervous. Luca did not appear shocked or scared by the noise, but continued down the passage. She suddenly went out of sight and Zale sped up. To his amazement, the passage opened into a great cavern, larger than any city he had seen and taller even than the sky. On the walls danced thin slivers of silver caused by light reflecting off a lake in the centre of the cave. The lake touched one of the walls where a beautiful waterfall fed it from a slit in the rock at least thirty metres wide. Surrounding the lake was an area of open grass that glistened with dew. Here and there were old tree stumps covered in green moss with purple flowers. A dense forest lined the cave except for where Zale and Luca had entered. The light that filled the cave came from sapphires the size of houses that could be seen poking out of the water. They were like precious ice burgs waiting to be discovered. Zale looked around in wonder. As his eyes travelled upwards, he could see a sea of stars above him, though, when he looked closer, he could see that they were not stars at all. They were fairies. Luca watched him silently, smiling as his face lit up with delight. Zale looked at her, speechless. He glanced back at the flying creatures and saw a few of them pointing and whispering, before darting off in another direction. Zale caught the sound of a beautiful song on the air, though he could not make out where it originated. The words were strange to him, yet that made him feel at peace. Luca began to walk away from him towards the lake. The light from the sapphires caught her dress and her whole body seemed to reflect it. Her deep blue eyes were more enchanting than ever. The fairies danced in the air around her as though drawn to her beauty. Zale followed her, noticing the ground turned silver beneath her bare feet. He was about to say something when the water stirred. It was then when he noticed an island, no larger than Luca's chamber, in the centre of the lake. Out of the water jumped what Zale thought to be a brilliant white horse. It landed softly on the island and gazed at him, its eyes shining silver in the light. In the centre of its head rose a single ivory horn, etched as if it were a spiral shell. Zale forced himself to look away and stared at Luca.

'It's a unicorn!' he said softly in surprise.

'Yes. He is called Silvarna.' Her voice was soft a melodic. Luca looked back at Silvarna and nodded. The unicorn leaped into the air and glided over the mass of water. He landed gracefully on the bank closest to Zale without even skimming the smooth, azure surface. Slowly, he stepped towards Zale. When they were eye-to-eye, Silvarna reached forwards with his nose and touched Zale gently on his forehead. He then gave one last glance at Luca and went back to the lake. He galloped round it until he reached the waterfall. There, he watched Zale for what seemed like an age, and then went behind the falling water.

Waking from his trance, Zale turned to Luca, jaw open.

'What did he do? I feel different.'

'He blessed you. You are more important than you know Zale. In time, you will learn. I brought you here to give you something that will help protect you.' Luca directed a hand towards one of the mossy tree stumps. In the centre of it grew a single purple flower. Luca flicked her fingers slightly and the flower broke away from its stem and floated into the queen's hand. Luca turned to Zale and showed him the simple beauty resting on her palm.

'Blessaynor silvinari.' With the Rayden's words came a cool breeze. It whirled around the flower and a burst of light came from its petals. The song around Zale changed, becoming louder and increasing in tempo. The light grew in intensity, filling the entire cave, forcing Zale to look away. The flower rose from Luca's palm, shrouded in light. There it hung, hidden entirely. The fairies darted away and into the trees. A moment later there was silence. The light had faded and the song had ceased. When Zale looked back at Luca's hand, he saw that where the flower had been there now lay a silver ring with a gem the same colour as the petals had been. Zale's eyes opened in amazement.

'This is for you. This flower has protected many before you. Do not lose it. It is a ring of unity. Do not ask what that means. You will understand with time.' Zale accepted the ring and placed it on his forefinger. For a moment he marvelled at it and then bowed to Luca.

'Come, I'm sure your chamber is ready. You must rest before your journey.'

'But Your Highness, where are we?' Luca could see that all that had happened confused Zale.

'It is no great mystery. If you open your mind to all possibilities, you will figure it out.' She smiled at him, watching him go through all possibilities in his head.

'Are we…we cannot be…but we must be…inside one of the Minar Mountains?'

'That is correct. Do not look so shocked. The tallest of them, Benza, is abnormally high. Have you ever noticed? It is not a true mountain. It was created by the magic of my ancestors after a great war, the one that drove the Histrims away from these lands. It is sanctuary to the last of the fairies and, as you have seen, the only remaining unicorn in existence. Silvarna would be hunted down and killed for money if he were in the wild. I protect him. Now, as I said before, I am sure your chamber is ready. Let us go back to the others. I have no doubt they are wondering where you are.' With that, Luca casually made her way back across the cool grass to the break in the trees and began back up the passage leading to the mighty cave.

When Zale was back in the entrance hall of the tower, he found the others waiting. They did not see where he came from, but did not ask. No one noticed the new ring on his finger. Milon was with them waiting to take them to their rooms. He led them through a door on the opposite wall to the one Zale had just come through and up a short spiral of stairs. It ended with a long corridor, eight crimson doors on each side spread widely apart.

'I hope the rooms are to your liking. There is food and wine in them.' He bowed and left them to choose their rooms. Each was identical to the other. In the centre, there was a large bed covered with pillows and cushions. The materials used throughout the room were red and gold. The floor and walls were also red. Each room had a balcony that looked out across the mountains around the tower. There was a table against the wall opposite the bed laden with food. The group said good night and made themselves comfortable in each of their rooms. The thick crimson curtains were able to completely block out the light that still filled the sky. All the time in that darkness, Zale could think of nothing other than what he had seen. He fiddled with the ring on his finger and wondered why Luca had thought him so special. His thoughts did not last long though as sleep took hold quickly.

When they woke, each of the warriors ate some of the food in their room, dressed, and left the tower. It was not long before they were all gathered outside the great oak doors. They readied their horses, which had been brought to them with their packs already adorned upon their saddles, and took one last look up at Luca's magnificent home. From her window, Luca could be seen watching them. The sun was still high when the warriors mounted their horses and began on their journey. Men and women stepped from their homes to see the group off and wish them well. Children looked on with excitement, gaping in awe at the sight of them. As the group left the city and rode through the villages, the citizens stood by their doors and felt reassured by the sight. Farmers lay down they hoes and nodded in respect at the warriors.

'So, you're sure that your horse knows the way?' Zale asked Bazyli with a smile as they passed the last wooden house.

'Yes, he knows. Only…I'm afraid,' replied Bazyli.

'Do not fear. We will all protect you.'

'It's not that. I haven't been afraid of death since my parents died.'

'Well, what is it then?'

'I'm afraid that I'll never see Damané again.' The two of them rode in silence. Zale had had the same fear, for, although he did not live there, he felt at home in Damané. He looked across at Harden. There was a distant look in his eyes. Zale decided to leave him to his thoughts. He knew that if Harden wanted to tell his secret, he would. Zale and Bazyli took one last look back at the dying land before crossing the eastern border to begin their journey.

Heat and Temptation

Due to the distortion of time, the days seemed to last forever. What would normally take four days of non-stop riding would seem like a two-week expedition. The weather would change without warning. This time distortion would begin at the Tower of Light and expand slowly until it engulfed the entire White Islands. In days to come, the events taking place within Damané's borders would appear to be taking place at a slower rate to the world around. This gave the group more time, as the slower time within the city would delay its break down.

As the group left, the sun was beaming down on the riders just off the eastern border of Damané. There wasn't a cloud in the sky. This was normal for the time of year. What was unusual, however, was the extreme temperature. During the winter season, the sun does not fade, but the heat usually leaves the air. At that time, however, the ground had begun to crack and the lush green grass was dying. Due to lack of water, the flowers had wilted and there wasn't any sign of life. No birds, no animals, not even the insects could survive. The ground began at first to rise steeply and then gently fall again as the group traversed the many hills to Damané's east. Due to the mud drying out, patches of loose stones caused the horses to slip every once in a while. To the south, the distant peaks of the Sincre Mountains could be seen just above the haze that now hugged the land.

Their course began due east, in the direction Luca could sense the crystal to be, but soon Bazyli turned them south into wilder lands. The land ceased to rise and fall, but the hills were replaced by thick brambles that were unaffected by the heat. The warriors had to dismount and cut a path through the undergrowth for their horses.

'Why is it that we come this way?' asked Sachiel once they had made it through their first barrier.

'My horse is smarter than you may think,' replied Bazyli. 'He sensed danger ahead and so has led us by a different route. Do not worry though. He will not get us lost.' Caden did not look convinced, but still he trudged on. Lysias smiled at Caden's ignorance, for the people of Damané have always had a strangely close connection to animals. They are somehow able to understand them and communicate with them simply through the power of emotions, as though they can sense what the other is feeling. Right now, Bazyli knew in his heart that his horse did not want to follow the eastern road.

The warriors' clothes got caught on thorns and whipping branches from overhanging trees scratched their faces. It seemed even warmer along their shaded route as it was a greater effort to get through. The horses held their heads low and whinnied incredulously at their masters for forcing them through the wounding vegetation. Beads of sweat slid silently down the men's cheeks as they continued to swing their swords to and froe in order to clear a path.

'You would have thought,' muttered Caden as he caught up with Zale, 'that Acacia would be able to get rid of all this somehow…you know…being the Princess of Earth and all.' Zale nodded and the two of them glanced back briefly to look upon Acacia's deceivingly slender form as she too slid her sword almost effortlessly through the thick brambles.

'Oh, she could more than easily do that,' commented Lysias, having overheard to conversation, 'though, do you think that one who in essence rules and protects the Earth would wish to destroy even the most minute part of it? This way she is only harming what need be harmed and nothing more. I'm sure that it is actually quite painful for her to see such damage being inflicted upon the entire world around us at this time. Without Nare and Baaron, she and Sachiel are helpless to stop it.' Lysias fell silent and drifted away from the two men. Caden and Zale contemplated for a moment what had been said and realised that they had been foolish to instantly expect a resolution to their problem in such a destructive form and not look upon the situation from all angles. Zale knew in his heart that this was the downfall of all men and wished that he could one day help change that.

Somehow now leading the group, Zale suddenly called out. So consumed by his own thoughts, he almost didn't notice that he had made it to the other side of the brambles. When the others joined him, they were relieved to feel a slight breeze cool their cheeks. Looking back, they saw what they had just come through and were glad they had not been able to see it from the other side. It was evident now that the ground had gently sloped downwards and was covered for miles with thick thorns and giant trees that now stood dead beneath the sun. They could see that their route had been the easiest way through, though how they managed to stick to it they could not tell. Before them lay a dusty plain, rarely interrupted by small hills. First, however, they had to make their way back towards the eastern road they had been on earlier. They followed the line of brambles, curving round until it turned north. There they had to lead their horses up the gentle slope until they reached the dirt track that veered east. Once they had mounted their horses again, Acacia decided to look west and see why they had taken a different route. Behind her, flames licked the sky as a village of houses burned.

'Look!' she called to the others, anger swelling inside her. 'Bazyli was right. There was danger.' The others turned and watched the last few houses burn. Harden searched the area cautiously with his eyes, trying to see if the enemy was still near.

'Come,' he said at last. 'We continue moving. There is nothing we can do here. It looks as though the enemy were here long before. Let us hope our passing goes unnoticed.' Lysias bowed his head, gently moving his hand in the air before him from left to right, then curving it up simply to bring it down as though tracing an ocean wave. After a final muttering of a prayer from the Kai-Rae, which the others could not hear, the warriors turned back to their road and set off on their journey once more.

After a few hours, the riders came across a dry riverbed. Fish carcases were scattered across the ground. The air had grown stale, all moisture gone. As they continued, they drank more and more of their water. It was apparent that if they did not find water soon, they would die of thirst. It was unnerving how silent it was, as though the whole world had turned against them. A little way on from the riverbed, Acacia tried to heal the earth with her powers. She dismounted and knelt down, placing a hand on the scorching ground. She whispered a few words in her natural tongue, but it was no good. She looked despairingly at the others and mounted her horse. They trudged on hopelessly and came to an open, sandy plain. Coming off their horses, the ground cracked beneath their feet. Caden looked towards the sky, cursing the sun for its heat. Their horses were suffering. Each gave their own horse some of their water. Before them, sand was being whipped up into small tornadoes by the wind.

'We're not going to survive like this. We need water.' Caden looked at the Elements as if pleading with them to do something. Acacia turned to Sachiel.

'Can you find no water at all?'

'No. There's nothing for me to draw my powers on. Caden's right. We can't last much longer.'

'Why is it so hot anyway?' asked Zale wiping his brow. His mouth was dry, the taste of the sandy air threatening to choke him.

'Jabari is using Nare against us. She controls fire. Who knows what he's doing to her. Xannon could have her under a spell for all we know.' Sachiel looked away, wanting nothing more than to be with his friends.

'Jabari! Not even I thought he would do something like this!' Harden turned from the others full of anger.

'Harden, please, tell me what happened.' Zale and the others looked at him eagerly. Harden turned back to his friends.

'Let's just say that Jabari has hurt me and my family over the years.'

'So you know him personally?' asked Sachiel curiously, raising his voice slightly to be heard over the growing wind.

'Yes,' replied Harden with distaste. 'My connection with him stretches back far into my past.' The others looked between one another sharing their confusion. They left Harden to wonder away from the group, consumed by his own thoughts.

'Surely Jabari cannot use Nare like this indefinitely,' said Bazyli.

'No, you're probably right,' said Acacia, placing a kind hand upon his shoulder. She did not express her fear, however, for what Jabari may do once Nare was of no further use to him.

'So it looks like our best choice is to simply continue on,' stated Zale, glancing across at Harden. Lysias made his way silently over to the pensive warrior. He lowered his voice when he spoke so as to not let the others hear their conversation.

'Why do you not tell them the truth behind your hate for Jabari?' Lysias asked almost suspiciously.

'I have the right to decide who does and does not know of my history do I not?' replied Harden contemptuously.

'Indeed you do,' said Lysias, not allowing Harden's display of anger to distract him. Lysias thought he noticed Harden reconsider his approach to the Kai'rae before he spoke again.

'I guess I just don't want the others to judge me, especially Zale. My link to this evil is too much for even me to bear. How would it affect them?' Harden looked into Lysias's eyes almost pleadingly.

'I know of your closeness with My Lady also,' said Lysias after a moment's thought. 'I do not want to see her hurt or worse…' Lysias paused to consider his choice of words, 'used?' Harden looked taken aback.

'You know of how I care for Luca,' he said suddenly. 'I would never *use* her. I could not. I understand that you disapprove of my fondness for her, and indeed her returning those feelings, but please do not let that affect your judgement of me.' Lysias nodded and walked away from Harden, still overwhelmed by a suspicious feeling. He tried to shake it off, telling himself that Harden was right. He did not approve of the Queen's relationship with this man and as such was bound to find some reason to distrust him.

'Well, we had better get moving,' said Caden, breaking the silence that now hung between them all. 'The sooner we are on the other side of that desert, the better.'

They all decided it was best to walk so as to not tire the horses too much and help conserve water. The sun blazed down upon their heads, forming beads of sweat on their faces. The going was tough. Every now and then, they came across an area where sand had been blown up into a dune that blocked their path. They thought it best to go over these rather than round so that they would not loose their way. The wind battered against them causing the sand to embed itself into their skin. After many hours of travelling, the group was separated in their line, each at least ten metres behind the next. The wind had become a warm breeze that gave no release from the scorching temperature. Harden, who was leading the group, suddenly looked towards the horizon. It seemed hazy, the heat streaming up off the sand. He thought he could see a figure in front of him. He reached out with his arm and realised it was Luca.

'Luca? What are you doing here?' She simply turned and began walking off some way to the left.

'Luca? Luca!' Harden let go of his horse and ran after her.

'Harden! What are you doing?' Zale called after him. Then he himself thought he saw a figure before him. To him, it appeared as though his brother was in the desert with him. He began to walk off some way to the right, Zale running after him.

'What is going on?' asked Caden, confused by what was happening.

'It seems as though this is the Desert of Temptation,' said Acacia fearfully.

'Draysa? Come back!' This time it was Bazyli who was running off, though after what the others did not know. Soon Acacia was running after Baaron and Sachiel was after Nare. Caden and Lysias were left alone with all the horses until the General saw his father before him and so he too was running off round the desert. Lysias, drawn by the heat itself, slipped into a dream world. His people thrived on heat, and indeed at times used it to bring about moments of pure pleasure. He had been able to resist it until now but the heat had grown in such intensity that all he could do was welcome it. The horses, shocked by the sudden rush of people, galloped away in the same direction they had been going before. This was the way of the desert. It lured wanderers off the path so that they were running round in circles after hallucinations, tiring themselves until death. None of the group saw each other, though some of them nearly collided in their hurry. Harden collapsed to the floor.

'Luca,' he said despairingly, sand covering his face, 'why won't you stop?' He looked up and saw her standing over him. She reached out a hand to him as if going to help him up. When he went to take it however, he missed and slumped back on the floor. After a moment, the desire to be with her took over him once more and he got back up, running after her hazy image.

Acacia's desperation had become so strong that she had begun to use magic to try and draw Baaron closer to her. She was shifting the sand so that the grains he stood upon moved towards her. Though, for all her efforts, Baaron remained some distance from her. All she accomplished was weakening herself until she could barely stand.

Bazyli ran round with tears streaming down his cheeks. Whomever it was he saw, it seemed to be distressing him greatly. Caden on the other hand was not upset by the apparent presence of his father. Instead, he was stood face to face with the hallucination and was duelling with it, trying to settle an old grudge that he had not been able to let go of.

After quite some time of stumbling through the sand, Zale stopped. His brother was no longer in front of him. Instead, there were the horses, stood on a patch of grass drinking from a small pool, the last of the water in those lands. He blinked twice, trying to see if they were real. When he turned around, he could see the desert behind him and realised he must have reached its border. When he looked down, he could see his ring glowing brilliantly in the sun.

'You're what brought me here aren't you?' said Zale, admiring his ring. He suddenly realised what had happened and knew he had to go back into the desert to save his friends.

'All I have to do is ignore the figures. They are not real. Ring, you must help me or else my friends will surely die!' He felt a bit foolish to be talking to a ring and for a moment believed himself to be going mad. Thinking back to the events in the great cave though, he knew that anything was possible.

He stepped back onto the sand, his ring glowing profusely. There before him was once again his brother.

'You are not real,' said Zale, trying to keep his head. Then his brother reached out for him.

Zale! I need you! Help me! Please, Zale! I cannot hold them back!

Zale was about to walk towards him when he felt a burning in his finger. His ring was now glowing brighter than ever. Zale was torn as to what to do. Tears filled his eyes. Then, out of nowhere, a beautiful white unicorn galloped towards him, stopping just before his face and rearing up on its hind legs. Zale raised his arm protectively over his eyes. The unicorn's front legs pounded down onto the sand and it snorted abruptly, tossing its head.

'Silvarna?' questioned Zale. Perhaps the creature was another hallucination. He reached out and touched the unicorn on his cheek. 'You're real.'

'Trust your heart.' A strong, male voice echoed in Zale's head. Silvarna was talking to him.

'My brother needs me,' said Zale with despair.

'Trust your heart,' repeated the voice. Then Silvarna simply blended into the haze, disappearing completely. There was Zale's brother, still before him, beckoning to him.

'You are not real!' Zale screamed at his brother, and, to Zale's amazement, he disappeared. He could feel his heart pounding in his chest. Wiping the tears from his face, Zale set off in search of his friends. It did not take him long to find them. They were all running round in the same area, reaching forwards after their hallucinations. Zale grabbed hold of Harden and shook him.

'They are not real!' he screamed. 'It is your imagination!' But Harden did not seem to hear him. He just pulled away from Zale and continued to run through the desert. Then Zale heard Silvarna's voice in his head again.

Knowledge and truth lie within you, even though they may simply trickle beneath the surface. To find the source of the stream is to control it.

'What do you mean? I don't know what to do!' argued Zale. There was no response. Zale realised he must figure out what to do on his own. Then he thought back to what Silvarna had said before.

'Trust your heart,' he muttered to himself. 'Of course! We always trust the ones we truly love, no matter what. But how does that help me?...find the source...those they love...control the stream...manipulate the truth...that's it! I must make them believe I am the one that they wish to follow. Then they will follow me to the edge of the desert.' He looked down at his ring and it glistened back at him. For a moment he lost faith in the idea, thinking Silvarna had been part of his imagination and the reassurance from the ring was a trick, but he soon realised that the plan was a good one.

'Over here! I am over here! I am the one you seek!' All of the group stopped and turned to Zale. Each could now see him as their hallucination and charged at him, calling for him to wait. He turned suddenly and ran as fast as he could out of the desert. Luckily, they all managed to keep up, even poor Bazyli who by this time was close to exhaustion. When they were away from the sand, they all stood still, blinking like Zale had done at where they were.

'They were hallucinations,' said Zale breathing heavily, proud to have been the one to save them.

'I know,' said Acacia. 'I knew it when Harden first called out, but they felt so real.' Embarrassed, they all fell silent. Their cheeks were bright red from the sun and there was a thin film of sweat covering their faces. They could see that the horses had drunk all the water that had been in the pool, though none of them blamed them. Hot and tired, they all were in need of some water.

'Where's Lysias?' asked Bazyli, looking around for his protector.

'He must still be in the desert,' said Acacia with fear.

'Why would he have not followed me?' asked Zale with surprise.

'Because he is a Kai-Rae,' explained Sachiel. 'They have Domai blood in them. The Domai are at their best in very hot conditions. Kai-Rae also thrive in heat, though as the temperature increases it begins to affect them differently. Lysias is probably out there somewhere lying blissfully under the sun.'

'Blissfully?' questioned Zale. 'You mean he's enjoying that?'

'Yes,' said Sachiel, 'though it will be against his will.'

'I will go and retrieve him,' said Acacia.

'No,' interrupted Zale. 'I was able to resist before, I can do it again.' With that he set off into the desert once more. His brother followed his every step, calling out to him for help. Each time Zale was about to succumb to the endless pleas, his finger burned with the intense glowing of his ring, bringing him back to his senses. Soon Zale stumbled upon the Kai-Rae kneeling down in the sand, his arms out to his sides as though waiting to be lifted into the air.

'Lysias,' called Zale as he approached. There was no response. 'Lysias!' Still the Kai-Rae knelt before him. Zale gripped his arm tightly and tried to pull him to his feet. Lysias's eyes opened and a deep hatred spread across his face. He bared his pointed teeth and gripped Zale's arms tightly. A great wind began to build around them as Lysias tapped into his magic. Fearing for his life, Zale kicked Lysias hard in the chest, forcing him to release his grip. The Kai-Rae was on his feet again in seconds, poised ready to strike. Zale turned and began to run as fast as he could away from him. Glancing over his shoulder, he saw just in time a beam of orange energy heading for his head. Zale darted to the side, still running as fast as he could. He glanced back again and now saw Lysias charging towards him with immense speed. Zale could see the edge of the desert just metres before him, but Lysias was almost upon him. Suddenly, without knowing how, Zale's own speed increased and he found himself next to the others. Lysias arrived right behind him and collapsed to the floor with exhaustion.

'What happened?' asked Zale bewildered.

'I could see what had happened and was able to move the ground you were running on so you reached us faster,' explained Acacia.

'Oh,' Zale panted catching his breath, 'right.'

'I am sorry,' said Lysias from the ground. 'I did not mean to attack you.'

'Yeah, about that,' said Zale. 'Why *did* you try and kill me?' Bazyli looked shocked and turned to Lysias.

'Do not fear Bazyli,' Lysias explained. 'It will not happen again. I was so affected by the heat that I was not myself. I am afraid I had no control over my actions. Once a Kai-Rae reaches a state such as the one you found me in, our instinctive reaction when approached is to attack as a means of self defence.'

'I can see how that makes sense,' said Zale. 'You are very vulnerable in that state of mind.'

'Yes,' said Lysias. 'Please forgive me.'

'There is nothing to forgive,' replied Zale, helping the Kai-Rae to his feet.

'So actually,' began Caden, 'it could happen again.'

'I suppose,' said Lysias, 'though next time I will place myself under an enchantment so that I cannot reach that level of awareness.'

'You can do that?' asked Bazyli, slightly concerned. Lysias looked down at him kindly and placed an arm on his shoulder.

'Yes Bazyli. I simply prevent my body from registering the rise in temperature. There is nothing to fear.' Bazyli smiled back at him.

'Well then, now that we are all reunited, we had better get moving again,' said Harden almost reluctantly.

'We need water first,' said Sachiel knowingly. He moved over to the area where the horses had been drinking. Placing a hand in the centre, he closed his eyes in concentration. After a moment of silence, cool, fresh water began to trickle out of the ground between his fingertips. Once it had subsided, the others could see that there was not much water, though it was enough for them all to quench their thirst.

'That is all I can find,' said Sachiel sadly. The others thanked him gratefully and began to drink. Once they had had their fill, they used what was left to wash the sand out of their skin. It helped cool them down and take some of the redness out of their cheeks.

'Now it is time we make a move,' said Harden as he stood up from the pool. 'Bazyli, what is it?' Harden could see Bazyli looking at something in the distance.

'Clouds! I can see clouds!' They could all see them, rolling towards them.

'Well, they certainly bring rain! Let's hope not too much though.' Sachiel looked slightly worried. None-the-less, they were all relieved, for the rain would replenish their water supply as the pool was now dry. They mounted their horses, all of which had waited for them, and set off again in the right direction. Lysias rode close to Harden so he could have another private word.

'You saw Luca, did you not?' he asked quietly.

'I did,' replied Harden.

'Then I know your heart is true. Please forgive my suspicions. I too care greatly for her.'

'As Zale said, there is nothing to forgive,' said Harden, taking Lysias's hand in a gesture of friendship. 'I would be worried if you were not suspicious of those who may influence the Queen.' Lysias smiled, appreciative of Harden's kindness.

A little way ahead, Zale was looking at his ring another time. Seeing the clouds before him and the ring glistening on his finger, realisation flickered across his face and he smiled to himself.

Magic

Before they knew it, it was pouring with rain. The sky went dark as a blanket of clouds hovered above them. A waterfall of rain cooled their skin and was able to replenish their water supply, but the temperature dropped dramatically. The air smelt fresh and alive, as though each drop carried the icy essence of new life. The wind howled around them. It was all the horses could do to keep moving. The sound was deafening. Sheets of water rushed past the riders' ears and thundered into the ground like piercing arrows. Pools of murky liquid formed in every hollow of earth, spilling over to form a thin film across the land. The horses' hooves splashed through them, sending missiles of freezing water up towards their riders.

'We must find a more sheltered route!' shouted Caden over the wind after half an hour of rain, 'Look at the boy!' Bazyli was shaking all over. His body was stiff with cold and his clothes were drenched. Acacia looked around the group. The horses' muscles were seizing up and the men were suffering. She glanced over at Zale and noticed for the first time how fragile his body looked. She knew he was strong but feared for him. He hadn't spoken for a long time and he had the least amount of clothing; he had given his cloak to Bazyli soon after the rain began. Acacia did not want to see Zale suffer for, though she would never admit it, she had grown quite fond of him. She did not know it, but secretly Zale had grown fond of her as well. Now, though, his mind was empty. The cold was taking over and he was finding it difficult to stay conscious. Not even the ring could help him now.

'Sachiel! Can't you do anything?' Sachiel looked at his fellow Element. He had slowly felt his energy growing with the surrounding water, though the freezing temperature smothered it slightly.

'We're not meant to use our powers against the natural cycle. Not long ago you wanted the rain. Now you want me to make it go away!'

'Do you think this is natural?' called Acacia. 'It may be the winter season, but these are the Sunar Plains. They have not seen a drop of rain for centuries. It's because the crystal is missing. Luca sent us with the men to help fight against nature when she is putting up a battle. At least make the water part for us.' Acacia looked at Sachiel pleadingly. She could make him do almost anything for her, as she knew he loved her like a sister, but she did not often use her power over him. He was very protective of her. With that, Sachiel summoned his powers. They came to him like warm blood trickling through his veins. His body tingled with the pulsing energy. He raised his hands before him in order to direct and manipulate the wild magic. It looked as if he was stroking the air until a great ball of blue light appeared between his hands. He pushed it away from him and it spread out to form a protective layer around the riders. No water came in, but the wind was still circling them.

'Why is the wind still getting through?' called Harden bitterly.

'Harden, I'm the Angel of Water. I cannot manipulate the air. That is what Baaron does.' Both Elements looked away. Tears filled Acacia's eyes, though she did not let the others see. She and Baaron were a couple, as were Nare and Sachiel.

'I'm sorry,' said Harden. 'Thank you for the shelter.'

With the horses able to move easier, they journeyed on. Lysias, also badly affected by the cold, rode over to Bazyli.

'Bazyli, can you hear me?' The young boy nodded. The Kai-Rae's speech was slow and difficult as he shivered profusely. 'I am going to help you stay warm, but you must watch me. My hand will be upon your shoulder. Keep it there until you see my eyes begin to close. Then you must remove it. Do you understand?' Bazyli nodded again. Lysias then stretched out his arm and rested his long fingers delicately upon the skin of the boy's shoulder. Bazyli held them there as Lysias began to use what little strength he had left to magically warm the child. He brought his powers to the front of his mind and tried to focus the image of them into a warm red liquid. He mentally sent the pulsing heat down his arm and projected it into the young boy. Within moments, Bazyli had his eyes fully open as he felt both comfortably hot and dry. He watched his protector's face carefully, ensuring he was ready if Lysias were to slip out of consciousness. Lysias continued to ride next to him with his eyes only half open. His vision was blurry and his head was spinning.

Acacia kept a close eye on Sachiel, for his powers were slowly draining with each passing moment. He was having to maintain the protection around the group. It would normally have been a simple task, though the wind was unnaturally cold and strong. It was as though it was directly attacking the Angel of Water, sapping his energy faster. Zale too was still in a bad condition. He needed rest and the warmth of a campfire's glow. Acacia pulled her horse up alongside Harden who was leading the group.

'We need to find some real shelter,' she said under her breath so as to not frighten the others. 'Sachiel is weakening and Zale is barely conscious. Now Lysias is slipping away from us as well.'

'I agree,' said Harden. 'There's a rock face up ahead to the left. It's the first sign of any landform we've come across. We might be able to find shelter there. If not, are you able to use your powers to create an overhang?'

'I will do what I can, but I make you no promises. This wind is strange. It is damaging Sachiel and I somehow. I think Jabari is using Baaron against us.' Harden nodded in agreement and quickened the pace, desperate to give the others a rest. With a burning on his forefinger, Zale stirred momentarily. His ring was glowing again. *Where there is danger, you will find safety also* said the familiar voice in his head. *Southwards does this foe come.* Zale glanced up to see a cave just to the left of the path.

'There,' he said in a hoarse voice, pointing in the direction of the shelter. Acacia saw it too and led them inside. Sachiel released his magic, sighing with relief as he did so. Bazyli lifted Lysias's hand off of his shoulder and thanked him greatly for the warmth. The Kai-Rae nodded, though he was still in a bad condition.

'We will stay in here until the rain passes,' declared Harden. 'We all need rest. We have had a long day. Try and sleep if you can, though two of us will have to stay awake on watch.'

'I will take the first watch with Acacia,' said Caden, 'if that is alright with her?' He looked into her beautiful green eyes hopefully.

'Of course,' she replied. 'We will wake Harden and Zale in two hours.' Zale nodded weakly, still mounted on his horse. Harden helped him off and lay him gently down as Sachiel started a fire near by with some dry leaves. Harden took a fresh blanket from his pack and wrapped it around Zale who had already fallen asleep due to extreme exhaustion. Lysias crept over to the fire and rapped himself up in one of his blankets, trying to dry his sodden clothes in the refreshing heat. Bazyli brought him a bed mat for the tired Kai-Rae to rest on and set his own next to him. The boy was very grateful for what the strange creature had done to help him. Now he wanted to do all he could to repay the debt. Sachiel, having now released his grasp on his magic within, set himself up quietly near the cave wall and settled down to a dreamless sleep. Harden watched Zale for a few moments, concerned for the young man's health, but he too succumbed to his weariness and slipped out of consciousness. Acacia and Caden were the only ones that remained awake. They sat near the cave entrance, huddled together in order to keep warm. Their backs were warmed slowly by the crackling fire. The only sounds came from the howling wind, backed by the eerie beat of the rain as it whipped the cliff face. Neither Acacia nor Caden spoke. They simply heated some water over the fire, to which Acacia added healing herbs that she had packed to replenish their strength. It was impossible to see out of the cave for the darkness that hung there. Still, Acacia's fingers rested purposefully on her bow and Caden'a hand never strayed too far from the hilt of his sword. Though they had seen no sign of anyone following them, the pair felt as though they were being watched.

After two uneventful hours Caden roused Harden and Zale. Acacia passed them both a fresh cup of the herbal tea, then lay down to sleep. She slipped into the land of dreams almost instantly. Caden followed suit, exhaustion taking hold of his body. After making sure Zale was recovered enough to keep watch Harden took him towards the back of the cave. He chose a spot where they had a clear view of the mouth of the cave, though they could not see anything but the sheet of water sealing them in.

'Why aren't we nearer the cave opening,' asked Zale yawning as he wiped the sleep from his eyes.

'It is not only the recovery of the crystal that brings me on this journey Zale,' Harden said seriously.

'What is the other purpose?' asked Zale hesitantly.

'Luca believes you would benefit from learning the ways of magic.'

'What?' said Zale, astonished, 'Why would she think that?'

'Her reasons are not important,' replied Harden. 'From now on, I am going to be your tutor whenever we have the chance.' Zale's heart pounded with excitement, though he kept a straight face. The last strains of tiredness in his veins disappeared.

'So,' continued Harden, 'how would you like to know how to speak the Ancestral Tongue? It is the only way we non-magic-born creatures can wield magic. Plus, you never know when you might need it.'

'You could teach it to me?' Zale asked, almost warily. Few people knew the ancestral tongue and he would be honoured to be one of them, but he did not know how Harden came to learn it. Sensing Zale's confusion, Harden explained.

'My father and my uncle taught me from the age of six. It is always best to learn a language from a young age. Then, when I reached the age of adulthood, I went in search of Loysa, the man who taught my uncle how to control magic, and asked him to tutor me. Having known my uncle, he was more than happy to.'

'So you can teach me right now?' asked Zale, still trying to make sense of the strange series of events unravelling before him.

'Of course. Right, where to begin? I know. I can get you to say your name and that you come in peace. A very useful phrase if ever you come across a Histrim. How is that?' Harden enjoyed authority so loved teaching Zale.

'That's fine. Anything will make me happy,' said Zale, still trying to contain his excitement. He felt like a young boy again, thrilling in the tale of an old legend.

'The words are: May tylanda hy Zale. Sino ryar op laywa.'

'May tylanda hy Zale. Sino ryar op laywa.'

'That's it. Now learn that well. It could be quite useful to you.'

Zale repeated the phrase a few times and was sure he knew it. He did not know when he may need the Ancestral Tongue, but was happy that he knew some of it. 'What next?' he asked eagerly.

'Well, I think I should show you what it feels like to use magic. I can't bombard you with phrases as I'm sure you'll get confused, and that can be dangerous. You must remember, magic feeds upon your own energy, so do not try a spell that will drain you quickly.' Harden gave Zale a sharp look, making sure he understood this completely. 'Eventually,' he continued, 'you will be able to perform a spell simply by thinking, but this can be extremely risky as your thoughts can become muddled, and, in turn, the magic mixed up.'

'Well, what should I do now then?' asked Zale.

'Repeat after me; Magnina.'

'Magnina,' repeated Zale.

'Good. Now, take a rock in your hand and focus your thoughts. Your aim is to turn the rock into a blue topaz, which is what the word means. Well, it means to transform, but your intent is what shapes it. Like this.' Harden picked up a rock from the ground and laid it in the palm of his hand. *Magnina.* With the word, the rock shimmered and transformed into a perfectly round topaz crystal, the firelight reflecting wildly off its smooth blue surface. Zale's eyes lit up with wonder.

'Now you try,' said Harden. Zale picked up a rock the size of his entire palm and tried to concentrate. *Magnina.* Nothing happened. He looked desperately at Harden.

'Try again. Remember; concentrate. Will the rock to change.' Zale sat up straight and focused all his thoughts on the rock. After a moment, he realised his mind was completely clear and the few words he knew of the Ancestral Tongue seemed to nudge against his mind, trying to force themselves forwards. He could feel them on his lips, desperate to be used. *Magnina.* This time the rock shimmered and became a beautiful blue topaz crystal. Zale took in a sharp breath as he felt a tugging at his heart. All his thoughts came flooding back and the blue topaz turned back into a dusty grey rock.

'What happened?' he asked Harden. 'Why did it change back? And what was that feeling I had?'

'You focused on the rock becoming a blue topaz, but you did not focus on keeping it that way. If you want something to be permanent, you must incorporate that thought into the spell, else the magic will keep feeding off you until your thoughts return and the spell ends. What you felt was the magic drawing its power from your life force. It is always a bit painful at first, but with practise simple spells use less and less energy and it is only the larger ones that affect you. Think of it as toughening up for a fight. You get used to the lighter hits after a while, but it's the sword to your side that you feel the most.' Zale nodded, trying to take it all in. The two of them sat in silence for a while, only listening to the wind outside. They glanced out of the cave and watched the water collect in a pool at the entrance.

'I think I will leave your training there for now,' said Harden abruptly. 'We will continue once we have moved on from here. You haven't had much rest and I don't want to push it. Once we are both fully refreshed and sleeping warm again, I will give you some more spells to play with.' Harden winked at Zale and smiled. Zale wiped his long, damp hair from his face and considered practising turning rocks into topaz. Harden noticed his expression.

'Don't try the spell too much. As I said before, it will drain your energy. If you must, then tell me first. Oh, and don't tell the others what we're doing. It might encourage Bazyli to try and listen in.' Zale nodded and looked over at the boy. He was sleeping soundly, as he should be. The two watchers sat and finished their herbal tea, thinking away the minutes.

'Harden?' asked Zale. 'Can Jabari use magic?' Harden looked up at him sadly.

'Yes, he can.' Harden paused. 'He too was taught by Loysa, though he had a much greater natural affinity for it than I. For that, I fear him.'

'How is it you know so much about him? I mean, of course one would know of one who had hurt them, but you seem to know about his whole life…or that's what I sense anyway.' Harden smiled.

'You are very intuitive,' he said happily. 'I'm sure the ways of magic will come to you quickly. Now, let's not talk any more of dark things. We should enjoy the peace we have while we can.' The two of them fell back into silence, Zale still desperate to know more of Harden's connection to Jabari. What truth could be so terrible that Harden could not trust him with?

Not more than half an hour passed when Zale looked towards the entrance of the cave. He could hear scuffing noises just outside. They were faint over the terrible wind, but he could just about make out the sound of splashing footsteps. He alerted Harden to the sounds and they both gently woke the others, instructing them to get towards the back of the cave. Sachiel dowsed the fire with a jet of water from the palm of his hand and they all sat in silence, straining their eyes and ears for any sign of what was outside. From nowhere, six silvery forms stood just before the entrance to the cave. The wolves paced back and forth, sniffing the ground to find the scent they were following. Their elegant forms were tense, their muscles shivering in the cold. The low hum of a growl escaped the lips of the alpha male. His white bushy tail lifted expectantly for a moment, but then dropped just as quickly. It was apparent they were frustrated with their loss and were desperate to find fresh signs of their prey. One looked briefly into the cave, and then continued past, the others following it.

'The rain masked our scent. We will have to be careful from now on,' said Sachiel. He was about to relight the fire when Bazyli called out in alarm. At the entrance of the cave, two jade green eyes stared at them all. The black she-wolf had been hidden by the darkness. Now she stood before them, flashing her teeth. She stood their silently, water from the cave roof dripping onto her midnight fur. The length of her back was scarred from old battles within her pack and her belly was bulging. She glared at the group contemptuously, as though they had done her some grave injustice. She darted forwards, but, just as she was about to sink her teeth into Sachiel's raised arms, an arrow struck her directly in the heart. Without a sound, the creature slumped to the ground, her eyes glazing over. The warriors all turned to Acacia who sat, still poised with her bow and another nocked arrow, ready to release.

'Nice shot,' said Caden. She smiled and walked over to the dead wolf.

'Who's hungry?' she asked simply. Harden, laughing, took out his knife and started to skin the wolf with Acacia's aid. They both paused briefly, staring at the creature's belly, but remained quiet and continued their work.

Lysias turned abruptly as he heard a low growling coming from the very back of the cave. The others stopped what they were doing and followed his gaze.

'Get back,' Lysias whispered as he positioned himself ready to defend himself and the others. The spikes on his ears grew slightly, as did his nails to give him claws.

'We cannot leave, not with those other wolves about,' said Harden, drawing his sword.

'There will be no need for you to leave this cave,' came a deep, growling voice from the darkness. A large shape moved in the shadows towards the group.

'Who are you?' demanded Lysias. His fingers were twitching, sparks shooting between his claws.

'One who is smart enough not to take on a Kai-Rae alone.' The creature stepped out into the light, its huge form reaching the height of Lysias so he could stare him straight in the eye. 'My name is Galzan, chief of the Wolvax.' Galzan's body was that of a wolf, though much larger and more muscular than those that had just attacked. Five thin silver lines scared his fierce muzzle. His fur was a rich blue-black, as though the night sky itself had stained the hairs. His dark yellow eyes bore into the surrounding warriors.

'I apologise for our intrusion,' said Lysias, bowing respectively to the Wolvax. His claws retracted and his form relaxed. This completely stunned the others.

'No apology needed,' replied Galzan, returning the gesture. 'I understand you were just sheltering from this unusual storm.'

'I am sorry,' said Caden, 'but I have never heard of your kind. Who and what are you?'

'He is a Wolvax,' explained Acacia, stepping forwards to show her respect for Galzan. 'The Wolvax are relatives of wolves, though they are some of the wisest creatures ever known. Their race was nearly wiped out when the Histrims were driven from these shores. And you are the chief of all that remain?'

'I am. There used to be thousands of us. Now, only a few hundred remain. We chose to protect the Histrims, and suffered greatly for it. Now a darkness attacks us once more. This evil that spreads across the land is hunting us down. It is all I can do to protect my kind. I have split up from my group so as to keep them from harm. The wolf packs are sent in search of me.'

'But you are far more powerful than they are,' said Bazyli. 'Surely they cannot defeat you.' Lysias looked at the boy and smiled.

'The evil lord sends the wolves after me in packs of dozens. He knows the Wolvax are a threat to him. Though he also knows that without a leader a power struggle will break out between us, depleting our numbers further.' There were scraping sounds near the mouth of the cave again as the white wolves came back in search of their missing companion.

'Stay with us,' said Harden, noticing the creature's giant form tensing. 'We will protect you. We go to fight Jabari.' Galzan laughed.

'I will only bring you more danger,' he said at last. 'Do not worry about me. This group seem small enough for me to handle. It seems as though your lives are much more valuable than mine if you are to do what you claim. I will draw them away from you.'

'You cannot just leave like that,' protested Bazyli.

'It is his choice,' said Lysias kindly. 'I only hope that one day we may be able to repay him.' With his words, Lysias looked gratefully into Galzan's strong face. The Wolvax slowly moved past them all, stopping only briefly to mutter something into Acacia's ear.

'I know your face…Grier.' A ghostly shiver ran down Acacia's spine as she hoped no-one had overheard. With that, Galzan left the cave. Moments later, snarling could be heard as the wolves spotted him. The battle cries faded into the distance, leaving the warriors to stand in silence, overwhelmed by the whole experience.

It wasn't long before the group remembered their stomachs. They half-heartedly roasted the wolf meat over the fire and ate quietly, their hunger dieing slightly but their thoughts with Galzan. The wolf did not have much meat on it, but it was enough to keep the warriors going for a while. Once they had all had their fill, they sat and talked for a few minutes to discuss what they had heard. It shocked them all to discover that other creatures on the White Islands were being attacked by Jabari. To Acacia's relief, none of the others had heard what Galzan's last words had been before he left the cave. All she could think of were those words along with the scars upon his muzzle.

As if the weather knew they were ready to move on, the rain stopped abruptly. The group packed up their things and saddled the horses. However, just as they stepped outside the cave, a thick mist enveloped them. It was almost impossible to see. The ground had softened and turned to thick mud. This did not help the horses' mood. They were already jumpy from the scent of the wolves and seemed to fear their disorientation. Still, the group trudged on blindly, keeping watch for the wolves and Galzan, but they were long gone. The ground rose steeply as it took them to the top of the cliff. For some time they travelled along a narrow column of rock with a sheer drop on either side, though none of them knew it. It was pure luck that kept them on course.

When the ground finally declined again, three long hours had passed. The fog was thicker than before, caught in the lower ground. The group rode within arms reach of each other so as to stop them from losing someone. The going was slow through the mud and the horses' legs tired quickly with the effort. To save the horses' strength, the group dismounted and continued on foot for another two hours. The thick earth buried their legs up to their knees. Bazyli sunk up to his waist, so Lysias pulled him out and placed a temporary enchantment on the boy's feet. They sparked with minute blue stars that stopped him sinking any further than the soles of his animal skin boots. None of them knew where they were going any more, not even Bazyli's horse. All they knew was that their only hope was to keep on walking, wherever that took them.

People of the North

Four hours on, back on the horses, Zale and Caden were at the head of the group, talking quietly between themselves as they kept a watch for danger. They had come across a route of drier ground and chose to follow it through the mist. Harden and Sachiel were also whispering together as they protected the back of the group. Only Acacia, Lysias, and Bazyli stayed quiet in the middle, lost in thought about their journey. Bazyli was growing tired and wanted nothing more than to rest, but he did not say as he knew it was best that the group covered as much ground as possible. His eyes drooped and head lolled slightly, only to snap back up again as he woke himself from his spells of sleep. It had only been nine hours since the cave, but they had only stopped then for just over 4 hours and the walk through the mud had drained him. The whole group would have benefited from staying in the cave for longer and each of them getting a few hours decent sleep, but it was not safe to do so with the wolves near by.

Bazyli stayed quiet for the next couple of hours, his head continuing loll to one side every so often as he drifted in and out of sleep. Lysias kept a close eye on him, at times using a quick pulse of transparent energy to keep the boy steady. The sun was barely visible above their heads, its rays blocked by the mist. Nevertheless, Caden thought he saw something shining in front of him.

'Zale, do you see that?' he asked, leaning forwards as if to get a better look.

'Yes,' replied Zale. 'I saw it there a little while ago, but it was smaller then and was swallowed up by this dense fog. I thought I was imagining things.'

'Well, I can definitely see something,' said Caden, 'though what it could be I cannot guess.' The two of them continued to lead the group towards the strange glow. As they got closer, they realised it was a lamp, hanging on a pole sticking out from a wall made of wooden posts. Beneath it was a large gate and above was a watchtower. Every now and again, a figure seemed to move within the tower. Caden and Zale soon realised that they were heading towards a guarded town. They stopped and waited for the others to catch up.

'What is it?' asked Sachiel as soon as he reached the two in front.

'There is a town ahead,' replied Caden in a hushed voice. 'It has a guard, but I do not think we have been seen. What do you think we should do?'

'Well,' said Harden thoughtfully after a pause, 'we cannot tell if they are in league with Jabari, but it is not like him to ask the aid of men from these islands. Bazyli, when you followed Xannon, did he come this way?'

'No,' said Bazyli shaking his head. 'As I followed him though, I could see smoke rising from the north. He seemed to avoid that route as best as he could. Where we are now however, I do not know. My horse does not seem to be in distress though, so that's a good sign.' He smiled broadly, proud to be the group's advisor.

'We must have turned north then,' said Acacia. 'The mist has stopped us from staying on course. That is the only explanation. If what Bazyli says is true and that Xannon tried to avoid this place, then I believe Jabari has no ties with them.'

After a bit more discussion, it was decided that Zale and Harden would ride to the town and ask for permission to stay a while. The thought of a good night's rest in a proper bed was too tempting after their experience in the desert and the cave to refuse.

As the two men approached, a horn was sounded and three armed guards came through the gate to greet them. They wore green weather stained garments, each with a brown leather belt upon which hung a silver sword open to the air. The lead guard had long auburn hair that blew out behind him with his black cloak. His eyes were dark and his chin was bristled as if he had been up many hours longer than he should have. This was the guard that spoke to Harden and Zale.

'Who goes there?' he called importantly to the night.

'I am Harden and this is Zale, son of Tre'ath,' called Harden as they drew up in front of the men.

'Tre'ath you say?' said the man with surprise. 'I thought his son Zale travelled alone now across the deserted lands.'

'Not alone,' said Zale. 'I met Harden on my journeys. We now come with five others and seek food and a good bed. We have travelled far and our horses are weary. Will you grant us entry?' The man looked Zale up and down and recognised the soft black curly hair as a trait of the late queen of Morsenden.

'Indeed I will,' said the guard. 'I am Gredin, second to General Pivloy of the People of the North. There is an inn you may stay at. May I ask who your companions are?' As he asked, Gredin peered round Harden and Zale, squinting through the fog as the rest of the group came up behind them. Caden had decided that if the people of the town were hostile, they would have heard some sort of commotion by now. He also felt that as General of Forthum, a major trading city within the lands, he may have some sway in negotiating a place to stay.

'This is General Caden of Forthum, Acacia, Princess of Earth, Sachiel, Angel of Water, Bazyli, our guide, and Lysias, a protector of Damané.' As Harden introduced each member of the group, they dismounted and walked closer towards Gredin.

'Well, may the stars have fallen!' said Gredin in awe. 'Elements! Two of the four are stood now before me! I would never have thought that. Come come! We must get you fed and rested. These days are dark and we cannot have you walking through the mist like this, even if the sun is high.' Gredin ushered them all through the gate and began to lead them up a cobble path towards the centre of the town as the town gates closed behind them. All around houses rose above them, each built with the same oak wood and four front windows; two at the bottom and two a floor above. They were set very close to each other, but none of them touching. Lamps were lit all down the path as the mist had taken away most of the light. However, there was no mist within the town itself. It seemed to avoid it and hung low above the roofs as if afraid to touch the houses. As they walked, Gredin told the warriors of how a dark cloud seemed to hang over the land. The days seemed to last an age and evil creatures were seen wandering the hills towards the mountains. With mention of this, he glanced at Lysias for his kind was strange to the soldier, though he did not suspect him to mean any harm to the town or its people. Lysias simply pulled up the hood of his cloak to hide the scales upon his face. He felt it best so as to not unsettle any of the town's inhabitants. Harden then told of the reason for the group's travel and a look of realisation came across the young man's face as if all the answers of the world had been bestowed upon him.

By the time Harden had recounted all the recent events, they had reached the inn Gredin had spoken of. It was triangular in shape as it split the path in two, creating two new roads down either side.

'Well, I am grateful of the news. Rest assured this town has nothing to do with this Jabari you speak of. A monster of a man he sounds! I will recite all to General Pivloy immediately. Then I must get back to my post. I am sure if this Jabari is capable of all you say he will try to find you. Go inside and say you are the travellers sent by Gredin. I already sent another of my guards to warn Dosain, the Inn Keeper, of your arrival. Everything should be ready.' The group thanked him and he took his leave.

Walking into the large room that was the bar area of the inn, the group could barely see through the smoke. There was a friendly atmosphere as men and women alike sat round large tables, laughing and drinking merrily. They took no notice of the strangers. To the group's left, there was the bar itself, surrounded by more people calling out orders and trying to move away through the crowd with their drinks. A young woman and a similar aged man were hurrying about behind the bar, serving customers and making drinks, though at the same time managing to have entire conversations with those they served. They both looked quite alike with blonde hair and brilliant green eyes. An older, taller man then appeared from a door that seemed to be between two barrels of beer at the far end of the bar. He bared a resemblance to the young man and woman, though he had curlier, brown hair and his skin was well tanned. He immediately spotted the group by the door and bustled his way over to them, pushing his huge form past the youngsters.

'You must be our new visitors!' he said with a large smile as he leaned over the end of the bar.

'And you must be Dosain, the keeper of this inn,' said Harden.

'I am indeed!' replied Dosain, almost a bit surprised. 'Gredin must 'ave told you 'bout me. Sorry 'bout me kids ignorin' ya.' He looked over his shoulder at the man and women. Both stopped for an instant, shrugged their shoulders, and went back to work. 'Never mind, at least I founds ya. Now, I 'ave saved you lot a space in one o' the booths o'er there.' Dosain pointed one of his large fingers towards the far wall. 'It's private like, so yous can talk wit'out disturbance. I'll send me daughter, Leylo, to see to all ya needs.' With that, Dosain went over to Leylo and took over her duties. She went off through the door he had appeared from and soon came out of another door closer to the booth. By that time the group had managed to work their way through the crowd and taken a seat.

'Me dad's already cooked you up some nice warm soup and a leg o' lamb will be ready soon. Would ya like me to get ya some beer?' The girl's voice was high and smooth and she looked at the group with a friendly smile on her face. The men all agreed to the beer, including Sachiel, but Bazyli, Lysias, and Acacia asked for water. The soup came almost as soon as Leylo had left them, brought over by a slender, middle-aged woman with straggly black hair wearing a heavily stained apron. The group ate in silence, cherishing the feeling of a warm stomach. Once they had finished, they decided not to think of the road ahead for a while but rather to speak of old times and tell stories each of them had. Bazyli sat and listened for he did not have many stories to tell, but was enjoying the adventures of Zale and Harden. Caden told of the glory of his army and the many battles he had won, while Sachiel and Acacia spoke of the beauty of the world and what the Elements can create when all together. Lysias told only a couple of stories of days long since past. He said little of what happened within the Tower of Light, though the others were eager to know of the life of Luca. As a Kai-Rae however, he was naturally secretive and did not want to disrespect Luca's privacy.

The lamb soon came and silence fell upon them once more. They could not tell when next they would have such a meal, so were content on enjoying it. All they knew was that it tasted a lot better than what little meat there had been on the wolf. It was moist and full of rich flavours of herbs and butter. Sweet potatoes and roasted vegetables lined it that smelt heavily of rosemary and thyme.

Their plates had been removed for some time and the stories flowed when an old man approached the group. He had been sat quietly in a corner of the room not too far away listening to all the strangers said. He wore a black cloak, but still the blue of his robes beneath could be seen with their delicate silver lining. His hair and beard were silver and his eyes were as grey as the morning sky.

'I hope I do not interrupt anything too important,' he said quietly. The warriors looked at him curiously. There seemed an air of authority about him.

'No, not at all,' said Zale who was closest to the man. He could see a band of silver on his brow with words of a language unknown to him carved into it.

'I have something important to discuss with you all. I have been waiting some time to do so might I add. There is a room off this one that I ask we talk in. All shall be explained there. I have instructed Dosain to take your belongings from your horses to some comfortable rooms and there they will wait for you.' Curious, the group got up from the table, still unnoticed by those huddled round the bar, and followed the old man.

The room they were taken to was only slightly smaller than the previous one and was only accessible by a hidden door at the back of the bar. The thick smell of incense lingered in the air. What little light there was came from five short, white church candles delicately placed upon a black chandelier in the centre of the room. Directly below this was a great round, metal table, carved into a ring, leaving an empty space in the middle. It shone silver in the flickering candlelight, giving it an almost enchanted feeling, as if the table itself were magic. Within the metal was carved various images and words in the Ancestral Tongue. As the group drew nearer, they could see various precious stones glittering in the shadows, embedded into the stone floor where the centre of the table was missing. Etched into the stone, giving shape to the jewels, was a great dragon curling round a man holding a sword high towards the heavens. The hilt of the sword was encrusted with sapphires and emeralds. Upon the man's forefinger, shining brightest of all, was a purple stone in the middle of a silver ring. Zale looked down upon his own forefinger and saw there in the darkness his own ring, the purple stone glowing brilliantly.

The Prophecy of Man

When the last member of the group had stepped over the threshold, the man closed the door silently behind them and walked to the other end of the table. The group now realised that low benches made of the same silvery metal surrounded the table. The man gestured for them to sit and obediently they did so. He then removed the black cloak from around his shoulders to reveal numerous silver chains around his neck with various pendants; some of dragons, some of symbols, some of men. His blue robes delicately stroked the floor, the silver lining now catching the light of the candles. They covered the length of his arms where they seemed to rest on the tips of his silver rings, three on each hand, each encrusted with sapphires. His face was old, like the trunk of an oak coming to the end of its days. His eyes seemed to now burn with an orange glow, though Caden was sure this was just the reflection of the candles' flames. Lysias did not mention it, though he recognised the greying man. He bore the resemblance of an old friend from Luca's past.

'Thank you for agreeing to talk with me,' he said in a deep, cracked voice, as though he had not spoken for some time. 'I am sure you have noticed this is no ordinary room. It has been here for many years, kept hidden from the rest of the world.' He paused for a moment and looked as though he was trying to remember some distant memory.

'I am sorry,' interrupted Acacia, 'but may I ask who are you?' The man looked up at them as if waking from a trance.

'Forgive me; my memory is not as it used to be. I did not realise I had not yet introduced myself. I am Restor, King of the Northern People.' The warriors began to murmur amongst themselves. Restor raised his hand and silenced them. 'However, I have not been thought of as king for many a year. The Northern People no longer need a king, and I am glad to be removed of responsibility. Many believe me to be dead, hence my disguise whilst in the bar area of the inn. Dosain, however, still looks to me as his leader and so grants me any of my wishes. I have told him of your reasons for being here as General Pivloy informed me. It is likely that none of you were even aware of my presence in the room.' He gave them a questioning look and received his answer from their gaze. A small smile crept to the corners of his mouth.

'Why is it you wish to speak with us in private, and why in such a sacred room?' asked Harden.

'This is the only record left of the Prophecy of Man,' replied Restor, raising his arms as if displaying the room. 'The Prophecy concerns part of your journey and so I thought it best to recite it to you, myself being the only one left with it in memory. When first discovered by the Ancient Folk, my forefathers agreed to keep it secret and only tell it to those who it concerned. There was much more to it, though it has long since been divided, each keeper of the prophecy passing down their sacred piece waiting for the day when they may recite it. For many an age we have waited, and here I am, the last of my house, now able to keep their promise.' The warriors looked at him with wonder. They already knew that they were part of one prophecy, but to be part of another at the same time was beyond their dreams.

'What part of our journey?' asked Bazyli with excitement. 'How do you know it is really about us?' Restor gave a short chuckle.

'A part that will soon come to pass,' said the old king looking fondly at the young boy. His gaze lingered on him for some time, as though he recognised him from a far off dream. 'I shall recite it to you, though no one knows fully its meaning. That is for you to understand at the end of your quest.' He cleared his throat and began to speak, his voice becoming lighter, almost as if he could hear a distant music and was singing.

'Dragons and men for an age
Live in peace with each other.
Yet a war filled with rage
Forever separates brother from brother.

'Both man and beast fills with hatred
Where love and friendship once lay.
Across the battle field none dare tread,
Even when the memory fades away.

'Many years do pass
Yet the wounds never fully healed,
Until, after centuries, at last
A man of strength is revealed.

'Upon his quest of worldly need,
The dragons are a threat once more.
Then is planted the immortal seed

That brings back the ancient lore.

'Scattered men reunite
And battle side by side
Giving back the dragons their flight
So no longer must they hide.

'Known to all by a secret symbol,
The man of silver strength does bear,
A ring with lilac crystal,
Making all his enemies beware.'

  The old man finished and sat down gracefully upon one of the benches at the table. The others looked at him in wonder, not sure what to make of the Prophecy. There was a silence that seemed to last forever.

  'Who is this man?' asked Zale at length, suddenly feeling the need to hide his ring beneath his cloak.

  'That is for you all to discover on your own. He is shown right there,' said Restor, pointing to the image carved into the floor. He did not look at it, but instead stared meaningfully at Zale, a twinkle in his eye. 'I do not know any more of the prophecy, or even if this man features anywhere else within it. The rest of it may have already been recited, its part played out. All I know is that there are three that know of this man of strength, yet he himself is unaware of his greatness.' With this, Acacia and Harden looked at each other, though Zale did not notice.

  'Do you mean,' said Bazyli at length, 'that this man, this brave warrior, is in this room?' His eyes lit up with the thought of it.

  'Indeed I do, though the Prophecy cannot come to pass if his actions are not honourable. Now, enough of this talk. I have done as promised and will now go to the north to live out my days in peace, if peace will indeed be found. The one you seek, Lord Jabari, is threatening my retirement!' Restor said this with a slight smile, though there was annoyance in his voice. 'I beg you; go to your rooms and think of this business no more. This night you may rest under the watchful guard of General Pivloy. He has instructions not to let any enter this town until you leave with the morning. Though, with the sun circling as it is, you may choose when that morning is! Stay as long as you wish. Feel not inclined to pay any fee for the promise also included generous hospitality for those whose future road was rough and treacherous. I will be here until you make your leave to answer any of your questions, but now it is time to sleep.' With that, Restor got to his feet, making the others do so in respect. He shook his head and smiled to himself whilst pulling on his cloak. He then went to the door and opened it for them. The bar area was now almost empty with only one or two customers left passed out over tables. He gave a short laugh.

'Just think,' he said quietly as if not to wake them, 'here we are talking of Prophecies and dark times, yet the people of this town go on about their lives merrily. Do you know why that is?' The warriors shook their heads. 'A spell was placed upon the town many an age ago protecting it from all dangers. You may have noticed the mist avoiding even the houses' roofs? It was set upon the walls so that the Prophecy could be kept safe and never lost to time. I think it has done well.' With that, he ushered them out of the room and locked it with a large, golden key. Dosain was there to greet them and show them to their rooms. Just as the group were lead towards a small, crooked staircase at the other end of the bar, Restor stopped Zale who had been walking at the back.

'Believe in yourself,' he said to him quietly. 'Trust your heart. Let yourself be guided by your feelings as all shall be alright.' Then, with a gentle smile, he walked away, back to the corner he had been sitting in before. Zale went over to stairs, but just before they wound out of sight, he looked back towards Restor to find he was no longer there. Like a ghost, he had vanished into the darkness.

The group found their rooms to be together so that none of them were more than a step or two away from anyone else. The rooms were paired so that the warriors could split and separately discuss the day's events. Acacia and Sachiel shared a room, as did Caden and Harden. Zale had offered to share with Bazyli who was more than pleased as he had long wanted to talk with Zale about what the future held. None of them spoke for long though as the experience in the Desert of Temptation and fear of the wolves had finally caught up with them. Sleep took them to peaceful dreams of better days when the world was absent of evil. Lysias chose to rest alone, taking the room next to Zale and Bazyli in order to keep watch over the boy. He did not rest as easily as the others. The thought of Restor unnerved him.

Careful not to alert the others as they slept soundly, the Kai-Rae slipped out of his room and down the stairs. The bar was empty now, Dosain having taken the drunken stragglers home. Lysias's hearing was heightened by the absolute silence that clung to the air. The smell of tobacco smoke lingered in the room. Lysias went over to the corner that Restor had watched the group from but found it to be empty. He was about to move away when he noticed a flickering of light escaping between a few slats in the wall. He pushed against them gently and they creaked open as a secret door. The Kai-Rae found himself stepping into a short narrow passage lit by a single candle held in a brass bracket on the wall. At the end of it was a small door opening onto the road to the left of the inn. The place looked familiar, as though Lysias had been in the town some time before. He followed the road past the sleeping houses, his muscles tensing at the slightest sound. For some reason the air felt different to when the group had first arrived at the town. The end of the road was marked by a grand house with a beautiful front garden. Instinctively, the Kai-Rae glanced to his left and saw an expanse of fields stretching out behind the other homes. Stood before them was Restor.

'I thought you would come to find me,' said the old king to the night. Lysias walked slowly over to him, his eyes sparkling in the darkness.

'How do I know you?' asked Lysias quietly. 'You seem to be the young king that Luca once knew so well, yet I know that man to have passed from this world a little more than one cycle of the sun ago.' Restor continued to gaze across the fields. He smiled sadly and slowly nodded his head. Lysias was confused. He knew of no magic that could be responsible for the man's presence other than of a secret creature, and he knew Luca's friend had not been of their kind. Lysias too looked out over the land and his eyes seemed drawn to the mist hovering above. Realisation flickered across his face. 'The enchantment.'

'Yes my old friend,' said Restor solemnly. His voice seemed empty now. 'I have been bound here in order to fulfil my task.'

'Once we leave this town, the mist will engulf it and you will be no more,' predicted Lysias. He looked at the man stood next to him and saw tears in his eyes. Restor faced the strange creature with a soft smile.

'How did you know I was no more?' asked the king.

'Luca was so fond of you she had one of my kind bond with your soul. She felt your death like it was her own.' The two of them stayed silent and turned back to gaze at the mist.

'I met a young girl on her own journey,' said Restor after a while. 'She too was special. Unfortunately, Jabari's servant, Xannon, came across her and saw her for what she was. Unable to track her down, he followed her path backwards. He killed her protector whilst trying to get information, and then he found his way back to me. I resisted until my end. Not one word passed my lips from the moment I saw him. Now I do not know if she is safe for I was bound to roam within these walls, until you arrived.'

'Once this is finished,' said Lysias, 'I will find her, whether she be dead or alive.' They fell silent again. Lysias was thinking everything through. It seemed as though Jabari had been working his evil into the world for some time. Then the Kai-Rae thought back to what was said in the sacred room.

'You said you were going to go to the north,' he said questioningly, 'yet you knew all along what would happen once we leave.' Restor looked pensive for a moment, as though choosing whether or not to share what raced through his mind.

'Do you know where my people come from?' he said at last. Lysias shook his head. 'We once ruled in a northern land. A war broke out and it took the death of one close to us to end it. We came here in search of a new start. Since then, my people have always believed that once we die we will travel back to our true home and be reunited with the one we lost. I too hope to share in my people's fate.' Lysias looked at the old man and thought he could see his essence fading. Restor bowed to him, signalling it was time for him to prepare, and then walked away. He disappeared into the grand house, leaving Lysias to stand alone. He could feel the silence around him like a thick blanket. He stared at the fields as he thought of the sacrifice Restor had made and the terrible knowledge he had had to live with, knowing he could never leave this life until he had fulfilled the task set to him.

The Kai-Rae stood there until his body began to ache. The journey was finally catching up with him. He made his way back to the inn and crept through the secret door. The bar was still empty, though the smoke had dispersed and its smell had faded. He silently made it up the narrow stairs and into his room. As soon as he lay on the small, dusty bed his mind succumbed to dreams.

After many hours of sleep, the warriors were woken by Dosain informing them that breakfast was being served in the bar below. He had prepared the booth that they had used before and was now simply waiting for their presence. They half heartily washed and dressed, longing for their time in the town to have lasted longer. They knew, however, that they must be on their way soon; else Damané would be lost forever. They made their way to the booth where they were greeted by platefuls of fruit and goblets filled with fresh water. Restor was once again in his corner and raised his own goblet to them. Lysias bowed his head slightly. He chose not to tell any of the group what he had discovered the night before. Many of the warriors had questions for the old king, but none had the heart to think of their future journey, so they all silently decided to set off that day unaware of what was to come. For some reason, each felt Restor knew far more than he had told but were aware that they were not meant to know at that time.

It did not take as long as the group hoped for them to finish their breakfasts. When they left the table, Restor had once again slipped silently away and was nowhere to be seen. Dosain informed them that their horses were waiting for them outside with fresh packs of food that would perhaps last them the day. He dared not give them more, for the horses also needed to carry them swiftly to their destination. He said his farewells and watched them leave the bar. He would have followed them to the town's border and watch them take their leave properly, but he was swept away by a flood of orders from fresh customers seeking a refreshing breakfast of their own.

The warriors' hearts were light as they made their way down the cobble streets past the quiet houses. The sun could still be felt trying to pierce the mist above them, though they thought the mist had thinned since the day before. When they reached the gates, Gredin was there to meet them.

'Good morning my friends!' he called when they were in sight. 'Now then, I hear you are of the hope to make your way back to the eastern road. I will give you the best directions I can to aid you, though it is mighty simple if you ask me.' With that, he waited for them to reach him and continued to laden them with information concerning the lands. Once he had finished, the warriors thanked him and he took one last look upon the fair faces of the Elements before watching them pass through the gates.

However, just before they had all left the safety of the town, a young woman began to call to them as she raced towards the gates. The warriors stopped and turned to greet her.

'Please,' she said as she drew near, 'please wait. How is it that you could have been here all this time and not have me hear of you?' She was panting from the run but stood with a cheerful smile on her face. She could not be more than 18 years old. Her short blonde hair was spiked like mountain peaks, similar to Lysias's, and her eyes were as blue as the ocean. Harden and Zale dismounted to speak with her and were surprised to find her to be just as tall as them.

'Why is it you wish to speak with us?' Harden asked. 'And who are you?'

'Me? Why, I am Zophia, the Turner of Minds!' Gredin watched all of this with amusement as Harden and Zale exchanged puzzled looks.

'She looks like a young woman who is as crazy as one who drinks scorpion juice,' said Gredin, 'but she knows what she's talking about.' He chuckled and stepped out of ear shot.

'I just have one thing to tell you before you leave,' Zophia said with an even bigger smile than before. 'White waters whisper the path of truth. When you find them, just listen.' Then she simply turned to leave.

'Hold on,' said Harden, 'what does that mean?' Zophia shrugged her shoulders, still smiling, but had a look of knowing in her eyes as she stared at Zale. Then she trotted off back up the cobbled street. Harden and Zale looked at each other and shook their heads with confusion. Zale looked to the others to see if they knew what Zophia had been on about, but they all looked just as stunned as him. Harden and Zale mounted their horses and the group went through the gates, their minds buzzing with the strange experience they had just had.

The Pass

As soon as they crossed the borders of the town, a blanket of mist once again confronted them. The gate's lights were soon swallowed up by the unnatural fog and left far behind. Lysias thought of how the town folk would now be shrouded in the same mist and that Restor would never be seen again. They continued on, travelling cautiously. They had been surprised by where the last fog had taken them and were now in no mood to find themselves lost again. The directions from Gredin had been precise, though they could not see any of the landmarks he had mentioned. Eventually, Caden dismounted and kept his eye on the ground so as to follow the stone path leading from the town. It was narrow, almost the same shade as the earth beside it. The others had to stay right behind the General so as to not get lost. The hanging moisture dulled their hearing and muffled the sound of the horses' hoofs. There was so much dust covering the road that after a while Caden took off his cloak and used it to swipe away some of the fine covering to reveal the path ahead. It wound mysteriously across the land, turning abruptly to avoid some unseen obstacle. This made it more difficult to track, though Caden felt they were at least generally travelling in the right direction.

Two long hours passed like this. Bazyli had begun to fear the mist as it seemed to draw in closer with the passing time and he thought he saw shapes flying past. In the back of his mind, the thought of wolves came to him. He kept imagining sharp teeth and yellow eyes appearing from the fog as they dived towards him. Lysias stayed close to the boy for reassurance, though he too could sense something moving out there. It was a strange feeling, like that of when he was near Restor. It was as though something was there but it could only be seen, not touched. Bazyli's fears did fade a little with the closeness of the Kai-Rae, though still he kept a watchful eye. Lysias was about to tell the others to stop a while so he could investigate when Caden called out. The path had stopped and he was not sure where to go.

'Well,' said Zale, 'I think it would be best if we tried to stick to the course we are already on. We cannot tell how long this fog will last so cannot attempt to wait it out. Besides, I sense a danger in this place.' The others had felt it too but none had dared to mention it. Lysias thought it best to let the group continue on so as to not add to all of their growing fears. Bazyli drew his horse in closer to Lysias's with the thought of the others also sensing a darkness. The Kai-Rae placed a reassuring hand on his shoulder and sent a pulse of warmth through him to lighten his spirits.

They journeyed on, Caden now back on his horse. He attempted to lead the group for a while in the direction he felt the path followed the most. There were loose stones beneath the horses' hooves and every so often Sachiel caught a glimpse of large boulders, until they were eaten up again by the mist. Shadowy forms seemed to glide past, though no one truly saw them. At times Zale thought he could hear whispers all around him, though he chose not to tell the others. He could not be sure if it was the effect of the mist, his imagination, or something darker. The horses were jumpy and had quickened the pace without instruction.

Many hours passed before the ground began to rise and they felt the sense of danger ebb away. The shadowy forms ceased to appear and the fog felt less intruding. The ground sloped downwards again and soon they found they were back on the sandy earth of the Sunar Plains. What the warriors did not know was that they had just passed through the Valley of Disinamorah. A great battle was fought there many ages ago between the Domai and the Western Wolves. The wolves had been invading the lands of those strange creatures and destroying its beauty. The Domai, as great warriors, took their stand in that valley, fighting the wolves as equals. It was a battle of claws and teeth, proving that the Domai, though magical, are as close to nature as the other creatures of the world. They chose that day, once the great had finally been won, to never loose their natural instincts and display their warrior claws proudly for all to fear. If the group had known the name of the valley they rode through, not even the Elements would have dared pass that way. It was said that all the souls lost in that valley continued to battle long into the years, still fighting for dominance in those lands, regarding any trespassers as enemies. Yet, even before this, an even greater battle had taken place; the one between men and dragons that the Prophecy had spoken of. The ground had been scorched and turned red with blood. All the surrounding lands had become barren and the island's creatures were in hiding for years after. It had gone on for many an age as the dragons fought for their existence. That war and all of its atrocities, however, had long since left the memory of men.

After an hour or so, Harden, who was leading the group, cried out as he almost rode into a wall of rock.

'What's the matter?' asked Zale as he joined his friend.

'The path is blocked. Bazyli, was this here when you followed Xannon?'

'Yes. There is a short pass somewhere around here.' The group stayed together and travelled along the edge of the rocky barrier, trying to find the pass. The strange wall rose high up next to them, disappearing into the mist. Its surface was smooth, almost perfectly flat except for small chips that looked as though it had been chiselled. Acacia placed a hand on its cool surface and sensed it did not truly belong there. Sachiel urged her on, knowing the unnatural barrier was delaying their journey too much and they had to find the pass soon. After an hour however, they ended their search and decided to make camp. Though the sun still gleamed above them through the mist, they had been travelling for over eleven hours without food or rest. Acacia was able to use her powers to grow four great oaks from the refreshed soil to provide them with some shelter. Their buds pushed up through the sand where Acacia's hand had been placed and wound slowly upwards, their delicate stems widening into sturdy, bark-ridden trunks. Fresh leaves opened around the branches and hung there, gently rustling in the breeze. There was no other vegetation as the Sunar Plains have always been too barren to support life. Grateful for the sense of security given off by the trees, the group rolled out their bed mats and lay down. Unsure if Jabari would send scouts to find them, Harden offered to take the first watch. Zale, unable to sleep, decided to stay up with him.

'How long has it been since you saw Jabari?' Zale asked quietly as he sat himself down against the rough trunk of one of the trees.

'Not since I was a young teen. He knows that I would kill him instantly for what he's done to me if ever I saw him again.' Harden's face grew cold. Zale looked at him sympathetically. He wished that there were something he could do to help Harden, but knew there was nothing in the world to take away his obvious pain. If only Harden would tell him what happened all those years ago. Clearing his throat, Harden tried to change the subject.

'Now, Zale, your swordsmanship is not what it could be. I mean, if I hadn't of been there when those Nicars were about, you would surely have died.'

'What? That's not true and you know it. I'll prove it to you.' There was a sparkle in Harden's eye as Zale said it. Zale's pride had got the better of him. They rose to their feet and drew their swords. Zale's technique was good, but Harden was obviously the stronger of the two. They became more and more competitive, each trying to get through the other's defences. After half an hour of fighting, Zale finally tired and Harden put the tip of his blade to Zale's throat.

'You have grown tired? I will have to teach you to go for hours without rest. We will train every time we camp, unless we find ourselves in a battle before then, in which case, lets hope you can muster enough strength to survive!' Harden's words were teasing but had meaning behind them too. He knew Jabari well. He was not the kind to let the enemy approach without trying to stop them first. The two of them sat down on a couple of large red desert rocks.

'Well,' said Zale, 'I'm sure I could get my way out of a fight by making blue topaz crystals!' The two of them laughed.

'That word, Magnina, does not only transform rocks to blue topaz crystals, but to any other form of rock you desire; diamond, for example. The magic can sense what it is you would like to do, so helps you in any way it can. Did you feel the Ancestral Tongue upon your lips last time?' Zale nodded. 'I bet Magnina stood out above all the other words.' Once again, Zale nodded in response.

'Transforming rocks still won't help me in battle though,' said Zale.

'Indeed. Therefore I think it is time I taught you two new spells.' Harden unsheathed his sword and held it out in front of Zale. 'At the moment,' he continued, 'this is a dangerous weapon to you. Yet, it can be tamed so easily.'

'What do you mean?' asked Zale, completely confused. To him there was nothing more dangerous than a sword other than an arrow.

'I see that you see metal as strength. Magic is more powerful than anything. Watch.' Harden muttered something under his breath and the centre of the sword began to glow white hot. With a sharp snap, Harden was able to split the sword in two.

'What did you do that for?' cried Zale thinking that Harden was now defenceless.

'A sword can easily be broken, whether it be by magic or another means. I can teach you how to protect your sword, making it stronger and much more deadly, and also how to repair it if you do not have time to do the first.' Harden said this with a sparkle in his eye. He found it fascinating how amazed Zale was to learn all these new things.

'What do I have to do?' Zale asked.

'It's simple,' continued Harden. 'Just repeat after me. Let's start with protecting your sword. There are many different incantations to do this, but my favourite is Syranor. Now, clear your mind as before. Pass your hand over your sword from end to end, and say Syranor.' Zale took out his sword and held it in front of his chest. As instructed, he cleared all thoughts from his head, concentrating only on his breathing. Then he opened his mind to the magic eager to be used and found what he wanted waiting for him. Remembering to also concentrate on making the spell remain, he passed his hand over his sword and said aloud *Syranor*. His entire sword glowed with a brilliant red hue. Zale released the link from his mind to the spell and was relieved to find the crimson light still there.

'Well done,' said Harden admiring his friend's work. 'I thought I could catch you out, but this spell seems to be lasting. Did you notice the difference?'

'What do you mean?'

'There was no pain.' Zale suddenly realised that Harden was right. This time there had not been a tugging at his heart.

'Why is that so?' he asked curiously.

'For two reasons; firstly, you were ready for it, and secondly, you only kept the connection to the magic for a short period of time. One piece of advice though,' Harden continued, looking seriously into Zale's eyes. 'In battle, or any other time for that matter, do not waste time choosing what incantation to use while you have the connection open. It is more difficult to do this when not speaking the spell aloud, but it is vital you try. As soon as you make the link, the magic begins to use up your energy. Know what it is you want before giving the magic control.' With a stern look from his tutor, Zale nodded his head to show he understood the gravity of Harden's words.

'How do I repair my sword?'

'That takes a bit more energy,' said Harden. 'The words are *departé chira yaytana*. They mean *silver strength healed*. This works for any form of weaponry. Take the parts of my sword in either hand and say the words, imagining all the while that the sword is being mended.' Zale picked up Harden's sword and began to clear his mind. He found it difficult to then imagine the sword coming back together and concentrate on the words. Frustrated, he glared at Harden.

'I can't do this. How can I imagine the sword being fixed, concentrate on it being permanent, and keep my mind clear of all other thoughts?'

'Stay calm,' said Harden. 'Close your eyes. See the magic as images as opposed to just words and commands.' Zale took and deep breath and tried again. Once his mind was clear, he closed his eyes and visualised the parts of the sword he held. He was surprised to find the image so clear. As if sensing what he wanted to do, he felt the magic pushing its way to his lips and could see it as a ribbon of colour dancing round the broken ends of the sword, preparing to mend it. Zale's voice rang out as he forced the two ends together. *Departé chira yaytana.* There was a blinding emerald light and the entire blade became molten in Zale's hands. After a moment of a scorching sensation in his hands, Zale felt the metal solidify again and he released the magic. Exhausted, he fell forwards, an even stronger pain in his heart than the first time he tried magic. Harden caught him just before his head would have collided with one of the roots of the tree. The two of them stayed there for a while, Zale breathing deeply as the pain gradually ebbed away. When he was strong enough, with the help of Harden, Zale sat back up against the tree.

'You said it was hard,' Zale panted, 'but that was one of the most difficult things I have ever done!'

'I know,' said Harden, 'but you had to do it some time. It will get easier. You were in connection with the magic for far too long. However, on the bright side, you mended my sword!' Zale looked at the sword that now lay at his feet. It looked as though it had just been made with no sign of a break. Then he looked down at his hands. They were a deep red and appeared as though they were going to blister.

'What happened to my hands?' he asked.

'You forgot to protect yourself from the magic,' Harden informed him. 'Then again, I forgot to tell you that the sword is fixed by being made molten and then reforming. Unfortunately, as a result, you have been badly burnt. I will see what I can do about that.' Harden took hold of Zale's hands and closed his eyes, muttering something under his breath. Zale could feel the heat leaving his hands and all signs of blisters seeping away.

'You healed me!' he exclaimed once Harden was finished.

'Not heal,' said Harden. 'We cannot use magic to do that. For us it is more complicated. I simply used a spell to draw the heat away from your hands. They may still hurt for a while, but it shouldn't last for more than an hour or so.'

'What do you mean *for us*?' asked Zale. 'You imply there are those who can heal.'

'That's because there are,' said Harden smiling, 'but as for them, you will learn more later. Our course leads us directly to them.' Zale looked quizzically at his friend, but no more was said of the matter. The two of them sat in silence. It did not take long for Zale to feel fully recovered from his experience, but both men were growing tired as the day caught up with them. Their watch soon drew to an end. They woke Caden and Sachiel and lay down to sleep, dreaming of peaceful times when magic was not needed to survive.

Throughout the night, the men and Sachiel took turns with the watch. Lysias chose to take the final watch alone, allowing the others to sleep through for a few hours. When they all woke, Acacia was angry that they had not woken her to take a watch just because she was a female. Lysias explained that it was his fault and that he had just wanted them all to get a decent night's sleep. She apologised for her outburst and smiled at him kindly. They ate some breakfast, no more than some bread and fruit, and packed up the camp, trying to leave no trace of them having been there. The men gathered together and started planning their next move. They had to find the pass quickly so as to not be delayed further, though it could be in either direction. They decided it would be best for them to split up, some going one way, the rest the other. One person would ride further ahead and start their search from their in case the pass was some distant away. The sun was still up and the mist still lingered once their plan was agreed. The men were about to set off to find the pass when they heard a shout.

'I've found it! I've found the pass!' Looking around themselves, they suddenly realised that Acacia had gone off ahead to find a way round. 'But I can hear falling rocks.' The next thing the men heard was a scream from Acacia. Her horse leapt out of the way of a large boulder that fell from the top of the wall.

'Are you all right? Is your necklace intact?' Sachiel galloped over to her.

'I'm fine. Besides, if my necklace were broken you would know. Bazyli, is there another way round? This way is too dangerous. The storm seems to have loosened the rocks.'

'The edge of the wall is a three sun ride in either direction and it's too high to climb,' said the boy.

'Well then, we will just have to chance it.' Acacia's words were final, though they all knew the pass was the only route they could choose to take. Any other way would jeopardise the safety of Damané.

Caden and Lysias were the first to go through the pass, followed by Harden, Bazyli and Sachiel. Zale and Acacia rode together at the back. They crept through the passage, keeping a watch on the boulders above as best they could. The mist was still thick and the horses found it difficult to walk on the fallen rocks.

'Why was Sachiel so concerned about your necklace?' Zale wanted to break the awkward silence that had fallen between him and Acacia.

'Each Element has one. If one gets broken then we will all die and the power of the Elements will be left to nature.'

'I see. So that's why Lord Jabari kidnapped Baaron and Nare.'

'Yes. He can kill us at any time, though why he hasn't, I am not sure.' Silence fell over the two of them once more. Zale was about to speak when someone called out.

'I've reached the other side!' Caden's voice echoed around the passage, disturbing the balanced rocks above the group. They could hear a great rumble and saw stones falling down the sides of the walls.

'Hurry!' Harden's horse began to canter, causing the others to do the same. They weaved in and out of the falling rocks, barely missing them. As he reached the other side, Sachiel turned to see a large boulder tilt and fall.

'Look out!' It was too late. The boulder hit Acacia on the head and she fell to the ground as her horse ran on.

'Acacia!' Zale turned round, rode towards her and dismounted. He picked her up and put her on his horse. He hit his horse on its flank and it rode to the end of the pass. The rocks were falling heavier now. By the smaller rocks being dislodged, the large boulders had begun to fall. Acacia's horse rushed past Zale as he ran from side to side. His arms and face were covered in blood where shards of stone had torn away the skin. Another large boulder landed right in front of him. He could see his horse rear up and come to a halt near the end of the pass to avoid a collision with the falling boulders, then continue on to safety. Zale looked around him. He now could not see through the falling rocks. The others' voices filled his ears as they tried to guide him to them. A rock the size of his head landed heavily on his shoulder, making him fall to the ground. He knew the pass would soon be blocked with him in it unless he got out quickly. Then, a gap appeared and he could make out the others ahead of him. He staggered to his feet and ran round the many boulders that littered the ground and headed for the mouth of the pass. Just as Zale reached the other side, the pass closed up behind him.

'Is she all right? Acacia? Can you hear me? Check her necklace!'

'Calm down Sachiel. Her necklace is fine but she's out cold.' Harden had taken Acacia from Zale's horse whilst Sachiel had frantically searched her for her necklace. Zale sat on the ground beside her, groaning with pain.

'Fine, no one ask me if I'm alright,' protested Zale as everyone's attention was on Acacia. Harden patted him on the back and pulled him to his feet. Zale winced in pain as Harden's hand touched the gash that now gleamed on his shoulder.

'Are you alright?' asked Bazyli.

'Don't worry, he's fine. Zale and I have had closer calls than that,' said Harden as he began to sooth Zale's wounds with a damp cloth. He smiled down at the boy, and then turned to see their route. 'Is there any way to wake her?' Harden's voice was grave.

'No, like you said, she's out cold. Why? What's the matter?' Sachiel stood up and suddenly saw what Harden was worried about. The mist had cleared for an instant to reveal nothing but marshes.

'Bazyli, why didn't you tell us about this?' asked Sachiel angrily. He was beginning to believe that Bazyli had been sent by Jabari to lead them to danger.

'I'm sorry Sachiel, but it wasn't here before,' replied Bazyli, fearing Sachiel's tone. He had never seen the Element like this before.

'Don't lie to me!' Sachiel raised his arm as if to hit Bazyli. The boy cowered before him. Zale grabbed Sachiel's arm and gave him a threatening look. The strength at which he did it startled Sachiel as he thought Zale to be weak. He did not even think that he could muster the amount of strength that Zale now had in him after a battering like that.

'Sachiel, how do you know that Bazyli's lying?' asked Zale, rage rising inside him. 'Lord Jabari has a sorcerer. Did it never occur to you that perhaps *he* has done this? And besides, what was once a dry plain could well be a marsh land after the rain we travelled through.' He turned to Bazyli and smiled. 'It's alright Bazyli, I believe you.' Zale put a hand on Bazyli's head. Bazyli wrapped his arms round Zale's waist. Zale was surprised at this show of affection, but then he hugged Bazyli back and suddenly realised just how young and brave Bazyli was.

'I am sorry,' muttered Sachiel, hiding his face in his hands. 'I did not mean any harm. I'm just so worried about Acacia, and now this.' Zale understood Sachiel's pain and gave him a nod of gratitude for the apology.

'Zale, please do not call him *Lord* Jabari,' said Harden suddenly.

'Yes, of course,' said Zale. 'I'm sorry, I should have known better.' Embarrassed, Zale looked away.

'Well, we had better get moving,' said Harden, changing the subject. 'It's a shame that Acacia can't just wave her hands and get rid of these marshes. After all, she is the Princess of Earth.'

'Is that all you think she's good for Harden? Is it?' snapped Sachiel, beginning to lose his temper again. The Elements' powers have been exploited by others ever since they were first known.

'Everyone stay calm,' said Zale. 'We are all tired and worried about Acacia. Harden did not mean anything by it.'

'No,' said Harden, 'I'm sorry. It just slipped out.' A sudden thought came to him. 'Lysias,' Harden began, 'do you think that your power is great enough to clear a path for us?' Harden looked around him for the Kai-Rae and then stopped in his tracks. 'Lysias?' He was nowhere to be seen. Looking back at the others, Harden realised Caden was missing too.

'Where are they?' asked Zale, he too now noticing their absence.

'We were all so caught up in each other's frustration that we did not notice they weren't here,' said Sachiel in horror.

'Lysias?' Bazyli called softly as he looked back towards the now blocked pass. The others followed the young boy's gaze.

'But they cannot be in there,' said Zale. 'They were at the front of the group. Caden was the one who called out to say he was at the other side.'

'That does not mean he actually left the pass though,' said Harden sadly. 'It appeared to be his shout that started the rock-fall did it not?' The others reluctantly agreed. 'Then it would be safe to assume that the greatest impact of his voice would have been on the rocks directly above both him and Lysias.' Tears welled up in Bazyli's eyes. The grief of loosing another person in his life filled his very being.

'But he cannot be gone!' the child cried. 'He is here to protect me! He cannot be gone!' Zale drew Bazyli into an embrace and allowed the boy to cry into his side.

'I'm sure they're alright, don't you Harden?' Zale gave his friend a meaningful look.

'Yes,' said Harden, though his eyes told a different story. 'After all, he is a Kai-Rae. I'm sure he and Caden are safe. Lysias will get them out of there. This end of the pass is completely sealed, so they will probably go the other way and just ride round the wall.'

'That's right Bazyli,' said Zale reassuringly. 'They'll catch up with us in no time.' Bazyli looked up into Zale's smiling face and bore an expression of gratitude. He knew deep down that Zale and Harden were probably just trying to spare his feelings, but he wanted to believe what they said and so took comfort in their words. He did not notice Sachiel silently whispering a prayer to Nature asking her to keep their souls safe as tears came to his eyes.

'Come,' said Zale abruptly, wanting to distract them all from the thought of Lysias's and Caden's fate. 'We will walk the horses through the marshland. We *will* find a way through. Sachiel put Acacia back on her horse and walk with her. Bazyli, stay between Harden and myself. I'll lead the way.' Sachiel wasn't used to being ordered around by men, but he did as Zale wanted. With that, the five of them reluctantly began their long journey through the marshes. They all knew that once they began to cross them, there was no escape. They would be more exposed than ever.

Marshes

They walked in single file through the thick mud and water. Their legs sunk to knee depth, making it difficult to move. Their muddy cloaks dragged behind them, covering their tracks. Flies swarmed around them. The mist was slightly thinner giving the warriors a better outlook on the marshes. They spread for miles in all directions like a blanket keeping the land warm. After an hour of strained walking, the group's progress was minimal. Bazyli was beginning to tire so Harden put him on his horse. The horses began to groan as their legs seized up with the effort of pulling themselves out of the mud. At one point, Sachiel fell into a pool of water to his left. Harden rushed to his rescue. His body was half covered in the muddy bed, making the water rise to around his chin. He continued to slowly sink as Harden found a branch for him to hold on to. When Sachiel had a strong grip, Zale threw him a rope that had been tied so it had a loop at one end. Sachiel put the rope around him so that it went under one of his arms. Zale and Harden then pulled Sachiel out of the water, causing him to land face first in the thick mud.

'Why don't you just take the water out of the ground?' asked Zale. 'That way there would be no risk of us falling into pools of water and the mud would dry up.'

'Because there is too much for me to move. Our powers are generated by us using up some of our own life force. If we try to wield too much power at one time, our life will be drained from our bodies. It is the same for all magical creatures.' Feeling slightly disappointed, and avoiding Harden's gaze, Zale turned and continued through the marsh. He knew Harden would be annoyed with him for not remembering his most important lesson in magic.

The minimal light that crept through the thick clouds above soon began to fade. The sunset seemed to last forever. Leading the group, Zale was stopped suddenly by Harden.

'What is it?' asked Zale, looking at the intense expression on Harden's face.

'I thought I heard something.'

'There is nothing out here but us,' said Bazyli sadly who had caught up with them, Sachiel at his side. The boy was inwardly mourning for the loss of his protector and felt more alone than ever. The horses began to whinny impatiently, tired from carrying Bazyli and Acacia.

'No, Harden's right. Something's approaching,' Sachiel was stood upright, alert.

'Lysias?' asked Bazyli hopefully. The others dared not look at him and pretended they had not heard his questioning voice.

'Can you tell where from? Are we in danger?' Zale looked at Sachiel and Harden who were both listening hard.

'It's coming from all directions. Draw your swords. Form as best a circle as you can around the horses. We cannot take any chances.' Harden's face grew tense as he looked around him. Sachiel put his hand to the ground and began to take some of the water from it. Each of the warriors and horses instinctively pulled their legs out of the moist ground as it solidified beneath them. A solid platform of mud formed around them and Sachiel stood up, taking a defensive stance. He strained his eyes and ears to try and discover what was approaching.

'They are Usari! Quickly, spread out!' Sachiel was panic-stricken. The others did as they were told and stared into the darkness, dread filling their hearts.

'What are Usari?' asked Bazyli, turning white with fear, still mounted on his horse. He could hear the movement too now and looked about him frantically.

'They are one of the most stupid creatures known to man,' replied Harden, 'but terrible warriors. They are six feet tall with scaled emerald skin. Their bodies are slender, giving them the ability to move at great speeds, yet their scales are as strong as mountains. They travel on foot, wearing hooded black cloaks to disguise their distinguishable features. They are mighty swordsmen with their necks as their only weakness, for the flesh is soft there. Yet, they are tactless and have no intelligence of any kind. They will do the biding of any who ask. Well, who ever pays them the most.' Bazyli began to breathe faster as his heart pounded inside his chest. Zale glanced at Harden, annoyed with his honesty for it made Bazyli's fear grow.

'Xannon must be controlling them with his mind, else they would never have made it this far without forgetting what they were meant to be doing,' added Sachiel. 'Find the one being controlled and kill it. That will make the others disperse.'

'How do you know that Xannon isn't controlling them all?' Zale asked with a note of fear in his voice.

'You really don't listen, do you Zale?' said Sachiel growing irritated. 'All those with magical powers can only use magic by draining some of their life source. If Xannon is controlling them, he has to reach a long way to do it. At the same time, he is protecting Jabari's keep with a spell, sapping his energy all the time. He is only a young sorcerer. He hasn't got full control of his powers yet. If he even dared to try and control all of the Usari, he would surely die.'

As he said it, ten Usari could be seen approaching them, their long legs barely even touching the mud, let alone sinking into it. They walked slowly, almost gracefully. Bazyli's heart pounded faster as he saw them. Beneath their cloaks he could make out long snarling snouts, sharp teeth glistening in what little light remained. Both sets of opponents paused for a moment, sizing each other up. Zale's breathing quickened, whilst Harden kept a steady hand. Blood from a recent meal dripped from one of the creature's mouths. Nothing moved. The wind swept the Usari's cloaks off their bodies, revealing a sea of glistening scales. Zale suddenly felt terribly exposed as he realised that he had no armour. The throbbing in his shoulder seemed to intensify as he prepared himself for battle. He thought about protecting his sword but felt there was no time. The creatures' eyes shone a brilliant orange, the colour of living flames. The Usari closest to the men tilted its head and snarled. The Usari charged and, in an instant, their bodies collided with the three warriors. Zale blocked a blow from one of their swords, then released his own from the hold and lunged forwards. His sword slid gracefully across the Usari's scales, leaving it unharmed. He spun away from the creature's sword and turned to face his opponent once more. Around him he could hear the sound of the clash of metal and the soft thud of flesh as Harden killed the first Usari. Zale cut through the air with his blade and was once again face to face with the creature. Their swords met, separated and rejoined many times before Zale crouched low to the ground. Beneath the creature, Zale could see his advantage and drove his sword up into the air. The blade slipped through the Usari's neck, killing it instantly. The Usari's dark blood trickled down the blade as Zale pushed its lifeless body off him. Blood began covering the ground as they all made their first kills. Zale, now free of attack, could see two Usari upon Sachiel. He ran forwards to Sachiel's aid. Together they killed their opponents swiftly. It was not long before the ten Usari lay motionless on the muddy earth. The warriors, exhausted from their efforts, looked at each other nervously. They were breathing heavily and wiped their brows. Though their enemy lay dead, it did not feel like a victory. Ahead of him, Sachiel heard a faint noise. Through the approaching darkness came more Usari, fresh and ready to fight. There were at least twenty of them, maybe more. Zale looked at Harden despairingly and saw his friend's face distorted into a vicious snarl as he charged to meet them. He angrily sliced through the air with his sword, killing three Usari with one stroke of his blade. Zale returned to the position he had originally been in as he saw two of the creatures run towards Acacia's body slumped over her horse. He dodged the blow of an Usari axe and knelt on the floor. He reached up with his sword and caught the Usari in the neck, the same way as he had done before. It was a good tactic, but slow. He then turned to see the second Usari almost upon

Acacia. To his surprise, he watched Bazyli take a dagger out of his shoe and kill the creature, blood covering his clothes. Zale nodded respectively at Bazyli and the boy wiped the dagger on his shirt.

To Zale's right was Sachiel, fighting for his life. Zale was about to help when another Usari attacked him. Through the corner of his eye, he could see Sachiel using magic to ward off the creatures. Streams of blue light were emitted from his hands as his life force slowly depleted. He killed the two that came from the front, but was blind to the third creeping up behind him. The Usari's blade went through Sachiel's back, straight to the other side. It pulled its sword back again and raised it for the final blow, Sachiel's warm blood caressing the creature's blade. Sachiel drew his sword, twisted his broken body, and pierced the creature's flesh below its jaw. The Usari fell to the ground. Sachiel staggered to his feet, his face twisted into a painful snarl. Before he had time to remove his sword that was embedded in the monster's neck, another Usari lunged forward. Harden, who had rushed to Sachiel's aid, blocked the blow. Zale could see Harden's arm dripping with blood from a deep gash that went the length of his upper arm. The sight of Harden and Sachiel both injured badly made Zale believe that all hope was lost. As he cut through the soft flesh of another monster, he kept glancing to see how Harden was fairing now fighting alone again. Zale saw him surrounded by six Usari. He ran to his aid but was blocked by a wall of green scales as ten more Usari stepped in front of him. They immediately began attacking. The situation was similar for Sachiel. Every time any of them tried to break free of their prison, more Usari came from the darkness. It seemed as though someone had told them to attack in groups rather than continue trying to get through the warriors' defences. Harden swung his sword from left to right, instantly killing two of his attackers. As he fought, his blade slid off the Usari's scaled skin, leaving it intact. One of the creatures managed to strike out with its sword as Harden fought off one of its companions. The smooth blade cut through Harden's leg and he howled in pain. Filled with rage, he lunged forwards, knowing he would not survive much longer. Harden and Zale's eyes met for a moment. In that instant, a feeling of sorrow and regret passed between the two friends. Determination welled up in their chests and they were once more filled with the desire to live. The emotion passed over Sachiel, and the Usari were shocked to find themselves being forced back. The creatures growled in pain as the warriors' blades reached their unprotected necks. About to retreat, the monsters suddenly seemed to gain courage once more. They attacked the men with greater force. Bazyli looked on hopelessly, sure that he was about to loose his friends. As Harden killed the Usari in front of him however, all the others ceased their fighting. They looked around themselves as if waking from a trance. The warriors took the moment to their advantage and began to slay all those before them, not even hesitating to try and work out what had happened. The Usari screeched in fear and fled the marshes, leaving the warriors breathless and relieved.

'That must have been the lead Usari you killed,' Zale said to Harden between breaths, putting a grateful hand on his shoulder.

'Must have been. I didn't think I could last much longer. How are your injuries?'

'Well, you my friend have a deep gash on your arm and Sachiel has been stabbed through the chest. Bazyli seems to be fine and I don't think I was touched. How's your leg fairing?'

'It's just a scratch, nothing more.' Harden looked across the Usari bodies that lay before him. His eyes fell upon Sachiel who was tending to his wound. Though the blade had gone straight through, it had somehow missed all of Sachiel's organs.

'Are you alright?' asked Harden concerned.

'I'll live. It is nothing a bandage can't fix,' replied Sachiel with a strained smile as he gripped his sword in pain. 'I'll let my magic work on it. So long as I surround the wound with a protective shield it shouldn't get infected.' Zale sheathed his sword and tore a piece of his robe off to tie around Harden's leg and another piece to clean the slash on his arm.

'Thanks. That was an intense battle. I'm surprised you came out unscathed. I could have sworn I saw you take a blow.' As he said it, Harden looked at Zale's neck in horror. He could see fresh blood seeping from a wound. 'You are injured! Give me that.' He grabbed the cloth from Zale's hands and began wrapping it around Zale's neck. Zale touched the wound in surprise.

'I didn't notice it. Is it bad?'

'I hope not. It's lucky I spotted it. You could have bled out.'

Once all the wounds had been attended to, the warriors decided that they had better keep moving. With the lead Usari dead, there was no likelihood of them returning, though they did not want to take any chances. They waded through the mud once more as the final rays of light ebbed away.

The Pit

Another hour passed before Acacia woke, though no one noticed. She looked around but could see nothing but blurry shapes. Her head was pounding and she felt weak. For a while she just lay there, feeling bursts of pain every time the blood pulsed through her head. She noticed her horse's slow, forceful walk, as if something were preventing it form moving forwards, but she was too dizzy to find out the cause. The sun no longer loomed above her but the mist was still hugging the landscape. She was aware of the others around her, but they were walking in silence. Her stomach ached for food and her hands trembled as she pat her horse. To her left, she could make out the small form of Bazyli on Harden's horse, his head lolling from side to side as he slept. The metallic taste of blood lined her mouth, though it seemed old. The smell of it however was fresh, though if it was hers or not she did not know. She was about to speak when she heard a cry for help somewhere ahead of her. The mist thinned for a moment, her vision cleared, and she could see Harden and Sachiel, apparently scanning the land for someone.

'Zale!' Harden could not see his friend.

'What's happened? Where's Zale?'

'Acacia?' They were all shocked to see her awake. 'I don't know. I cannot find him. One minute he was in front of me, next minute he's gone.'

'Acacia, are you alright?' asked Sachiel.

'I'm fine. Don't worry about me. We need to find Zale.'

'Are you up to using your powers? Apparently these marshes were not here before so you are allowed to get rid of them.'

'Allowed? Since when did I have to ask permission to use my powers?' Sachiel looked away shamefully. She did not mean to be so forceful and knew that he was just trying to help, so softened her voice. 'I am weak but I will try.' Just as Sachiel had in the rain, Acacia began to stroke the air. A ball of green light appeared between her hands and she pushed it away from her. It made a line down the centre of the marshes and shot out to the sides, wiping them away. Acacia's head throbbed even more and she fell forwards onto her horse's neck. Her breathing was heavy as she tried to rebuild her energy. Sachiel placed a concerned hand on her back and looked at her gratefully. He helped her off her horse so she could stretch her legs and steadied her with an arm. Ahead of them, two inches from his feet, Harden could see a pit with Zale lying at the bottom.

'Zale, are you all right? Are you hurt in any way?' Harden was down on his knees, leaning over the pit.

'I'm fine. I cannot believe it. Why does everything have to happen to me? I mean, one minute I'm dodging falling boulders, next we're in a battle and I get stabbed without realising, and now this.' Zale gave Harden a frustrated look.

'This is no time to complain,' said Harden, half laughing at his friend's situation. 'What can you see down there?'

'There seems to be some sort of passage. It appears to cut right under the marshes.'

'Acacia's awake. She got rid of the marshes.' Harden glanced at the edge of the pit. The sides were vertical. It would be impossible for Zale to get out.

'We are going to get you out of there. I promise.'

'Don't lie to me Harden. I can see the steepness of the walls just as well as you can. Leave me. Go on ahead. I will try following the passage to find a way out and catch you up.' Zale smiled up at his friend. Harden looked down at him for a moment, and then lowered his voice, making sure no one else was in earshot.

'I can teach you an incantation that would get you out of there.'

'I can't risk losing my energy again. You know that.' Zale gave his friend a reassuring look. 'I'll be fine.' In the end, Harden stood up, took one last look at Zale, and began to walk on.

'No! You can't leave him there!'

'Bazyli, I'll be fine. Go on. I'll catch up, I promise.' Bazyli looked upset. He had grown to like Zale more than the others. He was considering asking him if he could join him on his adventures when this one was over, though he knew Zale would refuse. At that moment however, all the boy could think of was all the people that had recently left him. He could not tell if this was another way to spare his feelings like with Lysias and Caden.

'Come on Bazyli. Zale will be fine.' Acacia ushered him on, gave a concerned look at Zale and mounted her horse. As she looked down upon him, she could see the bandage on his neck. Looking around, she suddenly noticed that they all had injuries of some sort and that there were absences. 'What happened? You're all hurt. And where's Lysias and Caden?'

'Don't worry Acacia, I'll explain as we travel,' said Sachiel, and she left the edge of the pit as he ushered her away.

Zale heard their steps fade and suddenly felt very alone. As he thought about it, he realised that he had never truly been on his own before. He looked doubtfully at the walls and knew that there was no chance of getting out of the pit. Sitting on the damp soil, Zale peered down the passage heading in the same direction as his friends. Above him he could see nothing but the mist beginning to thin and stars starting to show through the evening sky. He looked back up at the slopes and thought about trying to dig small holes in it to make steps and climb out. Touching the earth, however, showed him that the rain had not soaked through deep enough to make the ground crumble. It was as hard as rock. The movement of his arm reminded him of the rock that had hit him in the pass and realised that even if he could dig small wells as footholds, his arm would not be strong enough to pull him up. He was surprised that it had not slowed him in battle, but thought that perhaps his fear had spurred him on. Then he looked down at the ring and suspected it had something to do with his apparent luck. He rubbed his shoulder painfully and sighed deeply. Zale's best bet was to go down the passage. He looked at the floor and could make out some strange scratch marks in the soil. As he studied the pit, he noticed similar markings on the walls. Though this disturbed him, he ignored it.

'Well, if you're ever going to go, you had better go now,' he said to himself. With a sigh, Zale got to his feet and started down the passage. Before he could get more than ten metres along, he heard Harden's voice somewhere above him.

'Zale? Zale! Are you there?' Zale ran the short distance back to the pit.

'Oh thank the stars. Did you see where that passage went?'

'No, I only just started down it. Why are you back? I thought you were going without me.' Zale could now see the whole group above him. He felt as though he was an animal being inspected before an auction. He knew that there must have been a problem or else they would not have returned, but inside, he was deeply grateful for them being there.

'We were,' continued Harden, 'but the mist thinned and we could see mountains ahead of us. Bazyli said that there was a pass leading through them but when we got there, we found it was blocked. That seems to be happening a lot lately. The Forbidden Valley is just beyond it but there is no way of going over the mountains. They are laced with snow. We would freeze to death before reaching the other side. We were wondering if the passage leads under the mountains.'

'I'm not sure. We can try it. From what I've seen, it goes in a straight line all the way, but it is very dark and gets deeper as you go further in.'

'Perfect. We will leave the horses and slide down. They know their way back to Damané. Bazyli,' Harden turned to the boy, 'do you know your way from the Forbidden Valley?'

'Yes, I think so. It is just on the other side of a ridge at the valley's further-most borders.'

'Good. Alright Zale, we're coming down.' One by one, they slid down the side of the pit. Zale helped them as they reached the bottom. Acacia, head throbbing and still weak from using her powers, asked if they could rest. Once again, they made camp and organised a rota for taking watch. After eating a small portion of bread each, they lay down. It was easier for them to sleep as it was dark and they were warm in the pit. Zale and Harden went part way down the passage so that Harden could teach Zale some more of the Ancestral Tongue without disturbing the others. They felt, however, that there was no need for them to practise their battle techniques as they had only recently encountered the Usari. Harden did not teach him much. By the end of the training, Zale could levitate objects, stun opponents, and touch another's mind, though he could not get past any barriers they put up to block the intrusion.

When they woke, two moons shone brilliantly down upon them. Judging by their positions, the sun would soon rise again.

'Why are the days much longer than the nights?' Bazyli asked Harden.

'It must be Jabari's doing. It is easier to track us in daylight.' Bazyli looked slightly frightened, but Zale gave him a reassuring smile to ease the boy's worries. They ate in silence, none of them wanting to go down the passage. It seemed so dark and foreboding. None of them knew what lay ahead, though their minds were cruel and made them think of monsters and creatures of darkness. Once they had packed up the camp, they set off down the dark passage, hoping it would lead them in the right direction.

Galzan

Caden forced himself to open his eyes. It was too dark to see. He felt confined. The air was dusty, making him cough and splutter, his throat parched. He could feel a crushing weight on his left leg and the taste of blood was overwhelming. A warm liquid ran down his cheek. His whole body ached. He tried to move but found that there was no space to manoeuvre. All he accomplished was making his body fill with a blinding pain as he attempted to shift his leg from under its captor. He cried out in pain.

'Caden,' came a voice next to him. 'Don't try to move.'

'Lysias?'

'Yes.'

'What happened?'

'We were crushed beneath the rocks as they filled the pass. I tried to stop as many of them as I could, but unfortunately your leg was still trapped. This was the most space I could give us.'

'Can you get us out of here?'

'No, I'm too weak. And there're too many boulders to try and move.' Caden sighed hoplessly.

'Are you injured?' he asked the darkness.

'I'm not too bad,' replied Lysias. 'A few bumps and bruises; nothing too serious. Once I've recovered some of my strength, I'll try to get that rock off your leg.'

'I'd appreciate that,' laughed Caden. The two of them sat there in silence. Caden did all he could not to think of all the boulders he lay beneath that could kill him at any moment if they were to shift and collapse. The only thing piercing the silence was his and Lysias's breathing. He had never known the world to be so quiet. As he sat there in the darkness, all the small sounds he took for granted came back to him; the whispering of the morning breeze over the hills, the singing of the Sappaie bird in the trees, the call of the crickets in the lush grass, the crashing of the waves against the rocks near his home. As he thought of the sea and home, he suddenly longed for the scent of salty air, the gentle warmth of the sun on his cheeks, the touch of his childhood sweetheart, Legarni, as they walked across the golden beeches holding hands. His heart ached as he though of her. He had left her without a second thought at the first threat of danger towards Damané. *The mind of a soldier* he thought bitterly. Now he may never have the chance to tell her what he felt for her. Feeling a lump in his throat, Caden knew he had to take his mind off his home.

'Tell me about yourself,' he said to Lysias after pushing the thoughts to the back of his mind.

'There's not much to tell,' replied Lysias.

'Please,' groaned Caden as a wave of pain shot up his side. 'I need a distraction. Besides, someone who's lived as long as you must have a story or two. How old are you anyway?' Lysias glanced at the shadowy form that was Caden next to him and reluctantly began to speak.

'When you're immortal you seem to lose track of your age,' he began, 'though I know I have lived for almost three millennia, if not longer.'

'Wow,' said Caden with awe. 'That's too long for me to even imagine. The world must have changed a lot over the centuries.'

'Indeed it has. I grew up in the lands known as Caldorn. They reside next to the homelands of Luca's people, Derisida. When I was just twenty I began my training as a protector of her kind. We all did. Each one of my kind is bound by and ancient vow to keep Luca's kin safe. I was not as keen as my sister to become a warrior. I preferred having the freedom to do as I pleased. Still, I had no choice. As it turned out, I was a natural. I could not believe my strength and power during my training. It almost scared me. Fortunately there was peace in the lands so my people did not have to use our abilities. It was not until the Raden chose to sail to the White Islands that we were really required. There was a ferocious battle with the dragons. It lasted centuries, and was only the first of many. The Raden, Luca's people, fought many creatures of these lands, but those horrors are best left to memory. They were the worst years I can remember. I have done some terrible things. That is why I now choose to fight as little as possible. My power is too great to be used so carelessly. I fear if I touch upon the true nature of my power it will reawaken the darker side of me I have spent so long trying to hide. The Raden abused it and I grew to hate them for it. Luca's mother was the first to see the terror her people were spreading through the islands. She stood up to her own kind with the help of an ancient power that brought to her four magical beings to watch over her. Luca has followed her mother's footsteps well in keeping the Islands safe and peaceful. Do you agree?' Lysias looked back towards Caden. There was silence. 'Caden?' The General made no sound or sign of movement. Lysias was glad that Caden had not heard. Luca was so different from the hearts and minds of those before her that he felt it best not to let the past taint her name. While Lysias thought back to those days of pain, loss, and suffering, he felt his mind begin to blur as exhaustion took hold. Before he thought any more, his world turned to complete darkness.

'Hello?' An almost unnoticeable trembling had roused Lysias. It seemed to pass beneath him from Caden's direction, though it was indeed very faint. For a moment, the Kai-Rae thought he had seen a flash of green light before shrugging it off as his imagination. Lysias strained to hear anything amidst the suffocating silence, but all that came to him were the small pained breaths of the General. It was getting warmer in the confined space. Caden began to shiver and broke out into a sweat, yet all the while remained unconscious. The heat was helping Lysias recover his strength faster. He knew, however, that there wasn't long before their air supply ran out. He was also very much aware of the poison that was starting to seep into Caden's blood from his wound. Lysias wished that there was something he could do for the General, but he knew that they would need a miracle to save them. Even if he could get them out, he feared Caden may still have no hope of recovering from the damage to his leg. Deciding it would be best to use his magic once at full strength, the Kai-Rae chose to try and sleep so as to slow his breathing and preserve the air supply. He forced himself to ignore his growing hunger and thirst and think of instead about distant times when he was free to roam the wild lands of Caldorn. He could smell its fresh, salty air, feel the cool wind against his skin, and see the vibrant flowers that littered the grassy hillside. Closing his eyes, Lysias knew no more.

A scraping noise followed by the sound of something large and heavy being shifted woke Lysias from his dreamless sleep.
'Caden?' Lysias reached out and shook the General's body. Caden grunted and began to move.
'What's going on?' he asked.
'I'm not sure,' whispered Lysias. 'Can you hear that?'
'Yes. It's coming from near you.' The two of them stared at the boulders to Lysias's right. Small bits of rock and grit started to fall out of place as the centre-most boulder shifted slightly. After a moment, a stream of light flooded their hollow as it filtered through a small gap in the rocks. With a few more crashes and bangs, the boulder directly next to Lysias was moved away and the large black snout of a Wolvax appeared.
'Galzan!' exclaimed Caden as he recognised the silvery scars on his muzzle.
'How did you find us?' asked Lysias.

'I was nearby when the pass was blocked and could smell fresh blood,' growled Galzan. 'When the smell remained, I knew there had to be living creatures trapped inside. I had hoped to find an animal of some sort.'

'You're not going to eat us are you?' asked Caden as he tried to draw away but simply caused himself great pain.

'Don't be foolish,' came the Wolvax's response. 'I had merely hoped that none of you had been trapped. Your journey is important to all the beings of these Islands. If you fail then my kind will surely be destroyed.' Caden relaxed slightly, but found that that also caused him suffering.

'Here,' said Lysias, shifting himself so that he faced Caden. He directed his hands towards the boulder resting on Caden's leg and muttered *trasferra*. The boulder shimmered for a moment and then turned into a pile of sand. The rocks above were balanced just right so they did not fall.

'Thank you,' breathed Caden after he stifled a cry of agony. Fresh blood streamed effortlessly out of his exposed wound as the feeling came back to his toes.

'Come, we must leave quickly,' said Galzan urgently.

'What's wrong?' asked Lysias, glancing nervously at the blood that now gently trickled from Caden's leg.

'I wasn't the only one able to smell you out. There's a pack of wolves not far behind me.'

'I can't go anywhere with my leg like this,' grimaced Caden, realising Lysias had had the same thought. He too looked down at the dark blood that was beginning to mix with the sand around him.

'You will ride on my back, though I allow you to with protest. I am no working animal.' Galzan grunted with the thought of it. Lysias used his magic to realign Caden's bones and then make him a splint. The procedure caused the General great pain and he cried out in agony. Lysias then helped the injured man onto Galzan's back. It was obvious Galzan did not like to be treated in such a manner, but he knew it was the only way for them to survive.

'Come now, you as well,' demanded Galzan when he saw Lysias was not mounting him.

'My strength is returning quickly. I will be able to keep up.'

'Suit yourself,' snorted Galzan, 'but do not think that I will return for you if you are caught.'

'I would not expect you to.' With that, Galzan sprang up the rocks, heading east. Lysias was right behind him. The Wolvax found the Kai-Rae's speed and agility incredible. Wherever he went, Lysias was able to follow. Lysias glanced back to see ten wolves clawing their way up the rocks not far behind them. It was not long before Galzan reached the highest boulders and began to make his way down the steep slope on the other side. The wolves were gaining ground quickly. As he too neared the top, Lysias found himself being brought down again by a tugging at his leg. One of the wolves had sprung forwards and just managed to grip Lysias's ankle between its teeth. The Kai-Rae scrambled at the rocks to try and get some sort of hold, but try as he may he slipped further and further towards the pack of hungry wolves. The silvery furred female dragged him with all her strength. Lysias suddenly realised that she was desperate to have the support of her companions before attempting to subdue him. Turning to face her, Lysias kicked out and hit her full on in the muzzle. She yelped in pain, releasing her hold on him. Her body rolled down the rocks, knocking into the others of her pack, slowing them down. Wasting no time, Lysias darted back up the boulders. He jumped over the top and began to slide down the other side with precision.

'Hurry!' cried Lysias as he spotted the wolves just a few metres behind them. Galzan leapt to the ground below, Lysias following suit. The Kai-Rae then turned on his heel and raised his arms towards the pass. A pulse of energy left his hands and collided with the rocks upon which the wolves ran. The boulders crumbled, sending the wolves to a crushing fate.

'Nicely done,' panted Galzan.

'There was nothing else for it,' said Lysias sadly. Caden remained silent as he had passed out from the pain in his leg. A single wolf appeared on top of the rubble, blood dripping from its muzzle. The female looked sorrowfully at the ground beneath her, then turned and walked away.

'Come, we must move on,' said Galzan after a moment's silence. 'How's your leg? You're bleeding.'

'Don't worry about it. It won't slow us down. She wasn't able to penetrate the skin too much.'

'Well, we cannot afford any delays. Caden's wound is fresh and weeping. Other creatures, far worse than wolves, will pick up on the scent soon enough.' Galzan took one last look towards the pass before moving away. Lysias silently limped next to him. A mist still clung to the air as the final rays of sunlight ebbed away. The three new companions journeyed eastwards towards a wall of mountains with the simple hope of finding the rest of the group.

The Passage

The passage seemed endless. It was hard to breathe and the damp smell made the group feel dizzy. They would not have been able to see if it had not been for the small cracks in the roof of the tunnel letting in slithers of moonlight. At one point, Harden became so frustrated with how long it was taking for them to reach an opening that he tried to make his own way out. He attacked one of the cracks with his sword but found that it would take him forever to tunnel his way to the surface. They were now tens of metres under ground with no way out. The walls were jagged, the ceiling sometimes dropping so low the group had to crawl to get through, and there were tree-roots sticking out in places. The further they went down the passage, the more rocks they saw lining the walls. They stuck out like spikes, blending in with the shadows. The floor became more and more slippery as water trickling down the walls dampened the soil. In places, the ground had turned to mud and at one point Sachiel almost fell. Acacia had managed to catch hold of his cloak and steadied him before he ended up on the floor. The going was easiest for Bazyli. His feet sank in the mud preventing him from falling over. The ground was at an angle, going deeper and deeper. As they went further into the passage, the air became thicker. They were all breathing deeply to try and get as much air into their lungs as possible.

No one was talking. It was as if they were creeping past a giant sleeping monster that they did not want to wake. After an hour, their spirits fell further as they saw a small hole in the left-hand wall. It could only have been the size of a small melon but a stream of water was flowing out of it. The water joined the passage making the group's way even more dangerous. Further down the tunnel, however, they came across a similar hole, though it was larger. It was lined with stone slabs and did not have any water flowing from it. Curious, the group stopped to examine it.

'What do you suppose it is?' asked Zale.

'Well, it's definitely not natural,' said Sachiel. The others looked at him as if to say 'that's obvious'. He cleared his throat and turned from their gaze. 'What I meant was that what ever built it must have done so for a reason. They may still use it.'

'Well, what are we waiting for? Let's go down it and see where it leads.' Acacia began scrambling into the tunnel when Harden stopped her.

'Perhaps you should let one of us go first. It could be dangerous.'

'Harden, I am perfectly capable of taking care of myself. Just because I am female, it does not mean I am a weakling. Now, stand aside and let me pass.' Her gaze was hard and her muscles had tensed as tried to keep her anger at bay. Harden did as she asked and gave the others a look. Zale just shrugged his shoulders and went in after her.

They crawled through the tunnel for at least an hour. It was damp with a strange form of moss lining the walls. The air tasted foul and old. There was barely any room to move. As they went further in, the air became laden with the smell of decaying flesh. It was impossible to see for there were no cracks to allow light in. Ahead of her, Acacia heard a low hissing sound. She stopped, worried she would alert whatever was making the sound to her presence. Zale crawled into her with a loud thump.

'Ouch! What did you stop for?' he asked, rubbing his head where the end of her bow had caught him.

'Shh. There's something up ahead. I can hear it.' They all fell silent and strained their ears. The others could now hear the hissing too. It was like a snake, only there was a slight growl behind it. Then there came another, higher pitched. Amidst the hissing noises, there were small grunts, as though there were a group of creatures talking together.

'Acacia, keep going, but only a bit further. Let's see if we can find out what they are,' suggested Zale, keeping his voice low to prevent it from echoing around them. They moved forward and came to a bend in the tunnel. There was a glow coming from their right where the tunnel split into two separate passages. There were torches clamped onto the walls as the tunnel widened and became tall enough for a man to stand in. Huddled together, tending to wounds, were five Usari. The group held their breath and slowly backed away. The Usari's sense of smell however, was better than the group had thought. There was a single grunt and the Usari fell silent. The group froze, trying even harder not to breathe. They could hear the Usari sniffing the air and then there was a loud moaning noise. The Usari ran down the passage, away from the warriors. Thinking they had just had a very close call, the warriors struggled to turn themselves around and hurried back to the muddy passage.

'Did you see them?' asked Acacia when they reached the end of the tunnel.

'Yes,' said Sachiel. 'They appear to be the ones we encountered earlier. They must have used this tunnel system to track us down. Who knows where else it goes to the surface.' Sachiel looked gravely at the others. The very creatures they wanted to avoid blocked their guaranteed means of escape. Turning their backs on the stone tunnel, they started back down the passage in the direction they had gone before, their feet splashing in the water. They had not gone very far when they heard the hissing sounds again. It was coming from the tunnel they had just left.

'They are coming back! They must have alerted the others!' said Harden, drawing his sword. Bazyli hid behind Zale, clinging onto his cloak.

'There is a bend in the passage just up ahead,' said Acacia keeping her eyes on the tunnel's entrance.

'Acacia, what do you mean to do?' There was a note of worry in Zale's voice.

'When you get there, work as fast as you can to block the passage. Use mud, rocks, anything!' She drew an arrow and raised it strung in her bow to eye level.

'No Acacia! You cannot defeat them by yourself!' Sachiel was in a panic. He knew she was a great warrior but he could not stand the thought of loosing her.

'Go now, or else we all die!' She glanced over her shoulder to see them all still stood there. 'Go!'

With that, Harden pulled Sachiel down the passage and the men left her there alone to fight off the Usari. When they reached the turning in the tunnel, as instructed, they began blocking the way. Bazyli was most useful as he was able to find all of the larger rocks that were hidden under the water that flowed round his feet. The men worked hard, knowing that Acacia had very little time before she would have to retreat.

Acacia stood motionless in the middle of the passage. She could hear the scraping of the Usari's claws on the stone and could now smell their stench. From the sound of their movements, she could tell that they had slowed down. There was a moment's silence, and then the first Usari stuck its head out of the tunnel. With a whirring noise, it was dead. Acacia could hear the fearful grunts of the Usari behind. Another Usari then decided to come out of the tunnel, not realising that it meant sure death. It clambered out and stared down at its dead companion, confusion on its face. The other Usari in the tunnel could see it in front of them. Their fellow Usari looked down the passage and, next thing they knew, he was dead on the ground with an arrow in his neck. Full of rage and hissing wildly, they all charged out of the tunnel. Acacia began letting off arrows faster than she had ever done before, never missing a single target. The Usari were falling like flies, but they were still managing to advance. As Acacia slowly backed away, behind her the men were working furiously to block the passage. All they could hear were the howls, grunts and hisses of the Usari getting closer and closer. Finally, there was only a hole just big enough for Acacia to get through left in their hastily made wall.

'Acacia! Get here now!' Sachiel called desperately through the gap. Nothing happened. Zale and Harden looked at each other fearfully.

'Acacia? Acacia!' Sachiel was distraught. It was all the men could do to pull him away from the hole. Just as they were about to block it up with two ready picked rocks, Acacia's body slid gracefully through to the other side of the wall, the Usari close behind.

'Close it up now!' she called at the top of her lungs. Instantly, Zale and Harden filled the gap. Breathless, Acacia smiled up at the group, hearing the sound of the confused Usari on the other side of the wall. She raised her hand, sending a jet of emerald energy into the wall. The rocks and mud became as one, now an impenetrable fortification.

'See, I told you I could look after myself.' Sachiel hugged her tighter than ever, relief flooding his mind like a river. Bazyli began to jump up and down clapping with joy.

'Acacia, I underestimated you,' said Harden, patting her thankfully on the back. 'Now, I am afraid we have no time to rest. The wall will not last long. When the Usari break through, it would be best that we were not on the other side.'

'The wall will last long enough. But you're right; we cannot be sure as to where Xannon is. He may be able to destroy the barrier if he is near.'

With that, the group began down the passage again. Bazyli wanted to know everything about what happened with the Usari, eager to know how the fight took place. Acacia happily told him what little there was to tell. Though they had no idea if there would be a way out of the passage where they were going, their spirits were lifted for a while and Acacia was now named the hero of the group. Harden cleared his throat when this was declared, trying to remind them of how he killed the lead Usari out in the marshes, so they named him a hero too.

Domai

As they continued, the stream they walked through turned into a fast flowing river as more streams of water joined the passage through similar holes to the one they first came across. They held onto the walls for support, using the rocks that stuck out as handles. The passage began to slope upwards, but the water was flowing so fast that the river never stopped. The warrior's ears were ringing with the sound of rushing water. The air had suddenly become less thick but it was laced with water vapour that seemed to soak them as if it were raining. The steeper it became, the harder it was for them to climb. The mud that Bazyli had been using before to keep himself from falling was slowly being washed away. They came to an area where two tunnels joined onto the passage on either side, both with their own fast flowing river.

'Sachiel,' called Acacia, 'can you slow the water at all? Try and make us a safe passage across or stop the water.' Sachiel nodded and directed his hands towards the two joining tunnels. He opened his mind to the magic hidden there and let it flow through him. A jet of icy blue erupted from each of his palms and shot towards the rivers. As it collided with them however, the energy bounced back and caught him in the chest. Sachiel collapsed to the ground, his body slipping under the water. Harden grabbed his cloak just before he was swept away. The Element came up coughing and spluttering as he grasped his chest in pain.

'What happened?' called Bazyli, hoping Sachiel was alright.

'I'm not sure,' said Sachiel as he recovered his strength. 'My powers could not affect the water.'

'It must be Xannon,' cried Acacia over the noise. 'Nothing else could stop our powers. He is growing in strength,'

'Jabari may be aiding him with his own energy,' commented Harden angrily. Sachiel reached out in a pushing motion before him and the water in his path became shallow and moved away. The gap was immediately filled with the rushing water from either side.

'It's only the adjoining rivers that are enchanted. They must have been created by Xannon.' Sachiel looked at the others helplessly.

'Why would he do that?' asked Zale. 'He could not have known we would come this way.'

'Perhaps he is hiding something further ahead that he does not want the Usari to find,' suggested Bazyli. The others looked at him and marvelled at his logic.

'No matter what's down there, that is our only route. How are we going to get across?' called Zale over the torrent.

'One of us will have to wade through to the other side with a rope and then pull it taught so the rest of us can use it for support.' Harden began to rummage around in his bag for the strongest rope he had. It was quite thin, but stronger than any other rope in the land. It had been made by Luca's ancestors and was very valuable. There was not much of it left to be found on the White Islands as most of it had been taken across the great sea to the Land of Hope. It shone, even in the dark, a brilliant gold like the sun. Bazyli looked at it in awe.

'Harden, give the rope to me. Acacia and I are lighter on our feet than men. I will go first and she will come last.' Sachiel took the rope from Harden and began to wade through the water. The others looked on despairingly, tensing with every slight slip Sachiel made. It was a slow process. He had to battle against the force of the water coming from both behind him and from either side, and at the same time try to climb upwards without anything to hold onto. Acacia held onto the other end of the rope tightly, bracing herself in case Sachiel should fall. The water seemed to part slightly for Sachiel, reducing the force against him, but the current was still strong.

After what seemed like an age, Sachiel reached the other side and flung himself to the wall, grateful for the support. He then turned back to face his friends and pulled the rope taught.

'Come on Harden, you first!' called Sachiel.

'No, let Zale go. I will follow him.' Suspicious, Zale stepped forwards into the water and was immediately thrown against the rope. Acacia and Sachiel took his weight and managed to stop him from being swept away. After a few moments, Zale righted himself and began to pull himself along the rope. His muscles bulged as they fought against the urge to be dragged sideways. Almost half of his body was submerged, his feet pushing against the loose stones that littered the ground. After one final tug on the rope, Zale was safe on the other side.

Next came Harden, making his way across in the same manner. Though he was of a larger build than Zale, Harden found the strain just as tough. It was then Bazyli's turn. He had not wanted to cross before the others for fear of the rope not being strong enough. Now that he had seen the rope hold two grown men in a row, he was prepared to cross.

'Be careful Bazyli. The water is fast and strong. What ever you do, do not let go of the rope.' Acacia looked down at him with concern.

'I will be fine,' he said, smiling up at her. As he stepped out into the water, however, the water was indeed fast and strong, much more so than he had expected. His legs buckled under him and he fell forwards, his face in the water. The others looked on hopelessly. They knew that if they went out to help him, they could make the situation worse. Sachiel risked lifting one hand off the rope to force the water to curve under Bazyli's face, allowing him to breath. Just as Sachiel could feel his grip slipping, Bazyli was finally able to pull his face away from the water but he couldn't get a strong enough grip on the rope and slipped. Luckily, the water from the passage was faster than that from the new tunnels. The water pushed him up past the men on the opposite side of the crossing to Acacia. As he went, he knocked into Harden, sending them both up the passage at great speed.

'Bazyli! Harden!' Zale began to run after them trying his best to stay standing.

Sachiel was forced to stay to help Acacia across the joining rivers. As soon as she was safe on the other side, they both turned to hurry after their friends. They were stopped, however, by a cracking noise followed closely by the low rumble of rocks crumbling to the ground.

'The Usari!' exclaimed Sachiel. 'They must have broken through the wall. It won't take them long to catch up with us.' Acacia looked down the passage behind her wit great concern before turning to look Sachiel in the eye.

'If ever there was a time for you to use your powers Sachiel, it is now.' He looked at her with resigned agreement and took a solid stance facing the direction of the Usari. Stretching his arms out in front of him, Sachiel closed his eyes in concentration. He raised his arms, sweat forming on his brow as his muscles strained against the weight of the water. It rose before them, filling the entire passage like a shimmering wall of liquid silver. With one last effort, Sachiel pushed his arms forwards, sending the water rushing towards the Usari. There was a moment of silence followed by the Usari's cries. Acacia caught Sachiel as he swayed forwards.

'That should delay them a while,' said Acacia, a look of gratitude on her face. Sachiel nodded weakly. 'We must go after the others,' she continued. 'Can you walk?'

'Better,' replied Sachiel with a smile. 'I can run.' Acacia smiled back and then, taking Sachiel by the arm, began to run down the passage. It did not take them long to catch up. They had to leap across rocks in the mud that had been forced down the passage by the water. On many occasions Zale nearly slipped, but Sachiel and Acacia were better balanced and so always managed to catch him in time and help him back to his feet.

'Sachiel, can't you stop the water flow?' called Acacia over the tremendous noise that now filled their ears.

'I'm sorry, but I can't. If I do that, who knows what will happen to Harden and Bazyli. The water is the only thing stopping us from sinking any deeper into this mud. It is removing most of the thick layer that would encase them. If I stop the water, they will sink into it and probably die. It's too risky. Besides, I do not have the energy to. I have not yet fully recovered from moving the water. I don't know that I could stop it all, and if I only stop part they may still be carried away if they are out of range of the spell.'

'I could dry up the earth as you stop the water. That would not take as much energy.'

'And risk them getting stuck in the earth forever? It is one thing drying the earth. You know how hard it is to soften it again. It's out of our hands now.' Acacia knew Sachiel was right. They carried on down the passage after Zale.

Further ahead, Zale began to panic for he could no longer see either Harden or Bazyli in front of him. As he came to another crack in the roof he looked down. By his feet there was a sharp rock with a piece of cloth caught on it. The water surrounding it had turned red. Zale ran faster, telling himself that his friends were all right. The Elements saw the blood and became just as worried as Zale. They sped after him. Acacia especially did not want to lose two let alone three of the group. They needed all of them alive to get the crystal and the other Elements back. Soon, Zale came up to a turning and saw Harden clinging to the wall with Bazyli under his arm. He noticed a deep gash on Harden's arm stretching from his shoulder to his elbow. When he caught up, Sachiel helped Zale get them up.

'Are you alright?' asked Zale as the group lined up against the wall again.

'Yes,' said Harden breathlessly. 'I was able to grab the rock, but we would have drowned if you weren't so close behind us.'

'Look,' cried Bazyli, 'there's an opening in the roof. We must be on the other side of the mountains.'

'Thank the stars!' Acacia had never been so happy to see the sky. She could feel a gentle breeze stroking her face. It was the most refreshing thing she had felt in a long time.

'Come on then, I'll help you up. You first Sachiel. Tell us if the way is clear.'

'I can get up there myself Harden.' As he tried to climb up, Sachiel slipped on the muddy walls and was almost taken down the passage by the river. Acacia managed to stop him in time.

'Come on Sachiel. This is not the time to show off. We do not want to have to run after you as you go speeding down the passage.' Sachiel glanced at Acacia and blushed. He then turned to Harden and allowed him to help him get to the surface.

'Right, now you Bazyli. Is it clear Sachiel?'

'Yes, send him up.' Harden pushed against the soles of the boy's feet as he took Sachiel's hand. Once Bazyli was clear, he turned to Acacia and offered her his hand.

'When we are up there, let me look at your arm,' she said kindly.

'It's fine Acacia. I'll live. Now let me help you up.' She gave Harden a look that told him she would look at it anyway, and then allowed him to help her. At that moment, Harden was glad that Acacia had come with them. It was good for them to have a woman around to keep the men in check. He was about to help Zale when he stopped. Zale appeared to be listening to something.

'What is it?'

'I don't know. It sounds like…' There was a faint cry from somewhere down the passage. 'There's someone down there.'

'No, Zale!' Zale ignored Harden. He began to run down the passage for a second time.

'Wait there! Get out of the passage. I'll be back in…' He suddenly cried out. Zale slipped on the muddy ground and was sent down the passage.

'Zale!'

'What's going on?' Bazyli was mad with fear. 'Where's Zale?'

'Help me out.' Sachiel pulled Harden up out of the passage and into the daylight. 'Zale thought he heard someone down there. He's gone to find them.'

'What was the scream for?' asked Acacia as she peered back into the passage below.

'He slipped on the floor and was washed away. I would go and help, but he told me to stay here. One thing I've learnt from spending time with Zale is to do as he says.' Harden saw the look on Bazyli's face and knelt down to him. He put a hand on his shoulder and said calmingly, 'I'm sure he'll be fine. He knows what he's doing.'

Zale sped down the tunnel. It seemed impossible for him to grip onto the walls as most of the mud just broke away. The cries of help were getting louder and louder as he sped through the darkness. Zale looked at where he was going and was surprised to see a light ahead. With the light came an overwhelming sense of doom as he could see that the passage dropped vertically creating an underground waterfall. Zale desperately continued to scramble at the rocks that flew past, but it was no use. He was thrown over the edge of the waterfall where he crashed into the opposite side and then forced back beneath the water. Tree roots sprouted out all over the walls. Zale managed to grip onto some as he fell towards the ground. He came to a stop, spluttering as the muddy water cascaded down upon him. Once he was able to secure himself properly so that his head was out of the water, he looked to the wall next to him where he could see some sort of creature also gripping roots.

'Please! Help me! I can't get out!' It was a female's voice.

'Don't worry! Just hold on!' Zale looked down to see how far it would be to fall. The distance was not great, but what awaited them was terrible. He could now see that the light was coming from torches held by a group of Usari. The foul beasts glared up at them hungrily. Thinking quickly, Zale decided that the creature next to him appeared light enough and so stretched out his arm.

'Take my hand.' The creature reached out and held onto Zale with a grip he had never felt before. It was strong yet gentle. Deciding to find out what the creature was when they were safe, Zale pulled her onto his back where she secured herself round his neck and waist. Slowly, he began to climb, choosing which tree roots to use very carefully. After what seemed like an age, Zale pulled himself over the ridge of the waterfall. The creature pulled herself onto her feet and helped him up, taking care not to allow the current to sweep either of them away again. She them clung to his waist as he pulled them along the passage using the protruding rocks that littered the walls. Every so often, Zale glanced at the creature in his arms, trying to see what it was, but the passage was too dark to make out any features. Finally back at the opening, he found the group looking down on them eagerly.

'Pass her up.' Harden stretched out his arm and took the creature from Zale. Once she was safe, he turned and reached for Zale's hand.

'Wait, give me your bottles. I can fill them up. We don't know how long it will be before we find water.' The others passed him their water bottles. They looked like coconuts with small holes in them that had cork stoppers to prevent water from escaping. Zale passed them back up once they were filled and was helped to the surface by Harden. He took off his cloak and began to ring it out when he was spoken to.

'Thank you. Are you alright?' asked the creature.

'I'm fine. What's your name? And what were you doing down there?'

'I could ask you the same thing. My name is Lankoa. I am a Domai.'

'A Domai?' Zale was shocked. He had never seen a Domai before. There was a small gap in one of the clouds and a stream of moonlight hit the creature. Her figure was that of a woman, but her features were completely different. Her ears ended in sharp, white spikes that looked lethal. Her smooth skin was a pale blue and glistened in the light. She had long white claws rather than fingers and her hair was short and spiked. It was the colour of snow. She had slits for nostrils and black, shiny eyes. Her teeth were all deadly, white spikes. Zale realised how frightening she looked and knew that if there had been more light in the passage, he would have probably left her out of fear. Yet, after a while of inspecting her, he thought that in a strange way she looked quite beautiful. She wore a strap of brown leather across her chest and a short, brown, leather skirt. As he studied her, he realised that she shared some features with Lysias.

'What were you doing in that passage?' Zale was surprised at how calm Harden was. As he looked round the group he could see that Acacia and Sachiel also had not been disturbed by Lankoa's appearance. Bazyli, however, looked ready to run.

'I was captured by Jabari. He is a man of magical powers. He has made his home at the end of The Forbidden Valley. I was out collecting synar moss for food when a group of Usari took me. He offered me my life in exchange for the power of healing. I refused. He ordered the Usari to take me into the tunnels and torture me. Before they had the chance, I escaped and ran. The tunnels seemed to be the best route for me to take. When I reached the passage, I found the river too fast for me to walk through and was swept away. If you had not rescued me, I would have been down there forever.' Her voice was soft, like water rippling past rocks in a stream.

'I am sorry for what Jabari did to you. We are on our way to stop him. He has stolen something sacred to the Land of Light, and if we do not get it back, the land will perish.' Harden's voice was filled with growing anger at what Jabari was doing to the land and all the creatures within it. 'We need to travel through The Forbidden Valley. Would you be able to show us the way?'

'But no one is allowed in our valley,' said Lankoa as though she had been stung. It was almost an insult to her that someone would ask for such a privilege.

'Please. We just saved your life. We need the Domai's help. The Land of Light will perish if you do not help us. Luca, Bringer of Light, has always protected your kind, as have the Elements.' Acacia seemed to have gotten through to the Domai.

'Alright. It is not all that far from here, though the ground is full of hills.' The group thanked her, though she looked reluctantly in the direction of her home. None of them, however, were in the mood to set off at once. It was agreed that they would make camp in the shadow of the mountains that they had just passed under. Acacia found it difficult that night to look at Lankoa. She could see the resemblance that the Kai-Rae have with the Domai and it pained her. She had not had time to mourn for their fallen friends and now grief touched upon her heart. She glanced up at the stars and muttered a prayer for Lysias and Caden.

Passage through the Mountains

Galzan and Lysias moved with haste, Caden lolling unconscious on the Wolvax's back. The wounded General had not woken for some time and it was beginning to worry Lysias. The bleeding had stopped but the wound was now covered in a sallow crust.

'I fear the wound may be infected,' he said between breaths as he ran.

'The mountains are not far now,' stated Galzan. 'We can stop there and check on him.' Lysias nodded in agreement. The moons were slowly rising in the north, illuminating their path. The ground was unnaturally flat, the earth seeming to have dried perfectly the instant each muddy grain had lined up. There was no sign of vegetation for miles. It was completely silent except for the soft thuds of running feet and the heavy breathing of the Wolvax and the Kai-Rae.

'Wait,' said Lysias, stopping abruptly. Galzan ground to a halt. There was a sound through the shadows. Galzan sniffed the air and scanned the area.

'There is a foul scent that lingers here,' he said with a soft growl. 'Look ahead. There's a light touching the ground.' Lysias strained his eyes and could make out a hazy orange glow not too far ahead. The two of them prowled forwards quietly. As they neared the light, they realised that it was not on the ground at all, but rather coming from within the earth itself. Lysias glanced at Galzan questioningly and received his answer as they edged forwards slowly. They had come across a pit in the ground, the walls too steep for them to risk going down in case they would become trapped. As the two creatures peered over the side, they were shocked to see an Usari seemingly talking to the wall. It was apparent that there must have been a passage leading away from the pit as its growls and hisses were answered by other strange noises.

'Silence!' The voice that echoed around the walls was deep and strong. Lysias and Galzan drew back slightly so as to remain unnoticed. The move, however, had dramatic consequences. During the travelling, Caden had shifted and become unbalanced. With the Wolvax's sudden movement Caden's body fell forwards and tumbled into the opening. Galzan darted forwards with lightening speed just in time to catch a hold of the General's broken leg. There, the two of them froze, Caden hanging dangerously close to the enemy's sights.

'Stop your muttering and face the fact that you lost the target!' By the voice's continued announcement it became clear that Caden's fall had gone unnoticed. There came a horrific scream and then the sound of something crashing to the ground. Hisses and growls filled the air shortly afterwards.

'I said silence!' Whoever the man was, he was losing his temper. 'He should punish you all for your failure! I, however, have convinced him otherwise. You may still be of some little use to him.' The swish of a black cloak could be seen in the flickering firelight. The man was pacing up and down before his audience.

'Now?' hissed the voice of the Usari visible in the bottom of the pit.

'Now?' responded the man. 'Now I have a different task for you. I have been informed that the Kai-Rae is no longer a threat by means of his unexpected death.' There was a chorus of snake-like laughter. The man continued. 'Our spy is getting very close to the target now, so our Lord does not feel that you will be needed as trackers anymore. Your orders now send you to the sea of trees where you will wait.' There was a silence. 'Go!' From the sudden scrapings and the disappearance of the Usari, Lysias and Galzan could tell that the creatures were making their way down the passage.

After a moment, Galzan slowly walked backwards, pulling up Caden to safety. He laid the General carefully on the ground. He was about to speak when Lysias forced shut his muzzle. The Kai-Rae gestured silently to the pit. The man had obviously heard something and had stepped out beneath the opening. Lysias and Galzan pulled back so as to stay hidden.

Sunai

A jet of flames shot into the air out of the pit. Lysias and Galzan remained still, the heat intense upon their faces. Once the flames had passed, the man simply turned on his heel and set off after the Usari. Deciding it was best to remain silent, Lysias quickly heaved Caden onto Galzan's back and they crept away from the scene, hoping to reach the mountains as quickly as possible without being followed.

Galzan had been right. After only an hour the three companions reached the foothills of the mountains. There was a pass similar to the one that Lysias and Caden had found themselves trapped in, though this one was already blocked.

'Do you think the others were caught in that?' asked Lysias.

'No,' replied Galzan as he sniffed the air. 'I can taste no dust nor smell no fresh earth. This pass has been blocked for some time.'

'Then they must have travelled through the passage. At least we know they were not caught.'

'How do you know that?' asked Galzan.

'That man was angry about the loss of a target. I would assume that target would be the others.' Galzan nodded in agreement. There was a groaning from Galzan's back.

'Caden?' growled Galzan as he turned his head to try and get a look at the General.

'Where are we?' muttered Caden, looking at the world about him.

'We have just reached the mountains. The passage through is blocked though. How's your leg?' Lysias began to inspect the wound.

'I feel no pain,' said Caden as he sat up. Lysias laughed.

'This is no time for man's arrogance,' commented Lysias, though his faced turned to awe once he had more closely inspected the wound. 'It has healed!' Caden slowly slid off the Wolvax and tried to put some weight on his leg.

'See,' he said proudly. 'I told you I felt no pain.'

'That's incredible,' said Lysias in a whisper. 'How do you explain that?'

'It must have been when he fell,' stated Galzan. 'I caught him by his broken leg. My saliva has healing qualities for my kind, but I never thought they would hold true for a man.'

'So you healed me,' said Caden as he tore off his splint. 'I am very grateful…wait…I fell?'

'We'll explain as we travel,' said Galzan. 'I know of another way over the mountains. Can you run?'

'I think so,' responded Caden, putting weight on and off his leg and practicing a small jog.

'Then follow me.' Lysias and Caden ran after the Wolvax. Galzan kept his pace quite slow so as to allow Caden to keep up. They travelled south, winding along the very edge of the mountains, their snowy peaks looming ominously above them. After just under an hour, Galzan turned east again, taking them up the grassy slopes of one of the smallest mountains. Large boulders littered the ground, but Galzan's eyes were best suited for the dark and so he led them around them easily. There was a dense forest ahead.

'Are we to go in there?' panted Caden.

'Yes,' said Galzan shortly.

'Do not fear,' said Lysias, 'I sense no danger nearby.'

'I am not afraid,' stated Caden defensively. Lysias simply smiled and ran on. The three of them entered the pine maze, darkness falling upon them like a thick blanket. Caden and Lysias relied entirely upon the shadowy form of Galzan to wind them through the surrounding trees. The undergrowth was thick with brambles, sweet berries spilling their juices as the companions ran through them. The smell of wild flowers, fruits, and pine hung thick in the air. Lysias revelled in the sounds of the forest; the wind softly weaving between the treetops, tickling their branches; the gentle thuds of hooves as a herd of deer pranced deeper into the darkness; the rustling of a bird in her nest hiding her young from the eager eyes of predators. Caden could appreciate none of this. His hearing was limited, as all human hearing is, allowing him only to hear his heart pounding in his chest, his feet crashing upon the ground, and his heavy breathing as his muscles yearned for more air.

'How much further?' breathed Caden, his pace obviously slowing. 'We've been running for hours.'

'We are half way there,' said Galzan. 'We must keep moving.' Though, as the Wolvax made his command, his pace slowed also. Ahead of the three warriors there stood a young girl. Her ebony hair danced lazily around her shoulders, shimmering in what little light there was. She had stopped dead still, staring at the small group with flaming orange eyes. The three companions moved gradually closer, their eyes never leaving hers. As they approached, they could make out an earthy tunnel to her left just large enough for a grown man to crawl through. The girl was stood in a clearing, though the absence of trees appeared unnatural. The ground felt hot, as though the earth had been warmed around the tunnel.

'Hello,' said Lysias kindly. 'We do not intend to harm you. My name is Lysias. This is Caden and Galzan.' He gestured to the others. 'Galzan looks ferocious, but he's nothing of the sort really.' The girl simply kept staring, her gaze now solely upon Lysias.

'What are you doing out here alone?' asked Caden, almost within arms reach of the child now.

'Leave the girl,' came a voice from the shadows. Caden and Lysias looked up to see eyes all around them; what form the creatures took they could not tell. It was at that moment when they realised that the Wolvax had stopped a little way back.

'Do not fear,' growled Galzan, 'they mean us no harm. They have been tracking us.' Caden was taken aback by this information.

'And you felt it best to keep that from us?' he said in a harsh whisper.

'You did not know?' said Lysias inquisitively. 'We are roaming the lands of the Dûr'baëns.'

'What?' said Caden in shock.

'As I said, do not be alarmed,' said Galzan. 'You know we do not wish you any grievance.'

'Yes,' came the voice again. It was female, so delicate, as though her voice were weaving silk ribbons out of the air.

'I am Galzan. Caden and Lysias here need to make their way towards the Forbidden Valley.'

'I am Korana,' said the female. 'I protect this child.'

'She has power,' said Lysias softly as he gazed into the girl's fiery eyes.

'And as such she should be left alone,' said Korana heatedly. 'You know what men do with power.'

'Exploit it,' said Caden. The remark caught the others off guard. 'Do not look so shocked. I may be an ignorant man but I know what some of my kin do to those with strange abilities, for that is what you speak of, is it not?' The young girl nodded in agreement. Caden suddenly noticed her dress and realised how old and worn it looked. It was torn and dirty, even scorched in some places, making him think that perhaps she had already been exploited in her life.

'I also know however,' continued Caden, 'that individuals with these gifts have no choice in the matter and so should be allowed as normal a life as possible, away from harm. Luca trusts your people, so you are probably the best creatures to give her that protection.'

'Thank you for understanding,' said Korana. An arm appeared, gently pulling the child back towards the surrounding trees.

'Would you like to know what my power is?' asked the girl quietly as she stepped forwards out of the shadows again. Caden looked into her amber eyes.

'No child, for that is the beginning of temptation in these matters.' The girl smiled and slipped away into the darkness, as though the eyes around her swallowed her up.

'She is strong,' said Lysias. 'One to be admired.'

'I agree,' said Korana. 'She has suffered greatly, though she does not show it.'

'Come,' said Galzan. 'We must take our leave. I can sense the evil's ambition growing. Will you let us pass? We are taking the Route of Gannathor.'

'Of course,' said Korana. 'Though your fastest route is to turn north along the Zalen track. You will not go far before coming across a small stream. Follow its winding path east. It will lead you to the edge of the mountains closest to the Forbidden Valley. Danger lurks the closer to Gannathor you get.'

'Thank you,' said Lysias. 'And please tell whoever leads you that our foe lies beyond the eastern edge of the valley.' Korana nodded with understanding.

'What does he mean?' came the quiet voice of the girl. Lysias smiled.

'Farewell,' said Korana and the eyes around them vanished. Without hesitation, Galzan began to lead Caden and Lysias northwards in search of the stream.

Stories

Setting up bedding and shelter, the five warriors and the Domai nestled themselves in the shadow of the mountain. That night, the air was cool and the sky was clear. The stars sparkled down upon them and the moons were full. Harden showed Bazyli how to make a fire with what little they had and they all sat round its great flames, laughing happily, trying all the time to keep their minds off the days to come.

'Oh, what I would give to have a nice piece of fresh meat right now, rather than eating this dry bread!' said Zale, laughing slightly as he finished his third piece. The same thoughts had been nagging at the others' minds also.

'Well, I know these parts better than any. I will leave you for no more than half an hour and shall come back with some food for you,' offered Lankoa. The others accepted the offer gratefully and watched her disappear into the shadows.

'Are all of your adventures like this?' Bazyli asked Zale.

'No, nothing of the sort!' laughed Zale happily. 'Usually, Harden and I are paid to rid villages of dark creatures. For example, when Luca summoned us, we had just killed five Nicars.'

'What are Nicars? What happened?' asked Bazyli eagerly. Zale looked at Harden who simply gestured for him to continue. Zale sighed heavily and began his story.

'Well, Nicars are horrible creatures of the sky. Their flesh stinks of decaying animals and their eyes glow like red flames. They prey on young children, especially babies, stealing them from their mothers. The village that we were helping lay at the base of one of the Sincre Mountains. That is where the creatures lived of course; high up in the mountain peaks.

Well, one day, Harden and I stumbled across the village and were asked to help in any way we could. They offered us much in gold and we happily took up the challenge. We would have done it for no charge of course, but the villagers were insistent. Anyway, we waited and waited at the base of the mountain for them to come back down for a meal. When they finally left their home, we were ready. Harden shot one down with an arrow as soon as they appeared, drawing the other four in. The next arrow was dodged and the leading Nicar took Harden's bow from him, tearing it up in an instant. That was when the real fighting began!' At that point, Zale stood up and drew his sword. Harden did the same and they began to act out the battle.

'We swayed our swords left and right, blocking blows and dodging claws. Then Harden swung up high and brought down the second Nicar. The others were filled with rage and all charged at him, teeth bared. I took the opportunity to kill another two from behind. The last one was so terrified, it tried to flee. Harden and I of course sprung forwards and brought it down to the ground where it shall lie forever more!' Laughing heartily, the two of them collapsed to the floor, both satisfied that their battle training was done for the night. Bazyli cheered and clapped in approval, as did Acacia and Sachiel. Silence fell upon them all quickly though as Acacia raised a hand to silence them. They all strained their ears.

'Something's coming,' whispered Harden, clutching the hilt of his sword. All five of the warriors readied themselves and stared up at the trees that lined the base of the mountain. All they could see was darkness and the shadowy shapes of trees waving in the gentle breeze.

'How many?' asked Zale.

'Not sure,' said Sachiel. 'Perhaps two, three at the most.' They continued to look deep into the gloom. The rustling sounds stopped. It seemed as though the group had been spotted. Just a moment later, three beings ran out of the trees.

'Lysias?' questioned Bazyli. 'It's Lysias! And Caden!' The boy ran towards his friends eagerly. The others also now recognised them.

'Is that Galzan with them?' asked Acacia, straining to put a name to the black form galloping in their direction.

'Those are his scars alright,' said Harden. The Wolvax's muzzle glistened with the five stripes in the moonlight.

'Harden! Zale! Sachiel!' said Caden as he reached them at last. 'And of course, Acacia,' he added, his cheeks turning a slight pink as he looked upon her beauty.

'You're alive?' whispered Acacia, a tear in her eye. She hugged him tightly, then turned to Lysias and did the same.

'What happened? Tell us everything,' said Zale, gesturing for them to sit down. They all huddled around the fire. Caden was about to begin when he noticed Galzan staying back, scenting the ground.

'What's the matter?' he asked the Wolvax.

'I cannot stay here,' Galzan growled. 'An enemy of mine is nearby. A Domai.'

'Lankoa?' asked Sachiel.

'You have seen a Domai here?' asked Galzan taken aback.

'Yes,' continued Sachiel. 'She is going to guide us to the Forbidden Valley.'

'Then this is where I leave you. I have brought you to your friends safely as I intended. May we meet again some day.' Lysias was about to speak but had no chance to as the Wolvax sprang off into the darkness of the forest. As a relation to the wolf, Wolvax and

Domai do not rest well together. Galzan had had enough confrontation in recent days. He was eager to leave before his scent clung to the earth. Free to roam wild again, he set off in search of his pack somewhere to the north.

'Goodbye,' whispered Bazyli. The boy then turned back to Lysias, clinging to his arm almost as if to stop him from leaving again.

'Right then, I'll begin.' With that, Caden began to tell the others of the journey he and Lysias had just taken. The Kai-Rae helped him fill in the blanks for the times when the General had been rendered unconscious. With mention of the man in the pit, Harden interrupted.

'A spy you say?' he asked quietly. 'So Jabari has sent someone after us.'

'It appears that is so,' said Lysias, 'and whoever it is was close enough to us to inform him that myself and Caden were thought dead.' Bazyli's grip on Lysias's arm tightened.

'Xannon,' stated Zale.

'What?' asked Caden.

'The man you saw must have been Xannon. But what was he doing so far away from Jabari's keep?'

'That's anyone's guess,' said Harden. 'Jabari is not a man that allows his enemies to foresee his next step.' Zale glanced at Harden with a yearning to know the truth behind his relationship with Jabari. Still, he held his tongue. After a moment's silence, Caden continued with the tale until it led him to that present moment. For some reason he did not mention the girl with fiery eyes, though he knew not why. Bazyli then eagerly told Caden and Lysias about his own adventure in the passage, the others laughing heartily every time he over exaggerated the situation. It was not long before their minds were back to the present and the wish to not look to the future took hold. They sat silently watching the flickering reds, oranges and yellows of the firelight.

After a while, Bazyli longed for more stories. He began to ask Caden about his battles and the events that took place when Luca helped save Forthum from the Bangai dragons. He recited the tale as best as he could remember, everyone listening intently. He described how the dragons had come from across the sea in search of a new food supply. Hundreds of them had taken to the air from their icy homes and travelled towards the warmth of the White Islands. When they reached Forthum, they began to destroy the city immediately and killed many woman and children. Their white scales glittered in the sun as they burnt the wooden houses. Even though the dragons were born on the ice and as such weaker in the heat, they were too great an enemy for Caden's army to withstand, so he had called upon the aid of

Luca. She travelled to Forthum herself and used her powers to force the dragons back. They had lived outside the world of magic for so long that they had forgotten what some creatures were capable of. They underestimated the queen and paid for it dearly. Luca, however, was not a lover of violence, so in the end had made an agreement with the dragons. They were free to live on the White Islands so long as they did not harm another man or woman, else they would be forever banished. They would only hunt for food when it was needed, not out of sport, and would do so as true predators. They must only pick out the weak and the sick of a herd and leave the strong to ensure the herds survival. That way they would not run out of food as they had done on the barren glaciers of their northern land. The dragons agreed to the terms and left the city alone. Luca remained to help rebuild Forthum. Caden vowed that day that if ever Damané was in need, Forthum would come to its aid.

By the time Caden had finished his tale, Lankoa had returned with a deer slumped over her shoulder and some herbs. The group could see the teeth marks in the animal's neck and the blood glistening on Lankoa's lips in the moonlight. That was the first time they realised just how fierce the Domai must be. It had been many hundreds of years since any man had killed an animal with his bare hands and no arrow or sword. They all knew it took great courage to look a creature in the eye and watch it die, especially when you know it has done nothing wrong to deserve such an end.

Once the deer was cooked with the herbs, all thoughts of the strength of the Domai had faded and the warriors dug into the first decent meal since they left the People of the North. They continued to laugh and joke and tell tales until the moons were past their peaks in the inky sky. They then collapsed onto their bed mats and let their dreams take sway. They had, of course, decided a rota for a watch as they knew that the Usari were still roaming the land. Once again, it was Harden and Zale who opted to go first.

'Now, Zale, Luca has a request. I have tried to teach you as much of the Ancestral Tongue as I can, but it takes much time and I haven't had many chances to develop your knowledge.' Harden's voice was serious, which concerned Zale.

'What is it? I have remembered all that you have taught me. I don't know what else I can do.'

'There is a spell I can perform to speed up the learning process. It is Luca's wish that you know the whole language fluently.'

'Well,' responded Zale, 'if it is what Luca wishes, then I ask that you do it.'

'I must warn you first; it can be a painful process. Do not resist the magic in any way. Do you understand?'

'I understand,' said Zale, slightly fearful of what was to come. Harden nodded to himself and placed a hand on Zale's head. Closing his eyes, his arm shuddered for a moment and Zale's head shot backwards. Zale's face was distorted with pain and his body began to tremble.

'Do not resist,' whispered Harden, covering Zale with a blanket. Zale stayed in that state for two hours. His mind was racing the whole time. He saw flashes of his past. There was his city. He saw his father die over and over. Then there was his leaving of Morsenden. He saw a young girl and had images of her violent death. These were not memories, but his mind's way of testing his fears. He relived their journey to Damané and saw creatures he did not recognise. He flinched as weapons flew towards him but none of them struck his skin. Fire rose up in front of his eyes, its heat burning his face. The orange fingers turned to ice and shattered, tiny blue crystals shooting out in all directions. Towards the end of spell, his mind became clear. He could see a vast array of colours before him and knew that each one had its own magic. It was the beauty of magic.

When Zale woke, he found Harden sat watching him, slowly drinking a cup of herbal tea.

'How do you feel?' Harden asked.

'I'm fine,' replied Zale. 'I'm not in pain now, nor was I during the process. It was more of an emotional strain.'

'I know what you mean,' said Harden. 'Now, you should know the Ancestral Tongue. Remember, use a word that you need, and then visualise what you intend to happen. I want you to burn that tree over there.' Harden gestured towards a lone oak standing about twenty metres away in line with the mountains. Zale pushed himself to his knees and wiped a line of sweat from his brow. He could not believe Harden was having him practise magic so soon after his ordeal. The two men stood up and walked a bit closer to the tree. Zale searched his mind, and then reached his arm forwards.

Sunai! As Zale spoke the word, a beam of golden light left his hand and hit the tree. It burst into flames before Zale's eyes.

'Well done,' said Harden. 'Now, put the fire out.' Zale reached forwards once more.

Rancorah! Another beam of light came from Zale's fingers, though this time it was blue. It formed a ball above the flames and then burst into a shower of water, putting the fire out. Zale sat down on a boulder, speechless.

'Good, good!' said Harden. 'I see you will have no trouble then. Just remember what Sachiel said; magic uses your life force. Do not use too much or else you shall die, though I think you have a good amount of strength in you.' Zale nodded with understanding, heading Harden's warning.

'That did not take up as much of my energy as the spells I have cast before,' commented Zale before they went back to sit beneath the stars.

'Indeed. You are becoming more resilient. Now, it is time we sleep. We have a long day ahead of us tomorrow.' With that, Harden instructed Zale to try and sleep and said he would wake Caden to take over the watch. Zale lay down and closed his eyes, his head buzzing with thoughts of what he was capable of.

When they woke from pleasant dreams, the warriors decided it was best that they set off as soon as possible. The sun had already risen, even though the stars had only been out for a few hours. It seemed as though the days had been drawn out on purpose yet the night had been left at peace. They ate what little there was left of the meat from the night before and packed up the camp.

The land was just as Lankoa had described; full of vast hills, each alive with colour where patches of flowers sprung out of the grass reaching for the light. They seemed to cover the entire earth. Once they reached the top of the first hill, the others stretched out before them. Far in the distance there appeared to be two slightly taller hills that Lankoa told them made the Forbidden Valley.

It was the first day the group had walked under the heat of the sun with their heavy packs. Each longed for their horse as sweat seeped down their faces. The pace would slow with the rising of hills and then increase as the hills went downwards again. Every so often, the group would come across a cave that looked invitingly cool, but they continued on their path towards the dreaded valley. At one point, Lankoa had to take them round one of the hills as it was covered with shingle and they could not climb the slope. It took them over an hour to complete the detour and yet they were only quarter of a league further than if they had climbed the hill as its base was extremely wide but had little height.

After another hour, the wind began to pick up as they came across a patch of trees. The shade cooled their faces, as did the breeze, but just before they entered the darkness, Sachiel saw thick black clouds heading towards them. His body tingled slightly as he gazed upon them, but kept his thoughts to himself as he followed the others.

The land no longer rose or fell. Instead, Lankoa had the difficult task of leading the warriors through the maze of tall trees that all looked the same. At times they would have to double back due to their path being blocked and would have to skirt round. Once two hours had passed and they were nearing the end of the trees, Sachiel suddenly stopped with a look of fear on his face.

'What is it?' asked Acacia who was walking at the back with him. The others in front also stopped and looked to see what was going on.

'It is just as I feared,' he said gravely.

'What is? What haven't you told us?' asked Caden, beginning to feel anger rising in his blood.

'Just before we entered the trees I saw clouds but they were too far away for me to tell what weather they were bringing. Now they are almost upon us and my blood runs cold.'

'What does that mean?' asked Bazyli sensing the fear in Sachiel's voice.

'They bring a blizzard.' With Sachiel's words, the others looked around themselves as if searching for cover. Sachiel approached Lankoa and spoke to her in a low voice.

'How far are we from the valley? Are there any more caves around?' he asked her softly.

'About an hour or so…maybe two. No…no, there are no caves. We have left them all…' Lankoa's voice faded and Sachiel could not make out her last words. Her voice was stuttered and her eyes had grown glassy. Lysias approached her and placed an arm around her.

'What's the matter with her?' asked Zale.

'Domai cannot survive in cold weather,' said Acacia. 'If we do not find a place to shelter, there is no knowing what will happen to her.' She lowered her voice, but there was no need. Lankoa already knew.

'I am afraid the cold will not have a pleasurable effect on me either,' said Lysias solemnly. The others stared at him.

'I feared that may be so,' said Sachiel. 'Kai-Rae and Domai share that weakness, just like with the heat.'

'Then we must try to reach the valley,' commanded Harden. 'Lysias, is there any form of spell that you may cast to protect yourself and Lankoa?' Lankoa looked up at the Kai-Rae hopefully.

'None that I know of that will last.' He looked into the Domai's fearful eyes. 'Though there is one I may try that will slow the effects of the cold.' He embraced Lankoa, holding her tightly to his chest. As he closed his eyes, a silver liquid-glow started to grow outwards from Lysias's stomach. The energy encased the two of them and lingered until it then seeped into their very cores.

'Heat,' whispered Lankoa. Lysias nodded.

'I do not know how long it will hold,' said Lysias sadly.

'Well, it's better than nothing.' With Harden's words, the warriors left the cover of the trees and picked up the pace. They were in desperate need of finding shelter or else they knew deep down that Lysias and Lankoa would surely die. Before the trees had even shrunk behind them, the snow began to fall. The wind that came with it was icy and chilled them to the bone. The snow's delicate touch felt like kisses of death as the flakes melted and water seeped through their clothes. It was so heavy that after only half an hour it was difficult to find a way through the mounds of powder that surrounded their legs. The wind howled round their frozen ears, making it hard to hear. They pushed on further, their pace growing ever slower. There was no form of shelter anywhere to be seen. Lankoa, who was now at the back, stopped and began to sway. Her skin was now pale and was turning white. Zale looked round and saw her there, almost disguised by the snow. He began to make his way over to her when she fell into the snow, out of sight. He ran to the spot he had seen her to be and found her. Her whole body shivered and her eyes had begun to stare. Zale took off his cloak and wrapped it around her. Then, carrying Lankoa in his arms, he went after the others, though now they were hard to make out through the snow. By the time he reached them, Bazyli had also succumbed to the cold. Caden was on his knees trying to keep warm and Sachiel and Acacia were sat in the powder snow. Lysias was trying to crawl on further, the scales on his face now the same silver-white as Lankoa. Harden was trying to wrap Bazyli up when he too passed out. Zale put Lankoa down and approached the others. It was then when he realised that all of them had collapsed. He was just feeling as though his legs would give way when he heard a soft music on the wind. It was so peaceful and calming that it gave him some strength for a moment longer. Through the snow before him, he saw a blue light getting slowly closer and brighter. He could sense the ring on his finger glowing, giving his hands a moment of warmth. Then he felt the cold of the snow hugging his shoulders and tried to blink snowflakes out of his eyes. He could no longer feel his body. All his limbs were beginning to stiffen. As his eyes closed, Zale thought he saw a figure standing over him, but could remember no more.

The Rostauru

When the warriors woke, they found themselves staring at the ceiling of what appeared to be a small cave branching off from another, larger cave. The walls were a pale grey, covered in a thin film of water that shone blue in a light that the warriors could see no source for. The gentle sound of trickling water could be heard all around them, calming their fears. Bazyli was the first one to sit up. The others were lying peacefully on the ground around him, each wrapped up in a white fur blanket, similar to the one he found round himself. They had been placed in a circle around a fire that burned blue-white in the darkness. Bazyli looked towards the entrance of the apparent room they were in and saw a tunnel running straight past in either direction, lit with hovering balls of fire, just like the one warming his feet. He stood up and looked down upon the others. They were all studying the ceiling of the cave as if making the huge decision of whether to move or not. However, there was no sign of Lankoa or Lysias anywhere in the room. Bazyli went over to Zale and shook him gently. Zale's eyes suddenly cleared and he looked up at Bazyli.

'Are you alright?' Bazyli asked quietly. His voice echoed around the room, snapping the others out of their own trances and forcing them to sit up.

'Yes,' replied Zale. 'Can you see where we are?' he asked, propping himself up on his elbow.

'No,' whispered Bazyli, though the others could hear him perfectly. 'There is no sign of Lankoa or Lysias either.'

'Well then, we should get up and look for them should we not?' said Zale with a friendly smile on his face. Bazyli's fears of what may have happened to the two creatures faded and he helped Zale to his feet. The rest of the group also got up and followed them to the entrance of the room. Peering down the tunnel in either direction they found the source of the light, not to be from the balls of flame, but from thin streams of water down the edges of the path that seemed to glow with magic. The streams were sunken into the floor. If any of them had dared look closer, they would have found that the thin streams they saw were in fact mere fragments of a great lake visible through the cracks in the floor. And if they had looked closer still, they would have seen that the floor was made up entirely of slabs of smooth, grey-white stone that simply hovered some fifteen feet above the water. As the others stepped gingerly out of the room, Zale held back for a moment. He could hear a faint sound coming from between the stone slabs. At first, the sound was nothing more than the echoes of running water. Then he realised there was an underlying whisper. Zale listened harder. The whispers were in a strange language, but to his surprise, he could understand it. The rest of the group oblivious to his actions, Zale bent low to the ground and concentrated on deciphering what the whispers were saying. As he did so, the memory of Zophia, The Turner of Minds, came back to him. *White waters whisper the path of truth. When you find them, just listen.* Zale's eyes widened with wonder as he began to hear the chant clearly. Zophia's riddle had now been solved, but now he faced a new one.

> *Follow the path of rising plains,*
> *To the valley of horrors unknown.*
> *When you have made two halves whole,*
> *Then shall you be ready,*
> *Then shall you have grown.*
>
> *Let your heart been torn by the winds*
> *And make what decision you know is right.*
> *Blinding light,*
> *Searing pain,*
> *Then shall your birth take flight.*
> *Belief is all you need*
> *To make yourself whole again.*

The whispers then continued to repeat the verses as if they had done so for an age. Zale stood up again and brushed the dirt from his knees, puzzling over what he had heard. At that moment, Harden turned to him.

'Are you alright?' he asked.

'Huh?' responded Zale, breaking away from his thoughts.

'You look troubled,' said Harden.

'No, no, I'm fine. It's nothing.'

After a concerned look from Harden, the group decided to venture down the tunnel to their left, as it was from that direction that they could hear a soft music.

'I heard this before I passed out in the snow,' said Caden. 'I thought I saw a blue light and a figure, but more than that I cannot remember.'

'I believe I saw that too,' said Zale.

'And I,' said Sachiel. 'Let's see what lies behind this mystery.'

They travelled as quietly as they could, for the echoes amplified their footsteps. Ahead of them, they could see the tunnel come to its end at another entrance to a room. A great blue light came from within and the music grew louder. They could now hear singing and every so often a silhouette would dance past. When they reached the doorway, they blinked in the light that shone on their faces. When they could finally see, they found before them beautiful men and women dancing and singing to music with no source. A few of them stopped to look at the strangers, but they soon went back to what they were doing, not bothered by their presence. The warriors edged further into the room, not sure what to make of it all. They now saw three long white tables running down the centre of the room, covered with fruits and meat. The walls were just like the tunnel they had travelled down and their previous room; pale grey stone, the film of water shimmering blue in the light of the underground streams. There were also the same balls of fire bringing light to the dancers' movements. The room was round, like that of a cave worn into the side of a mountain. On the far side of this hollow, they could see three thrones, two either side of one larger one, standing tall and white amidst the apparent celebrations. Upon the centre throne sat a man who appeared older than all the others in the room, yet had a face of youth and beauty. His silver-blonde hair seemed to blend with his pearl robes as it hung long and loose around his shoulders. The robes themselves appeared to have the same blue shimmer as the walls. Resting on his brow was a wreath of crimson flowers. His expression was calm and knowing, making the warriors believe the dance was in his honour. To his left there sat a young woman, more beautiful than any ever seen. Her hair was the same silver-blonde as the man by her side but she wore an elegant blue dress that hugged her body until her waist where it fell delicately to the floor. The sleeves ended with a single point at her middle finger where they seemed to be attached to a silver ring. Her skin was pale, making her eyes look even more dazzling. They were silver, lined with the ocean's blue. A single tear-shaped sapphire rested in the centre of her forehead, held in place by a thin silver chain that disappeared into her hair.

'I have heard of these creatures,' whispered Sachiel, 'but only in myths. Few have seen them, but all in dreams.'

Harden gestured towards the thrones with his head to the others and began to make his way over to them. The rest of the group followed, unable to take their eyes off the woman. Once before the man, they bowed respectfully and waited. The woman rose and the music stopped. All in the room turned to look at the strangers.

'Welcome,' she said in a soft voice. It was a sweet melody to their ears. 'I am Alana, daughter of Onofre, king of the Rostauru.' With the mention of Onofre, Alana gestured towards the man still sat upon the throne before them. He bowed his head to the warriors, who then bowed again in return.

'We brought you here,' she continued, 'as you were wandering off your path and would surely have died in the blizzard. We normally stay hidden as it is forbidden for any other than our own kind to see us, but we did what we had to.'

'What does she mean?' asked Bazyli.

'The Rostauru,' replied Acacia 'are the Protectors of the White Islands. They are immortal keepers of peace when darkness creeps back into the world. I am guessing they were aware of our journey and so knew that they must save us in order to protect Damané.'

'You are quite correct,' said Alana. 'However, we can do no more for you now other than to dine you and give you rest. If you are wondering about the Domai and the Kai-Rae you travelled with, they are being tended to. They were both close to death when we found you but will soon recover. I believe you can spare one more day of rest from your journey to allow their full recovery?' She said this questioningly and turned to Onofre who nodded with approval.

'Thank you,' said Zale, bowing once more. 'May I ask where we are?' Alana smiled gently and seemed for a moment to be even more enchanting.

'When we found you, you had managed to wander far off your course towards our mountain. Now, you stand beneath it in one of the many halls of the Rostauru. It has, however, given you an advantage. The path you followed was blocked by an unnatural growth of thick trees, but now you may come out of the other side of the mountain looking out upon the Forbidden Valley itself. It has saved you much time. Now, enough talk for this day. Though to your eyes we are celebrating, this is a day of mourning. My dear brother's body was discovered slain the night we found you by Lord Jabari.' With this, Alana indicated towards to empty throne. 'That was our main purpose for being away from our home. Each day, Jabari comes nearer to finding our borders; a task he must not succeed in. Enjoy our music and eat our food. The Domai and Kai-Rae will be sent to you as soon as they are fit enough.' Alana then sat back down and the music began. The other Rostauru took up their songs and dance again as if there had been no intermission, casting many a wild shadow upon the walls.

The warriors went to the centre table and piled some food on a plate for each of them. They then looked back to the thrones and saw Alana watching them with a smile.

'There is something strange about her eyes,' whispered Caden.

'Indeed,' said Sachiel. Bazyli looked directly at Alana, and to his astonishment, though she peered in his direction, her stare was empty, and yet full of life.

'She is blind,' he exclaimed, as quietly as one can. The others all looked towards the mysterious woman and realised Bazyli was correct. Yet, though the Rostauru were blind, they all had an acute sense of where everything stood in the world and what was beautiful.

The group went to the side of the room and sat on some cushions that appeared to have been recently laid. There they watched the figures dancing about them and ate in silence. The display was like nothing they had ever seen. The dancers were more beautiful than anything in the world and had the grace of the wind. Their coloured robes gently caressed the floor with such delicacy it was unbelievable. It was as though the ground would shatter if anything more than a silken touch fell upon its surface.

Zale looked around the room with awe. His gaze fell upon the thrones. The figures around him seemed to blur into thin wisps of white smoke weaving in and out of each other. The Rostauru's eyes shone silver in the fire light, except for Alana's and her father's. Theirs reflected the brilliant purple hue of Zale's ring. As Alana's blank stare bore into him, Zale felt his right index finger tingle and warmth spread down his arm and through his body. All around him melted together into an opalescent sea. All thoughts were swept from his mind. The only sound was a clear young woman's voice, more beautiful than the evening star in an azure sky.

Breso ka Silvana si dom prixira tala moostah

Kiro dom tala estraysal vondra

Ay termina prendo

Visikar ome ay mé dono niander fisku sy

Bennor fo tinna scor sy

Lyanna bet eht skillia

Sonometre si ob latrommi milyda

The next thing Zale knew, he was back in the first room they had found themselves in with Acacia looking at him closely, a sparkle of knowing in her eye.

'What happened to you?' asked Caden. Brining himself back to reality, Zale turned to the General.

'What do you mean?'

'Well, you seemed to be in some sort of trace,' said Sachiel. 'You didn't hear anything that we said on our way back here. You didn't even seem to hear what Alana said to us before we left the hall.'

'What did she say?' asked Zale eagerly.

'Not much,' replied Harden. 'She was just saying that we could wander these halls if we so wished but to use our time here for rest before our journey. Are you sure you didn't hear her?'

'Yes,' replied Zale. 'I'm sorry, I don't know what happened.'

'That's strange. She was looking at you the whole time,' said Sachiel.

'Well, we'll just leave you to your thoughts then,' said Caden. 'We're all going to have a look around, apart from Acacia who seems content in staying here and resting.' With that, Harden, Caden, Sachiel and Bazyli left the room; Zale and Acacia remaining sat on the floor.

'So?' Acacia asked with a smile.

'So, what?'

'So, what did she say to you?'

'How did you…?'

'I just know these things,' said Acacia mysteriously. Deciding to simply accept the fact that Acacia appeared to know all, Zale continued.

'It was the strangest thing. All I could see was her. Everything else faded from existence. Her voice was so different to what we've heard, and she spoke in the Ancestral Tongue.'

'Could you understand her?' asked Acacia, suddenly thinking that she should be careful as to what she said to Sachiel in her own tongue.

'Yes…as if it were my own tongue. Harden's spell worked well.'

'Was it Ancestral Whittador or Ancestral Elecantra?'

'What's the difference?' asked Zale, thinking there was only one Ancestral Tongue.

'Ancestral Elecantra is what Sachiel and I speak,' replied Acacia.

'It must have been Ancestral Whittador then because, from what I remember of your words outside the Tower of Light, I can't understand you and Sachiel.'

'Oh right,' said Acacia, feeling she had got some of her privacy back. 'Please, continue. What was it she said?' Zale thought hard for a moment, trying to remember what it was he heard. Then, translating it, he spoke.

'Silvana's gift is more precious than jewels, worth more than eternal gold, and forever lasting. Remember him and he shall never fail you. Beware of those around you. Danger lines the sky. Betrayal is an immortal enemy.'

'You know Silvana?' asked Acacia with surprise.

'Yes, Luca took me to him.'

'But how?'

'What do you mean?' asked Zale. 'He lives in Damané. I mean, I was surprised too. I didn't think there were any unicorns left in the White Islands.'

'He was in the form of a unicorn? He must truly have had a strong spirit then.'

'What do you mean 'in the form of'?'

'Zale,' said Acacia looking at him almost with sympathy, 'Silvana is Alana's brother. That's who they are mourning.' The two of them sat in silence for a moment. Zale was confused by what Acacia had just told him. After a while, he spoke.

'How is it that I saw him and that he has been with me if he was still alive here?' he asked.

'It is said that those of strong spirit, such as the Rostauru, take the form of unicorns after death,' replied Acacia. 'If Silvana had felt his death near then he could have separated his soul so as to prepare for death. The separated part would have formed the unicorn you saw. As he has now passed from this world, the unicorn is his entire soul.'

'How would he have sensed his death?'

'No one knows,' said Acacia. 'The Rostauru have powers beyond even my understanding. He may have known for years and made the transformation a while ago. That would explain him living in Damané. It would be a safe place for him to stay until his task was set.'

'What task?' asked Zale, slightly nervous of the answer.

'To protect you. He is connected to you somehow. The reason why will be revealed soon enough.' They once again sat in silence. Zale thought over all that had happened since Luca had called upon his aid. It was as if there was a great weight upon his shoulders, though he knew not what caused it.

An hour passed before the others returned. They found Zale and Acacia lying on opposite sides of the room, apparently overwhelmed by their own thoughts. When they arrived, Zale sat up.

'Find anything interesting?' he asked.

'Not much really,' said Harden. 'The cave system is extensive with many rooms. We saw some of the Rostauru's maps of the White Islands and other lands within the seas. The water that gives light to these walls has some form of enchantment on it.'

'They are very kind people,' said Bazyli. 'They said that if there was anything else we needed just to ask. They have filled our packs with fresh food and water.'

'They are kind. It is lucky for us that we came across the Rostauru,' said Zale seriously. 'Without Lankoa, who knows what the Domai may do to us. How are they to know we are friends? The world is dark, especially in the lands closer to Jabari's keep.' Harden nodded. They all sat down and fell back into a silence only filled by the distant singing of the Rostauru.

For the rest of the day each warrior stayed mainly to themselves, every once in a while going back to the great hall and watching the dancing. By the evening, Lankoa had appeared and seemed quite cheerful. She seemed at peace with everything, her eyes with a look as if she could see the distant stars. This was the effect of the Rostauru medicine on a mortal. It sets ones soul at ease, lifting it to the surface of the mind. Lysias soon followed, though his expression remained as it always did; full of knowing. Bazyli hugged him tightly, glad that he had returned. The two of them sat in a corner talking together. Through the general conversation, Lysias was secretly teaching the boy defence techniques and ways of hiding oneself from enemies. Bazyli had no idea he was taking in all of this new knowledge, but simply continued to tell Lysias of his days with his mother and father, and with Shethar.

Just as the group was going to lie down to sleep before the journey ahead of them, Alana appeared in the doorway of their room. Not one of them had seen her arrive so Bazyli was startled to find her stood there when he turned around.

'I am sorry to disturb you,' she said softly. 'My father has asked that you rest for the night in a room closer to the edge of our caves. It will mean less time travelling through these tunnels in the morning.'

'Of course we will,' said Harden. 'Your hospitality has been far beyond what anyone could expect.'

'We are the Protectors of the White Islands. That means we are obligated to provide all the needs of any a wanderer who stumbles upon us in the darkness. Please, follow me.' Alana then turned and led them down the passage away from the great hall. It took them nearly an hour to reach the end of the caves where a room was found on the right just twenty metres or so from the mouth. In the inky sky outside the stars could be seen shining down on the world.

'This is where I leave you.' With Alana's words, Caden lowered his head with disappointment. 'Do not worry General Caden. I will make my brief farewells in the morning. I will send some guards who will watch your leave. I am afraid there is nothing more we can do. If the White Islands were under threat from those across the seas, we could intervene and give aid to the people. However, this is a dispute from within the lands and the people that reside there. Only when destruction is immanent can we help.' On this note, Alana turned and went back down the passage, her blue gown billowing behind her.

The room was just like the previous one, the only difference being that there were two extra blankets for Lankoa and Lysias. Unable to shake their sense of peace, the warriors laid their heads down without a thought of Jabari and the dangers ahead. It did not take long for pleasant dreams to find them.

The Forbidden Valley

When the sky outside began to pale, the group woke and stretched their legs after a good night's sleep. The birds were singing as if the world was at peace and, for a moment, the warriors believed it was so. The soft yellow of the sun melted the morning mist that hugged the grassy hills. Each dewy blade sparkled like a diamond amidst the array of golden flowers. Delicate bluebells lifted their heads to the warmth of the new day, sheltered by the emerald giants of a nearby forest of bay trees. A young fox cub trotted to the edge of the cave mouth and peered in curiously before its mother appeared to usher it away into the undergrowth. The sight of the Rostauru guards in their shimmering green robes reawakened the warriors' minds to the dark cloud hovering over the land. The blind sentinels waited patiently to take the party of men, Elements, and Kai-Rae to the borders of their land. The group half heartily got dressed and packed up their belongings. They were given a small breakfast before they took their farewells of Alana and her father who met them just outside their room.

'May you go in peace,' said Alana, 'and be met with peace in return.'

'That is very kind,' said Caden, 'but I fear we will not be met with much peace from now on.' He lowered his head, though it was not times ahead that troubled his mind.

'We will meet again brave General,' whispered Alana, raising his chin with an outstretched hand and staring into his eyes. Caden was filled with a feeling of hope, as if he knew everything would turn out right. It was as though Alana had given him a small truth about what was to come and for moment he thought he could see himself returning home in his mind's eye.

'Thank you for everything,' said Lankoa. Onofre accepted her thanks with a nod and then spoke for the first time since the warriors had arrived.

'I am only sorry that we cannot intervene at this time. We know that Lord Jabari is doing wrong for this land, but our laws are strict. When the time comes, he shall meet his punishment.' With that, Onofre turned and began walking back down the passage towards the great hall, his scarlet robes skimming smoothly along the floor.

'Farewell,' said Alana. 'Do not look for us after this day, for your search would be in vain. We will find you, if the time calls for it.' Then she too walked away from the group, not once looking back. The group was sad to see her go. Her air of wisdom had been comforting, even for Lysias who had existed long since she was born.

The guards led the warriors to the edge of the cave system and told them that they would stand and wait until they had passed into the valley. The group then turned as one and saw before them two tall hills making a valley. Though it was mid-morning at the passage entrance, the valley was cast into shadow. Its opening was guarded by a thick fog, far more dense than the one the group had previously travelled through. Fear spread through the group.

They left the security of the Rostauru's home behind them and made their way down a grassy slope, the brilliant orange flowers that grew there gradually disappearing. As they approached the Forbidden Valley, each member of the group was silently wishing that they didn't have to meet the Domai. Though Acacia, Sachiel, Lysias, and Harden did not fear them, they did not want to trespass on their ground. They were very secretive creatures and did not welcome visitors kindly. Harden was reassured by the presence of Lankoa. She could stop the Domai from attacking, though he did not think they would help the group if asked. They usually choose to stay out of others' problems and conflicts. Lysias felt more wary. He knew of the Domai's capabilities of stealth attacks and did not want to be forced into using his powers to defend the group. Though the Domai have the ability to heal, the magic he may be forced to unleash would be devastating. Sachiel was at that moment thinking of their healing capabilities also, though he was seeing it as a great ally. To have creatures with them in battle that could heal wounds would give them a much better chance as they fought alone against the dragons Bazyli had seen. In the back of his mind, however, he knew of the Domai's reluctance to heal creatures other than their own kind for the gift of healing is then passed on to the one who has just been treated. They could not risk their one main advantage spreading through the world.

It only took a quarter of an hour to reach the steep slopes of the two hills. They towered above them like small mountains decorated with lush forests and woodland. The group did not pause to admire their beauty but simply entered the fog guarding the valley's entrance without hesitation. They discovered the fog to be only about five metres thick, designed to scare off trespassers.

'This is where I leave you. You cannot follow me on the route I must take to my home. Good Luck. I shall warn the Council that you are coming.' Lankoa gave Harden an apologetic look and then sprinted away from him.

'Lankoa? Lankoa!' She had gone. They looked around to see if there was any sign of where she went, but there was none. The group left the fog and shuddered as they saw the valley. Razor-sharp rocks covered the slopes and the ground was scorched. There seemed no way to get round the rocks, not that they really wanted to. They all would have preferred to turn back, but Luca had insisted that they asked the Domai for help. There was no sign of life in the valley. All the trees on the slopes were either dead or severely burnt, though there seemed no source of fire. Above them, the stars glistened brightly. For a reason unknown to the warriors, it was night in the valley though the rest of the land was filled with light. Each of them took a few cautious steps forward, looking around them all the while. At that moment, a tremendous roar came from behind the first turn of the valley. Bazyli hid behind Zale.

'I heard that noise when I was following Xannon but I was too high up to see where it came from.' The boy shook with fear as he noticed small animal bones scattered around the boulders. They were scoured with teeth and claw marks that he did not recognise to be from any predator he knew.

'It is alright Bazyli,' said Zale reassuringly. 'Just stay behind me. Harden, any ideas?'

'I haven't got a clue. Does anyone else know what we are about to face?' Caden and the Elements shook their heads. Lysias had a look of concentration upon his face as though he was still analyzing the sound. His eyes peered cautiously about him at the numerous marks on the barren earth.

'What ever it is, it must be what was responsible for the disappearance of my men,' said Caden. 'We should just leave and traverse the top of the valley like Bazyli did.'

'No, Caden. Luca wants the Domai's help. They are Damané's allies. Now, let's get moving.'

'I do not think that is wise,' said Lysias as he knelt to the ground and placed a hand on a patch of scorched earth. 'There are few creatures I know of capable of making these marks and I desire to come face to face with none of them.'

'See,' said Caden, 'Lysias agrees with me.'

'We have no choice,' said Harden, beginning to move forwards. Reluctantly, Caden followed Harden towards the turning in the valley. They had to climb over large rocks and skirt round boulders. Zale stayed with Bazyli to help him over rocks he could not manage to traverse by himself. As the men went ahead, Acacia knelt down beside Lysias and studied one of the scorch marks on the ground. They were shaped like ovals as if the heat source had come from above at an angle.

'A dragon?' she said to herself curiously. 'A dragon! Wait,' she called at the top of her lungs to stop the men, 'It's a dragon! Stop! Don't go round that...' It was too late. The men and Bazyli disappeared from her sight. She and Lysias heard another roar and the sound of flames rushing through the air. They ran round the corner to find the men huddled together behind a group of boulders.

'Acacia! Lysias! Get down!' Before Acacia could follow Caden's instructions, Acacia felt her arm being warmed by a tree on fire to her left. The dragon was attacking her. She looked up to see a mass of black scales. The dragon was ten metres tall with wings twice the length of its body. Its claws were silver and its eyes were a fiery yellow. Its two powerful hind legs were bent into a protective crouch whilst its front legs were held ready for attack. The beautiful beast looked at the Element threateningly, its eyes turning a piercing red. Lysias dragged Acacia behind the group of boulders as the dragon prepared to breathe fire once more. The Kai-Rae was just able to create a protective shield around all of them as the dragon attacked once more.

'What do we do now?' asked Caden as flames soared over their heads, coursing round the transparent energy.

'I don't know,' said Harden. 'We cannot go back and we cannot go forward. Any ideas Sachiel?'

'None. But you're right; we appear to be trapped.'

'I think I could subdue the creature, though I would have to do it alone,' said Lysias gravely. The young boy next to him gripped his arm.

'She's just trying to protect her children,' said Bazyli.

'How do you know that?' Zale was stunned by Bazyli's calmness.

'Did none of you see? There's a nest behind her. She obviously thinks we want to harm her young.'

'Either that or she wants to feed us to them!' Caden could not see anything positive about their situation. They had no means of escape other than to face a mighty beast with the added strength of being a protective mother.

'I have an idea. The Ancestral Tongue is what the dragons used to speak. I don't know if they still use it, but it is worth a try.' Harden gave the others a determined look, and then stepped out from behind the boulder.

'Harden, No!' Zale reached for his friend, but Harden was too far away. Behind the rocks, Lysias began to draw upon the source of his powers. He could sense the cool, magical liquid of his mind starting to stir wildly. Before he could summon it to his fingertips, Harden drew himself up and began to speak.

'May tyla…' Before he could say any more, the dragon's snake like tail swung from behind her and knocked Harden across the valley floor. His head hit a rock and he lay unconscious on the ground. The dragon turned to him and snarled. Slowly, she began to approach him, but was stopped when she heard another voice.

'May tylanda hy Zale. Sino ryar op laywa.' Zale had stepped out from behind the boulder and looked upon the beast without fear. She turned her head and eyed him cautiously. A short, low growl came from her mouth and she tilted her head. Zale was suddenly overcome by a sharp pain in his mind. He closed his eyes and cried out in agony. He felt his knees crash to the floor. Then, as if from nowhere, there was a voice. It was in his head alongside the pain. It was soft and smooth, that of a female.

'May tylanda hy Freyna. Sino juli unu ly rass. Sino kino prosini may breya. Sanchu, ryar mil gransa das tora.' It was the dragon. She was speaking to him through his mind. The pain suddenly dissolved and he could see again.

'Zale! What is it? Are you alright?' Caden was calling to him from behind the boulder. Lysias was stood over him staring at the dragon, a newly formed sphere of cerulean energy in his hand.

'Don't attack. I'm fine. She spoke to me.' His words were soft and his breathing was sharp.

'What did she say?' Bazyli looked at the dragon fearfully from over the top of the boulder. She still had her head tilted to one side as if examining them, all the while keeping a watchful eye on the spell resting upon Lysias's fingers.

'She said her name is Freyna. She said she means us no harm and that she must protect her young. She asks that we come out from behind the boulder.' The others simple looked at him, unsure whether his translation was correct. Realising that Zale had not convinced his friends to come out from hiding, Freyna went over to Harden's body, the red from her eyes dissolving back to yellow. The group held their breath. Lysias raised his arm threateningly. She gently picked Harden up in her jaws and turned back to the others. Freyna slowly walked over to them, her long neck stretched out low to the ground. Once her head was next to Zale, she placed Harden's body on the ground and touched his head with her nose. Harden's eyes slowly opened and he started. He had not expected to wake with a dragon in front of him. Freyna glanced back at Zale, and then backed away, curling herself up around her sapphire eggs that lay in individual wells in the ground. Harden looked at Zale with surprise.

'What happened?'

'I'm not sure. Freyna knocked you unconscious and then I spoke to her in the Ancestral Tongue. I felt a terrible pain in my head and heard her voice. Now she has just made you wake up and backed away.'

'You spoke to her? Do you know how dangerous that was! You could have been killed! When a dragon connects to your mind like that, they have complete control over you.' Zale looked away from Harden's eyes shamefully. He had not known what was going to happen when he spoke to a dragon and now felt like a foolish child.

'I'm sorry, but you were unconscious and she was about to attack you. I didn't know what else to do.'

'Well, what did she say?'

'May tylanda hy Freyna. Sino juli unu ly rass. Sino kino prosini may breya. Sanchu, ryar mil gransa das tora.'

'Well that's good news! That's why she woke me then.' Harden suddenly felt a wave of pain from the back of his head and touched it to check for blood.

'She really woke you? So she truly means us no harm?' Sachiel was leaning as far out from the boulder as he dared to hear their conversation.

'You were able to translate it?' Harden asked Zale, turning to his friend.

'Yes, but I'm not sure that the others had faith in my understanding,' Zale replied with a smile.

'Come on,' said Harden. 'Zale's right. She was just protecting her children, but now knows we don't mean to harm her.' The others looked relieved and came out from hiding. Lysias released the energy back into his being, his body glowing blue for an instant. Freyna looked up with an obvious smile on her face. Zale looked at her appreciatively and noticed her eyes were no longer the fiery yellow they had been before. They were now jet-black, reflecting the starlight. As the moons crept out from behind some light clouds, Freyna's scales glistened brilliantly.

As the group began to approach Freyna, they heard the sound of a battle horn from the surrounding slopes. Freyna looked through the darkness, her eyes turning red once more, as the others searched the slopes nervously. They formed a circle, Bazyli hiding in the centre, and drew their swords. Acacia nocked an arrow in preparation for a fight. Lysias brought forth the magic he had just released and held his arms out in front of him, sparks flickering from one hand to the other. As if from nowhere, hundreds of bodies charged down the slopes. In the darkness, the warriors could not see who their enemy was. Their hearts began to race as the sound of feet pounding on the ground filled their ears above the war cries. Just as

Lysias was about to release a deadly spell to destroy almost half the army, a mass of black moved in front of the group. Freyna was standing on her hind legs, roaring as a stream of flames went spiralling into the air. Her jaws slammed shut as her forelegs crashed to the ground and her tail began cutting through the air, warding off the enemy. The sea of bodies came to an abrupt stop as Freyna stared them down. Now that there was silence, the warriors could hear a voice from half way down one of the slopes.

'Stop! They mean us no harm! Don't hurt them!' As he strained his ears, Harden realised that he recognised the voice.

'Lankoa?' The Domai was pushing past her kin to get to the front of the army. She reached the warriors panting hard from her efforts.

'Thank the stars! I warned the council of your arrival, but the guards were not informed in time. They were watching you from the slopes. Because Freyna did not harm you, they thought you had put her under a spell. I am so sorry.'

'It is quite all right. We are used to being attacked now!' Harden said with a short laugh. 'We did not put her under any spell. I tried to communicate with her, but she pushed me aside. Luckily, I had taught Zale the Ancestral Tongue so he was able to speak with her. I was about to explain to her why we are here when your army charged us.' Lankoa dropped her eyes from Harden's gaze. To their right, Freyna made a small howling noise, and then went back to her eggs. She curled herself around them protectively and kept a cautious eye on the Domai army. The air was still as the army inspected the warriors. Through the silence came another voice.

'Brilliantine!' With the word came a shower of sparks and tiny lanterns appeared like specks of dust in the sky. They hovered silently in the air. From them came a brilliant glow that filled the valley with light. The army parted, forming a path between the warriors and an older looking Domai surrounded by five others. They all wore white robes that shone against their red skin. They were taller than the Domai that made up the army and had a presence of authority. Unlike Lankoa, they had long, slender fingers rather than white claws. The Domai leading the five others appeared to be the oldest and held a staff. It had been him who had uttered the word that had brought forth the light that now filled the valley. When he reached the warriors, they bowed respectfully, presuming he was the one in charge. He bowed back and drew himself up.

'I am Ersona. I am the head of the Domai council. I am sorry for the misunderstanding, but my guards are under orders to presume any intruders are hostile. After all, times are dark of late. If it had not been for Freyna and young Lankoa, it is likely that you would be dead by now.' His voice was slow and cracked, as if he had not spoken for quite some time. Though he looked like Lankoa, his face was etched like the bark of an old oak. His head was bald and his red skin was covered in gold writings from the Ancestral Tongue. Looking around, Bazyli noticed that all of the male Domai had bald heads and, to his surprise, the army consisted of both male and female Domai. Unlike Ersona however, the entire army had blue skin and ferocious claws, just like Lankoa.

'We did not mean to trespass, but this was our only means of contacting you. Luca has sent us to retrieve one of the sacred crystals of the Land of Light. She requested that we ask for your help.' Harden bowed his head again out of respect. Ersona's face turned pensive as he thought over what the warriors asked. He nodded to himself and looked at the five other red Domai around him. They bowed their heads in agreement and Ersona turned back to Harden.

'In the depths of Snolye Forest, amidst the ceaseless brambles, there lies a clearing. Streams of light filter through the canopy above, catching on tiny creatures floating in the air. The grass sparkles with dew, each blade an emerald. A soft breeze sweeps across the ground, making the leaves dance to the music of blue birds. The surface of a river ripples as it gurgles past small rocks left from when the land used to be a series of mountains. Its crystal clear waters reflect the light around, giving a hidden cave an enchanted feel. In the centre of the clearing stands a mighty oak, taller than five men with leaves as large as an adult hand. Its branches fan out above its trunk, casting the world beneath into shadow. Squirrels and birds alike nestle together among the acorns high above the ground. As day turns to night, and the stars begin to shine, the moons cast great shadows through the forest. One lonely beam of moonlight finds its way into the clearing. It lands upon the back of a fine stag. His antlers reach up to the heavens. His majestic being stands motionless in the still air, a splash of black on his muzzle. Grey clouds roll towards the oak and release a torrent of rain. Lighting flashes across the sky like great fingers. Thunder echoes around. Animals everywhere run for shelter, but the deer stands his ground. Not a drop of water touches his fur. This is what the waters of sight have shown me, as what I currently desire most resides there. I believe they would show you the same thing.' The warriors looked at each other wondering what the old Domai meant by his words. He smiled to himself then began to explain.

'The forest I speak of lies at the top of a mountain. This mountain is where Jabari has your crystal. The stag I speak of is no deer at all.' Ersona's face became solemn. 'He is our royal in disguise, though his disguise did not fool Jabari. He has him prisoner. That is why no light touches the land around you. Just as Luca gives the Land of Light the sun, our royal, Shaynar, lets light reach out its fingertips into our valley. Without him, the Forbidden Valley shall forever be cast into shadow. We will help you, but you must swear that you will not return until you have rescued Shaynar.' The warriors looked around each other and nodded in agreement, just as the Domai council had.

'We will return your royal to you. Jabari has two of the Elements prisoner. We may be lucky and find them together.' Harden sheathed his sword at that point. They had kept themselves armed in case the Domai did not wish to help them and became hostile once more. The others followed Harden's lead and put away their weapons.

'Very good,' said Ersona, obviously relaxing now that the warriors had shown their trust of the Domai. 'I will send two of my personal guards with you. Silvio, Dempe.' As Ersona beckoned to them, the two guards came forwards and bowed. Once again, they were different to the surrounding army. They too had slender fingers rather than claws, though for what reason, the group could not tell. Their skin was a turquoise colour and they appeared stronger than those around them. They did not, however, carry weapons.

'May I ask why you do not carry a sword?' asked Caden curiously.

'They do not need weapons,' replied Ersona. 'They have been trained to use magic and magic alone to defeat the greatest of enemies. I have taught them how to fight without draining too much of their life force. Now, I am sure you are tired and wish to rest before you continue on your way. Unfortunately, none are allowed to look upon Shaynar's kingdom or learn of its whereabouts.' Ersona raised his arms and clicked his fingers. Nine female Domai came through the army carrying plates of food and drink.

'Here are some refreshments. Silvio and Dempe will stay with you as you camp here. May Disuff leave you in peace during this time of violence.' The female Domai placed the plates before each member of the group, including Silvio and Dempe, and then turned back to the army. After bowing to Ersona, they and the Domai army began to walk back up the slopes to their home. Ersona bowed farewell and walked away, the five other council members following him closely. Just before he went out of sight, Ersona turned back and spoke once more.

'A shadow may appear a haven when merely it is a shadow. A cave may appear a shadow when inside it conceals the truth.' With that, Ersona disappeared over the top of the slope, leaving the warriors even more confused than when he told the tale of the deer. The only one who did not appear puzzled by Ersona's remark was Lysias, for he had listened to him carefully and found his meaning in his other words.

Lose One, Gain Two

The warriors began to eat greedily. They had not had that much food since before leaving Damané. There were apples, pineapples, oranges, grapes, and other strange and wonderful fruits. There were also large slabs of roasted meat, though the group did not know of what animal. Silvio and Dempe watched them from a nearby rock upon which they sat.

'They do not look very strong,' commented Caden in a low whisper, giving the two Domai a side-glance. 'In fact, I think that I could knock them down with a wave of my hand.' Caden and Zale tried to stifle their laughter. Harden glared at them.

'If you really believe that, then do it.' Caden stared at Harden for a moment, trying to decide whether he should take the challenge and then nodded.

'That would not be wise,' said Lysias suddenly. Caden ignored the Kai-Rae.

'Fine. I will show you that we do not need them.' Caden got clumsily to his feet, a large grin on his face. When he reached Silvio and Dempe, they turned to face him, their eyes staring blankly into his.

'Excuse me, but I wish to prove to the rest of the group here that we are stronger than you. I know it is rude of me, but I mean, look at you. You look weaker than a twig in a storm!' Caden roared with laughter and turned to see the reaction of the group. Silvio and Dempe looked at each other and nodded. They were on their feet in a flash and sent out a beam of orange light from their hands. Instantly, Caden was thrown to the floor. Startled, and rather annoyed, he got to his feet and drew his sword. As he charged at the two Domai, Silvio simply said 'Would you like the honour?'

'Oh no dear brother, I insist, you have some fun.' Dempe casually sat back down on the rock and watched Silvio happily. Silvio stretched his arms, cracked his fingers, and reached forwards. By this point Caden was almost upon him, belting out a war cry. With a flick of Silvio's wrist, Caden's sword flew out of his hand and hung in midair. Caden came to a complete stop and stood, dumbfounded, staring at the sword. Silvio then moved his hands and the sword mimicked their movement. The blade went and poked into Caden's neck where it hovered, waiting for further instructions. Beads of sweat began to roll down Caden's face.

'Well, I see you have had much practise. You know, I was only joking.' Caden shuffled nervously, keeping his eyes fixed on the blade beneath his chin. 'May I have my sword back please?' Silvio looked at him for a moment and then let the sword fall back to the ground. The group began to laugh, including the two Domai, whilst Caden turned red.

'See Caden? They are stronger than you think. Not all battles must be fought with a sword,' said Sachiel. Harden was very amused with what the Domai had done and later told them so.

'I am glad someone has finally taught him that men are not all that powerful in this world,' said Harden laughing. The two Domai smiled back and nodded.

'We enjoyed ourselves. It has been a while since we have been challenged by a human and I am glad we can still win!' said Silvio.

'Yes, I would have thought that you men would have learnt the ways of magic by now!' laughed Dempe, suddenly realising just how primitive men still were.

'Well,' began Harden. 'There are a few of us…' He held his hand palm up before him. There, without so much as a whisper, he created a ball of blue flames. The Domai smiled and nodded.

'I am impressed. Who taught you?' asked Dempe.

'Loysa.' When they heard the name the Domai's eyes opened wide with wonder.

'He is the greatest teacher any could have,' remarked Silvio.

'Yes, he is. I am afraid to tell you however, that Jabari has also had his training. He is a mightier enemy than most know.' The Domai looked down and shook their heads gravely.

'That must be how he was able to capture our prince so easily.' With Dempe's words, the three of them stood in silence.

'Curse Jabari for doing this!' Harden said suddenly. The Domai were taken aback. Zale heard the outburst and decided it was finally time to challenge Harden.

'Why is it that you hate him so?' asked Zale. 'We all have reason to, but your hatred runs so deep nothing could ever touch it! Yes he killed your father, but there seems more to it. I would truly hate any that murdered any of my friends or family, but the extent of that hatred depends upon the manner of the killing. If it was war, then so be it, but another way? Some terrible way…what did he do to you and your father?' Everyone stared at the two of them. They stood facing each other, each trying to stare down the other. Zale could feel his heart racing. He had never demanded anything of Harden, but now he wanted to know the truth.

'I suppose you have the right to know,' said Harden at last. He reluctantly released Zale's gaze, his eyes falling upon the dusty floor. 'When I said before that Jabari killed my father, it wasn't the whole truth. In fact, it was far from it.'

'What do you mean?' Zale looked curiously at his friend.

'I'll tell you the whole story. It was many years ago. Jabari was…well, is…it's hard for me to admit this…'

'It's alright Harden, take your time.' Acacia stepped forwards and placed a hand on Harden's shoulder as she looked sympathetically into his eyes. He smiled back at her then moved away from the group. After a few moments, he turned back to address them.

'Jabari is my uncle.' Zale was shocked. It could not be true. Harden was so kind. He could not be related to a monster. Before he could interrupt, Harden raised a hand and continued.

'He was my father's brother. They were very close, and I was close to him also.' Harden looked down, ashamed.

'We lived near the Tower of Light and were good friends with Luca. Jabari had always been gifted with intelligence. He was a genius, and still is or else he couldn't have done this. He was Luca's advisor. One day, Jabari discovered how powerful the dragons are. Yes, we hear stories of their might, but you cannot truly believe it until you meet one. Well, Jabari came across hundreds when they were out on a feed. He was overwhelmed by their immense strength and ingenuity; the way they worked together and used their jets of fire to herd the prey instead of harm them and damage the meat. He wanted to use their power to protect the city, but everyone knew that they could not be trusted. Since the battle against them they have not been allies with many creatures. Without permission, he went to the dragons and spoke to them about a deal.' Seeing the confusion on Caden's face, Harden explained, 'He can speak the Ancestral Tongue. That is how he communicated with them. Just as Zale spoke to Freyna. They said they would protect the city if they were granted one human child. Foolishly, Jabari asked Luca for a child to be sacrificed "for the good of the city". Of course, she denied the request and was appalled by Jabari's behaviour. She said that she no longer wanted him as her advisor. Well, Jabari was not pleased with that. He went to my father and told him what had happened. He wanted my father to leave the city with him and live as enemies of Damané. Jabari said that they were too powerful to be controlled by such a "pathetic" queen. You see, Loysa had taught them both how to use magic at a young age, and I do not exaggerate when I say Loysa is the greatest of all magicians. I was to be instructed in the ways of magic once I reached the age of adulthood. Anyway, my father refused to leave. He knew that Luca had been right to deny the dragon's request. He and Jabari had an argument. In the end, Jabari turned to me and said, "I'm sure your son would come with me." My father was furious. He tried to get me away from Jabari, but Jabari stopped him. Next thing I knew, Jabari's voice was in my head. He was telling me to pick up my father's sword from next to the table. It was irresistible. Then Jabari said to my father "your son will do my bidding, even if you won't. Harden, kill your father!" I tried to stop myself but couldn't. My father could have used his magic against me to stop my attack, but he just closed his eyes, opened his arms, and smiled kindly. The sword pierced the left of his stomach, granting him a slow death. The look on my dying father's face still haunts me.' Harden looked away, tears in his eyes. The group were stunned. They knew there was nothing Harden could have done, but it was so awful.

'Harden, it wasn't your fault. You cannot blame yourself.' Acacia had her arm round him again.

'That's what Luca always tells me.'

'What happened next Harden?' Caden asked what everyone else was thinking.

'I woke form the spell and saw what had happened. I was distraught. My hand had slain my own father. I turned on Jabari and rushed forwards. I wanted to kill him. Before the blade came within arms reach of him, he waved his hand and I found myself frozen to the spot. "Neither you nor your father ever knew how advanced my powers were, did you?" He was laughing at me. I could see my brother at his side. He was only the age of Bazyli here. Jabari took him as his sacrifice to the dragons.' The tears now began to silently stream down Harden's face.

'So that's why Jabari was banished.' Sachiel was almost thinking out loud.

'What was it that Luca said to you before?' Harden looked at Zale with determination in his eyes.

'Luca gave me her blessing in the Ancestral Tongue. I have now been granted the right to murder my uncle with no risk of punishment, whether it be done when Jabari is armed or not.' Zale looked at Harden astounded. For a moment, he could not believe that Luca had granted such a thing. Then he thought of how much anger he would feel if his brother were ever to be murdered out of greed and selfishness. Zale nodded with understanding and held fists with Harden showing his loyalty to his friend. Lysias watched Harden carefully, a look of suspicious anger in his eyes.

'Now you know.' The group was silent; all thinking of the terrible things Jabari had done, both past and present.

'We are now even more eager to help you fight this evil,' said Silvio suddenly. 'Will you help us stop him from killing another innocent soul?' Harden brushed the tears from his face and nodded; his appreciation apparent from his face. He cleared his throat and walked over to the Domai. Eager to change the topic, Harden spoke again.

'Why is it you do not have claws like your army?' he asked curiously. The others listened to this enthusiastically, all of them desperate to think of kinder things.

'We are trained in the ways of magic. Magic needs a gentle touch, and so our claws simply became fingers, like yours. The army is not trained to use magic because their claws can be very useful for close combat and are very effective at scaring off the enemy,' replied Silvio, smiling happily, proud of his kin's strength. The rest of the group sat down in a circle, choosing to leave Harden to his conversation with Silvio and Dempe.

The three of them then began to talk about their lives and adventures and, most of all, Jabari. The Domai were keen to find out all they could about their enemy so as to be prepared for anything. They also used their knowledge to find Jabari's weaknesses, though he had few. The only one Harden could come up with was how Jabari feared being vulnerable. How they would force this upon him, they did not know.

Meanwhile, the rest of the group sat huddled together silently. Caden refused to look at anyone since his recent embarrassment with his fight with the Domai.

'I think they're amazing,' said Bazyli after a while. 'Just like you Lysias. I would love to be able to use magic.' Acacia laughed at this.

'Well,' she said, 'one day you may be able to.'

'Really?' asked Bazyli, his eyes lighting up with wonder.

'All it takes is the right teacher.'

'Why do they not say any incantations when using magic?' Zale asked glancing at the Domai talking away with Harden.

'When one is born with magic,' replied Acacia, 'they need not use words to summon it. Like Sachiel, Lysias, and I, the Domai use thoughts alone to control their powers.'

'I have heard that can be dangerous,' said Caden, deciding he ought to join in the conversation.

'It can,' said Acacia. 'It is unwise for someone who has merely been taught magic to use their thoughts to wield it. However, if you have been using it since birth, you know how to separate your thoughts and not confuse the spell.' Zale began to think back to the first spell he had done. He had found it so difficult to clear his mind. It was hard for him to contemplate how anyone could use magic so rapidly with thoughts alone. Zale became lost in his thoughts as Bazyli questioned Acacia about magic and how she used it. Caden turned to Lysias for conversation.

'So you can use magic without saying anything?' he asked.

'That's correct,' said Lysias.

'Then why did you use words when we were trapped in the pass to free my leg?'

'I was still weak. It takes less energy to use words than to use thoughts alone,' explained Lysias.

'Well, so far I have not seen any of you continually use magic. Instead, I can simply see the drain it takes upon you. I thought that as magical creatures you could keep using magic for as long as you liked.' Sachiel chose to interject at this point.

'Acacia and I,' he began, 'can use a great deal of power if we prepare our bodies for it. We did not want to keep the magic alive at the front of our minds for the journey for we knew that we would not need to use much of it until we neared the end of our task.'

'And we are weaker when not as a whole,' said Acacia suddenly. Bazyli had run out of questions for the Princess of Earth and so the two of them decided to join the other conversation. 'When the four Elements are separated,' she continued, 'our energies become singular. Once together again our individual power will be multiplied by four giving us a great advantage. That is why Jabari did not take all of us; else we would have been likely to escape using our combined strength.' Acacia stopped speaking abruptly. Talk of her friends in the enemy's grasp brought a lump to her throat. Sachiel also sat with a distant look upon his face as he thought of Nare's beauty and how he missed her so. Seeing this, Lysias chose to take over the conversation.

'I do not feel the need to use much of my power at this time,' he said quietly. 'I was going to when the Domai were attacking, but luckily Freyna put herself in my path. She would have been very much aware of what I am capable of.'

'Would you have destroyed the army?' asked Bazyli with excitement.

'Half of it, yes,' said Lysias solemnly, 'though I would never wish to cause such destruction if it was not necessary. At the time I could see no other option.'

'Could you do that to any enemy?' asked Caden.

'No,' said Lysias. 'I fear the battle to come for my strength is minimal compared to the dragons we will soon face.' They all fell silent once more. Their minds raced with thoughts of the fight to come and what great danger lay beyond it. If they could go any other way, they would all happily follow another path. As it was, there was no time to try and skirt the barrier of dragons. They would have to fight their way to the mountain, and they all knew it.

As the day wore on, though time was hard to judge beneath the unnatural stars, the warriors set up camp. Soon, they were all sat round a fire laughing and joking like the night they were reunited. Even Silvio and Dempe had decided to join them and were happily telling stories of the Domai past and listening intently to the lives of the others. As the Domai are very secretive people, they do not know much about the customs of others. They were especially interested in Lysias, for they saw him as a blood cousin, though the Kai-Rae did not divulge much about himself. The Elements told the most tales as, after Lysias, they had been alive the longest. Bazyli was most interested in this and asked the most questions.

Fatigue began to eat away at them and they decided to sleep before moving on. The bed mats were unrolled and the talking died down. Silvio and Dempe offered to take the first watch, even though there was no need seeing as the Domai army were always watching from the top of the slopes. They also had Freyna a little way off who would kill any who tried to hurt the friends of the Domai. She was curled up around her nest with her eyes closed, though the group knew that she was secretly watching them.

After an hour or so, Silvio went and woke Harden who in turn woke Zale. The two Domai were then about to rest their eyes when they heard Harden using the Ancestral Tongue.

'You can speak the tongue of old as well as wield magic?' asked Dempe.

'Yes,' replied Harden.

'I thought you had to know how to speak the Ancestral Tongue to be able to use magic?' said Zale curiously.

'Not necessarily. You can use magic simply by knowing a few words,' responded Dempe. 'What do you know of magic anyway?' he added suspiciously.

'Luca has asked me if I could teach it to Zale so that he too can learn the ways of magic,' explained Harden.

'Is that so?' asked Silvio, turning to Zale.

'Apparently. For some reason she thinks me special, though I do not know why.' As he said it, Silvio looked down at Zale's forefinger and saw his purple ring. He looked up in surprise at Harden who gave him a look that told him not to mention it. Unfortunately, Zale picked up on this.

'What is it? What are you not telling me?' He looked down at his ring and saw it glowing. 'What is so special about this ring?' Zale was becoming impatient and Harden knew he would not let it drop. With a sigh, he chose to tell Zale some of what he knew, though not the whole truth.

'Luca also has the power to see the future,' began Harden. 'She knows things that no one other than the Rostauru does. There is something about you that is special though I honestly do not know what it is. If she were to tell you, however, what ever it is you are meant to do will not happen.' Zale looked surprised. He had never thought himself special in any way, but now he knew that there was something big planned for his future.

'Alright,' he said, still suspicious that Harden had not told him everything. 'I will leave it be. Though I am shocked that Luca did not mention anything; not even that she can see future events. And you imply that the Rostauru can do the same?' Harden nodded. 'So be it. Shall we continue with the lesson?' Silvio and Dempe decided that they would stay up and help hone Zale's skills with magic, especially how to block magic. Harden then chose to focus on Zale's battle techniques. By the end of two more hours, Zale was exhausted and said he had to get some sleep. Harden, Silvio and Dempe understood. They knew that the repeated use of magic had drained much of Zale's energy and they did not wish to risk his life any more than necessary.

When Zale lay his head down on the ground he could still hear Harden, Silvio and Dempe talking in low whispers. He knew it had something to do with him and his ring but try as he may he could not stay awake and listen. In no time at all, his dreams took sway and he heard no more.

The sun was high over Damané when the group woke the next day, though above their heads stars still littered the sky. They were surprised to see that some fresh plates had been brought out with some food for them during the night.

'They came not all that long ago,' said Acacia when she saw the confusion on all the others' faces.

'They said not to worry about clearing the camp. Apparently there are some Domai waiting at the top of the slopes for us to take our leave. They will take care of everything.'

They rolled up their bed mats and gathered their belongings. It was not long before they were saying their farewells to Freyna and calling up the slope their thanks to the Domai. Silvio and Dempe led the group as they weaved their way through the rocks heading for the eastern border of the Forbidden Valley. It was a long and difficult road, mainly due to all of the rocks they had to traverse. The path had not been travelled on for many years, except of course for when Xannon used it to return to Jabari's keep. There were some areas where fresh boulders had rolled down from the slopes of the valley, blocking the way completely. The group had great difficulty in traversing the rocks before them. It was hardest for Bazyli. Harden, Zale and Caden's feet slipped on the rocks, but Bazyli could not even get over the steepness of the boulders. Struggle as he may, he just slid back down the boulder's face, annoyed with himself for being so small. Dempe, with no word at all, went to the back of the group and helped Bazyli all the way with the aid of Lysias standing upon the rocks to help pull him up and over. The boy was very grateful for this and enjoyed his chance of studying the Domai. He watched the way they were so light on their feet and how they could jump great distances with ease and not even make a sound on landing. Bazyli also noticed their great strength and how not once did Dempe strain himself pulling Bazyli up the steepest slopes. He was then also able to see the similarities and differences between the Domai and the Kai-Rae. It seemed as though Dempe was stronger than Lysias, though Lysias had lived longer and held more wisdom in his gaze. Which of the two was more adapt at using magic, Bazyli could not tell, though with what he feared was to come he knew he would soon find out.

After many hours of travelling like this, the warriors came to the base of an almost vertical slope covered in shingle. As they looked up, their eyes came upon the sky. There was a perfectly straight line stretching from horizon to horizon where the black sky of the valley met a brilliant pale blue. On the other side of the slope the group could see that clouds were skimming across the sky. They had reached the border of the valley.

It was agreed that they would make camp as best they could between the rocks and wait for dusk on the other side of the valley before climbing over. They knew that if there were any dragons on the other side waiting for them, it would be hardest for them to see during the sunset as it would cast many strange and wild shadows that would confuse them. A fire was lit, which the group huddled round wrapped in blankets as an icy wind swept through the boulders. Silvio and Dempe went off in search of some animals that they could eat, rather than having to begin back on bread again. When they returned, they had two young bucks with them.

'I am sorry, but this is all we could find. The dragons have been hunting down all of the animals. There are signs of them everywhere,' said Silvio, throwing the small deer on the ground next to the fire.

'So they are definitely there then?' asked Acacia.

'I am afraid so,' replied Dempe. 'And from the looks of things there are many of them.'

The warriors' spirits fell. They roasted what little meat there was over the fire and ate in silence. The smell of both fresh and cooked meat warmed their hearts and fed their memories, but the setting cold and soundless evening chilled them to the bone. Harden and Zale decided not to work on any magic or fighting. A dark cloud of fear had blown across all of their minds and they felt as if everything that had happened so far had been leading to that moment. None of them slept very well for thoughts of what was waiting for them just over that ridge consumed them.

As the light over the ridge slowly began to fade and the embers of the fire dwindled, the group gathered their belongings and made their preparations for battle. They knew there would be no other way into Jabari's keep than past the dragons. Zale and Harden sharpened their swords on a sharp rock they had found as Caden looked for anything that could be used as armour or a shield. There was nothing around strong enough to protect them from the deadly claws of the dragons. Acacia checked her bow to ensure it had not been damaged by the journey as Sachiel meditated to bring his magic more easily to him. Silvio and Dempe sent sparks between their fingertips to warm up the energy flow within them. Lysias simply knelt down to Bazyli who gripped his dagger tightly.

'Do not fear young one,' said Lysias kindly. 'I will be by your side the whole way. It is my duty to protect you, and that is exactly what I shall do until my last breath. I feel honoured to have been chosen for such a task.' Bazyli smiled and looked up into Lysias's kind dark eyes. The Kai-Rae made him feel safe and had become a close friend. He simply longed for Lysias to turn to him and say that it was all over and he could take him home again.

Just as the group was about to set off, horses' hooves could be heard echoing around them. They drew into a circle, expecting an attack from Jabari's army. Twenty horses then appeared at the top of a ridge to the north, fifty metres from the valley's border. They charged down the slope, heading straight towards the warriors. Straining his eyes, Zale stared in amazement at the banner the lead rider bore. It was black with a silver sword wrapped in a green serpent. He now noticed the riders were men wearing black cloaks and emerald green armour. They were men of Morsenden, Zale's home.

'They are from Morsenden! They are my people!' cried Zale. The others looked confusingly at each other.

'What are they doing here?' asked Bazyli. 'Did you send for them?'

'No. That is what's worrying. Something must have happened.'

The horses stopped ten metres in front of them and the leading three men dismounted.

'King Zale!' said the man closest to the group, removing his helmet and bowing. His face was old and there were streaks of grey in his auburn hair. The other two men also bowed. 'I bring grave news.'

'You are a king,' said Bazyli with awe. The warriors looked at Zale with surprise.

'No, I gave up the title to my brother,' said Zale with fear. He looked down upon the men with apprehension. 'Why is it that you call me king?'

'That is the news I bring,' replied the man, lowering his head. 'Your brother is dead.' With these words, Zale almost fell to the floor. He clutched his heart as if it had just been run through with a sword. Harden held him steady. Acacia put her hand to her mouth with sorrow. None of the warriors could believe the news Zale had just been brought.

'How did it happen?' asked Harden, knowing Zale could not speak for grief.

'The city of Morsenden was attacked by an army of men from the Lonely Shores. We believe them to be from Breynoris,' said a slightly younger man behind the first. He stepped forwards, obviously of lower rank to the one who had first spoken.

'I speak as an eyewitness. I am Trenith, General of Morsenden's army.' As he stepped into better light, the group could now see his face scratched with wounds inflicted by a blade. There was a deep scar across his left eye that seemed to have only recently healed.

'I remember you well, General Trenith. You were a close friend of my father, were you not?' asked Zale as he pulled himself together.

'I was. He was a great man. You would have ruled well in his stead. As it was, your brother, Lokar, ruled equally well.' Trenith dropped his eyes from Zale's.

'Now I must rule, whether I wish it or not. My brother has no heir and there is no other who can take my place.' A single tear rolled down Zale's cheek. Acacia stepped forwards and put her arms round Zale to comfort him.

'How did you find us?' asked Sachiel.

'We heard of Luca's need and knew she would call upon Harden. It was also in our knowledge that Zale travelled with Harden on his adventures. We went to the Tower of Light and she told us all she knew of your whereabouts. It took us so long to reach you as we had to traverse the top of the valley for fear of the Domai,' explained General Trenith.

'May I ask your name?' asked Caden to the first man.

'There is no need,' said Zale. 'I know who he is.' The group looked at him in surprise. Zale had made no sign of knowing who any of the men were other than General Trenith. 'He is Beornad, second to the king. He is to stay with the King of Morsenden at all times. He has come to crown me and take me back.' Beornad nodded in confirmation and gestured for the third man to come forward. He held in his hands a black velvet cushion upon which a silver crown sat encrusted with emeralds.

'Zale, son of Tre'ath, please kneel.' Zale stood up tall and walked forwards. He then knelt at the man's feet.

'I, Beornad, advisor of Morsenden, crown you rightful king of the city of swords.' He took the crown from the cushion and placed it gently on Zale's head. 'Rise, King Zale.' As he did so, all the men behind Beornad dismounted and knelt. The warriors also knelt with respect.

'Do not kneel to me my friends!' said Zale, pulling Bazyli off the floor. They rose and looked upon him in a new light. Though he was the same man as a moment before, he was now a king.

'I am no different now. We have been through so much together. Harden, you are my best friend. Acacia, Sachiel, you are the Elements! You are protectors of nature itself. Caden, you are as great a king as any, though your title may be General. The people of Forthum look to you for guidance. Silvio, Dempe, you are personal guards to the greatest of all Domai. You are wielders of magic! You are greater than most men I know. As are you Lysias. Your wisdom stretches far beyond anything I could ever imagine. And finally, Bazyli, we would be nowhere without your guidance. You are the bravest boy in all the land. You saw danger, left in safety, and yet returned when you did not have to. I am proud to be your protector.' Bazyli looked up at Zale smiling, tears beginning to roll down his face. He knew that Zale was going to leave him now to face his own enemies.

'Zale, I am sorry, but we must leave. We believe the army was sent to Morsenden by Jabari.' When Trenith said this, Zale's face turned to rage. He looked at Harden and placed a hand on his shoulder.

'Kill him Harden. For you and for me. For your father and both our brothers.' Harden nodded a look of determination on his face.

'Come King Zale. We must make hast. The army still resides in Morsenden. We only just made it out in secret to get you.'

'What? They are still there? Why did you not say before? Hurry!' Zale gave his friends one last look and then went with Beornad back to Morsenden's men waiting under the stars. They had a great black stallion, much like the one Xannon rode, waiting for him. Then, without a second thought, Zale rode off away from the Forbidden Valley's border, unaware of his ring glowing brightly upon his finger.

'Good bye Zale', whispered Harden. 'Choose your path well, or we are all doomed.'

Dragons

Hearts were heavy as the warriors began to make their way up the rocky bank of the Forbidden Valley. Zale's parting had been sudden, leaving them all in shock, not really taking in the fact that he was no longer with them. Bazyli took it worst of all. Zale had become a true friend to him, looking out for his safety ever since they left the Tower of Light. Bazyli saw him as an older brother and could not bare the thought of never seeing him again. The warriors knew that they were on a desperate quest. There were likely to be many more dragons than them, decreasing their chances of even getting near Jabari and the stolen crystal. When Caden had seen the men of Morsenden, he had secretly hoped they had come to aid in the battle, only to find they had their own battle waiting for them back in their own city. He dared not think of his sister ruling alone in Forthum and the possibility that she could also be under attack.

The Domai were the first to reach the top of the slope and chose to lie flat to the ground and look over the edge. When the others reached them, they did the same. To all of their surprise, there was nothing there. All that lay before them was a dry plain of earth, barren, unable to support life.

'There is nothing here,' said Dempe, beginning to get up. 'We must have come to the wrong place. Either that or Jabari has moved.'

'No!' shouted Bazyli, pulling him back to the ground. His eyes were wide, looking left and right. His face had turned pale and he was shaking.

'What is it Bazyli?' asked Harden. 'What do you see?'

'Dragons. They are everywhere!' There was fear in his voice. Acacia moved over to him and put her arms around him to calm him down.

'I can see them. They are like shadows giving birth to flames! Their eyes are searching, great red orbs embedded in scales. Can you not hear them? Their deafening screeches, the pounding of their wings, I cannot bare it!' Bazyli clamped is hands over his ears and shut his eyes.

'It is all right Bazyli. I am here,' said Acacia reassuringly. The warriors looked at each other nervously.

'Well, there is nothing else for it but to go down there and see for ourselves.' As Caden said it, the others nodded with approval.

'Bazyli, where is the barrier?' asked Sachiel.

'It is just over the ridge; only a few steps away.' The others could not believe that there were dragons right in front of them yet they could not see them.

'Do not fear Bazyli,' said Lysias as he moved over to the boy, 'I will protect you. Stay behind me. What ever you do, do not leave my side.'

With Bazyli's warning taken to heart, the warriors made their way down the other side of the ridge and passed through the invisible barrier. Like beacons of death, a sea of dragons blanketed the sky, glistening in what little light could filter through. From a distance, they appeared to be precious stones, each taken from the earth and gently placed amongst the clouds. However, from where the warriors stood, all the beauty held by the mass of creatures was overwhelmed by the burning hate within their eyes. Before the brave group, the dragons tested each other's strength, warning off enemies with a burst of fire.

As soon as the barrier was breached, the dragons turned as one and flew towards their enemy. The warriors dived for cover behind some rocks that had now appeared before them.

'What are we going to do?' called Acacia over chilling shrieks as the dragons sped towards them. 'There are hundreds of them!'

'We must fight!' shouted Harden over the noise. 'For Luca and the Tower of Light! For Zale! For the White Islands!' There was determination in his voice. They all feared it was the end, but Harden's words brought forth courage in them all. Even Bazyli pulled out his dagger and prepared for battle.

'We fight!' called Harden, holding his sword high above his head. The group of friends got to their feet and charged at their enemy. It was a strange sight. Four different races all fought together against a mutual enemy. There were only eight in total, all with no armour, only their swords to protect them. Acacia began to shoot down a few dragons with arrows, but it did nothing to their numbers. The dragons met the men, Domai, Elements and Kai-Rae with full force, knocking them off their feet. The battle had begun. Already, each of them was wounded with deep gashes from the dragons' talons. However, the dragons did not go unscathed. Many of them were also injured. Some even lay slain on the ground as it turned crimson with blood. Caden swung his sword back and forth as it slid over the dragons' scales, rarely piercing the flesh of their soft underbelly. As his sword slipped through one of their necks, blood shot out across his face, though this was mixed with his own. The dragon had also managed to strike, forcing its mighty talons into Caden's shoulder. He cried out in pain and fell to his knees. The dragon before him was stood on the ground, its breathing becoming faint. There was pure hatred in its eyes as it began to approach Caden, its legs, like four great trees, shaking the ground. Caden stared at it but had little strength to raise his sword. At that moment, Bazyli appeared from behind a rock and ran in front of Caden. Taken by surprise, the dragon was unable to protect itself from Bazyli's knife as he plunged it deep into its eye. With one final shriek, the dragon lay dead. Bazyli then ran over to Caden to make sure he was all right. Caden suddenly sprang to his feet and flung Bazyli on the ground as he ran forwards, sword raised. Bazyli turned to see the source of Caden's new strength to find him fighting off another dragon that had almost seized Bazyli in its jaws. Bazyli then got to his feet and stood on top of a great boulder, stabbing at the dragons above him. Lysias appeared from nowhere and pulled Bazyli from his platform. The Kai-Rae pushed upwards with a great wave of energy, knocking back five dragons that threatened to snatch Bazyli from the ground. The creatures' necks snapped with the force of the magic thrust upon them and their mighty bodies crashed to the ground. One of their lifeless tales whipped out towards the boy. Lysias threw himself on top of Bazyli and focused all his might on creating an invisible barrier to protect them from the tale's bladed tip.

'I told you not to leave my side,' said Lysias panting from the energy he had dispelled.

'Thank you,' whispered Bazyli. Lysias pulled the boy to his feet and dragged him to an area where he was sheltered by two boulders.

'You can defend yourself from here. I will be right there,' Lysias pointed to a spot just a few metres away. Bazyli nodded with determination and raised his dagger to the skies. Lysias unsheathed two long, thin, curved swords from his side and charged at three dragons coming his way. He swung the blades with deadly precision, ready to await the next onslaught.

Sachiel had just slain a great scarlet dragon when he heard his voice being called out over the sound of metal against scales.

'Sachiel!' called Acacia as she fought off three dragons.

'What is it?' called back Sachiel from behind a sea of blue scales. He fired a ball of exploding cerulean energy into the eyes of the beast before him.

'I am sorry we could not get back Nare and Baaron. I want to thank you for always being there for me. I love you Sachiel. I always will.'

Tears welled up in her eyes as a dragon's wing clipped her shoulder, sending a sharp wave of pain down her arm. As it drew back for the final blow, she had just enough time to gather her energy and send forth a beam of green light that hit the dragon in the chest, leaving it dead on the floor. The other two dragons took to the air, making way for their uninjured companions.

'I love you too Acacia,' called Sachiel as he thrust his sword deep into the heart of a dragon approaching from his left. The battle was without hope. Each time a dragon lay dead, more and more came. Bazyli was thrown to the ground as he was hit with a tail in the stomach.

'Bazyli! No!' screamed Harden when he saw the boy motionless amongst some rocks. His mind was filled with rage and he killed five more dragons in an instant, but his strength soon faded again. His arms grew weak as blood trickled down his face from a gash on his brow. Two dragons landed just in front of him and began to prowl forwards, smelling his fear. He turned and jumped on a boulder behind him. The dragons paused for a moment, but then charged at him. Just as they opened their jaws, Harden leaped forwards and landed on one of their backs. The dragon let out a mighty shriek as the other's teeth snapped shut on air. Harden sunk his sword through the dragon's head and jumped off just in time. The other dragon had swung its tail at his head but missed. It raised itself up on its hind legs in desperation, leaving its underbelly unprotected. Harden took the opportunity and lunged forwards, sword first, killing the beast instantly. He stood, breathless, trying to gather his strength, just to find another dragon flying straight towards him. With a great effort, he raised his sword and went back into the heart of the battle.

Silvio and Dempe stayed together, each trying not to let the other lose too much energy from using their magic. Though they were trained to survive many hours continually using the mystical energy against their common enemy, the onslaught from the dragons was too great. They had each conjured magical golden bows that barely seemed to exist as they shimmered in the Domai's hands. Silvio aimed at a russet coloured dragon that flew towards him and drew back his arm. As he released his hand, an arrow magically appeared and brought down the creature. Dempe did the same to a grey and an ashen dragon that prowled towards him on the ground. Both fell to the floor with a loud thud. Though the brothers were keeping the dragons before them at bay, others still circled round behind them and struck them in their backs, tearing the skin from their shoulders to their hips. The wounds drained their energy, making it more and more difficult to conjure their weapons. Dempe chose to switch to stunning spells so that the others could slay the dragons as they lay motionless on the floor. He could not keep this up however as there were too many for him to continually hit. If he got his aim wrong, his magic would slide off the dragons' scales, just like a mortal weapon. As magical creatures, this was the dragons' main defence, though they could not use magic themselves.

Lysias was now protecting Bazyli's motionless body. The boy had been thrown by the tail away from where the Kai-Rae had left him to a more open area of rocks. There was no protection from the bursts of flames that were now being sent in his direction. *Rancorah!* Lysias created a wall of water around Bazyli in an attempt to keep out the burning flames. He continued to slice his swords through his enemies' flesh as he struggled to maintain it. The Kai-Rae had to dive from side to side as a dragon turned its back on him and cut through the air with his tale. Lysias's swords did little harm to the heavily scaled weapon. Instead he just used more and more of his energy. The dragon lifted its tale high for an instant as if to bring it down upon Lysias. The Kai-Rae took his chance and dived between the dragon's back legs. His body slid across the dusty ground, placing him beneath the dragon's chest. Without hesitation, Lysias thrust his swords into the dragon's belly and rolled out to safety. The great beast collapsed to the floor, no spark left in its staring eyes. Seeing his companions struggling and Bazyli still motionless within his watery shelter, Lysias reached up to the sky and pushed forwards with all his might. 'Close your eyes!' he called to the others desperately. *Taydira!* A rippling wall of crimson energy rushed towards the circling dragons. The warriors all shielded their eyes. Those dragons on the ground saw this and instinctively did the same. As the energy reached the dragons in the air, the creatures were instantly blinded and screeched in agony, flying upwards in search of safety. Lysias fell to his knees, the wall of water crashing to the ground behind him.

Even with the momentary relief, the warriors knew in their hearts that it was the end, but none of them would have wanted to be anywhere else. The dragons on the ground turned back to face them, snarling in anger for the colossal attack. They prowled forwards, six of them singling out Lysias. Dempe ran towards the Kai-Rae, somersaulting over a dragon between them, and conjured a shimmering blue whip. It lashed out at the dragons, which were now almost upon Lysias, scaring their sides and faces. The magical rope created wounds that would not heal. Blood seeped effortlessly from between the dragons' scales. They roared in agony and fell to the ground, their breathing strained.

Caden and Harden were at the front of the others as they chose to form a tight group. The two men readied themselves with their swords as Sachiel and Silvio fired countless spheres of icy magic at the approaching dragons. It numbed the creatures' ability to create fire, protecting the group from that threat. Meanwhile, Acacia stood on a raised area of ground behind them, bow raised, releasing arrow upon arrow into the midst of the nearing enemy. Her aim was precise, allowing each loosed arrow to slide easily into the soft skinned necks of the creatures. This did not keep them back for long though. All that the group achieved was to anger the dragons further.

Above them, the dragons regained their sight and charged even more ferociously towards their enemy below. The ground assault was upon them all. Harden and Caden were slicing through the air with their swords, the mighty blades deflecting off the dragons' scales. The creatures were using their greater strength and weight against the warriors, knocking the men with their sides and fiercely protecting the soft skin of their underbellies. The companions knew they were going to die for a cause each of them believed in. They called out their farewells as Caden fell to the ground, the smell of earth filling his nostrils as blood ran from his injured leg. Lysias dragged himself to his feet and continued to slice his way through the sea of scales before him, side by side with Dempe, but he knew that soon there would be too many dragons around them to fight off.

Just as the warriors thought the dragons would send them to their deaths, they heard the faint sound of a horn blowing on the breeze. The dragons began to retreat in fear back up to the sky. The warriors were confused as they heard war cries coming from behind them. As the dragons fled, the group turned to see an army of at least five thousand heading towards them from the valley slope. This, however, was not an army of men. It was the Dûr'baëns. Luca's allies had arrived.

The Dûr'baëns were like nothing any of the warriors had seen before. They had the torso of a man and the body of a horse. The lead Dûr'baën was male with long, curly black hair and the body of a black stallion. He had a bow slung across one shoulder and a belt holding a sword around his waist. As they approached, the warriors noticed that the army was made up entirely of female Dûr'baëns, except for the leader. They all appeared to be incredibly strong and carried similar bows and swords in the same manner as their leader. Each was extremely beautiful and they all seemed to be relatively young. There were groups that wore different coloured bands around their heads that the warriors presumed indicated different ranks. The group staggered gratefully over to them, Harden holding up Caden and Lysias bringing Bazyli who had woken soon after the water had washed across his face.

'You are the warriors sent by Luca I presume,' said the male Dûr'baën in a deep voice.

'Yes we are,' said Harden. 'You could not have come at a better time. You are the Dûr'baën army?'

'We are indeed. Luca must have told you about us. My name is Zilnar. I lead this army.' As Zilnar said it, five Dûr'baëns came up behind him, each with a different coloured band around their heads. Harden realised that the colours must represent different regiments and that these were their commanders.

'Zilnar, the dragons are regaining their courage. They will not wait much longer. We must prepare for battle.' The Dûr'baën who spoke wore a blue band and had long golden hair that shone beneath the rising moons.

'Jameela is right. We must attend your wounds and prepare. There are more of us now. Do not fear. We will live through this.' Zilnar spoke with such confidence that Caden let go of Harden and stood up tall.

'I am ready to fight. The city of Forthum is forever in your debt.'

'Calm now General Caden of the Old City. You are wounded more than the rest. We will fight this battle without you at first. As soon as you are bandaged up, you may join us.' With that, Caden and Bazyli were taken towards the bottom of the slope that the Dûr'baëns had recently charged down and attended to.

'Harden, I am aware that you have the need to get past these beasts and go in search of both the crystal and the missing Elements,' said Zilnar.

'Yes. How is it that you know our names?' asked Harden curiously.

'I have had scouts following you for some time now. I am sorry we could not join you as soon as we were told of your destination but there was trouble in the mountains. The men from the Lonely Shores attacked us. We forced them to retreat, but I am afraid they have come to Jabari's keep to help protect him.' Harden's anger grew. He had to walk away from Zilnar for a moment to stop from screaming out with rage.

'Will he not stop?' asked Harden angrily. 'Will he continue like this until he has destroyed the entire White Islands?'

'Please Harden,' said Zilnar. 'Do not let Jabari get to you like this. You cannot win a battle if you lash out in rage. You must keep a cool head and use tactics. Else you will drop your guard and be killed.'

'I know. I am sorry. It is just that Jabari has stolen one of the sacred crystals, killed Zale's brother and now attacked you. If anyone deserves to die today, it is him!'

'You are right Harden, but I must tell you my plan quickly, before the dragons attack again, or else you shall never have your chance of revenge.'

'What is it?' asked Harden, calming himself down slightly.

'My army and I will distract the dragons whilst you and your friends head towards the Maze of Rocks over there.' Harden had not noticed the maze and was grateful that he had been warned of it. He and Zilnar quickly discussed what was to be done and then Harden relayed it to his fellow warriors.

Before long the sun set completely but to everyone's surprise, the dragons did not attack. The Dûr'baën army stood motionless, waiting for a wave of scales to head towards them, yet nothing happened. Instead, the dragons landed at the base of the mountain and watched them. Half of the dragons curled themselves up and went to sleep whist the others stood guard. The Dûr'baëns and the warriors looked at each other nervously, not sure what to do. After an hour of waiting, it was decided that the army would get some rest, leaving one regiment to keep watch. Harden and Zilnar spoke for a while, discussing what the dragons may be doing, but they had no answer for it. Soon, they lay down to a restless sleep, waking every so often to see if there had been any movement.

Over in the city of Morsenden, a great battle was taking place. The men from the Lonely Shores were burning down all buildings as women and children fled to the mountains. Zale, followed by his army, rode through the streets and cut down all in his path. The men from the Lonely Shores were outnumbered and fled to the Plains of Grator that opened out beneath the slopes of the mountain that the city of Morsenden resided on. Zale led his army after them, cries of victory filling his ears. When they reached the plains however, all cheers ended as the men from the Lonely Shores stopped and turned. Both armies stood facing each other, neither advancing nor retreating. The army before Zale suddenly parted and through their middle walked a dark, cloaked figure. He stopped half way between the two armies and removed his hood. His scar on his face shone silver in the light as he called out to Zale.

'I am Xannon. I have heard rumours of your training in the ways of magic, young Zale.' His voice was deep and enchanting, as if his words were some form of spell. Zale's eyes turned to that of hate. 'I would be most interested to see what it is you can do.' A smile flashed across the sorcerer's face and his eyes sparkled.

'You do not fool me, servant of Jabari,' cried Zale. The title removed the smile from Xannon's face, replacing it with a snarl. 'If it is a fight you wish for then so be it. Just remember this; even if I do fall, my men will drive you out of these lands and send you back to the hovel you came from.' Zale then rode forwards, now able to see Xannon's anger. His plan had worked. One must be calm to perform magic and never lash out in anger. With Xannon's mind filled with rage, the magic would not come to his fingertips so easily. When

Zale reached him, he dismounted and faced the sorcerer. His horse galloped back to the Morsenden army. The two opponents stared at each other for a moment and then Xannon, without warning, muttered something beneath his breath and hit Zale with a blast of orange light. Zale stumbled backwards and found his head to be bleeding. Muttering a stunning spell, *Yandarl,* Zale reached forwards with his arms. From his fingertips came a shower of blue light that made Xannon fall to his knees.

'You have been taught well,' Xannon remarked as he pushed himself up off the floor. 'However, I think you forget that, as a sorcerer, I have lived with magic my whole life. *Restrarni!*' Xannon reached out his arm, sending fine golden threads towards Zale. When they reached the new king, they wrapped round his body, restraining all of Zale's limbs. Zale closed his eyes in concentration. He knew the words he needed to release himself, but also knew that if he were not careful the spell would use up a lot of energy. Xannon drew his sword and began to walk towards Zale. Sure he was ready, Zale opened his eyes. *Relinqui mi verna dan trava tak tor zifarla.* The golden threads unravelled and shot back towards Xannon. In a panic, Xannon dropped his sword and crossed his hands in front of his face. *Dienta!* The golden threads fell to the floor and vanished. Xannon glared at Zale. Without hesitation, Zale reached forwards, muttering *Pi'lira!* Xannon raised his arm as if to block the spell but was still forced backwards. He stumbled to the floor, shock spread across his face. He looked at his shaking hands and saw his veins turning black. Zale looked at this with horror. He had merely used a spell of force against the sorcerer. Xannon pulled himself to his feet and shook himself off, as if pushing the image of his darkening skin to the back of his mind. Zale raised his arm again, this time sending out a shower of silver sparks towards his opponent. Xannon simply brushed the spell to one side and continued his approach. Zale tried again, but the sorcerer once more pushed the magic away. Then a strange thing happened. Both Zale and Xannon sent forth beams of light simultaneously, each conjured by a different incantation. The blue and the orange collided and froze, creating a bridge between the two of them. Zale pushed forwards with his mind and found that the blue light went closer towards Xannon. Seeing this, Xannon also pushed forwards and proved to be stronger. The orange light went far beyond half way between them and came inches from Zale's hands. Zale could feel his strength failing and found he could not force his power any further forwards. The world around him was turning black. The magic being released from his hands began to burn, turning a bright white. Xannon starting advancing again, all the while maintaining his spell. Images began to flash through Zale's mind of Damané and Luca, his brother and his father, Alana and the Rostauru, Harden and the others. The orange glow was almost upon him when his mind decided that enough was enough. It was up to him to save his people. There was no one else there. Harden was not going to appear and come to his rescue. There was only him and Xannon. Not even the armies could do anything. Zale then pushed forwards with all of his strength and the blue light went straight towards Xannon. It hit him full on and sent him flying through the air. Xannon landed painfully among the men of the Lonely Shores who fled with fright. Their leader had been defeated; or so they thought. After a few moments, Xannon staggered to his feet and stared at Zale. His whole body was shaking. The darkness within his veins had spread right up his arms now.

'We will meet again, you and I.' Xannon's voice was weak. He turned and, with a flash of light, disappeared. The army of Morsenden gave a roar of triumph and Trenith, who had been watching fearfully, began to ride over to Zale. Zale turned to look at his people, his face pale. Raw blisters erupted on his palms and sweat rolled down his cheeks. His eyes began to stare and, with no strength left in him, he fell to the ground, breath no longer leaving his lips.

Harden, Caden, Acacia, Sachiel, Lysias and Bazyli all woke with a start. The image of Zale's pale face still burned in their minds. They looked fearfully at one another and knew immediately that they had all had the same dream. They sat in silence, the stars still above them. None of them wanted to admit that they had seen Zale die. As Bazyli lay back down to sleep, silent tears rolled down his cheeks. The others also tried to fall back into dreams, but the thought of Zale haunted their minds.

More Than a King

A woman ran out across the Plains of Grator, her brown hair flowing delicately in the breeze, and reached Zale's body even before his army. She turned him over in her arms and held him, tears streaming down her face. Zale's men dismounted and removed their helmets in respect.

'No,' whispered the woman. 'You cannot leave us now. Your house shall not die this night.' She brushed his dark hair away from his eyes and softly kissed his forehead. The beautiful lady pulled a white cloth from the sleeve of her dress and used it to mop away the dirt and sweat from his white face. The fallen king was motionless in her arms. She hugged Zale's body close to her and quietly sobbed into his shoulder.

'Please,' said General Trenith gently, 'there is nothing more we can do.' The woman gradually pulled away, but to Trenith's surprise, her face was not sad, but filled with wonder. It had not been his words that ceased her tears, but the ring on Zale's finger, which now shone brightly. The burns on his palms faded away and some colour came back into his cheeks. Zale took in a deep breath and opened his eyes.

'It is a miracle!' cried one of the soldiers.

'I would never leave you,' said Zale in a strained voice. His breathing was laboured, but his strength was growing. The woman smiled and wiped away her tears. 'It's good to see you, Queen Synae.'

'My title was removed with the death of my husband, good king,' she said with a smile.

'You shall always be a queen. My brother's death would never take that from you.' Synae nodded appreciatively and helped Zale to his feet. The entire army before them knelt. Synae took a step back and curtsied, a broad, mocking smile on her face. Zale bowed to her in return and then realised he did not quite have his strength back and staggered sideways. Trenith caught him before he fell.

'I think, my King,' said Trenith, 'that you should get some rest.'

'That sounds like a fine idea,' said Zale, 'but there is no time. Have the men from the Lonely Shores truly left?'

'They have,' replied Trenith.

'Then we must help in the battle against Jabari. I feel there is something I must do here first however.'

'What is that, my Lord?' asked Synae.

'I am still Zale, the boy you grew up with Synae. Call me by my name.'

'As you wish,' she said grinning. Zale laughed briefly and thought of how he had forgotten her beauty. She stood proudly before him, her green eyes sparkling in the light of the setting sun. Her black dress of mourning hugged her pale skin, reminding Zale that, although she looked upon him with a smile, the loss of her husband was all too recent.

'I must pay my respects to my brother,' Zale said after a moment.

'Then we shall take you back to the city,' said Trenith. With a supporting arm around his king, Trenith helped Zale walk back to the city of Morsenden. As they walked through the streets, the people of the city cheered and bowed respectively, only pausing briefly to admire their new king before returning to tending wounds and putting out the last of the burning houses. The small wooden homes had lined the base of the city so as to be close to the farmlands. The timber now smouldered beneath the sun. The main stone structures of the city had not been affected by the battle as most were carved into the base of the mountain upon which the city resided. It was a long winding walk though the tiers of the city to reach the Black Palace, the second highest structure within the settlement. Above it were the armouries and training grounds for the soldiers. This protected them from attack and allowed direct access for the palace guards if needed during an assault on the city.

A great ivory archway stood as the entrance to the palace. The interior was the same throughout; black speckled marble walls and white marble floors. The group of men slowly walked through the long halls, each person they passed bowing respectively to their king. There was an unnatural silence within the palace. All who walked its halls were dressed in black, like shadows flickering in the candlelight. Colossal paintings hung on the walls, each depicting a different tale of war, hunting, and the ways of Morsenden's people. Zale glanced to his right to see a great oak door reinforced with iron. He thought back to younger days when he would sneak through it to the magnificent gardens that rolled out down the side of the sandy mountain. A scent of lilies lingered in its wake as royal gardeners prepared the grounds for the upcoming funeral just beyond its wooden beams.

A short distance on from the gardens' entrance was the throne room. It was significantly different from the rest of the palace in that it had ivory pillars running down its length, each carved with a different ruler of the past. Zale glanced sadly towards the most recently added pillar. He knew it awaited carving with the figure of his brother.

'Please,' Zale said to Trenith, Synae, and the group of guards that had followed him in, 'leave me. I will call you when I am ready. Prepare the army. It will not be long until we leave.' Trenith bowed and left, ushering the guards out with him. Synae placed a concerned hand on Zale's shoulder and kissed him lightly on his forehead. Then she turned and followed the steps of Trenith out of the room. Zale placed a hand briefly on the new pillar and then walked over to the ivory throne that stood at the back of the room on a raised marble platform. He sat on the black velvet seat and ran his fingers down the arms of the throne. It felt cool and smooth beneath his skin

'Why did all this have to happen?' he asked the empty room. His voice echoed softly around him. He placed his head in his hands and began a prayer for his brother, as is tradition when mourning the loss of a loved one in the Black Palace.

'When the sand falls upon the dune, it knows which side will best allow the hills to grow,' said a strong male voice.

'What?' said Zale, lifting his head and looking around the room. He could not see anyone there.

'One of many answers, though one so true,' said the voice again.

'Who's there? Show yourself!' commanded Zale, standing up and looking about him for the source of the voice. His eyes fell upon the ring on his finger and saw it glowing. 'Silvarna?' he questioned the room.

'Now the sands have stopped altogether and await their calling. Only one may choose the light from the dark,' replied the voice.

'Why didn't you just say it was you?' Zale said, slumping back into the throne with relief. 'Why are you always so mysterious?'

'In the shadows or beneath the burning sun?' continued the voice. 'The wild stallion runs more free than the ox, though the ox has the ability to move earth and still have freedom. Become a leopard? Or lead the pack of wolves. Freedom over ropes? Solitude over love? Does the freedom overpower the love? Or are the ropes strong enough to hold you together?' A hidden door suddenly opened in the wall on Zale's right. He stared at it in wonder.

'I do not understand. What must I do?' Zale's voice trembled slightly. He feared to go through the door. So much had happened in recent days that he wanted only to focus on the battle ahead and not have a new journey thrust upon him.

'Only one can give them their calling,' said the voice. 'Choices are lonely things.' Zale rose from the throne and walked cautiously towards the secret door. He knew that Silvarna was guiding him towards it. A strange light filtered through the gap, highlighting specks of dust in the air. Zale reached forwards and pushed the door fully open. Before him was a stone passageway, similar to the one Luca had taken him down all those suns ago, but this one led upwards. He unsheathed his sword and began to make his way along the tunnel, turning back every once in a while to make sure no one was following him. The light gradually grew in intensity until it was nearly blinding. Some time passed before the passage opened out onto a hidden room. It was the largest room Zale had ever seen. Its domed ceiling was decorated with coloured paintings of battles and grand cities of stone. Pillars thicker than tree trunks spiralled up to join the paintings, adding their own images to the room. The walls were of white marble, covered with golden writings in the Ancestral Tongue. The floor was made of solid gold, reflecting daylight around the room that came from oval holes in the ceiling. Zale tried to see where the holes led to, but the light was too blinding.

'How is there light?' he muttered to himself. 'The sun must have gone down by now.' He looked around the room with awe. It was the most magnificent structure he had ever seen. After his eyes had fully adjusted to the light, he noticed a monument in the middle of the room. Sheathing his sword, he silently walked over to it, unable to take his eyes off it. It was a narrow pillar, carved out of pure ruby. It rose to Zale's middle where it was capped with a hand made of white gold. The hand lay open with a mighty sword balanced carefully in the centre of the palm. The hilt was encrusted with sapphires and emeralds.

'I must make a choice, mustn't I?' Zale asked the room. There was no response. The air around the sword shimmered. Zale reached forwards and found that he could not move his hand through the invisible barrier. He moved away from the monument and began trying to decipher the writing on the wall. The symbols were unfamiliar, though he knew they were indeed in the Ancestral Tongue. Instead, he chose to study the images on the pillars and the ceiling. It was then when he realised that they told stories.

'But they're not right,' he said to himself. 'The stories are wrong. There's Harden and I battling the Nicars. It did not happen that way. There were only five, not twenty. And there; I did not drag my friends out of the desert. I tricked them into following me. How have these stories been painted already? They have not yet been told.' He moved about the room, from pillar to pillar, pointing out all of the mistakes in the stories. Then he stopped, realisation flickering across his face. 'This is how they would be told if I left. The truth would be lost. The stories would be glorified to make me seem more heroic. If I choose freedom, a life away from responsibility, then my people will never know the truth, and I would be alone. I must become the ox. I will be able to make a difference in this world. Change things for the better.' He looked back at the sword. Its presence seemed to call out responsibility, making Zale think to times ahead with him bound to serve under Morsenden's flag. Then some movement on the wall to his left drew his eyes away. A new image began to form. It showed Zale defeating Jabari single-handedly, his army surrounding him with admiring faces. Once again,

Zale looked to the sword, then back to the new image of him as a hero. After a moment's hesitation, he turned to leave, thinking of how much in the world he had not yet seen and how wonderful it would be to be thought of in that false light. Then he thought of his friends, fighting alone against the dragons. He thought of the people he had seen in the streets and how their eyes were filled with hope, even though their homes were burnt. Then he felt the anger within him for Jabari and all he had done to the people of the White Islands. He turned back to the monument and walked swiftly to the sword. He knew the responsibility that came with taking up that sword, but for the first time in his life he was not afraid to be a leader. With words from the Ancestral Tongue, Zale said in a bold voice, 'I vow to lead my people. I vow to do all to protect them. Sealed with magic, I will forever hold to that promise!' With that, his hand passed smoothly through the magical shield. He took the sword into his hand and held it high in the air.

'I have made my decision!' he called to the air. The ground beneath him began to tremble, yet he continued to stand there, holding up the sword. The pillars started to fall, one by one. The walls were crumbling around him. Still he stood there. The monument fell to the floor and smashed. One by one, the paintings were destroyed. The room around him collapsed and an even brighter light filled his eyes. A brilliant white horse reared up in front of him. He put a hand protectively to his eyes.

'Silvarna?' Zale whispered, awestruck. He heard hoofs collide with the floor and saw a white mare before him. He smiled to himself and patted the horse. Zale found the source of light to be the two moons high in the sky. The collapsing of the room had opened a hollow in the face of the mountain just above Morsenden's armouries. He could now see all the people of the city staring up at him. Zale mounted the horse and raised the sword high into the air once more. The people below him cheered. A massive cry rose up.

'Hail King Zale! Hail the King of all men!' Zale looked questioningly down upon his people. King of all men? He was only king of Morsenden.

There was a mountain path that led down to the palace where Zale found his army congregated.

'Are you ready to leave, my Lord?' asked Trenith.

'Yes,' replied Zale. 'Why did they call me the King of all men?'

'Because, my Lord,' said a woman's voice, 'you hold the sword of men.' Synae stepped forwards.

'I do not understand,' said Zale.

'There is an ancient lore that states: *Any he who bears the sword of men has put his love of his people before all else. For this, he is worthy to rule all the people of the land. He can be trusted with any secret and shall lead the people well, until his final day, when the secret citadel is restored and the sword is hidden once more.*' Zale looked away for a moment.

'You say this is an ancient lore?' he asked at last. As his mind raced, he thought back to an old book he had once read during his childhood. Those words seemed to echo in his mind.

'Yes. Have you heard of it?' asked Synae curiously. Zale's mind went back to the Prophecy of Man the old king had told him and his friends. He shook off the thought and brought himself back to the matter at hand.

'We must help those that are attempting to fight the dragons,' he said in an authoritative tone. 'How many do we have?'

'Twelve hundred strong,' replied Trenith.

'Good. General Caden has two thousand more split between Damané and Forthum. General Trenith, take three hundred to Forthum and ask for five hundred of Caden's men to accompany you to Damané. Call upon the aid of his neighbouring cities as well, and any of ours that have shown their allegiance in the past. If they do not agree…'

'They will agree,' interrupted Trenith.

'How can you be sure?' asked Zale.

'There are already rumours that you bear the lilac ring. Now you hold the sword of men, the eternal flames will have reignited. There is one in every great city. The world of men already knows you have arrived.' Trenith smiled at his king and mounted his horse.

'Well then, let's not disappoint them,' said Zale cheerfully. Hope had filled his heart once more. 'I will take the rest of the army to Damané. We must move with haste. Beornad!' The second to the king stepped forwards. 'You must remain here and watch over the city. Jabari shall not attack now. He believes me to be dead. There is no point in him wasting any more men.'

'Of course,' said Beornad, bowing respectively.

'Oh, and look after to this for me.' Zale threw him his crown.

'But, my Lord!' protested Beornad as he caught it clumsily, 'the King must always wear his crown!'

'I am off to battle, not dinner,' laughed Zale.

'If that is so, my Lord, then take this.' Beornad handed Zale a horn, which Zale took appreciatively. 'This shall call your army to you when you are in desperate need.'

'Thank you,' said Zale. He then turned to his men. 'We ride for Damané!' With that, Zale's army mounted their horses and he led them out of the city and turned west.

'Hold on my friends,' Zale muttered to himself as he rode. 'Just a little longer.'

Reinforcements

The different regiments of Dûr'baëns had kept watch all night, switching every few hours to allow each of them some rest. Their hooves had scrapped away most of the sandy film that clung to the barren earth. As they guarded the sleeping warriors, they had gone off in groups to practise their face-to-face combat, the sound of metal against metal ringing in the air. The sight of the Dûr'baën army was intimidating, even to the dragons that now lay peacefully on the other side of the open plain. A few of the mighty creatures paced quietly, carefully watching the Dûr'baëns prepare for the imminent battle. Their polished scales glistened in the light of the moons. One of the females, a beautiful crimson creature, was more restless than most. She snarled and snapped her jaws, scrapping the ground with her colossal claws. She soon took her heavy form to the back of the sleeping giants where her growls could still be heard.

When the sun had risen, it still found them there, army watching army, neither daring to attack. It appeared as though the dragons were formulating a plan, though what it could be the Dûr'baëns did not know. Dempe and Silvio took one of the Dûr'baën regiments out in search of food for the entire army. When they returned, the dragons lifted their heads to the smell of freshly killed meat and sent their own scouts into the air to gather food. The Dûr'baëns thought the dragons were making their move so jumped to their feet and prepared to battle. Yet still, the dragons kept their distance.

The day lingered on, and a long day at that. The sun was in the sky for over nineteen hours. Harden grew impatient, thinking of nothing other than Damané slowly dying and the strange dream he and the others had had. Acacia went over to him and they began to talk quietly.

'You do not think it was real, do you Harden?' she asked, hoping for reassurance.

'We all saw it,' he said sadly. 'The only way for us to have the same vision is if the one close to death has sent it to us. Zale must have wanted us to know so that we did not have a false hope.' He lowered his head trying to hide his tears. Acacia put her hand on his shoulder.

'But it cannot be true,' she said softly. 'Luca has seen that he comes with us. I will not believe that her premonition was false. She has never been wrong.' Harden looked at her sympathetically and nodded. He thought it best to let Acacia believe that Zale was alive, even though he knew deep down that he could not be. She left him to his thoughts and went over to Sachiel. They all tried to turn their thoughts back to the battle that awaited them.

It was common belief that as soon as night fell, the dragons would finally attack, well rested and fully healed from their previous battle. As the sun began to disappear behind a grand mountain, at the base of which the dragons slept, the Dûr'baëns gathered their weapons and stood facing them, ready for the creatures to take flight. When the moons had risen high in the sky however, the dragons remained quiet on the ground as if waiting for something.

That night was just as long as the day. The warriors sat in a group just to the left of the Dûr'baën army, talking in low whispers, trying to decide what to do. Zilnar sat with them, just as concerned.

'Any idea what the dragons are doing?' asked Sachiel.

'None. They seem to be waiting for something,' replied Zilnar, looking cautiously over at the mass of scales under the moon.

'Perhaps they are waiting for us to attack them,' suggested Caden. 'And if you ask me, I think we should. We have to get through to that mountain behind them. That has to be where Jabari is hiding. Have you noticed its unusual plateau? It looks as if someone has come along and cut off the peak.'

'Yes. I have never seen anything like it before. I do not even think myself capable of creating such a landscape,' said Acacia pensively. 'But I do not think we should attack the dragons. I am aware of Damané slowly fading, but we cannot risk dying now. We have come too far and there is too much at stake. We need the diversion that Zilnar has offered us.' Zilnar bowed his head appreciatively.

Whilst the others spoke, Bazyli sat away to their left on a rock, listening to all that was being said and trying to put bits together. Lysias sat a little way from him. The Kai-Rae had not left his side since the battle, punishing himself for allowing Bazyli to be struck by the dragon's tale. Bazyli tried to tell him it was not his fault, but Lysias knew deep down that if it happened again it could be the end of the boy's life. As Bazyli looked out over the sea of dragons, he thought he saw some movement on one of the slopes of a valley that joined onto the Forbidden Valley. It was as if something were moving towards the dragons. He saw another movement, and then another. There were creatures joining the dragons.

'Lysias, Silvio, Dempe, can you come here?' The two Domai and the Kai-Rae went over to Bazyli and followed his gaze. Meanwhile, the rest of the group continued to talk.

'What I do not understand,' said Harden, 'is why the dragons did not just kill us before you, Zilnar, arrived.'

'Maybe they had orders from Jabari. He would know that the Elements are with us,' suggested Caden. 'If either of them were to die, so would Nare and Baaron.'

'That may be true,' said Harden, 'but he would not need Nare or Baaron if we are no longer a threat. It would take too long for anyone else to reach Jabari other than us in order to save Damané.'

Over by the rock, Bazyli spoke with the Domai and Kai-Rae in a quiet voice, as if not to arouse suspicion in the dragons.

'Your eyes are better than mine. Do you see what I see?'

'Where?' Just as Dempe asked, he saw a group of ten men slide down the slope and hide behind the dragons that lay motionless, watching the Dûr'baën army.

'Men?' muttered Lysias.

'They are men! They are joining the dragons!' Silvio's voice alerted the warriors who all stood up and looked out. Sure enough, there were men moving in large groups through the darkness towards the dragons and joining their ranks.

'They are the men from the Lonely Shores!' exclaimed Zilnar. 'They have come to help the dragons!'

'There appear to be a great many of them,' said Sachiel, a note of fear in his voice.

'Yes,' said Zilnar pensively. 'There are more than those who attacked the Dûr'baëns.' Acacia let out a short gasp and tears filled her eyes.

'What is it?' asked Sachiel.

'Zale.' Harden had also had the same thought.

'What do you mean?' asked Bazyli, half guessing his answer and beginning to shake.

'For the men from the Lonely Shores to have swelled in numbers,' began Harden, his voice breaking slightly, 'then the ones in Zale's city must have joined them. The only way for that to have happened is if Zale is dead.' A deep silence fell upon the warriors, all of them caught up in thoughts of Zale lying slain on his new thrown. The group looked out sadly towards the dragons, none of them sure what to do.

After more discussions with Zilnar, they decided to still wait for the dragons to make their first move. The group sat far apart, none of them wishing to talk. Each would often glance at the men joining the dragons, knowing they would not win a battle against so many. In total, eight thousand men joined forces with the dragons that night. A Dûr'baën scout informed the army that, from a closer look, there appeared to be at least two thousand dragons now beneath the mountain. More had been secretly joining them from behind, skulking low through the plains. The warriors' hopes were failing. The Dûr'baën army sat restlessly, each regiment taking it in turns to try and rest. They would need all of their strength for the upcoming battle, and each of them knew it was likely to be the last battle they would ever see.

Broken Borders

Zale and his army rode all through the night and half of the following day before they reached the borders of Damané. The horses were exhausted. Many had grazes across their chests from thorns and branches that had barred one of the forest roads they had taken. The men were in need of food and rest, but none of them complained.

'We need not all enter the city,' said Zale, brining his horse to a halt in the shadow of a hill. 'I will take twenty men to the Tower of Light and the rest of you must wait here and gather your strength.' Zale's army murmured in agreement and dismounted. Zale chose twenty of his strongest men and began to ride up the final slope that signified Damané's border. He had to urge his mare on, whispering promises that this part of their journey was almost over and she could rest soon.

'Have any of you ever looked upon the ruling city before?' Zale asked his men. They all shook their heads. 'Well then,' he continued, 'this is a treat for you indeed.' When they traversed the top of the slope however, a sight lay before Zale that he had never expected. Beneath thundering black clouds and flashes of lightening, Damané was under attack. Caden's men and the Damané guard fought together against a force of men from the Lonely Shores. Plumes of smoke filled the air as farmhouses burned. Archers lined the inner-city houses' rooftops, loosing arrow after arrow in an attempt to drive the enemy back. The Tower of Light and the Masdour remained defended. What stopped Zale in his tracks was not, however, the sight of the onslaught. Only a few metres before him rose a transparent dome high above the city, encompassing it completely. What was stranger still was that all within the dome moved at a greatly reduced speed to normal. It was as if Zale was watching the battle in slow motion. He glanced up to see a bird flying towards the dome. When it passed through the transparent barrier, its wing beats slowed and its progress forwards was greatly reduced.

'What is this magic?' asked one of Zale's men, his eyes unable to move off the city.

'I do not know,' said Zale, awestruck. He found it difficult to believe his eyes. Shaking himself off, he drew his sword. The men around him did the same and looked towards their king. 'We must fight. If we can, we must hold off the enemy forces until General Trenith arrives. Cut me a path through them and I will attempt to reach the Tower of Light.' The man next to him turned back down the slope and called orders to the army. Then, with nine hundred men behind him, Zale charged down the slope towards Damané.

As they passed through the dome, it was as if each man had been sliced with cold. A tremendous noise that sounded like crashing waves filled their ears, soon to be replaced by battle cries once they were through the transparent barrier. The scene before them became faster, returning to normal speed, disorientating the men. Still they held true to their course. Zale veered to the left, allowing his men to ride before him as a column eight men across. The men from the Lonely Shores had little time to react when Zale's men were upon them. The army began to fight their way through Damané's enemy. The strange men around them fought on foot, swinging long, curved swords with precision. They were mighty warriors, their muscles bulging beneath their black chain armour. Some wielded metal clubs topped with spikes that were curled into a spiral. These hammered against the horses' body armour as Zale's men sliced down their enemy below. Damané's guards had seen the army coming and the archers now focused their attention on aiding their mission. They directed their arrows towards the men that posed an immediate threat to Zale's army. Unable to shield themselves from the air assault, the men from the Lonely Shores began to fall fast. After almost ten minutes of pushing forwards, the army had managed to cut a divide straight through the enemy that surrounded the ruling city. His men advancing slowly to either side, Zale was given enough room to ride directly through the middle and reach the Tower of Light. He looked back briefly to watch his men hold back their enemy, and then he proceeded to enter the tower.

In the grand entrance hall Zale found a ring of ten royal guards surrounding an oak table. Standing over the table was who appeared to be a high-ranking guard discussing battle tactics with a figure Zale could not see. With a gesture from the figure, the guard stopped speaking and took his eyes off the many papers beneath his hands to look at Zale.

'You have arrived at last,' said the guard. 'I had my doubts.' Zale looked slightly puzzled.

'When will you learn to trust what I say?' said a woman's voice calmly. The guard stepped back to reveal Luca sat behind the table. 'It is good to see you again Zale.'

'And you, Your Highness,' replied Zale, bowing in respect. She looked even more magnificent than when Zale had first laid eyes upon the queen. Her blonde hair was drawn back, showing off her long, slender neck, and her expression was full of knowing. The sparkle had long since left her beautiful blue eyes, yet she appeared stronger than ever.

'A king that bows,' said Luca mockingly, 'how refreshing.' She smiled kindly at him and he felt a bit more at ease. 'Come,' Luca continued, waving him forwards. 'You wish to speak with me. This is Milon, my personal guard.' The man that had been talking with Luca bowed to Zale then joined his fellow guards protecting the queen. Stepping closer, Zale could now see that the queen looked pale and he realised for the first time how old her eyes looked. Her youthful features had hidden her age well, but now Zale could see the effect time had had on her.

'How has Damané been caught so undefended?' Zale asked her. 'Its borders are protected with enchantments that prevent any from entering with destructive intentions against the city.' Luca looked away shamefully.

'The fault lies with no one but me,' she whispered. 'I let down the defences so that a friend could do what he must.'

'What do you mean?' asked Zale.

'I'm sure Harden told you what I said to him all those suns ago? By allowing an act of sin, in this case murder, and giving my blessings for it to occur, I opened the borders of Damané to other acts of sin. That is how the enchantments work.' Luca looked up at Zale and held his gaze. He could see she was finding it difficult to hide her emotions, yet she seemed adamant against letting her guards see her distressed.

'Then why did you do it?' asked Zale gently.

'Because otherwise Harden said that he would not be able to do the task. No matter what Jabari had done to him, he knew that when it came down to it, he would not be able to make the killing blow to his uncle. If he had my blessing, then the task would be in the name of Damané and its protection, rather than in the name of his vengeance.' Zale found this remark strange. *Harden is full of so much anger and hatred. What would make him think himself incapable of killing his uncle?* Brushing the thoughts aside, Zale glanced away for a moment, trying to think of a way to help Damané. Those fighting Jabari had little time left and he had to leave.

'It will be all right,' said Zale, his voice growing in strength. 'I have my army with me and more men on the way. They will be here shortly. They will help defend the city. All is not yet lost.' Luca began to shake her head sadly.

'You must take your men to the others and get the crystal back.' Her eyes were filled with determination.

'Five hundred of Caden's men are on the way with three hundred more of my men. How many still fight within Damané's borders?'

'Eight hundred and sixty of Caden's men remain, along with four hundred of my own. The fairies are keeping me informed.' It was only then when Zale noticed the small beads of light darting in and out of the Tower's windows. When he looked closer, he could make out the minute forms of the fairies, their wings almost twice the size of their elegant human bodies. 'They are able to fly over the battle undetected,' continued Luca. 'They have also been updating me with the growth of the dome.'

'What is that dome?' asked Zale.

'It is the distortion of time taking effect. The dome is slowly expanding. Soon all of the White Islands will be covered by it. Then its growth will accelerate, no longer tamed by the magic within these lands, and eventually nothing will be able to escape it. Those within it see time passing at the usual rate. It is only as an outsider that all appears different. I am sure you observed that upon your approach. Once the dome reaches its maximum size, all within it will be encased in flames.' Luca's voice trembled slightly as she mentioned the doom that awaited them all if the crystal was not returned.

'What of Damané's people?' asked Zale.

'The have taken sanctuary in the mountain where the lake I took you to resides.'

'So they are safe then, for a while at least.' Luca nodded.

Before Zale could ask more about the situation, an emerald green fairy flew straight towards Luca and began to talk wildly by her ear.

'General Trenith approaches,' said Luca once the fairy had flown away again. 'There are at most one thousand. Only five hundred are from Forthum, but that is plenty.'

'What do you mean?'

'You cannot afford to spare any more time or men. You must leave at once; else there will be no chance of returning the crystal. Remember, though you have only been here a short while, much time has passed outside the dome. Leave no more than five hundred men here. If you do, I will send them to follow you. Instruct the men to maintain an attack from the outside of the city inwards. Perhaps being trapped will scare the men from the Lonely Shores into fleeing.' Zale was about to protest when Luca raised a hand to silence him. Knowing she would not change her mind, Zale bowed to the queen and left the entrance hall, the sound of Milon's voice beginning to suggest tactics once more echoing around him.

When he left the Tower of Light however, Zale's exit was barred. His men had been forced to retreat towards the edge of the dome to prevent any loss to their numbers. Zale looked hopelessly for some other means of leaving the city, but there was no clear path. He mounted the grey mare he had left in front of the tower and rode from side to side along the length of the battling armies.

'Why haven't you left?' called a woman's voice. Zale turned to see Luca stood in the great doorway of the Tower of Light.

'I have no means to,' Zale called to her. 'My men have been pushed back. There is no way through.'

'There is one way,' said Luca, her face set into a look of determination. Milon ran to her side.

'No, Your Highness,' Milon protested. 'You do not have enough strength!'

'It is the only option. I have caused this, so I must act in order to stop it!' With that, Luca raised her arms towards the sky and began to chant in the Ancestral Tongue. As her voice echoed around the city, Zale could not make out her words. Her eyes shone a brilliant yellow and her body began to shake. The clouds above her head slowly moved apart, allowing a beam of golden light to penetrate the dome's surface. Those it landed on were blinded and tried to move towards the failing light they were adjusted to. This created a gap straight through to Damané's border. Zale stared at Luca in disbelief. The queen collapsed to the floor, her whole frame trembling from the effort.

'Go!' demanded Milon, cradling Luca close to him. Zale looked upon her with great concern. 'Go now, before the light fades!' Zale turned and rode down to his army, just making it before the gap closed.

'What was that?' asked General Trenith with awe.

'That was proof that Damané is still strong,' replied Zale. He turned to the army before him and saw banners of familiar cities. 'Men of Forthum, Drasdorin, Haytana, and all other cities present! Luca, Bringer of Light, asks that you help defend the ruling city. Any who wish to leave, go now. No one will hold it against you.' All the men stayed before him. 'I am glad the men of this land are still loyal. Five hundred of those from the nearest cities must remain here and attack from this side. You are the least weary and so have a great advantage over the invading men. Do not let our enemy rest.' Knowing their new orders, a group of men split from the army and turned as one, riding towards the battle. Addressing the remaining men, Zale continued. 'I know you are tired and in need of rest. I too am weary. Pair up together. One of you sleeps whilst the other guides you. Change hourly to ensure you are all refreshed when the time comes to fight.'

Without another word, Zale turned his back on the slowing events within the city. General Trenith joined him at his side and they rode away from Damané together, seventeen hundred loyal men behind them.

'So now we ride straight into battle,' said General Trenith.

'Not quite,' replied Zale. 'We have one last stop to make.'

The Last Battle

At daybreak, the men stopped arriving and the dragons began to get restless. They would walk around and eye up their enemy, unafraid to reveal the men with them who still hid, protected by the dragons' scales. The sun was in the sky for twenty-seven hours that day, burning brilliantly all the while, not a cloud in the sky. The Dûr'baën army had some shade from a few trees that lined the Forbidden Valley, whereas the dragons and men from the Lonely Shores were left to sweat in the scorching heat. Both sides knew that battle was drawing near. It was to begin at nightfall. For the Dûr'baëns, there was little hope. Their five thousand now stood against ten thousand. There was almost no talk during those sunny hours. Bazyli did not even eat for grief. Discussions only began as the sun grew closer to the plateau. Zilnar and his lead Dûr'baëns spoke at length about their plan. Their best chance was to take down as many dragons as possible before the men attacked so as to anger them. Their rage would focus their attention on the Dûr'baëns, allowing the small group of friends to head towards the maze unnoticed.

Tensions grew as inch by inch the sun slipped further behind the looming mountain. The Dûr'baëns stood in their regiments, row upon row, facing the dragons across the plain. A gentle breeze danced the sand and dust into golden tornadoes separating Dûr'baën from dragon, man from man. The sound of shifting horse hooves filled the silence. The odd clang of metal rang in the warriors ears as a Dûr'baën changed from bow to sword, trying to decide which weapon they should use as they charged across the plain. The rear three rows of Dûr'baëns stood perfectly still, like stone sentinels, each with a nocked arrow aimed towards the sky, ready to release when their enemy came into view. The warriors marvelled at their steadiness. For over an hour they stood their, not one of them dropping their aim. Their arms were rigid, frozen into position, awaiting the command from their regiment leader.

Just as had been suspected, the dragons attacked as soon as the last rays of light faded. The great flying beasts pushed themselves heavily off the ground, sending tremors towards the Dûr'baëns, filling them with a sense of dread. The might of the dragons was apparent as they soared into the sky, their colossal wings pounding the air beneath them. They grouped together, circled for a moment, and then dived down towards the ground for a second time. The Dûr'baëns and the warriors, beyond any fear, went to meet them in the middle of the rocky plain. Arrows shot across the sky, bringing down at least a hundred dragons before the two armies collided. Swords were raised as the dragons swept down upon the Dûr'baëns and warriors, slicing through the air with their talons. This time, the dragons began to breathe fire, killing ten Dûr'baëns at a time. Both armies were losing numbers rapidly. The dragons were sweeping down, picking up Dûr'baëns in their claws, flying them high into the air, and then leaving them to fall to the ground. There was a sudden blast on a horn and the Dûr'baëns split into their five coloured regiments. They formed a large ring around the flying dragons, leaving a patch of bare earth beneath them. At least half the dragons landed heavily on the ground and snapped their jaws at the Dûr'baën army. It was just as they had planned. Zilnar signalled to Harden and Harden began to lead the warriors away to the right towards the maze. The dragons did not notice for they were too concerned with the Dûr'baëns surrounding them. The mighty beasts struck out with their claws and whipped their tails through the Dûr'baën army. Flames roared above their heads as the dragons in flight tried to defend themselves from the arrows that still soared through the air. Most skimmed off their tough scales, though some pierced the soft flesh of their underbellies, sending dragons crashing to the ground. The warriors ran towards the group of rocks, hearts racing, and the sound of their heaving breathing filling their ears. Lysias gripped Bazyli's arm, spurring the young boy on. Silvio and Dempe were at the front of the group, closely followed by the two Elements. None of them dared look back at the battle behind them. All their focus was on reaching the maze. It was at that moment, however, when the men of the Lonely Shores started their march towards the battle. They had seen the small group trying to escape and quickly blocked their path. Rows of men headed straight towards them, long pikes aimed at their chests. Harden called a few commands and the group hurried back to the mass of Dûr'baëns, now fewer in numbers than ever. The Dûr'baëns rose up on their hind legs, kicking at the dragons' eyes whilst at the same time swinging their swords to and froe. On the ground, the dragons were vulnerable and started to fall rapidly. The Dûr'baëns clambered over their massive bodies, reaching into the heart of the plain. Each time a dragon tried to take flight, a speeding arrow shot it down. The Dûr'baëns had organised themselves so a circle of archers were on the outside of their main ring, attacking the dragons above, allowing the Dûr'baëns fighting with swords to concentrate on their ground enemy.

     Silvio, Dempe, Sachiel and Acacia, surest on their feet, went to the front lines to help. Harden, Caden, Lysias and Bazyli cut through the Dûr'baëns in search of Zilnar. They found him at their centre shouting orders to any who listened.

     'Zilnar!' called Harden over the noise. 'Look to your backs! The men are upon you!' Before Zilnar could respond, the men reached the archers and began to slay them without them even hearing their approach. Before they knew it, men were mixed with Dûr'baëns, forcing the archers to draw their swords. Seeing their opportunity, the remaining dragons on the ground took flight, soaring high above their enemy. From the thousand that had first landed, only three hundred remained. Still, the dragons totalled at nine hundred, and now they were free to come down upon the Dûr'baëns unchallenged. From it looking as though the Dûr'baëns would win the battle, the dragons now seemed to have taken over. With the help of the men, the Dûr'baëns began to fall, one by one. It seemed hopeless. The dragons had paired themselves together so one could swoop down a take hold of a Dûr'baën whilst protected by the roaring flames of the other. Any Dûr'baëns that were able to break free from the crushing claws of the dragons were left to fall upon the awaiting blades of the men. The men from the Lonely Shores were used to battle, and much stronger than the Dûr'baëns, though the Dûr'baëns had greater speed. They galloped around their enemy and were able to slay them from behind. Their height and powerful legs were also an advantage as they were able to run down their enemy with ease. Yet still the Dûr'baëns fell. The attack from above was too much to handle along with the onslaught from the ground.

'Zilnar!' cried Harden. 'Thank you for coming to our aid, even if it was in vain!'

'Not in vain my friend!' called back Zilnar. 'We fight for a cause. We shall now die believing in it! Good luck! Farewell!' Harden then saw Zilnar charge forwards and cut down ten men, but more followed. A group of twenty had been sent into the middle of the battle in search of Zilnar himself. Unable to fight them off, they stabbed at him with their swords, covering the ground with his blood. He fought until death gripped at his heart and it beat no more. Harden looked round him desperately. Only one Dûr'baën leader remained. She lead what was left of her regiment to the edge of the Dûr'baëns, meeting the oncoming men face on. Each one of them fell that night. As the moons slowly crept across the sky, the remaining ninety Dûr'baëns and eight warriors gathered in the middle of the battlefield, surrounded by four thousand of their enemy. They held their swords high, determination on their faces. No words needed to be said. Each knew they would fight until the end, no matter how soon that end would be. The warriors did not even look at each other. They knew how close they all were now. In their hearts, each of them felt they were fighting for the memory of Zale. They had finally come to the bitter end of their journey. They had failed Luca and the White Islands, but they had never given up hope. Through the darkness, they could see their enemy closing in on them. The final stand was nigh.

Survivor

The dragons, now sure of victory, landed on the bloody ground behind the approaching men. They roared furiously, licking their lips with the smell of fresh meat. The men, tattooed with blue symbols, raised their swords in the air, preparing to charge. Their long, curved blades glistened with blood in the moonlight. They approached slowly, grouping tighter together to ensure there was no escape. They were like shadows in the night, their black armour covering their mighty forms. The dragons could be seen behind them like an opalescent sea rising with the darkness. The warriors and Dûr'baëns stood staring at them nervously. Lysias held Bazyli close to him, determined to protect the child. He was concocting a plan to save him, though he knew he had to act soon. The Kai-Rae knelt down to the shaking boy and looked into his frightened eyes.

'Bazyli, look at me and nothing else. I want you to think of Damané. Picture the Tower of Light in your mind.' Bazyli nodded and stared at his protector. He did not notice the Kai-Rae's body begin to glow softly. Lysias smiled at him and opened his mouth to utter some words in the Ancestral Tongue. At that very moment, one of the Dûr'baëns called out with surprise, pointing to the ridge behind the dragons. The light seeped back into Lysias' form and he rose to follow the Dûr'baën's gaze. Both men and dragons all turned to see what the Dûr'baëns were looking at. There, sat tall on a horse at the top of the ridge, was a man. His black hair blew wildly in the wind and upon his forefinger a purple ring glowed brilliantly with the sunrise.

'Zale?' said Harden to himself in shock. It was true. Zale had returned. For a moment, the men and dragons were slightly confused. Then, a small group of them were sent in Zale's direction now that they realised he was just one man. Just as they reached the slope, Zale raised his sword high in the sky and called out a mighty battle cry. Hundreds of men, all on horses, came up behind him, swords raised and ready.

'Zale has come to save us!' cried Acacia. 'I knew it! I knew he was alive!' The small group of men and dragons hurried back to their army in complete bewilderment. The men at the top of the ridge were all calling out their own battle cries, filling the air with the sound of war. The dragons hissed and snapped at the air, unsure of what to do.

'Harden,' called Caden from the other side of the circle of Dûr'baëns. 'Harden, he has my army with him! And the army of my neighbouring cities! They have come! Men have united and come!' As Harden now scanned the men on the ridge, he too could see all the different armour and coloured banners. It had been centuries since men had put aside their differences and fought as one against the same evil. Now it appeared to be happening again.

'To friends!' Zale's voice galloped over the air as the new army charged down the slope. The dragons were about to take flight when a dark creature flew up from behind the ridge. It was another dragon. Behind it came twenty others, smaller in size. It was Freyna and her young. Her eggs had hatched and her children had grown already to half her size, shooting flames across the sky. They swept down in front of Zale's army and began attacking the dragons. The men from the Lonely Shores were in complete confusion. They regrouped and split in two. Half went to the Dûr'baëns and the other half went to Zale. Filled with a new hope, the Dûr'baëns ran out to meet them. The battle began again. The sound of metal against metal rang in the warriors' ears as they fought to get to their friend. Though confused, the men from the Lonely Shores were just as strong as before. Their swords sliced through the leading Dûr'baëns, sending them to their deaths. The warriors amongst them took revenge on the front row of men, Silvio and Dempe firing orange stunning spells into their midst. Acacia cut through them with her sword, as did Lysias, but Sachiel chose to use incantations that filled his enemy's bodies with pain. Still the men were advancing, gradually depleting the Dûr'baëns' numbers.

'Zale!' called Harden. 'We need you here!' The men from the Lonely Shores were breaking through the Dûr'baëns' defences. They were overwhelming them.

'To the heart of the battle!' called Zale as he led his soldiers from Morsenden to the centre of the rocky plains where the Dûr'baëns now fought. When he was safe with his friends behind a wall of fighting Dûr'baëns, he dismounted and embraced them all, relieved to find them all alive.

'I am sorry it took me so long to reach you,' he began. 'There was something I had to do in Morsenden. Then I rode to Damané to bring more aid, but found the city under attack.' Seeing the look on his friends' faces, Zale quickly added, 'do not fear. I have left more men there to defend Luca. I now know now what it is Luca saw me doing. I was to unite men. As soon as I had made the choice required of me, ancient fires were lit and now they shall burn until I die. All men, deep in their hearts, knew of the Prophecy of Man, where one man would unite all men, bearing a purple ring, exactly like mine. I am that man the King that the Northern People spoke of!' Zale had not fully realised how important he was until that moment, but now he had said it out loud he felt a great weight of responsibility fall upon him. He looked out at the battle and felt a great need to bring peace to the lands once more to ensure his people were free. Harden put a reassuring hand on Zale's shoulder.

'I know,' Harden said in almost a whisper. 'Luca told me your destiny. If I told it to you however, you would have made the choice to lead men out of others expectations, not from your heart. Or worse, you would not have made the choice at all.'

'You knew?' asked Zale surprised. 'It is strange to think that all this time you were aware of what I was to face. I must admit I nearly turned my back on my people. Then I realised that I could never turn my back on all of you. So here I am, ready to fight. Where is Zilnar? My scouts told me he was the leader of the Dûr'baëns and was here with you.' Zale began to scan the plain but saw no sign of him or the other Dûr'baën leaders.

'He did not make it,' said Acacia sadly, 'nor did the other regiment leaders. They all fell this night.' Zale was filled with a rage he had not known before.

'I came too late!' he cried. 'Now the Dûr'baëns are leaderless. It is my fault!'

'No,' said Sachiel, grabbing Zale by the arm. 'You were needed by your people. You have saved us still. If you had not come at all, we would be lost. We were out of hope. We all saw you fall. We all had the same dream where you faced Xannon and fell.'

'You saw?' said Zale, slightly confused, and yet happy at the same time. 'Then it worked. I tried to show you all that I was in trouble with the hope that you may not have attacked the dragons and would be able to send aid. I am sorry to have scared you like that. To die is an unusual thing, but what happened after that is stranger still. However, that is a story for when this is all over.'

'Well, I am glad you are all right. Bazyli was distraught,' said Harden. Zale then knelt down and Bazyli gave him a hug, unable to believe he was seeing Zale again. At that moment, one of the men of the Lonely Shores broke through the falling Dûr'baëns and charged at Zale. One of Zale's men stepped in front of his king and took the blow. He fell dead to the ground. In rage, Zale drew his sword and began to duel with the man. Their swords clashed loudly. The man attacked in ways Zale had not been tested against. He brought his sword down from up high just to avoid Zale's sword by swinging it to the side. He then manoeuvred it to head straight for Zale's legs. Zale blocked the blow with a quick flick of his wrist and used all his might to force the man's sword back up again. He was stronger than most men Zale had ever fought, but he made a fatal mistake. The man suddenly pulled away, appearing to be awestruck by the sight of the purple ring. Zale took his chance and struck the man to the floor. He lay dead at the king's feet.

'Zale,' said Caden, 'we are fighting a desperate battle. How many men do you have? They must get through to here, else the Dûr'baëns will not survive.'

'I have seventeen hundred strong that follow me. Another two thousand are making their way here now from the People of the North.'

'You must call your men here,' said Silvio desperately. 'The other two thousand will not make it here in time. We must force the dragons and their army to retreat.' With that, Zale took a horn from his horse's saddle that was carved from the tusk of a great Rasnor, a long since dead race of cat-like creatures. He knelt down to Bazyli and handed it to him.

'Bazyli, this has lived in the palace of my city for many generations,' he said. 'Will you do me the honour of calling all men to the King?' Bazyli looked up at him with wonder in his eyes and nodded. Bazyli raised the horn high into the air and gave a long, deep blast. The entire army of united men began to cut their way through the warriors. The horn sounded again, filling the dragons with fear. Freyna and her young flew to Zale and his friends and landed among them. She walked over to Zale and curled herself around him. Zale looked at her thankfully and raised his sword high into the air in triumph as the dragons and their army of men became overrun by Zale's army.

'Look,' whispered Acacia to Harden. 'It is the image from the sacred room in the town of the Northern People.' As Harden looked over to Zale, he too could see the carving of the dragon around the man with a lilac ring brought to life.

'There is the proof,' he said quietly. 'All that the prophecies speak of shall come to pass, and we will all live to see it.'

The dragons and men from the Lonely Shores tried to fight off the united men, but were outnumbered. They fled to the base of the mountain where they had watched the Dûr'baëns during the days before, terrified of the new force against them. A great cheer erupted as the sun rose steadily higher. The men had won.

Mercy

As the heat began to rise with the sun, the men and few remaining Dûr'baëns sat relaxing on rocks, drinking wine and ale from supplies Zale's men had brought with them. There was, however, a constant guard to ensure the dragons' army would not attempt to attack them as they drank merrily. Meat and fruit was piled high on metal platters, relieving the men's hungry stomachs. Altogether the atmosphere was one of victory. Zale's army was fifteen hundred strong after the battle, but only forty Dûr'baëns remained. The dragons' army however, due to being taken by surprise, had fallen in number from ten thousand to a mere two thousand. Bodies littered the ground, their blood still glistening in the heat.

A ring of boulders was formed with the nine friends all together at one end. The other leaders from the cities that had joined Zale were sat with them. They were laughing and enjoying the sound of the Dûr'baëns' soft voices as they sang sweet songs of hope and peace. Behind their words, however, they sang of mourning in the Ancestral Tongue, paying their respects to those who had fallen. Zale understood their words and stood, goblet raised to the sky.

'Men, Dûr'baëns, Domai and Elements!' he said in a loud voice so all could here. His voice was filled with a new confidence and Bazyli noticed his appearance of authority. Freyna cleared her throat and gave a short growl. 'And, of course, dragons.' Zale bowed his head to Freyna and her young and she likewise to him. Lysias sat next to Bazyli, choosing not to have his race added to the list. 'We have earned a great victory this night.' With his words came a booming cheer from the crowd around him. He raised his hands in silence and the noise died down. 'Our enemy still waits next to us, hoping for a chance to get their revenge. They have faired worse than us, yet we have still lost. I not only raise my glass to you now in gratitude of your loyalty, but also in memory of those who are not with us now. To the memory!'

'To the memory!' called all who stood there. Each raised their goblets and drank to their dead friends. Many that night had lost fathers and brothers. For the Dûr'baëns, entire families had been taken. The few Dûr'baëns stepped forwards and began to sing softly once more. Acacia stood by them and joined in their mourning.

Gracia dai sunar
Brekon sway arnana
Tillu oundar magar

Brestonia quai soolu ama

Histoni lai westunu
Singra may inlanda
Shinogh, shinogh, misaley!
Losway, nitawa yishore

As they sang, the men fell into a trance. Sadness, deeper than they had ever felt, entered their hearts.

'What are they singing about?' asked Bazyli.

'They are remembering those who are gone,' replied Lysias, staring dreamily at the sky. 'Their words are carrying their souls to the next life where they will be free from war and grief.'

The song continued for what seemed an eternity. The men slowly made their way to the plain where the battle had taken place and rested a single white flower on each body that lay there, including those of their enemy. The flowers grew just on the other side of the slope from which the men had come from. Bazyli thought it strange that even the enemy were being honoured until Silvio told him that the dragons had been enslaved by Jabari and had no choice other than to do his bidding. Freyna and her young were the only free dragons left in the land.

The men from the Lonely Shores looked out at their dead with sorrow and longing. After what looked like a long discussion, one man mounted a horse and rode out to the middle of the plains. There he stood, awaiting a response. Zale mounted his horse, Harden about to do the same.

'No my friend,' he said quietly. 'Allow me to speak with him.' Harden nodded with understanding.

'It would be wise if I joined you,' said Lysias suddenly.

'They may see you as a threat,' said Zale. 'You are a more powerful warrior than any here. I should go alone.'

'That I understand,' said Lysias, 'however, you will require one to translate your conversation.' Zale looked towards Harden.

'They do not speak our language?' Harden simply shrugged.

'Their tongue is somewhat different to ours,' said Lysias earnestly. After a moments thought, Zale nodded in agreement to the Kai-Rae's offer. He expected Lysias to ride out with him, but the Kai-Rae simply walked along side Zale's horse so as to not appear a greater threat than he already could be. The man they met on the plain was extremely muscular, his arms and face painted with delicate blue symbols from his country, though in his eyes there was a great sadness that could not be measured by any account.

'Eh kharn yo kachdor ihk breys dakfira.' The man's voice was deep and strong, yet he faltered slightly as he spoke.

'He wishes to collect his men's bodies,' said Lysias. Zale looked all around him. The men from the Lonely Shores deserved as much respect as his own men. War is war. No solider chooses who he must fight or when.

'Tell him he may do so with my blessings,' said Zale at last. The message was relayed and the man bowed respectively towards Zale. Zale mimicked the gesture and rode away. The man raised a hand to his fellow soldiers watching and a small group of them ran over to him carrying a stretcher, cerulean flowers intricately woven between the strips of bark. They took it over to the body of the man that had attacked Zale and carefully laid him upon it. The air was then filled with their own song of mourning as the men carried the body back to the dragons. Zale watched curiously from the other side of the plain, though no one spoke as they saw each of the dead taken back to their fellow friends.

The sun was soon at its highest point and Zale's men were discussing how to help the warriors skirt round the dragons to the maze.

'We need a distraction,' said Harden, speaking to Zale. 'If you split your army into its regiments and have them encircle the dragons and their army, then we can go behind them unnoticed, protected by a shield of armour. As soon as we are in the maze, we will be safe from them.' Harden began to draw in the soil with his finger, outlining his plan.

'I thought that you were going to ask for something like that,' said Zale, 'but you do realise that I am coming with you.' There was a determined look on Zale's face. Harden dropped his gaze.

'Yes, I know you are coming with us.' Harden's voice was solemn and knowing, waking Zale's old suspicion once more.

'What is it that you know?' asked Zale cautiously.

'It is nothing,' said Harden, clearing his throat and standing up dismissively.

'There is more to this prophecy, isn't there?' Harden turned from Zale and began to walk away. Zale got up and followed him. Once he caught up, he spun Harden round and stared him in the eye.

'Tell me what you know! Why do you fear the future?'

'Because all that has been foretold has come to pass!' said Harden in desperation, tears filling his eyes. Zale was shocked to see this. He had never seen anything give Harden so much sadness other than what Jabari had done to his brother. 'I fear the future because I now know that the rest of the prophecy, a part that has been lost, will certainly come to pass. I know that I can do nothing to stop it. Luca has seen our future.' Zale let go of his friend in bewilderment. He did not know of what Harden spoke, but he knew it was grave. Looking round, he saw the army of men staring at them. Acacia walked up to him and placed a hand on his shoulder.

'Please Zale,' she said softly, 'do not ask any more of Harden. He is forbidden to tell you what is to come to pass. Luca should not have even told him, but someone had to teach you the ways of magic.'

'Do you know what lies ahead?' asked Zale in a quiet voice so Acacia almost could not hear.

'Yes, but only I other than Harden. For what reason, I cannot say. Now we must prepare for our attempt at reaching the maze.' With that, Zale walked away, his mind racing with ideas of what was to happen to him. He gathered his weapons and sat alone on a boulder away from his army. Harden did the same, angry with himself for saying so much.

Lysias sat with Bazyli, their backs to the dragons. Bazyli seemed to have been disturbed by the outburst from Zale.

'He only fears what may happen to Harden, you, and the rest of us,' said Lysias quietly.

'I know,' said Bazyli. 'I wish this was all over.'

'And soon it will be,' said Lysias. 'I will stand with you proudly when we look upon all this as a memory.'

Somewhere high upon the mountain, a bird, darker than the night's sky, spread its wings and took to the air.

'Are you afraid,' asked Bazyli suddenly. Lysias looked down upon the boy thoughtfully. Bazyli wished he knew what was going through the Kai-Rae's mind. He was so wise and knew so much of the world.

The bird gradually flew over the dragons, gazing down upon the bodies between them that now lay still. Its delicate shadow moved gracefully over the dusty ground, rising and falling with each body it touched.

'I only fear not being able to protect you,' said Lysias. 'You are the future Bazyli, and I am charged with protecting that. I know of no greater honour.'

The bird drew nearer Zale's men and the Dûr'baëns. Its silky black feathers glistened in the sunlight. It cocked its head slightly, as if curious as to the ways of men.

'I am glad you are here,' said Bazyli as he clung to the Kai-Rae's arm. For the first time in a long time, Lysias smiled. The strength this young boy had was overwhelming.

The bird suddenly changed course. It dived towards the ground, flattening its wings against its sides. Its black feathers burst into sparks of gold. Its body began to elongate, taking the form of an arrow.

'What's that?' called one of Zale's men as he spotted the fiery arrow heading straight for them. All eyes turned to the strange creature. Lysias spun round and pushed Bazyli to the ground.

'No!' screamed Acacia as she ran towards Lysias. The Kai-Rae turned his hand towards her and used a pulse of transparent energy to force her back. One of Zale's men put himself between Lysias and the arrow. The golden missile passed straight through him without even scratching the man. Lysias closed his eyes and muttered a short prayer. As he did so the golden arrow pierced his flesh, running straight through his heart. Bazyli cried out as the Kai-Rae crashed to the ground, his face contorted into a silent scream of pain. His eyes were wild, searching the sky above him, as his body writhed. Bazyli crawled over to him but was stopped as Sachiel caught him in his arms.

'Do not touch him,' demanded Sachiel. 'We must wait!'

'Let me get to him!' screamed Bazyli as he tried with all his might to get away from Sachiel's grip.

'No!' shouted Sachiel. 'This is magic far greater than any of us. Do not let his fate doom you as well!' There was nothing they could do other than watch Lysias thrash from side to side in agony. His veins turned black as the poison spread through his body. After what seemed like an age, he stopped moving. His breathing was sharp and his eyes were beginning to stare. Bazyli broke free from Sachiel's grasp and ran to his dieing friend.

'No Lysias!' Tears began to stream down the boy's face. 'Not you too…you cannot leave me…I need you…' His words turned into sobs as Lysias's breathing finally came to an end. His eyes softly closed and his body relaxed. The entire army was stood watching Bazyli as he tugged at Lysias's lifeless arm.

'Come Bazyli,' said Zale quietly. The king pulled Bazyli to his feet and held him close to his chest, allowing the child to cry into him.

'Acacia.' Zale looked towards her fragile form now threatening to be overcome with grief. 'Acacia,' he said again softly. She looked sadly at him. 'What was that?' She could not talk for sorrow.

'It was Death Magic,' said Silvio, still staring at Lysias's body. 'A truly powerful spell conjured to kill a creature of magic. It will harm none other than one who has unlocked the mystical energies of the mind and allowed them to flow within them. It takes such energy to create that I cannot believe I have just witnessed such an evil.' They all stood in silence. Harden looked to the sky. The sun was nearly its peak.

'We must burry him,' said Harden solemnly. The others slowly nodded in agreement. Bazyli moved away from Zale and knelt next to Lysias's body, his tears now silent. He didn't take his eyes off him, as though he was afraid he would vanish if he did. Acacia moved over to the slope of the valley. There was an area where a group of boulders had formed a tight semi-circle. The Princess of Earth reached forwards and placed the palm of her hand in the centre of the rocks. The ground shimmered for a moment and then began to change. A small hole appeared where Acacia had touched the sandy ground. It grew outwards, stopping when it touched the boulders. It then started to carve into the side of the valley, creating a cave large enough for ten grown men to stand in. There it stopped and solidified, the boulders now an elegant archway guarding the room. Silvio and Dempe then entered the tomb. They held hands and closed their eyes. A breeze picked up around them and their bodies began to glow. The white light emanated outwards, filling the room. The Domai released the magic and there the light stayed. They stepped to one side with Acacia.

'Help me bring him,' said Harden to Zale sadly. Zale whispered to Bazyli to stand with Acacia. The boy moved as if in a trance, his eyes still locked on his protector's body. Zale and Harden stood at either end of Lysias. Muttering under their breath, the two of them used magic to raise Lysias's body and move it to the centre of the tomb. They were about to lay him down when Sachiel stopped them.

'Allow me to give him the crypt he deserves.' Zale and Harden nodded and held the Kai-Rae's body at waist height. Sachiel took a goblet of water and moved over to the body. He tilted the cup, his eyes turning white and his body perfectly still. The cool liquid danced around Lysias, filling the entire space beneath him. Short walls formed beside him before all of the water solidified. Zale and Harden then released their magic, leaving Lysias to lie on his icy bed.

'This solid shall never melt, erode, or fade in any way,' said Sachiel softly. Caden then brought Lysias's swords and placed them delicately across his chest, crossing the Kai-Rae's arms over them.

'So all that see him shall know of his strength and courage,' the General said as he moved away. The group stood around Lysias's still body, silently wishing him farewell. The army of men waited patiently outside. Bazyli walked up to his dead friend and placed a single white flower on his hands.

'Goodbye,' he whispered. He gripped Lysias's hand briefly and walked away. No-one there noticed the darkness seeping away from the Kai-Rae's veins.

'Let us seal it,' said Acacia sadly. The friends stood in a circle around the crypt. Acacia took a handful of sand and released it over Lysias. She, Sachiel, Silvio, Dempe, Harden, and Zale muttered a single word under their breath. The sand spread across the entire crypt and froze in a thin block as it touched its walls. The crypt was sealed. Each had thought of a different stone, causing the surface to be formed of diamond, ruby, emerald, sapphire, and topaz. The colours seemed to blend together, shielding Lysias's body from view, except for a small oval around his face. There the sand had formed a completely transparent window so all could pay their respects to the fallen warrior. Acacia stepped behind the crypt and placed the palm of her hand on the cool soil. She whispered a few carefully chosen words, and then walked away again. From where her skin had touched the earth a pure white flower bloomed. All around it, green shoots began to sprout from the ground, giving life to identical white flower buds. The creeping plants spread all across the tomb, reaching up to the entrance where they stopped. All at once, every bud burst open to reveal beautiful white flowers, their centres brushed with lavender.

The group stood around Lysias for a few moments, then walked back out into the sunlight. The men around them took up a song of mourning. Sorrow filled each of their hearts. Tears welled in men's eyes and voices wavered with the strain of staying strong. The small group of friends walked between them and sat together on some rocks. Bazyli gripped Acacia's hand as if he feared to let go else she would leave as well.

The sun had long since passed its peak by the time Zale next spoke to Harden. All thoughts of his previous outburst had slipped from his mind. His voice was calm and there was no sign of anger or irritation in his eyes; only a sadness he endeavoured to mask.

'It is time we made for the maze,' said Zale softly. 'The dragons prefer fighting at night, so this sun should give us an advantage.' Harden nodded. Zale went and informed his army as Harden got the small group of warriors ready.

'Bazyli,' said Harden, kneeling down to the boy. 'I would like you to stay here. You have helped us get this far and have shown us Jabari's keep. I do not want to have your life at risk any longer.' Bazyli looked up at him, his eyes still red from crying.

'I am coming with you,' said Bazyli defiantly, 'even if I must hide in the shadows and follow you to do so. If not that, then I shall stay and fight this enemy. I have lost to this evil just as everyone here has, so I have the right to punish those responsible.' Harden smiled and put an arm on Bazyli's shoulder.

'You are the bravest boy I know,' he said honestly, 'and I am proud to fight beside you.' He rose to his feet and indicated with a nod to Zale that they were ready. Zale gave his last instructions to Trenith, who was to lead the army, and then joined his friends.

'So, is everyone prepared for battle?' asked Caden.

'I think so,' replied Silvio as he and Dempe conjured magical swords that glinted with a golden hue. 'Let us just hope that the men are victorious. There is a strange feeling on the air, and it is not sorrow.'

'Oh?' said Harden questioningly. 'What type of…?' At that moment, a voice was heard on the air coming from where the dragons waited.

'Zale!' called Xannon. He had secretly made his way through the dragons' camp and now stood before them. He looked taller for some reason and his voice was filled with power. A wave of fear went through Zale's army. 'I told you we would meet again. I see all of your friends are still alive. They are stronger than I thought. Oh wait, what's this? Where has the Kai-Rae gone? Fled in fear perhaps?' Bazyli could feel the anger swelling inside him. He did not know whether to shout out or simply charge across the plains at the sorcerer.

'Leave this place Xannon,' called Harden, gripping Bazyli's shoulder tightly, 'if you value your life.'

'Harden! I did not see you there. Tell me, do you still see your father's face at night?' Harden tried to run forwards in rage but was held back by Zale and Caden. A menacing laugh came across the plains from Xannon. It was suddenly drowned out by an even greater clap of laughter. Somewhere on the mountaintop, Jabari was listening. Zale's army jumped back in shock at the sound of his voice. Even Xannon flinched.

'Anger weakens the mind, Harden.' Jabari's voice echoed deeply around the plains. It vibrated through every bone in the men's bodies. 'You have seen my true power now. Do you not realise I have been merciful with your lives. To kill each and every one of you would be simpler than swatting a fly. I give you the chance now to turn back, though I doubt you will listen to reason. So if you must fight, then fight you shall.' With that, Xannon turned and was hidden once more behind the sea of scales. It was then when Dempe called out. A great black cloud was approaching fast, covering the sun.

'How is he doing this?' asked Bazyli nervously.

'He must be using Baaron's powers to force the clouds to us,' said Acacia, a note of hatred in her voice. She turned to Sachiel and saw him frozen to the spot. 'Sachiel? What is it?' With that, the Angel of Water began to shake. His feet lifted just off the ground.

'Sachiel!' There was nothing Acacia could do. As the dark cloud drew nearer, an icy blue shadow of Sachiel's form was seemingly sucked out of him. It coiled into a tight ball and shot towards the black mass. As soon as it hit them, the clouds burst with water. The rain came thick and fast, making it difficult to make out the enemy across the plains. Sachiel's body crumpled to the floor.

'Sachiel? Are you alright?' Acacia had her arms around him and was helping him to his feet.

'He drew upon my powers,' said Sachiel weakly. 'I should have been protecting myself, but he caught me off guard. Now I know what Nare and Baaron have been going through.' The others looked at him gravely.

'Will you be alright to fight?' asked Caden abruptly. Sachiel nodded, pulling himself up straight and readying his magic.

'The time is now,' called Zale. With his words, the army of men charged forwards. The dragons immediately took to the air once more where Freyna and her young met them. The two armies of men clashed on the plains and fresh blood began to seep into the ground. Lightning flashed through the clouds, sending wild shadows across the land. Metal against metal rang in the air. Dragons dived down, only to soar up high again, men clutched in their talons. Freyna's young were attempting to create a ceiling of fire above the battle in order to stop the dragons, but they still swooped to the ground, their scaly hides resistant to the flames. In some cases, however, the dragons misjudged how high they were and crashed into the muddy earth, snapping their necks instantly. Any that survived the fall were overwhelmed by men, stabbing at their eyes and softer underbellies.

The small group of warriors stood and watched as men began to fall and dragons fell from the sky. Freyna had already lost two of her young when Harden led the group around the battle. They had to climb a ridge and hide behind a line of rocks so as to not be seen. From the sky, two dragons caught a glimpse of Zale's ring and swooped down over them. Their talons could not reach into the gaps between the boulders, but still they attacked. Acacia fired a few arrows into the air, but they could not pierce the scales. The warriors began to crawl along the ground so as to make some headway, but the dragons flicked their tails between the rocks, stopping them from going anywhere. Suddenly, the dragons sent shrieks of pain into the air and fell onto the rocks below. Their eyes were glassy and their breath was cold. Silvio climbed one of the boulders to see what had happened and saw the remaining Dûr'baëns at the bottom of the slope, bows raised. He bowed with gratitude and they went back to the main body of the army. The warriors were now free to continue on their way.

It did not take them long to reach the maze. It loomed above them, dark and mysterious. From inside, there was absolute silence, as if the world had been blocked out. Behind the warriors, the battle continued, filling the air with the sound of metal against scales and arrows piercing flesh. Now, however, their main concern was getting through the maze before them, unaware of the danger waiting inside.

The Maze

The warriors stepped cautiously through the rocks along a path made of gravel. When they were about twenty metres in, the rocks suddenly vanished and were replaced with thick trees that could not be passed. The warriors spun round to find that the entrance to the maze had been sealed and there was a mocking laugh on the air.

'Xannon,' said Harden with a scowl. 'He has set us a trap. Be on your guard. You never know what may be lurking behind these corners.' The sound of the battle could no longer be heard; the only noise was made by the warriors' feet shifting the small rocks beneath them. They knew that Jabari was probably keeping the crystal somewhere on the mountain so decided that any passage that lead upwards was the one they would take. They seemed to be travelling a long way to the right so chose a path that led them down again, but further left. The trees towered darkly above them almost blocking out the black sky completely.

'I do not like this place,' said Silvio. 'There is cloud of danger lingering on the air.'

'He is right,' said Caden. 'It weighs heavily upon my heart like that of a deep guilt that one cannot shake.' The warriors looked at each other nervously. They could all feel it. There was danger ahead to be sure, but in what form they could not tell.

'We cannot go back,' said Dempe. 'We were travelling too far south for my liking. We will have to turn off again though and travel eastwards as soon as we can. Let us hope danger does not befall us before then.'

They continued on and after a while came to a turning in the path. Their road did not split but instead turned east as they had hoped. Before they could reach the next corner however, they heard gruff voices in front of them. The warriors stood absolutely still, pleading that whatever was around the corner had not heard them. It sounded as though two creatures were having an argument as they stood guard, though their language was unfamiliar to any of the group. Acacia raised her bow and nocked an arrow. The others unsheathed their swords and stood motionless. They had just come to the idea of retreating when the voices stopped and a sniffing sound came upon the air. A slight breeze had picked up as if from nowhere sending the warriors scent right to the creatures. There was a mighty growl and the sound of heavy feet before two trolls sped round the corner and skidded to a stop in front of them. For a moment, both parties stood perfectly still as if contemplating what to do. Then, as if their minds had become one, the warriors charged forwards together, swords raised. Acacia fired an arrow, piercing one of the troll's legs. It bellowed out in pain and grunted to its partner who leaped forwards to meet the attackers. Harden slashed at its chest and Caden cut open its arm as Silvio, Dempe and Zale skirted past its giant body and headed for the other one. The first lashed out in rage, hitting Bazyli full on in the stomach, sending him flying through the air. He landed with a painful thud on the ground and sat up blinking, more in shock than pain. Harden and Caden, along with Sachiel who had joined them, thrust their swords upwards and opened the troll's neck to the world. It fell to the ground with one final roar, nearly crushing its killers. By this point, Silvio and Dempe had been able to use the trees' branches to climb onto the other troll's back and begin stabbing at its head. Its skull, however, proved too hard to damage. The troll swung its arms wildly at the Domai, trying with all its might to get them off. Zale took the distraction as an opportunity to attack the troll's face. His sword slid effortlessly through its eye and he removed it quickly before the creature swung a great arm at him. The Domai hastily jumped from its back to avoid being thrown off. Acacia, now with a clear view of the troll as its partner lay on the ground, fired three arrows with one shot at the beast. They pierced its neck and, with a look of despair and confusion, it too lay dead on the crimson soil. She then ran over to Bazyli to ensure he was all right. The boy looked up at her with a smile and got to his feet.

'Is everyone alright?' asked Zale, checking they were all still there. The warriors nodded.

'We should keep moving,' said Silvio. 'Danger will surely find us if we stay here. Something will have heard the commotion.' With that, the small group continued through the trees, their pace quickened. Here and there Bazyli thought he saw shadows dart past. Where they came from he could not tell. The group had just managed to turn north once more when the ground began to shake.

'What is this madness?' called Caden and the sound of crumbling rock filled their ears.

'Beneath us! Run!' As Sachiel shouted out the demand, the others could also feel the ground beneath their feet sagging. As they ran, the earth behind them crumbled away, leaving a burning crevice filled with flowing lava.

'Hurry!' called Zale as he glanced behind him and saw the crevice was upon Acacia. She did not seem to be focussed on running. Her mind was racing as she collected the energy within her to stop the destruction following her. Just as she was about to use her powers, her foot slipped off the edge. Instinctively she sent out a wave of emerald energy, which stopped the progress of the collapse. She gripped onto the edge of the crevice with all her might, the heat of the lava chocking her. Sachiel turned on his heel and sped to her aid. He reached down and swiftly pulled her to her feet.

'Thank you,' she whispered breathlessly. Sachiel bowed slightly and held her steady. Acacia then turned back to the crevice a directed her palms towards it. Ripples of amber magic began to knit a tight mesh over the deep pit. After a few moments, the mesh turned to solid ground again, sealing the molten rock beneath.

'What else could possibly be waiting for us in here?' asked Bazyli, half jokingly and half frightened.

'Let's not wait to find out,' said Harden. 'We cannot be too far from the way out. I can feel a cooler breeze with fresh air.' The others could also feel it. With renewed hope, they continued on. It was not long, however, before Dempe thought he could hear hissing noises around them. The group stopped, straining their ears. Instantly, the sounds paused, as if whatever was creating them knew they had been discovered. Zale gestured for them to slowly continue, still listening hard for any sign of danger. As soon as they moved on, the hissing started once more, quieter this time, and the snapping of twigs beneath feet could be heard. The group moved faster. The response to this was the sound of rapid footsteps and no sign of the hissing being covered up.

'Quickly! Xannon has sent his slaves after us!' As Harden spoke, he ran round the corner to find the passage leading to the end of the maze. It was no more than four hundred metres away. The warriors ran as fast as they could, but to their horror, they were being pursued by Usari. The creatures were swifter on their feet than even the Domai, yet they did not have time to catch up with the warriors in front of them. They had only just turned the corner when the warriors were upon the end of the passage. Zale, who had over taken Harden, heard a whooshing noise and a loud thud behind him. He shuddered to a halt and turned around slowly, not sure if he wanted to see what had happened. The others had also stopped and could already see what had come to pass. Harden was stood stock still, an arrow protruding from his chest in the place of his heart.

'No!' Zale's voice echoed all around as Harden's body fell to the ground. He ran over to his friend, tears streaming down his face.

'Harden, get up! Come on, please!' Harden's breathing was deep and shallow. Already, his eyes were beginning to stare.

'Zale?' he whispered to the growing darkness.

'I am hear Harden. Don't worry, I will save you.' The Usari had slowed their pace, sure that the others would not leave without their companion. They skulked towards them in the shadows.

'No Zale. You cannot. It has been foretold.'

'What?' said Zale with shock. 'This is what was seen?'

'Yes, and more. Listen to me Zale.' Zale was shaking his head, not wanting to believe what he was hearing. 'Listen! Do you love your people? Answer me honestly.' Zale had to choke back the sobs threatening to take over.

'Yes Harden, I do.'

'Would you die for them?'

'Yes.'

'Good. Make me proud Zale. Remember, always follow your heart.' Harden's eyes closed with pain, each breath an effort.

'Come Zale,' said Acacia urgently, placing a hand on his shoulder. 'We must leave.' Reluctantly, Zale moved away from his dying friend. Bazyli stood frozen to the spot, unable to believe they were going to leave Harden behind when he was still alive. Caden picked the boy up and he cried out for them to go back, reaching towards Harden's motionless body. As the group fled the scene, Silvio and Dempe fired magical arrows of protection at the pursuing enemy. When the Usari reached Harden, they looked down upon him with satisfaction. He still lived, though barely. Harden reached up with is sword in an attempt to kill one of his enemies, but found he did not have the strength. Through the mass of scales came Xannon, laughing.

'Go on then. Kill me!' shouted Harden at the sorcerer. The Usari above him tilted its head and snarled. Xannon raised his hands in preparation and released a beam of silver light.

All that the group heard as they ran on blindly out of the maze was Harden's screams.

Snolye Forest

Tears were streaming down the warriors faces when they finally decided to stop running. There was no longer the sound of any pursuit. They looked back upon the path they had run, finding it to be a mere dusty road surrounded by long grass. The maze could not be seen through the darkness still held by the black clouds. If the rain had even fallen upon this part of the mountain, it had now stopped completely. The warriors walked on in silence, the sound of Harden's death still ringing in their ears. The ground was flat, as if they had reached the mountain's peak, though none of them felt any triumph for their accomplishment. The path was winding, taking them left and right as the grass became taller and taller until they could not see round each bend. It felt like a sea of sandy green had risen up around them. There was a chill breeze and a faint scent of salt on the air.

'The mountain must overlook the sea,' said Silvio, his steady voice hiding the grief within his heart. Zale cleared his throat.

'I think you're right,' he said, not daring to look at the others. 'I can hear what sounds like waves far below. Be careful where you tread. There may be a cliff near by.' The group tried desperately to see through the darkness. Sachiel, who was now at the front, suddenly stopped, drawing himself up and groping the air as if looking for support. Caden pulled him backwards and the two of them staggered to the side.

'What's the matter?' asked Acacia now rushing forwards.

'Zale was correct. There is indeed a cliff,' said Sachiel steadying himself. The group peered down at the path where he had just been. There was a sheer drop ending where the ferocious sea crashed against the rocks.

'This path has been designed as a trap! We allowed ourselves to be lead to the edge of our doom!' Caden's voice was full of rage.

'Calm down Caden. Sachiel saw it in time. There is no harm done.' Zale's words seemed to make Caden's anger swell. He began pacing the ground, pulling himself away from Acacia's arm offering comfort.

'We're never going to get the crystal in time. We have lost Lysias and Harden, the strongest of all of us, and now our road is blocked. Damané will fall and there is nothing we can do about it!' Zale ran forwards and grabbed Caden by his shoulders, staring him in the eyes.

'Listen to me! Get a hold of yourself! This is exactly what Jabari wants us to do. If we fall apart now then yes, Damané will fall. But all hope is not yet lost. I more than anyone here feel the loss we have suffered. It is all I can do to stop the grief from eating away at my courage. But we must stay true to our course. The White Islands are depending on us and I am not going to fail them!' The rest of the warriors watched as Zale and Caden stared at each other. Zale's words had instilled hope in them once more. Caden nodded, a new look of determination on his face.

'I suggest we move off the path,' said Dempe.

'Yes, I think you're right.' Zale looked at them all for a moment. 'I will lead you on from here. From the base of the mountain I could see a forest up here. That is where we head for. Come Bazyli, walk with me. You have keen ears.' Bazyli went to Zale's side and looked up into his face.

'What is it you wish me to listen for?' he asked.

'Do you know the Midnight Dancer?'

'Yes. They fly the hills of Damané often.'

'I heard one not too long ago. They like to nest in woodlands so I am guessing there is a family of them living in the forest. I am counting on you to guide us towards their call.' Bazyli nodded. A smile appeared on Zale's face. He admired Bazyli's courage. He had not shown any indication of wanting to give up at any point on their journey, even when death threatened them. Now he was willing to be the first to walk into the next spell of danger.

It did not take them long to find the first of the aged trees that made the plateau's forest. Of course, none of the warriors were aware that this was Snolye forest, the one they had been told about by Ersona, the head of the Domai council. At the bough of the foremost tree, Zale and Bazyli stopped. Silvio stepped forwards and felt the bark, his eyes widening with wonder.

'What is it?' asked Sachiel.

'Have any of you heard of Tarren Oil?' said Silvio. They shook their heads, except Dempe who stepped forwards, also reaching out towards the furred wood.

'You do not think…?' Dempe's voice trailed off.

'What's the matter?' asked Acacia. Silvio and Dempe looked at each other curiously before responding.

'Tarren Oil,' began Silvio, 'is a great and rare liquid that can only be drawn from the tears of a Domai. A royal Domai.' The others looked at him. 'It was said long ago that at the beginning of all time, there were two of every creature. There they stood, a bare earth before them. It was decided among them that each would give a gift to the earth and in return the earth would provide for them. I am not sure what all the gifts were, but I know this. What the Domai gave were their tears, for they were filled with all the love and protection any could desire. The tears seeped into the ground and from them sprung forth the greatest trees any had seen. The trees we look upon now are the same.' As he finished, Silvio looked up towards the giant acorns scattered amongst the great leaves.

'What does it mean?' asked Caden. 'How could these trees have survived?'

'A royal Domai must have come here recently and replenished their thirst,' said Dempe.

'Well then,' said Bazyli, 'we ought to go and find them.' And with that he boldly stepped past the tree and into the forest. Slightly bewildered, the warriors followed.

The further into the tress they went, the thicker the air became. It was rich with the smell of decaying leaves and the sound of birds high above. After some time, the brambles that surrounded them became so wild that Zale and Caden had to cut them aside with their swords. Acacia and Sachiel stayed at the back of the group ensuring no creatures crept up on them. Acacia delighted in the beauty around her. The forest was so natural and untouched that she felt more alive than ever; as if she were in her own forest. Bluebells and daffodils laced the ground. Brilliant crimson berries glistened with dew amongst the brambles. A small group of deer hid in the shadows, though the Princess of Earth could sense their presence.

Bazyli was the first to hear the sound of running water. He called with delight as he saw a parting in the trees just wide enough for a small river. The warriors made their way to its edge where they drank long and deep, quenching their thirst.

'I think it best we follow the stream,' said Sachiel. 'It is sure to lead us to the other side of the forest.' The others agreed and they began to pick their way slowly along the edge of the meandering water. The riverbank was narrow and slippery and more than once Bazyli almost lost his footing. If it were not for Silvio keeping him steady, he would surely have fallen in.

The stream bubbled gently next to them, swelling in places where pebbles had knocked together to form a dam. Small silver fish darted between the aquatic plants as they were danced by the current to a silent melody.

After some time, the clouds above unleashed a tremendous bellow of thunder before releasing a torrent of rain. Like the edges of broken glass, lightning stretched across the sky, illuminating the narrow path the group travelled on. It was not long before they were all shivering, their clothes soaked through. It was just as the warriors thought they would never leave the forest when Dempe paused for a moment and looked at his arms.

'What is it?' asked Zale.

'My clothes…they are drying!' It was true. All the water that had been weighing down the Domai was slowing seeping away. Dempe looked at Silvio in amazement, just to find the same thing happening to him. The others looked at them curiously.

'Are you doing this Sachiel?' asked Caden.

'It is not I,' replied the Element, eyes wide. 'I know of no force that could be doing this other than myself.' Silvio suddenly looked at Dempe, realisation spreading across his face. Dempe shared his expression, then, as if running from a predator, the two of them ran off through the trees. Acacia was the first to follow, causing the others to do so. The Domai did not take them far. When they had caught up, they found Silvio and Dempe standing in a clearing where the trickling river seemed to end in a hidden cave. In the middle of the clearing stood a mighty oak, beneath which a handsome stag slowly stepped into view. Bazyli gasped, as he noticed no water touching the stag's back.

'The Domai prince,' he said, almost in a whisper.

'Who?' asked Caden.

'See the splash of black on his muzzle?' asked Sachiel. 'It is the royal Domai that Ersona told us of.' The group seemed to stand there for an eternity, staring at the creature before them, his fine antlers stretching towards the sky. The rain stopped as the clouds moved away, revealing a midnight sky scattered with stars.

'Is it really you?' Dempe finally asked his voice cracking. In response, the stag reared up on his hind legs. A mass of shimmering silver specks formed around him, shielding him from view. They danced upon the breeze, whipped up into a frenzy. Each gave off their own beacon of light as they hummed around the being. When they finally dispersed, a Domai, as black as the sky above, stood before the group. His silver eyes bore into each of the warriors, making them subconsciously withdraw. The tips of his long fingers gave out golden sparks as he rubbed them together. Silvio and Dempe stood, grinning at each other and then to the new Domai. He, however, did not return the gesture. Acacia was the first to speak. She took a step forward, bowed, and then addressed him with a formal tone.

'I am Acacia, Princess of Earth, and this is Sachiel, Angel of Water.' She motioned towards Sachiel behind who bowed. 'This,' she said, continuing the introductions, 'is Zale, King of Morsenden, Caden, General of Forthum and Bazyli, a mighty warrior.' With that, Bazyli gave the biggest bow he could and gave Acacia an enormous smile. She then turned at last to Silvio and Dempe. 'I believe you already know Silvio and Dempe. We have all been sent…'

'I know why you are here,' interrupted the Domai. 'Lord Jabari told me about your actions.'

'May I speak, Royal Shaynar?' asked Dempe, going down on one knee in a bow. Shaynar gave a slight nod of affirmation.

'I am surprised Jabari would tell a prisoner such as yourself of our attempts of retrieving the crystal and you.' A broad smile appeared on Shaynar's face.

'*Lord* Jabari,' said Shaynar, making Zale wince with thoughts of Harden, 'told me everything about your journey.' Dempe looked as if he had just been granted a deep understanding that he did not want to believe. He took a step or two back, his fingers flicking together.

'*Lord* Jabari?' asked Silvio confused, also preparing his fingertips. Zale noticed this and secretly placed his hand on the hilt of his sword. Shaynar's smile widened further with amusement.

'That's right, *Lord* Jabari. He and I spoke of all the recent events as we walked beneath these beautiful trees in the evenings.' He gave a short laugh. 'Did that old fool, Ersona, really think that I would *allow* myself to be captured by a human? And to think the people almost worship him!' He laughed again, his eyes flashing with malicious glee. 'Lord Jabari is the one with all the power now. It is foolish to fight against him. Oh, Zale, Lord Jabari asked me to give you a gift, welcoming you to your new throne.' Shaynar stepped to one side and snapped his fingers. A rustling sound came from between the branches as something heavy began to fall. Zale looked up to see Harden's body falling through the amber leaves. *Shwaysa!* He reached forward with his arms and a beam of white light left his fingers. As it hit Harden, his arms recoiled as if they now held a great weight. Beads of sweat forming on his forehead, Zale gently lowered Harden to the ground next to him and bent down over his friend. He took a deep breath, and then slowly turned Harden over so that he looked upon his face once more. Zale jumped back with surprise. Acacia ran over to him.

'It's alright,' she said softly, but Zale did not take his eyes off Harden's face. Acacia followed his gaze and she too gave a short gasp. Lying before her was Harden, his mouth, hands and feet bound and his eyes looking up at her, blinking with life. After another moment, Zale hurried back to Harden's side and took off the binds.

'You're…you're…' Zale could barely speak. Bazyli ran up to Harden and hugged him with all the force he had.

'Zale, I am so glad to be back with you.' Harden put a hand on Zale's shoulder. 'Xannon did not kill me, but rather healed me.' Zale was about to respond when Harden stopped him. 'There is no time to talk now. I was used as bait. Shaynar's about to attack and you now cannot afford to use magic.' As Harden finished, Sachiel called out as a beam of orange light headed towards Acacia. Sachiel pushed her out of the way just in time. Silvio and Dempe then stepped forwards and retaliated, sending forth their own beams of magic. At the same time, Acacia loosed an arrow, but Shaynar was too powerful. He managed to block both the spells and the arrow. Sachiel then stepped in and added his powers to the attack. Acacia soon resorted to magic and the four of them attacked the royal Domai. Caden and Zale were about to help when Harden pulled them back.

'No, you must go after the crystal. It is not the moonlight that illuminates that cave, but the black crystal beneath the river's waters.'

'What about you?' asked Zale.

'I am no use to you now for I am too weak to fight. Go!' Zale and Caden left Harden crouching on the floor and headed towards the cave. Before they could reach the hollow however, Xannon appeared before them.

'Caden, go for the crystal,' ordered Zale. 'Do not let anyone reach it, and whatever you do, do not touch it.' Caden nodded and continued towards the cave.

'I will enjoy killing you this time,' sneered Xannon. Zale could see that the black dye spreading through Xannon's veins had now reached his neck and were threatening to creep up around his face. 'I must admit Zale, you are the only one strong enough to have even the smallest chance of defeating me. But now, you cannot use your powers.' Xannon cackled, his voice echoing around the clearing.

'It is unwise to underestimate me Xannon. When you last attacked me I was unprepared for your strength. Now I know what I am up against and am ready.'

Zale drew his sword and charged forwards, reaching Xannon just in time to stop him from releasing a spell. Instead, Xannon instantly created a shield of protection around him, but he could only sustain it long enough to save him from Zale's blow. Stepping back, he drew his sword and engaged Zale.

'Oh yes, that's right,' said Zale between strikes, 'You're wasting energy trying to maintain Jabari's keep.' Xannon lunged forwards and caught Zale in a hold.

'That may be so, but at least I do not fight alone.' Xannon laughed and looked behind Zale. Just as Zale was about to follow his gaze, Xannon pulled back and struck out once more.

Behind Zale, Harden was getting to his feet. As he looked upon Zale, his eyes were not filled with concern, but hatred. He slowly drew his sword and stalked towards Zale and Xannon.

'No longer will I pretend to ally myself with such futility,' Harden muttered, raising his sword. Zale turned to see him just as he was upon him. An overwhelming disbelief crossed Zale's face. Before Harden could bring down his sword however, he felt a searing pain in his shoulder and cried out. Zale managed to move out of the way of Harden's blade and dived behind a rock before Xannon's spell reached him. He turned to see what had happened to Harden and saw Bazyli clinging to his throat, a dagger in Harden's shoulder. Bazyli jumped off him, pulling the blade out of Harden's flesh, ready to defend himself. Harden turned in anger and moved towards Bazyli.

'Run Bazyli!' called Zale. The young boy shot off to the left just in time to evade Harden's blow. Harden turned back to Zale.

'I'll be back to finish you off, My King,' muttered Harden before setting off after Bazyli. Zale came out from behind the boulder to see where Xannon was just to find himself having to duck out of the path of a beam of cerise energy. Zale took a deep breath and focused his mind. Stepping out into the open, Zale reached forwards and hit Xannon with a spell that seemed to push him into the ground. Xannon screamed out in pain, and then threw out his arm, sending another spell through the air. Zale collapsed to the floor, half to get out of the way and half due to the sudden energy loss he felt gripping his heart. Xannon got up slowly, but before he could take a step towards Zale, he was hit by a shimmering blue light that emanated from Sachiel's hand. Zale muttered *Garanor* under his breath. Distracted, Xannon could not block the blow from Zale and felt a searing pain shoot through his legs. Yet, Xannon was still fast enough to return the attack. He shouted *Synancar* and his sword burst into flames. The burning weapon swept past Zale's head as the king dived to avoid it. He jumped to his feet and blocked the next blow with the sword of men. Sparks burnt Zale's cloak as he struck forwards again and again. He was a better swordsman than Xannon, but the sorcerer's blade was stronger. So it went on, the two opponents consistently swinging their swords at the other, neither giving in. With every move Xannon made, the darkness of his veins spread. In its watery prison, the black mist seeping from the Crystal of Death was thickening.

Death and Shadows

Not too far behind the battle between Zale and Xannon, Caden reached the cave. He made as if to pick up the crystal, but then remembered Zale's warning.

There must be some way in which the crystal can be transported thought Caden. *Perhaps one of the Elements could move it.* Caden looked behind him at the various battles taking place. Both the Domai and the Elements were fighting Shaynar, apparently not enough to overcome the powers he was managing to draw from the forest. Zale and Xannon were locked in what seemed to be an eternal duel, both highly talented swordsmen. The flames of Xannon's blade had recently fizzled out giving Zale the confidence he needed to force the sorcerer back. Then Caden saw Harden and Bazyli, the boy just managing to avoid strike after strike coming to him from Harden. Caden realised that Bazyli needed help and was about to assist when he heard a noise.

'Look at the trees!' called out Acacia as she launched a whirl of green energy at Shaynar. Caden followed her gaze. In front of him, the mighty trees of the forest had begun to move as tall figures darted between them towards the clearing. 'Usari!' Zale could see them too, though he could not withdraw from his fight. There had to be at least one hundred of them. Caden drew his sword. It took only moments for the Usari to reach the clearing. Caden ran to meet them, trying his best to fight them off and stop them from attacking the others. They came out of the trees five at a time, each new wave surrounding the lone warrior. Caden swung his sword high over his head, catching the bare necks of a row of Usari, but there were too many of them. They encircled him, his blade sliding effortlessly off their glistening scales.

'He needs help,' cried Sachiel. 'He cannot keep them back for long.'

'You two must go,' called Dempe. 'Silvio and I will deal with Shaynar.'

'He is too powerful,' said Acacia as she sent forth another beam of green energy that trembled the ground beneath Shaynar's feet.

'Do not worry about us,' said Dempe urgently. 'Go to Caden's aid.' With that, the two Elements left to fight the Usari. With the extra strength against them, the Usari were unable to get beyond the tree line. Acacia threw Sachiel her bow.

'Keep them back with this,' she called to him. 'You are as good with it as I.' Sachiel knew this was not entirely true, but still he was adept enough to hold the scaled creatures back. Acacia continued to draw upon her magic. The forest itself was aiding her as she was within her element. She pulled the trees together, forcing the Usari to come from the same narrow path. Caden was then able to attack them one on one, his battle skills much greater than theirs as he had decades of experience behind him.

As Xannon and Zale continued to battle, Zale could slowly feel his strength returning. His blade started to glow with a purple hue that trickled down from his ring. The light seemed to give the weapon increased strength and accuracy. The sorcerer was taken off guard. Xannon reached inside his mind to conjure forth a new source of power and enchanted his blade, making it glow with ebony strength. He blocked blow after blow from the king and realised Zale was preventing him from concentrating on his magic. He tried to draw upon it once more but found something to be blocking it. The sorcerer knew he had to drive Zale back enough to break the two of them apart. Only then would he have the chance to use his inner strength. Still, the sorcerer started to simultaneously fight against the force keeping his magic trapped.

More and more Usari were lingering behind the trees as a new batch joined the fray. Zale could see this but was unable to reach Caden's side. Some way behind them, Silvio and Dempe could also see what was happening and hastened their attempts to overthrow the one they once protected. It was in fact Zale who gave them the opportunity to make the final blow. As he raised his sword above his head with the aim of striking Xannon to the ground, a single slither of lilac leapt from the tip and struck Shaynar directly on the head. For a moment he was left unable to tap the magic from his fingers. It was then when both Silvio and Dempe pushed forwards with a combined spell, striking Shaynar in the heart. His eyes cleared for an instant, and then misted over as he fell dead to the emerald earth. Without further thought, Silvio and Dempe rushed towards the encroaching Usari and produced a moonbeam bow and quiver of arrows. The Usari immediately began to withdraw as the new force overwhelmed them. Dempe ran to Caden, taking a sharp breath at the sight of his bloodied face.

'Do not fear, it is not my blood,' said Caden, 'though it would have been had you and your brother not arrived when you did.' He pushed Dempe to the side as another Usari approached, slaying it on the spot, before turning to him again. 'You must go and help Zale,' he continued.

'No, you and the Elements need help here. Only Zale can defeat Xannon now,' Dempe said looking back at the King in battle, concern in his voice. 'He must draw upon all of his strength to finish his task. Only then will the Usari flee.' Caden and Dempe looked hopelessly at the beasts advancing towards them, unsure if the battle would ever end. Then they saw Harden almost upon Bazyli, but were blocked from helping the boy by a barrier of green scales. The Usari had broken through Acacia's barricade and come round the side of them. With a new wave of determination filling their hearts, Caden and Dempe threw themselves back into the battle alongside Silvio and the Elements.

Zale glanced around him and saw the despair on his friends' faces. He knew that the battle would soon be lost if he did not do something to end it all. He pushed off from Xannon's sword and staggered backwards. Xannon, with little strength left, took the opportunity to mutter *Disinamorah* under his breath, the strongest spell he could muster. Suddenly, a swarm of blackness enveloped Zale. His heart began to race. Strange shapes darted past him, blocking out all light. The shapes were whispering to him. He tried to cut them down with his sword, but the blade simply passed through them. They were getting closer and closer to him.

'Zale!' cried out Bazyli as Harden's sword caught his arm.

'Zale,' called Acacia, 'what are you doing?' She had seen him slicing the air recklessly, ignoring Xannon's approach.

'They're everywhere!' Zale cried out. 'I cannot stop them!' Xannon laughed and waited quiet calmly as his strength slowly returned.

'There's nothing there,' said Sachiel.

'Look!' said Zale desperately. 'The black figures!' Acacia suddenly realised what was happening.

'They're shadow creatures Zale. They feed on your fear. They are in your mind. Do not let them take over you.' Hearing her words, Zale stopped and closed his eyes. *They do not exist* he said to himself. Opening his eyes, he found the creatures to still be there.

'You do not exist,' whispered Zale, yet still the creatures remained.

'You do not exist!' he cried out. A great white light spread out from him in all directions and pushed back against the darkness, eliminating its power. Catching his breath, Zale slowly turned to face the spot where Xannon stood. Zale drew his sword before his face and muttered a spell under his breath. Xannon, not yet fully recovered, drew upon the last of his energy and unleashed the deadliest spell known to him in the form of a beam of black energy. Zale's sword struck Xannon's spell and sent forth its own lilac energy. It was now a battle between Zale's and Xannon's strength. Xannon's beam of black light met Zale's purple hue exactly half way between them.

'You cannot defeat me,' said Xannon, straining against Zale's force. 'I still have more energy than you. You expelled yours when you saved Harden.'

'But you forget,' said Zale, a smile growing on his face, 'I have Luca's ring, and with it, I have the love of my people.'

'What?' said Xannon, his eyes flashing with fear. 'You found it?' Zale's smile broadened as an image passed between them.

Zale was in Morsenden, standing in a great domed room. Intricate paintings covered the walls. In the centre of the room stood a great pillar upon which rested a mighty sword. From Zale's scars it could be seen that he had just fought Xannon on the Plains of Grator. He walked determinedly to the centre of the room, each step a separate echo, and took the sword into his hands. The room began to crumble. Through the falling of the ancient room, Zale did not take his eyes off the sword. Once the dust cleared, all the people of Morsenden stood in the streets below him and a cheer filled the air.

Xannon's black magic began to involuntarily withdraw as the sorcerer shook his head with disbelief.

'That's right Xannon,' whispered Zale, 'the love of my people is behind me for my love of them is true.' Xannon looked closer at the sword in Zale's grasp and saw the pattern of precious stones in its hilt that he knew symbolised the sword of men. The purple hue touched Xannon's fingertips, then his hands, and then crept up his arms, until, finally, it cloaked him. The link between the two opponents broke. The blackness in his veins covered Xannon's face entirely now. The mark of the Crystal of Death was complete. Xannon's body shook wildly as it absorbed the lilac hue around it. For a moment, the world seemed to become perfectly still; no sound, no movement, just Xannon frozen in time. Then, without warning, Xannon's body burst into a shower of golden sparks. As the sparks hovered before Zale, the entire forest burst into the same shimmering fragments. The Usari fled faster than they had ever before. The dragons on the plain at the mountain's base roared with a mixture of anger and delight and took to the air, leaving the barren lands. The group could see them soaring over the forbidden valley and heard the faint cried of victory from the plains below. The air was filled with a strange sound, one of peace and yet sadness. Once the sparks had dispersed, all that remained on the plateaux was the warriors and the black crystal. The warriors staggered towards each other, relief being all that kept their limbs resisting fatigue.

'How did you do it?' asked Silvio. 'I thought you did not have the energy.'

'When I was in Morsenden,' said Zale, 'I was seen worthy of this sword. As my love for the people of my lands was true, I was granted the power of the sword when my need arose.' Dempe shook his head with wonder, but before he could comment, Caden called out. Behind them stood Jabari, Baaron and Nare hovering next to him, one on either side. The thought of Bazyli struck Zale and he looked around him frantically. He saw the boy laying on the ground not too far away, a deep gash down his side. Harden was nowhere to be seen.

Silvio made as if to prepare his magic but was stopped as Jabari raised his arm. From his hand dangled the two Elements' necklaces, each glowing brilliantly.

'The world is a strange place,' said Jabari in a deep voice, his jade eyes glistening curiously. 'Men can kill without thought and make unlimited sacrifice, yet when one they care for is at risk, their minds go blank and fear grips their hearts.' The warriors stood motionless, unable to decide what to do. Zale glanced backwards to where Bazyli had been to find him missing.

'What is the matter Zale?' Jabari asked. 'Is the great king finding his new leadership too much to handle?' Jabari's face broke into a smile. A slight breeze blew back his long, sapphire cloak, revealing a glimpse of his strong body clad in dark linen.

'No,' replied Zale calmly, turning his gaze to meet Jabari's. 'I am merely wondering how best to kill you.' Jabari threw his head back and laughed. The sound echoed around the group, sending a shiver down their spines.

'Why not show us how great you truly are?' asked Acacia, her green eyes blazing. Jabari paused for a moment, and then gave a short nod. He carefully placed the necklaces back around the Elements' necks and turned to face the warriors.

'You wish to see how powerful I can be?' he said questioningly. 'Well then, I think it best to have it demonstrated by ones who know.' With that, he snapped his fingers, releasing Nare and Baaron. They fell to the ground before drawing themselves up and stepping forwards. Acaica and Sachiel looked delighted for a moment, until they looked into their friends' eyes. Both pairs were jet black, no sign of the real Elements remaining.

'What have you done?' cried Acacia as she went to cast her magic upon Jabari. Baaron raised his hand and blocked her magic, sending it back to her twice a powerful. The combination of her energy and his was overwhelming. The Princess of Earth was sent flying backwards, her body crashing into the ground. She staggered to her feet.

'You would have us fight our family?' she hissed with hatred. Jabari laughed and sent Nare and Baaron forwards. Acacia and Sachiel had no choice but to defend themselves. Nare sent a spiral of flames towards Sachiel. The Angel of Water drew icy liquid from the ground to create a chilling barrier to dowse the flames. He then sent the wave crashing towards his partner, tears in his eyes. The water hit her with full force, knocking her off her feet. Icy blue sparks began to attack her body, preventing her from drawing upon the fire within.

Meanwhile, Baaron was sending giant tornadoes at Acacia. They emanated from his palms, drawing in the air around him and forcing it towards her. It was all she could do to stop them. She raised the earth before her, but it was stripped away by their strength. In desperation, she made the earth beneath Baaron's feet sink and used boulders to block him in. Jabari, seeing Nare and Baaron almost overthrown, sent out golden threads to pull the two of them back to his side. Acacia and Sachiel instantly withdrew their attacks and were relieved to see the colour returning to Nare and Baaron's eyes. They smiled weakly at Acacia and Sachiel, now forced to hover next to their captor once again.

'Now now you two' said Jabari sternly, 'we cannot have them die. Why should I let you have all the fun?' The warriors looked at each other with concern. 'Let it begin,' he said simply. Nare and Baaron immediately tried to draw on their powers but were prevented from finishing their magic as their bodies were bound by tight golden bands unleashed by Jabari's hands. Silvio and Dempe however were able to finish their spells, just to find the magical spheres rebound towards them off an invisible shield surrounding the great magic wielder. Jabari then pushed his arm forwards, sending a stream of flames towards the group. Sachiel protected them all by creating a wall of water half way between them. Caden and Zale then ran forwards, swords raised, as Acacia shook the ground beneath Jabari's feet. Unable to concentrate, Jabari only had enough time to raise himself above the ground before drawing his sword to block both blows from Caden and Zale. The others then rushed forwards to help in the fight. Yet Jabari was still able to fend them all off. He created spell after spell, knocking them all back. Acacia, finally giving in to her desperation, attempted one last time to get to Jabari as he was fighting off Zale with his sword. As she was about to reach him, Jabari pushed Zale backwards and turned on his heel. He lunged forwards with his sword. The blade went straight through Acacia's chest, piercing her heart. Everyone was motionless. Acacia gasped for breath as the silver shine left her skin. Warm blood trickled from the skin around the blade and stained the ground. Shards of emerald light shot out from the wound, illuminating the whole area. The light could be seen from the plains at the mountain's base for it was so bright. Then, without warning, Acacia's body was immersed in the light and a green nova erupted from her very being, not a trace of her body left behind. The warriors looked on helplessly as her necklace fell to the ground and smashed. The remaining Elements closed their eyes. Their own bodies then disappeared in a nova of light; crimson for Nare, yellow for Baaron, and sapphire for Sachiel. The group were dumbstruck, no one knowing what to do. Jabari turned to the others, ready to finish his destruction. He was, however, caught off guard as a pain gripped at his side. Looking down, he saw Bazyli's dagger deep within him. The young boy stood to his left, tears streaming down his face. Jabari pushed him with all his might across the ground. Filled with rage, Caden rushed forwards and pushed his sword through Jabari's chest. Jabari looked down at the blood seeping from his wounds in disbelief and then fell to the floor, his eyes staring and his breath cold. The land was silent. Nothing moved. There was no cheer of victory, no sighs of relief. The only tears were not of joy, but of sadness.

Life

Silvio was the first to speak. His voice cracked as he tried not to think of what he had just seen.

'It is done. Now we must return the crystal before it is too late.' Zale looked at him and nodded slowly. Then, with a shock, he thought of Bazyli. Looking around himself frantically, he saw the child lying on the floor.

'No' whispered Zale. Bending down to Bazyli, he realised that he was dead. The wound on his side had been too deep and his blood loss was severe. He had been the one strong enough to look past his grief and do what needed to be done to prevent Jabari from succeeding in destroying the White Islands. Now his body lay limp in the moonlight.

'This cannot be,' said Caden quietly. 'How can they all be dead?' Zale looked at the General helplessly. Then the four of them froze as they heard a faint voice on the air.

'With the new age, let there be new life.' Night became day and a light shower fell upon the warriors. The water was cool and fresh, as if the first water to ever fall upon the earth. New shoots of grass came from the soil and a fresh, salty wind filled the air. The sun beamed down upon them all, bringing warmth to their hearts. There was a small hope that the world could still be healed.

Zale was the first to look back at Bazyli. This time tears rolled down his face and he had to look away. Silvio and Dempe stepped towards the boy and held their hands above his body.

'Look,' said Caden, forcing Zale's gaze to rest once more upon the boy. His eyes widened as the air shimmered beneath the Domai's fingers. Bazyli's skin filled with colour and he took a deep breath. Blinking wildly, he sat up. Caden and Zale both rushed forwards and embraced the boy. Bazyli looked around him desperately.

'Was it all a dream?' he asked.

'I'm afraid not,' said Zale. 'But at least you are safe.' Zale stood up and looked at the two Domai that had stepped away.

'Thank you' he said. Silvio and Dempe bowed.

'Teach him not to abuse the gift we have given him,' said Dempe. 'Keep him safe.' Zale bowed in response.

'What gift?' asked Caden.

'He now has the power to heal, if the need arises,' informed Silvio. Bazyli's eyes widened in awe and he looked at his hands as if expecting them to be transformed. Silvio and Dempe laughed.

'The power is within you,' added Silvio. 'One day you will work out how to use it.' Bazyli looked at the Domai and smiled. Then he looked slightly beyond Zale and the others followed his gaze. There, hovering in the middle of the plateau, rested the black crystal.

'We are too late,' said Zale. 'There is no way we can get it back in time to save Damané. The time distortion by now is too great. I do not yet have enough energy to transport it that far. All that we have done has been for nothing.' He looked down in despair.

'Not for nothing,' said a strong male voice behind them all. The warriors turned and saw Alana walking towards them, her father, Onofre, walking in front of her. The warriors bowed in respect.

'You have all shown your loyalty to these lands,' he continued. 'It has now reached a point where the Rostauru can step in.' Zale looked at him with disbelief.

'I thought you could not help us,' said Caden.

'We are protectors of the White Islands,' said Alana. 'It is our duty. We may only intervene, however, when our actions are beneficial to all those in the White Islands and are not bias.' With that, Onofre stepped forwards and reached towards the black crystal.

'Wait,' said Dempe. 'If you touch it you will die.' Onofre looked at him and smiled.

'Indeed I will,' Onofre replied simply.

'Father?' asked Alana, fear and confusion in her eyes. Onofre turned to his daughter and embraced her.

'I have now lived to see the end of another age. It is time for a new generation to continue. As my daughter, it is your responsibility to lead the Rostauru.' A single tear rolled down Alana's soft cheek, but still she nodded with understanding. Onofre then approached the crystal once more and took it into his hands. He muttered something under his breath that could not be heard by any of those stood around him. Raising his arms, a brilliant silver light shot out across the plateau, causing even Alana to shield her sightless eyes. The crystal disappeared, as did Onofre.

'It is done,' whispered Alana.

'Thank you,' said Zale, nodding appreciatively to her. The beautiful woman then walked away from the group and faded into the horizon.

'Come,' said Zale after a moment, 'it is time we began our journey back to Damané.' He helped Bazyli to his feet and the group slowly walked down the side of the mountain. All of the vegetation had vanished. All that was left of the maze was a collection of boulders littering the steep slopes. When they reached the bottom, they saw men and Dûr'baëns walking amongst a sea of lifeless bodies looking for their loved ones. Freyna and the four of her young that survived the battle were huddled in the shadow of the Forbidden Valley. Above the valley peaks, the army of dragons could be seen just about to disappear over the distant mountains.

The warriors were about to set off with the gathering men when a flicker of light caught Zale's eye. He moved over towards the shining object on the ground and picked it up. In his hands he held a medium sized dagger, priceless diamonds lining the hilt. A look of shock and fear crossed Zale's face and his eyes searched the plains frantically as if looking for something.

'Is everything alright?' asked Bazyli. Zale looked down at the young boy.

'I hope so,' he said. With one last look across the plains, the warriors headed off towards Damané, a line of men and Dûr'baëns marching wearily behind them.

Lightning Source UK Ltd.
Milton Keynes UK
20 October 2010

161605UK00001B/153/P